THE HORROR AT PLEASANT BROOK

KEVIN LUCIA

Let the world know:
#IGotMyCLPBook!

Crystal Lake Publishing
www.CrystalLakePub.com

Join the Crystal Lake community today
on our newsletter and Patreon!
https://linktr.ee/CrystalLakePublishing

Download our latest catalog here.
https://geni.us/CLPCatalog

ISBN: 978-1-957133-33-1

Cover art:
Kealan Patrick Burke—www.kealanpatrickburke.com

Layout:
Lori Michelle—www.theauthorsalley.com

Proofread by:
Paula Limbaugh

ALSO BY KEVIN LUCIA:

Hiram Grange & The Chosen One
Things Slip Through
Through a Mirror, Darkly
Devourer of Souls
Things You Need
October Nights
Mystery Road
The Night Road
October's End
When the Lights Go Out
Joey Leonard's Last Horror Movie Marathon

PRAISE FOR KEVIN LUCIA

"Kevin Lucia is this generation's answer to Charles L. Grant."

—Horror Grandmaster,
Bram Stoker Award-Winning Author, Brian Keene

"Kevin Lucia's writing is both scary and smart, a lethal cocktail that makes for mesmerizing storytelling."

—Tosca Lee,
New York Times Bestselling Author of *Demon: A Memoir*

"Lucia writes tales that stick with you, that are memorable. And believe me, they are the best kind."

—Bram Stoker Award Winning Author,
USA Today Bestseller Tom Monteleone

"Kevin Lucia writes my favorite kind of horror . . . the subtle breed, the sort you don't see coming until they're already upon you and you realize it's too late to catch a breath."

—Kealan Patrick Burke,
Bram Stoker Award-winning author of *The Turtle Boy* and *Kin*.

"Kevin Lucia is a major new voice in the horror genre."

—Jonathan Janz, author of *Marla*

"Lucia is a true craftsman of the horror story, with a fine sense of the genre's best traditions."

—Norman Prentiss,
Bram Stoker Award-winning author of *In the Porches of My Ears*

WELCOME

TO ANOTHER

CRYSTAL LAKE PUBLISHING

CREATION

Camilla: "You, sir, should unmask."
Stranger: "Indeed?"
Cassilda: "Indeed it's time. We've all laid aside disguise but you."
Stranger: "I wear no mask."
Camilla: "No mask? No mask!"

"The King in Yellow,"
by Robert W. Chambers

"The Thing, they whisper, wears a silken mask
Of yellow, whose queer folds appear to hide
A face not of this earth."

H.P. Lovecraft

"The dead travel fast."

Dracula, by Bram Stoker

October 31st, 2020
Pleasant Brook
Adirondack Park, New York
7:45 PM

1.

LISA OWEN KNEW what she had to do. As she paced back and forth through the kitchen, smartphone ringing against her ear, headache pulsing in her temples, she understood it was finally time to accept the inevitable. Time to stop delaying what she'd put into motion. The shadows in the corners of the room stretched along the walls, whispering promises she could no longer ignore. Whispering that their time had come.

Still, she wanted to give Robert one last chance. To answer his phone. To be her lifeline, so she didn't have to . . .

"Hi, you've reached Robert Owen, Lifestyles Editor for The Poughkeepsie Journal. Please leave a message . . . "

She slapped the kitchen counter open-handed, savoring the sting in her flesh. She hit redial. One more chance. Just one more.

It rang two times, clicked, and then: " . . . *Lifestyles Editor for The Poughkeepsie Journal . . .* "

Rather than slap the counter again, Lisa hugged herself with one arm and pressed redial with her thumb. She thought *just once more* as she glanced around the kitchen, then out into the den. Despite the bright lights blazing in both rooms, the shadows swelled in the corners. Whispering promises to her. Things they'd give her if she'd only let them in.

She closed her eyes and bit the inside of her cheek.

"Not yet," she mumbled. "Not yet."

She opened her eyes and clenched the smartphone tight. Her gaze darted back and forth from kitchen to den. She peered into the corners, daring the shadows to crawl towards her. They quivered, but for now, remained still.

She shivered again and clutched the smartphone tighter. Telling herself she didn't need the darkness and what it offered because everything was fine.

Just fine.

But that wasn't true, was it?

Things *weren't* fine. Not after years of a barren womb. Years of miscarriages. Years of growing distance between her and Robert, pushing them farther and farther apart until they weren't even husband and wife anymore. Now they were nothing more than roommates. Cohabitants living under the same roof and moving around each other mechanically, every day both locked in a distant dream of how things used to be before she'd failed to produce the children Robert so desperately wanted. Before he'd given up on her.

Before the parade of other women.

Things weren't fine.

Nothing was fine.

At all.

She hated her life and everything it had become. Loathed it in a furious but quiet way, with every fiber of her being. She'd even come to hate what she'd once loved. The art surrounding her where she worked at the Munson-Williams-Proctor Arts Institute in Utica. She wanted to smash hundred-year-old vases to pieces. Slash decades-old paintings into ribbons.

In fact, the only thing good about her job as the Art Curator was how it had given her access to something which could take it all away. Something which could let the shadows in and cover everything and make her forget, if only she had the courage to make it happen . . .

" *. . . if you'll leave a name and number . . .* "

She pushed away from the kitchen counter, suddenly unable to stand still. She resumed pacing, mindful of the shadows in the corners. Had to remain alert, lest they think she wasn't paying attention. It didn't matter that she was having second thoughts. If she took her eye off them, they'd rush in. Even if she *didn't* complete the invocation.

Eight months ago she'd embarked on her final journey. She stopped taking the pills and herbal supplements Dr. Kontis had been prescribing for years. Stopped going out and visiting friends who had children of their own and didn't understand what it was like to be barren Could *never* understand. She pulled even further back from Robert. Gave up on him and their sham of a marriage when she found something else. Something which offered comfort and answers that pills and Robert couldn't. Something which whispered that if only she let the darkness in, she could forget.

All she had to do was give in.

So, she locked herself into her study for hours at night, pouring over electronic documents and journals about ancient Celtic myths and the Festival of Samhain, which she'd downloaded through the museum's intralibrary loan system, studying lore about something which offered to take her pain away, if only she was willing to sacrifice everything. All while Robert shuffled along his numb little way, ignoring her torment and burying his own between the legs of other women.

All the while, she watched the shadows grow in the corners of the room as she learned how to call forth darkness. Learned what It promised if she appeased It. She *believed* the darkness could give her peace. Believed it so much, she'd abused her position at the museum, forging signatures, falsifying records, and lying to get the thing she needed to bring the darkness to life.

"*. . . I'm away from my phone . . .*"

The small flickering light of hope inside Lisa guttered and finally died. She tapped the red phone icon and laid her smartphone down on the kitchen counter. She looked into the corners where the shadows trembled. They were hungry. Twisting and sinuous, and so near. She'd been flirting with them for months, and they were tired of waiting.

So was she.

All her thoughts fell still. She emptied her mind—as she'd taught herself these past eight months—leaving it void. Lost in a dream deeper than the one she'd suffered the past ten years, Lisa Owen turned and walked out of the kitchen to the stairs leading to the second floor and her office. The darkness followed her. Whispering of an end to pain, an end to everything. She clung to that whisper and its promise, as she drowned in an oily black sea.

2.

ROBERT OWEN DROVE home, a combination of dull shame and annoyance swirling in his guts. Annoyance, because he'd spent the whole night at Mahoney's chatting up a moderately attractive middle-aged blond woman named Cindy (with an admirable rack and very few laugh lines to boot) who'd ultimately turned out to be nothing but a tease. She'd let him buy her drinks all night until she smiled sweetly, pushed back from the bar, and sashayed away, tossing a breezy "Happy Halloween!" over her shoulder as she walked out the door.

He felt shame, of course, for the lurid fantasies he'd entertained of what he would've liked to do with said woman in the nearest flea-bitten motel. Shame, because while he wanted to spend the next few hours plowing a stranger, his wife was sitting at home, probably staring at the four walls, or locked in her office again, doing God knew what.

After he'd left Mahoney's Pub, a strange instinct made him check his phone, when normally he'd be more than happy to ignore it until the next morning. To his surprise, he'd missed dozens of calls from Lisa, which was odd, because it had been years since she'd bothered to pepper him with calls when he "got drinks with the guys after work." Even odder was his response. He'd obeyed a strange compulsion to call Lisa's smartphone and the landline several times, with no answer.

Of *course*, she didn't answer. She was in her office researching something she wouldn't tell him about. Par for the course from the woman with whom he shared a house. A woman he'd once considered his *wife*. He shouldn't be surprised.

He turned off Route 82 onto Main Street, and crawled through Pleasant Brook, passing Martinkovic Park on his right. Flicked on his left blinker and turned onto Pleasant Brook Road. Another left, onto Howe Road, which, five miles later, led him to their two-story Victorian.

When they'd first moved here, it seemed like a nice, quiet place to live. Pleasant Brook wasn't even a town. More like a hamlet, (not much more than a Main Street and a collection of side streets), but it had enough shops for them to get the groceries and goods they needed without always having to travel to Utica or Poughkeepsie, and Pleasant Brook itself was deep in the Adirondacks. At the time, it had felt rustic and idyllic.

Now, it only felt isolated and lonely.

He pulled into the driveway, parked, shut off the car, and got out. He shut the door, turned, and looked at his home. Lights blazed from every window. A curious dread stirred his guts.

Something was wrong. What, he didn't know.

Robert walked stiffly to the front door, unlocked it, threw it wide, and entered. He passed through the kitchen and looked up the stairs, which led to the second floor.

Yellow light spilled over the top step.

The door to Lisa's office was open.

"Lisa? Hey, it's me. Sorry I'm late. Lost track of time. Everything okay?"

No answer.

His unease swelling, Robert numbly climbed to the second floor. Once there, he walked down the hall. When he reached the office he didn't pause but stepped through, for fear he'd be paralyzed and unable to enter the room at all.

He stumbled to a halt. A strange relief, surprising in its intensity, flooded through him at the sight of Lisa's back. She stood facing away from him, staring into the corner of the room at something only she could see. She gave no evidence she'd heard him enter.

Which didn't make any sense. She'd protected her office with dogged persistence the past several months. Refusing to let him in, or even peek at what she'd been studying. That she would so casually stand there without ordering him out was disturbing.

Then he noticed it. Her shoulders, swaying ever so slightly. She was also humming a wavering, odd tune he didn't recognize, and didn't like. It sounded wrong. Off-key. Almost *foul* and *obscene* for some reason, but he didn't understand why . . .

His gaze traveled downward. Fear blazed anew in his heart when he saw the bright red slick running down her left forearm and dripping into a widening pool on the floor. Her right hand was out of sight; pressed against her belly, away from him.

He took a tentative step toward her, filled with a near hysterical panic. "Lisa? It's Robert."

Lisa shivered once and fell still. The humming stopped. She cocked her head slightly.

Another step. Robert raised both hands, unsure of what to do with them. What part of Lisa should he grab? Should he grab her at all? Even though he didn't think she was sleepwalking, he couldn't stop thinking about the old adage of not disturbing a sleepwalker for fear they'd hurt themselves. "Sorry I'm so late," he said carefully, taking another slow step. "I should've come straight home, I know."

Lisa giggled.

The sound curdled Robert's stomach. She sounded drunk or high, which of course was certainly possible. She had stashes of booze and weed around the house. Usually, she tried to hide her use, however.

She shook her head sluggishly. Still staring away from him, now up at some indefinable point on the ceiling.

Another step. His hands raised and out, though he still had no idea what to do with them. "Lisa? What's going on?"

Another shiver rippled through her. She sighed in what sounded bizarrely like post-coital bliss. Her right hand was still hidden. Her left, almost completely covered with blood which pattered sickeningly against the bare wood floor. Still, she said nothing.

Only two arm-lengths away. One more step and he could reach out and touch her shoulder . . . except, suddenly, he didn't want to. Though his wife was probably experiencing a suicidal break, and her blood was dripping into an ever-widening crimson pool at her feet, the compulsion to turn and flee filled him so powerfully that he was only able to stand his ground through force of will alone.

This was his wife. Maybe she no longer loved him. Hell, maybe she hated him, but she had good reason to. He'd been a shitty husband. Had been selfish and petty when she'd needed him most. He was a self-centered, self-pitying, cheating asshole. But he would not run. At least, at this moment, he could try and be worthy of the title "husband."

"Lisa." He reached out a trembling hand and forced himself to grip her shoulder. "Honey, listen to me. You need help. *We* need help. Let's go downstairs and . . . "

She laughed. Shivered again, as something orgasmic rippled through her. Then, she spun faster than humanly possible and plunged a bright and shining knife into Robert's guts. The knife sank into his belly all the way to its hilt. A tremendous cold sensation exploded inside.

He stared into Lisa's face . . . except, it *wasn't* her face. It was a mask. An oval, wooden mask, like something found in a museum. Stringy hair—not Lisa's—hung from the mask, which was split by a carved, crazed grin. He could see Lisa's teeth through it. Her wide pupils glittered madly through its eye holes as she twisted the knife against his soft insides.

Wordlessly, he mouthed *Why*? This wasn't revenge for being a bad husband, for all the times he'd cheated on her and ignored her, or for anything earthbound. As the lights dimmed in his head, he realized this was something far more horrible.

With another twist, she yanked the knife from his belly and shoved him, her hand flat against his chest. His knees buckled and his legs folded beneath him as he flopped to the ground. He gagged, spitting and coughing, his hands fluttered weakly and uselessly at the ragged gash Lisa had torn into his belly. As he felt his warm blood leak from his body, he thought that, most likely, it wouldn't be long before he was gone. Though that scared him, it also comforted him. Soon, the pain would be over.

Lisa towered above him, grinning mask staring down, knife held to her side. He saw with a dim sort of horror that her shirt was unbuttoned and her bra was off, nipples barely visible through the shirt's fabric. In a terrible irony, it was the most intimate she'd been with him in three years, and would certainly be his last image of her. But he felt no arousal or desire. Only a dim nausea.

Lisa dropped the knife to the floor and mounted him, grinding her pelvis into his, as if they were about to make love. Closing her eyes, muttering something which sounded strange and alien, she plunged both hands into his open belly and rooted around, probing his guts.

Robert arched his back and screamed. Lisa pulled her right hand—coated with his red, dripping viscera—out of his slit belly, and with two fingers, paint streaks of blood on the mask's wooden cheeks and forehead. All the while, she continued to whisper in an unknown language.

Robert was dying. He knew that. Even so, as Lisa chanted softly and painted the wooden mask, a deathly chill filled him. He didn't know why, but she couldn't be allowed to finish whatever it was she was doing. If she did, he thought that maybe things wouldn't end with his death. Thought maybe something else would happen to him. Something *worse*. He didn't know how he knew that. Only that he did.

The chill inside deepened as Robert saw the mask on Lisa's face . . . soften. Melt. Wriggle, and stretch like rubber.

Somehow, he found the strength to grope at his side with his right hand. His fingers curled weakly around the handle of the knife she'd dropped. He squeezed it and lifted the knife off the floor.

She kept painting the mask with his blood. Chanting in that whispering monotone. Eyes glittering madly behind the now liquid, spreading mask.

Robert swallowed. Took a deep, hitching breath, and swung the knife up toward Lisa with all his remaining strength.

Despite his fading mind and the pain roiling inside, his aim proved true. The knife buried itself in the base of Lisa's neck, up to the handle. Blood spurt from the wound. Somehow, she managed to turn and gaze down at him, eyes glassy behind a mask which was suddenly nothing more than a grinning wooden mask, now.

Behind the mask, through its carved grin, he saw her mouth open in a wide O. Blood flowed down her neck. He squeezed the knife's handle, twisting and digging it deeper. A flood of red erupted from Lisa's mouth and out through the mask's grin, splattering onto his chest, pooling in his belly's wound.

It didn't matter. The hand which had been painting his blood onto the mask flopped uselessly. The chanting faded as Lisa's mouth opened and closed silently. Feeling a strange sense of triumph and satisfaction, Robert finally let go. His hand slipped off the knife's handle and thumped to the floor next to him. He fell into a warm blackness.

As Lisa slumped over on top of him, the mask fell off her face, and onto the floor. Then, as his mind darkened further, and as Lisa's insides mixed with his, Robert thought he heard something skitter away. Like a large beetle, scuttling for the safety of darkness. But that didn't matter. He'd traveled beyond such concerns.

Two Years Later

Monday
October 20th
Pleasant Brook
The Tipper Inn, Main Street
10:00 PM

3.

CONSTABLE GRACE MATTHEWS—the lone "arm of the law" in Pleasant Brook—was sipping from her third Jack and Coke when her smartphone buzzed against the Tipper Inn's rough, pitted bar. She picked it up and smiled at the name which flashed on the screen. Book Wench. She unlocked the phone with her thumb, put the phone to her ear, and said, "Hey, you. To what do I owe the pleasure?"

"*I'm at the library. Was staying late to organize the collections, but now I'm reading Emily Dickinson and drinking.*"

Grace snorted. "Crown Royal?"

"*Absolutely. And, I found the perfect poem for us!*"

Grace smiled as she sipped her drink again. Sage Hunter, Pleasant Brook's town librarian, was *always* drinking Crown Royal and calling her with what they'd decided was the "perfect poem for us." Even though Sage and Grace hadn't dated in four years, like clockwork, every Monday night when Grace was holding up the bar at The Tipper Inn, Sage called with another "perfect poem." Grace supposed maybe it should annoy her (they weren't a couple anymore, after all) but for some reason, she found it endearing.

She drank her Jack and Coke, swallowed, and said, "Hit me."

"*I'm nobody! Who are you? Are you nobody, too? Then there's a pair of us! Don't tell!*"

Grace chuckled and raised her glass in a toast Sage couldn't see but would certainly reciprocate if they could. "Hear hear. To the Nobodies." She tipped her head back, drained the glass, and tapped it against the bar.

Jim Hutchins, the scowling, craggy-faced bartender, appeared almost instantly and mixed her another. When he finished, he slid the glass to Grace, and she nodded wordlessly in thanks.

"*You at the Tipper?*"

"Of course. Ladies' Night, you know."

Sage snorted. "*You, my dear, are* not *a lady.*"

It was an old joke. Oddly comforting, like the weekly "perfect poem." Grace replied, "That may be. But I'm the only one here who even vaguely qualifies, it's Ladies' Night, so here I am."

"*Better go easier than last week, or you won't make it into work until noon, again.*"

Grace shook her glass lightly, watching its ice cubes clink against each other. "So what if I don't? I'm my own co-worker *and* supervisor. It's not like the county is checking to see if I'm reporting in the same time every day. Besides, the phones are routed to my Android, so . . . "

"*You're terrible.*"

"You would know." Grace took a healthy swallow of her drink and set it down. "Sage . . . you ever think it's a little pitiful that the one place we were so desperate to escape is now the place we're going to spend the rest of our lives in, and probably die in?"

"*Don't look at me.* You *got out, and then came back. Could've stayed away if you wanted.*"

Grace looked down into her glass. "Couldn't stay in Utica. Not after . . . well, y'know."

"*Your record was spotless, and they owed you. Could've gone anywhere else you wanted.*"

Grace shrugged. "I reported a cop to IA. That sort of thing gets around."

"*Even so. There had to be better gigs than a county-paid constable position in place which barely qualifies as a town. You could've done better, Gracie.*"

"Maybe. Maybe not. What about you? Graduated top of your class. National Merits Scholar. Determined to write the next Great American novel. Took a summer job at the library after senior year, and never left."

"*Hey. I'm still working on that novel.*" (They weren't; Grace knew). "*I'll get it done. Eventually.*" (They wouldn't; Grace knew this, too). "*And after Mom died, Dad fell apart and could hardly function, and then he died . . .* "

"Ah, shit. I'm sorry. That was a cheap-ass shot. I wasn't thinking."

"*It's okay. No one's fault we never got away, or couldn't stay away. We didn't. No real reason, I guess.*"

"Hardly anyone ever gets out of Pleasant Brook, anyway. Not for long."

Sage paused and then said, "*Pretty sure I saw Jesse Simpson the other day, driving a beat-ass pick-up truck away from the Sip and Go. Heard tell he and Bobby Lee Haskel got kicked out of the Army. Drunken disorderly, or something like that.*"

Grace frowned. "Great. Pleasant Brook's finest, back for an encore. How long they been around? Tiffany Carter know Bobby Lee might be sniffing around?"

"*I don't know, and I hope not. Hopefully, they're just passing through.*"

"Amen to that." Grace lifted her glass and tossed back the drink in one swallow, ice clinking against her teeth. When she set the glass down, Jim moved toward it, but Grace waved him off, thinking Sage had a point about going easy on the drinks tonight.

"*Hey. You . . . want to come over to the library for a nightcap, after the Tipper closes?*"

Grace chuckled. "How much of that Crown Royal you got left? Cause it sounds like you've had a bit too much."

"*Definitely enough left for one drink each. If . . . if you want to, that is.*"

Grace opened her mouth and was about to crack a joke about this being a "booty call" but thought better of it, realizing Sage was probably going to regret being so forward the next morning.

Instead, as lightly as possible, she said, "Can't. Probably going to have to babysit, tonight." She looked into the Tipper's deep shadows in the back at a man wearing flannel and jeans. He was passed out, face-down on a table, CAT hat lying on the table next to his head. "Looks like Lester got into some of that backwoods moonshine again. Gonna have to drag his ass back to the station, hook him up with our luxury accommodations."

"*Oh, well. Yeah, better get him tucked in. Don't need him suffocating in his own puke.*" Sage paused, then added, "*Y'know, it's something I'll never understand. Why some folks—like Marty Crenshaw—can go dry on their own and start a new life, but someone like Lester won't ever be able to sober up, no matter how much help he gets.*"

"Marty's drinking was his own fault, and he decided to face it and own it. Lester's wife up and left and took his kid without a word of explanation. Not even a letter, and he started drinking so he could forget. Two different cases, I suppose."

"*I guess. Hey . . . Grace? Can we forget about me asking you to . . .* "

Sage trailed off into an embarrassed silence. Grace said gently, "Already forgotten. Enjoy your Crown Royal . . . but not *too* much."

"*You too. See you around.*"

"Night."

Grace hung up, feeling the same conflict she always did when Sage slipped a bit and tried to invite her over. Even though experience had proven they were better and healthier as friends, she still found it surprisingly hard to turn down Sage's occasional entreaties. Even so, common sense—and the acrid memory of their last fight, four years ago—always won the day.

She glanced at the time on her phone; thirty minutes remained until closing. Glanced into the bar's shadowed depths at the peacefully sleeping Lester McDonough, thinking, *Fuck it*, and tapped the bar next to her glass.

Knowing her as well as he did, Jim was already moving to get her a refill. Grace didn't know if that was comforting, or disheartening.

Old Owen House
Howe Road
2 AM

4.

BOBBY LEE HASKEL *loved* fucking. He never stopped to consider *why*, exactly. His reasons lay on an instinctual level, and though Bobby Lee was many things, introspective he wasn't. Hand-wringing and obsessive navel-gazing wasn't his thing. That was more Jesse's scene, the fucking limp-wrist.

If he had any inclination to think about it (which was unlikely ever to happen), Bobby might realize he loved fucking so much because he loved *power*. Loved *control*. Women didn't have sex with him, they didn't fuck him, he fucked *them*, and that was how he liked it.

At one time in his life, Bobby Lee *had* been in complete control. Of his life, and his environment. Ever since his athletic prowess blossomed his freshman year in high school, transforming him into an unstoppable force as linebacker on Pleasant Brook's tiny and often unfairly dismissed varsity football team. In one season, he'd gone from being a surly nothing who lived with deadbeat welfare parents in a trailer on the outskirts of town to a football star all the girls wanted, and all the guys wanted to be.

He took his future into his own hands and made it his bitch. He threw himself into weight training and conditioning. When he set division sack and tackle records his sophomore year, Bobby Lee Haskel knew he had it made. Football was his ticket out of this shit town, the key to bigger and better things.

He did well enough in school, (with help here and there from smart girls he was banging), so he knew he didn't pose a risk to schools offering scholarships. By junior year, he'd received six full ride offers, an unheard-of accomplishment in a town as small as Pleasant Brook. His picture was on the front page of the county news periodicals, his exploits—merciless sacks on hapless quarterbacks—consistently making the county's television sports highlight reels.

He owned the Pleasant Brook High's varsity team. Everyone knew it, including coach. Instead of cheerleaders hanging off quarterbacks and wide receivers, they hung off Bobby Lee. He was a "good boy" and attended all his classes (most of the time) and didn't skip school. Even so, everyone there—including good old Principal Williams—knew who was in charge.

He was.

Until that day. That *fucking* day in April, his senior year. When everything changed. When it all went to *shit*.

He'd signed his letter of intent to play Division I football at Syracuse University that Friday afternoon, accepting their full-ride offer, in the packed crackerjack box gymnasium at Pleasant Brook High. He had big plans to celebrate that night. Was going to a kegger with the boys behind the old abandoned barn on Burns Hill Road, and he planned on fucking Tiffany Carter (his cheerleader girlfriend; with shiny blond hair, apple-bottom ass, and huge knockers) until neither of them could stand. He was the king of Pleasant Brook. He planned on partying like one that night because the world belonged to him.

That didn't happen.

It all went to shit. *Everything* slipped out of his control, and the world was never his, ever again.

And even though he never thought about it much, that was why he loved fucking so much, even more than he had in high school. When he fucked skanks however many ways he wanted, he tasted—if for only a little while—the *control* he used to love. For only a minute, it felt like the old days . . . before it all went to shit.

Naked, Bobby Lee shifted in his sitting position on the floor in one of the bedrooms of the old house they'd been squatting in the last two weeks since returning to Pleasant Brook. He cracked his neck. He'd already used up tonight's fuck; some slut he'd picked up at a dive bar in nearby Smyrna. She was on an old mattress in the middle of the bedroom, where he'd been fucking sluts since they'd returned. Lying on her back, staring at the ceiling, seeing nothing.

He wasn't thinking about her at all, though. All he could think about was the weird fucking mask he held in his lap.

He brushed his fingertips down the mask's smooth wood. It didn't feel like wood, though. Not exactly. It felt soft. Almost like rubber, but not quite. Though he knew it wasn't possible, it almost felt like . . .

Human skin.

Light from the propane lantern next to him flickered over the mask's features. It didn't look like anything, exactly. An oval-shaped face, oval eyes, straight nose, and grinning mouth. Fake hair (though it felt real) hung from the mask's scalp.

He'd been sitting there for maybe an hour, his raging erection straining against the mask in his lap. It felt good against him. So good he thought about dropping the mask and rubbing one out on it, right now. A good thing to do. The right thing to do, even. Like putting money in the offering plate at church, but instead of an offering to God, it'd be an offering to the mask.

He didn't know why, but Bobby Lee thought that would be a good thing. But not right yet. For now, he wanted to keep holding the mask and looking at it. Even though it was giving him a headache, and making his guts feel funny, too. If he had to, he supposed he could always use that slut some more to help relieve his hardness. It wasn't like she'd complain. Fact was, he thought maybe he'd broken her, because for the first time . . . he'd worn the mask when he fucked her.

It had done something to him.

Changed him.

Made him go longer than he usually did, and Bobby Lee usually went for a *long* time. At some point, the slut, about at the end of her rope, had started fighting him off. Telling him to stop. Saying he was hurting her. He hadn't listened. She'd looked different, somehow, through the mask's eyesholes. Distant. Unreal. Not human. A sketch of a human.

So he'd kept pounding away. At one point she started hitting him, slapping him, gouging his chest with her fingernails, but he kept thrusting. She'd even tried to yank the mask off, but the weird thing was, it wouldn't come free. Like it had gotten stuck on his face. Glued to his skin, almost. Finally, he'd hauled off and decked her twice in the face. Hard enough to break her nose and splatter blood everywhere.

She didn't give him any grief after that. He went on until he finally finished. He figured he could do whatever he wanted to her now, and he smiled and got harder, thinking about it. His erection throbbed even more. He was definitely going to need another round with her, broken or not. Which meant he was going to leave quite a mess tonight. Worse than the last one, down South. Jesse would flip shit when time came for him to help clean up, but fuck Jesse anyway. Bobby Lee had been a good boy for almost three years. He was due another mess.

Bobby Lee frowned, thinking about Jesse. Used to be, Jesse was up for anything and everything. Back in school, (before it all went to shit), Jesse was Bobby Lee's constant tag-along, like a faithful dog that adored you even when you kicked it for shitting on the floor. Jesse followed him everywhere and did whatever Bobby Lee said, no questions asked.

It was the same in the Army, the only place that would take Bobby Lee after it all went to shit. He and Jesse attended Boot at Fort Benning, Georgia. Then they both shipped out to Kabul in the same unit. The Army hardened Jesse and made a man of him, finally, but he remembered the good old days and did whatever Bobby Lee told him to do, whether they were on duty, or chasing the local whores wherever they were stationed.

(Of course, that had gone to shit too, hadn't it? He could hardly be blamed for that, though. He hadn't known those last three girls were underage.)

These days, though, Jesse was a fucking pussy. He was no fun anymore. Used to be, when Bobby Lee brought sluts home, Jesse would help himself to sloppy seconds after Bobby Lee finished.

But that was before they'd moved into this abandoned house. Since then, Jesse had turned into a fucking loser. Lying around downstairs in that ratty chair. Smoking weed until his eyes popped. Moaning about how they shouldn't be here. How he could feel the bad mojo because some crazy wife and husband had killed each other in the room where Bobby Lee liked to fuck. Said they were going 'pay the reaper' one of these days, for sure.

Bobby Lee smiled as he slipped a hand beneath the mask and grabbed himself. He started stroking smoothly, up and down. Waves of hot pleasure flashed in his hand's wake.

Maybe squatting in a house where nasty shit happened was crazy, but it was *his* kind of crazy. The kind of crazy that had made him the best grunt in Boot. The kind of crazy that made him always volunteer for the most dangerous duty. The crazy that juiced him up so high he loved busting down doors, assault rifle blasting away. The kind of crazy which had saved Jesse's ass dozens of times, whether on maneuvers or in bar fights after they came back home.

Light from the Coleman propane lantern nearby flickered over the mask, making it look like its lips were moving. Like it was alive. Like it was hungry.

His hand burned. His member throbbed, harder than ever. He stopped stroking. In one smooth motion, he lifted the mask and put it on. Pressed it against his face, feeling that soft, skin-like material glue itself to his flesh. An acidic burning spread across his forehead and bloomed on his cheeks. It felt like a thousand insectile pincers were digging into his skin, as the mask sunk its roots into his face. He felt blood oozing and pooling beneath the mask. His face burned.

But he felt *good*. Better than he'd felt in a long while. In fact, he hadn't felt this good since the old days. When he'd been the boss of his life, in control of everything and everyone around him. As the mask started to *melt*—fuck yeah, it was actually *melting*—sink *into* his skin and glue itself to his fucking skull, Bobby Lee thought—no, he *knew*—thanks to the mask, he'd never be out of control ever again.

5.

JESSE SIMPSON STRETCHED on a moldy couch in the abandoned house's ruined den and took another drag on his joint. He held the smoke in for a few seconds, then let it trickle out his buzzing nostrils.

He stared up at nothing, ignoring the dark shadows flickering in the ceiling's corners. The shadows never went away in this damn place; no matter how many propane lanterns were burning. Even in the day, when it was light, the shadows always hung around.

Jesse took another hit and closed his eyes. Hard to believe he and Bobby Lee had ended up back home in a dump like this after twelve years in the Army. They'd had a good thing going until Bobby Lee got himself tangled up with those underage Afghani girls. And him saying he "didn't know" was bullshit. He'd *known* they were under sixteen. Like he'd known if he went down, Jesse'd go down with him. But in typical Bobby Lee fashion, he hadn't given a fuck.

They'd bounced around the country for three years before returning home. Spent some time in Louisiana learning to brew the 'shine Bobby Lee now sold to the hill folk around Warren County. This wasn't rot-gut shine, either. This shit was pure and sweet. Absolute fucking rocket fuel. Bobby Lee had turned out to be a home-spun distilling genius.

After Louisiana, they'd rambled around a bit (barely getting out of some serious shit in Georgia, where Bobby Lee had gotten himself mixed up with *another* fucking underage whore), and—without even realizing it—eventually worked their way home to Warren County and Pleasant Brook.

They'd been home for two weeks. Nothing much had changed, of course. Same boring-ass town full of boring-ass people doing the same boring-ass shit as always.

Holding his dwindling joint in one hand, Jesse rubbed his face with the other. He'd never forget that night. Bobby Lee calling him from the constable's office (Pleasant Brook was too pissant-small to have an actual police force) after the accident. An accident Bobby Lee caused (drunk on his old man's booze) after he'd plowed his pickup truck into a mini-van driven by a soccer mom, and filled with kids. Two of her own, and their two friends.

No one died, but everyone in the minivan ended up in the Warren County Hospital. Two of the kids were touch-and-go for weeks with serious head trauma. The mother suffered a concussion and a broken wrist.

Bobby Lee walked away without injury. *Physical* injury, anyway. He was eighteen, no longer a minor, and got slapped with a DWI, and his license taken away for five years. Somehow, he managed to avoid time in Warren County Jail, but Jesse figured that was only because no one died.

The Syracuse scholarship went away. So did all the other offers.

So he'd hightailed it to the Army, which took him in spite of the DWI conviction. And, stupid ass that he was, Jesse followed him. Like he always did, until he eventually followed Bobby Lee all the way home. The crazy part, though?

It seemed like no one cared or remembered. Granted, they hadn't seen any of the guys they ran with back then, and Bobby Lee certainly hadn't bumped into Tiffany. It wasn't like they socialized with anyone in Pleasant Brook. They'd been mostly invisible since returning. Jesse was okay with that.

Bobby Lee was another story. Jesse supposed Bobby Lee had *expected* to get hassled, had expected to take shit for what he'd done fifteen years ago. Had geared himself up for it, the way he used to gear himself up for football games, or deployment.

But when nothing happened? When they were practically ignored? Bobby Lee didn't show it much, but Jesse figured it was like someone took a needle to his ego and popped it. Bobby Lee had become so insignificant; he wasn't even despised anymore. Worse?

He was a *nobody*.

Jesse rubbed his face again, took another hit from his joint, and held the smoke in until he felt his edges go soft. Then he exhaled, shivering. He hated this fucking house. Had hated it from the start. A kind of dark shadiness lived in the corners. Jesse also swore he heard whispers late at night. Bobby Lee called him a pussy and a paranoid pot head. *He* had settled in fine, so what was Jesse's problem?

Jesse exhaled again, after what felt like forever. Weed did that to him, sometimes. Stretched time out like a big glop of taffy and made things go slow as hell. He liked it that way. Made it easier to deal with this place.

He looked up at the mottled stucco ceiling where greenish water stains throbbed, alive and hungry. He and Bobby Lee had crashed in lots of places the last few years. All of them shitty, but Jesse hated this one the most. According to a shinehead they ran into a few weeks ago in Moose Lake, two years ago a couple killed each other in this house, doing some weird-ass ritual. Right up in that room where Bobby Lee liked to fuck. Of *course*, soon as Bobby Lee heard that, he was determined they squat here. Jesse thought Bobby Lee liked to fuck in that room *because* of the shinehead's story. That was Bobby Lee down the ground.

Jesse had never been much of a church person, but he'd always liked horror movies. In horror movies, moving into a murder house never ended well. He looked down at his hands, curled and trembling in his lap. He hated this place with a passion.

Jesse blinked and cracked his neck. Tasted his dry, cotton mouth. Shit. He wanted another hit already. That was a bad sign, but it was the only way he could stand being in this place. Fly high all the time.

Knew he couldn't push it, though. Weed was tricky that way. Floating free was only a puff away from freaking the fuck out. One of their first nights here, while Bobby Lee was screwing in that damn room, Jesse had puffed once too often and found himself cowering in the corner of one of the upstairs rooms, losing his mind. Convinced dark things swirled and oozed toward him along the floors, slimy things that would EAT him, soon as he closed his eyes. There he'd sat, rocking back and forth in that corner, eyes wide open all night.

Bad as this house made him feel, that night had been way worse, so he stayed careful. Didn't need to go through that shit again. No way.

He shifted back and propped himself up, elbow on the couch's armrest, cheek on fist. Scoping out the smoldering joint which was almost gone. That was good. He didn't need any more hits right now, no matter how bad he wanted them. He'd ride this one out, let himself coast almost all the way down, and . . .

Shadows loomed over him.

Side-by-side, flanking him. Two hands grabbed both his shoulders and pressed down with inhuman strength, pinning him to the ratty couch. Jesse looked up, eyes wide, mouth opening and closing, as fear stole the breath from his lungs.

It was Bobby Lee. Naked, and wearing that creepy damn mask he'd found in this fucking house not long after they'd moved in. But what the hell was he doing?

He looked over at the other figure. It was the slut Bobby Lee had brought home. She was naked also . . . and wearing the same mask as Bobby Lee, yet not exactly. Hers looked similar but narrower. More feminine. Rivulets of blood ran from under the mask, down her throat, and across her breasts.

And in her hand, she held Bobby Lee's favorite knife.

Jesse finally found his voice as he began to struggle against Bobby Lee's iron grip. "Hey. Hey, hey what the hell is goin' on here? I don't want to play any of your kinky games, man. I ain't in the mood. Let me fuckin go, man . . . "

He jerked, wrenching his shoulders against Bobby Lee's grip. Bobby

Lee didn't say anything. He cocked his head, his face . . . no, his mask . . . grinning. Frantic hysteria taking hold, Jesse threw his entire body weight against Bobby Lee's hands, but it did no good.

"C'mon, man. Let. Me. Fucking. Go!"

Before he could heave upward again, the slut—where the hell did she get that mask?—darted in. She pistoned the knife down, straight into Jesse's guts. She stabbed him repeatedly with the rhythmic clockwork of an uncaring machine. Blood splattered everywhere. Onto the girl's mask; onto Jesse's neck. Blazing electric pain exploded in his abdomen as steel cut through muscle and fat, over and over.

Blood flooded Jesse's throat. With a great intestinal heave, he spat a wad of it at the slut's mask, more out of a desperation to breathe than anything else. The bloody clot splattered against the cheek of her mask, and then . . .

It faded.

Disappeared.

No. It sank into the mask itself as if the mask . . .

Drank it. The mask drank his blood.

With that last fading thought, the essence of Jesse faded to a pinpoint. His head flopped back. An immense, yet somehow comforting cold filled him. The torn mess that was his guts ached distantly, but he took comfort in the fleeting hope it would all be over soon.

But it didn't end.

Bobby Lee let go of his shoulders, grabbed both sides of his head, and positioned his face over Jesse's. What little remained of Jesse exploded in white-hot panic as Bobby Lee's mask melted. It turned into a mass of goo and poured over Jesse's face, burning his eyes, filling his mouth and throat, until there was nothing left but darkness, and burning, and hunger.

Tuesday, October 21st
Pleasant Brook
Constable's Office, Main Street
10 AM

6.

"HONEY? I'M HOME."

Saluting the quiet with a cup of coffee from the Sip-and-Go, Constable Grace Matthews smiled as she entered what passed for Pleasant Brook's police station, a two-room rectangular building (three if counting the cell) at 8 East Main Street, right across the street from the Pleasant Brook Public Library (a two-story rectangular building not much bigger than her office), where Sage spent their days.

Grace's smile faded slightly as she saw a red 5 blinking on the station's outdated answering machine. More than likely, a collection of recorded complaints and requests which would, as usual, take all day to address.

Grace sipped her coffee and winced. It tasted like warmed up dishwater, but she'd slept through her alarm this morning and hadn't time to make her own. That's what she got for staying up late and having too many drinks at The Tipper Inn.

Can't say Sage didn't warn you.

She shook her head and made a tsk-tsk sound as she rounded the desk to pull out her chair. "Grace, Grace. What *would* your mother think?"

A snide voice in her head chuckled. *Probably the same thing she thought when you left for Utica, and the same thing she thought when you came back home and took this job, instead of joining her and Dad down in Florida. That you're a never-ending disappointment who refuses to live up to her God-given potential.*

Grace snorted as she continued her one-sided conversation, setting her cup down on the desk. "Whatever that potential is. She was never clear on that point. Was she?"

She reached for the answering machine, but paused, her finger hovering over the 'PLAY' button. "What's it going to be today? Pastor

Yorkins complaining about the 'godless heathens and liberals?' Leslie Winter complaining about those 'punks' in their cars playing that 'godawful' Five-Fingered Death Punch when they drive by her house? Someone complaining about Miles Treverow's non-eco-friendly Humvee?"

The silently blinking red 5 on the answering machine was her only answer.

"Fuck it," she whispered as she punched the PLAY button. "May fortune favor the foolish, and all that shit." The machine beeped and played its first message.

"Constable Matthews, this is town selectman Bob Pacione. You've absolutely no right to make the arbitrary decision to cancel this year's Halloween festival! I insist that the festival go on. We'll mask, we'll social distance, but there's no reason to cancel. Please, call me back at your earliest convenience."

Grace smirked. "Whole county's back to remote schooling because of COVID spikes, and you want a Halloween festival? Not likely. I'll let you keep the Corn Maze at Goodlow's. Be happy with that."

BEEP.

"This is Pastor Yorkins from First Baptist again. *I can't believe you have the temerity to cancel our Fall Faith Festival. It's a gross over-reach which violates our constitutional right to assembly . . . "*

"For fuck's sake. None of you wear masks, you're all anti-vaxxers, and you *refuse* to social distance." She paused, and as Yorkins took a breath, she whispered, "C'mon. Say it. You know you want to. Call me a godless liberal lesbian. It will *make* my day."

"Call me, or I'll file a complaint with the county. Goodbye."

CLICK

"Dammit. Someday."

Shaking her head, Grace pushed out of her chair, stood, and walked over to the moderately-sized refrigerator in the corner, where she kept several boxes of microwavable sandwiches. She had to get Lester fed and off to work, even if there wasn't much for the custodian of a school on remote learning to do. If he lost his job, that would simply mean more time for him to drink.

Grace opened the freezer, grabbed a package of frozen sausage and egg sandwiches, and sighed again. Just another glamorous day as Pleasant Brook constable.

7.

LESTER MCDONOUGH WAS enjoying a soothing dream that Holly had never run off with their only son Bobby. It was Saturday morning. He and Bobby were sitting at the dining room table, while Holly bustled around the kitchen, making pancakes and humming a light, breezy tune. Holly had always been a wonderful cook. Her pancakes were to die for.

Of course, it had been quite some time since she'd made pancakes for them. Too long, actually . . .

Lester frowned at the thought, which was an odd one. Holly always made them pancakes Saturday mornings. Why did it seem like forever since he'd eaten them?

He'd been sleeping in more Saturday mornings. Had been staying out later on Friday nights the last year or so. Drinking more and more. Didn't much feel like pancakes with a hangover on Saturday mornings. Lester didn't like those thoughts, so he pushed them away.

As Holly cooked, she cast a beaming grin over her shoulder, washing away his strange doubts and troubling thoughts. He smiled in return and said, "Smells delicious. And we're starving. Right, champ?"

He turned and reached out to tousle Bobby's blond hair, but his hand froze mid-reach, because the chair next to him was empty, which didn't make sense. He'd been talking to Bobby about fishing for trout down Pleasant Brook after breakfast. Hadn't he?

A cold sensation formed in Lester's gut.

Because he hadn't taken Bobby fishing Saturday mornings in a while. Hard to do when you're hungover. Last thing you want to do is tramp deep into the woods with a four-alarm headache pounding in your brain . . .

"Hey, Lester. Rise and shine. You hungry?"

Confused, Lester turned back to a voice which didn't sound like Holly's at all. Instead of a plate of syrup-drenched pancakes, he saw a paper plate with two wrinkled and sad-looking microwavable breakfast sandwiches on it. The other hand held out a bottle of water.

"C'mon, Lester. Gotta get you up and into work by noon, or Principal Williams is finally going to fire you."

Lester blinked.

The bucolic, warm image—many years old now—broke apart into fragments and dissolved. His entire perspective shifted, as he found himself lying on his side, on a cot's thin mattress. Holly's smiling visage faded into Constable Matthews' concerned and bemused expression.

Right about then, the headache started up, pounding in his temples triple-time. "Oh," he muttered, weakly reaching up and rubbing his face, "fuck me."

"Sorry, Lester. You're not my type." Sensing, maybe, that he wasn't sitting up any time soon, Matthews sighed and set the paper plate and its sandwiches on the floor, the bottle of water alongside. She straightened and said, "Whenever you're ready. But I gotta tell you, it's ten. Only got about two hours to pull yourself together and get to work."

Despite how shitty he felt, Lester chuckled gently, so as not to jostle his pounding head. "10, huh? Getting in to work a bit late yourself, huh Constable?"

Matthews snorted as she turned and eased herself down on the cot opposite Lester. "Bite me, Lester. I spent an hour getting your drunk ass from the Tipper to here, and then I sat up with you for another hour to make sure you didn't puke and drown in it."

Shame pulsed through Lester, as it always did when the full impact of the night's escapades dawned on him, as they inevitably did. Of course, it wouldn't be enough to stop him from drinking later. Rather, it would serve as additional motivation to get trashed, so he could forget the shame, if only for a little while.

He smiled weakly. "Appreciate the concern, constable. But maybe drowning in my puke is the best thing all around. Would save me further humiliation and save you and other folks trouble."

Matthews frowned but didn't respond to this directly. She'd given up on the "rah-rah make yourself a better man" speech a long time ago, which, quite frankly, he appreciated. Instead, she said, "You're in worse shape than usual. Jim said you came in last night already smashed to hell, ordered one beer, then passed out at your table. You get into some bad hooch last night, Lester?"

She raised her eyebrows. "Maybe some backwoods shine? That shit'll rot your brain, Les."

He rolled over onto his back—slowly—and laid an arm over his eyes. "I cannot tell a lie; indeed 'twas the shine."

Matthews grunted. "Anyone I know? Someone local?"

"A gentleman never kisses and tells, Constable."

"Whatever." The cot squeaked and Matthews' boots scraped the cell's concrete floor as she stood. "When you can, get some water and food in you. I've got coffee—real coffee, and not the shit they sell at the Sip and Go—brewing. I know with the school on remote you're the only one there, and you could probably sleep the rest of the day and no one would notice. But get yourself together so I can take you over to the school, and then you can sleep it off there."

"You're an officer and a gentleman, Constable." He uncovered his eyes and gave her a small smile. "And I mean that not just because you like girls instead of boys."

Constable Matthews smirked and flipped him off. "Fuck you, Les." She said it without heat, of course. They'd been doing this dance for a while, after all.

She was halfway out the cell when he said, "Hey. Grace." His voice felt rough with tears he no longer shed.

She stopped. "Yeah, Les?"

"Why'd she leave? I was drinking more and more. I know that. I was neglecting her and Bobby, was turning into a shit husband and father. But why'd she leave without *saying* anything? Or leaving a note? If she'd said something, I could've tried . . . "

He trailed off and swallowed. Grace said nothing, expression somber. Finally, she said, "I dunno, Les. Not exactly an expert on relationships." She nodded at the plate on the floor. "Try to get those down. Coffee's almost ready."

He nodded. She nodded back, tapped the cell's bars, and left. He rolled over onto his side and did what he always did at this point. Silently mourned all he'd lost and all that he'd thrown away.

Pleasant Brook Library
11:00 AM

8.

AS IT ALWAYS was this time of day, the Pleasant Brook library was empty and still. The only patron at the moment hardly counted, Jasper Riley, the fifteen-year-old malcontent member of the Riley family, sitting in one of the computer kiosks against the far wall. Principal Williams had asked Sage—rather half-heartedly because no one liked dealing with the Rileys—if Jasper could do his remote schooling at the library because the Rileys had no internet at their farm. Sage reluctantly assented, which, of course, in turn, made them feel bad. As the only progressive non-binary with an MFA in town, they should be more accepting and tolerant.

Right?

Jasper Riley, however, unsettled Sage. They didn't know why. It wasn't his checkered upbringing, his torn jeans and ragged heavy metal t-shirts, or his mullet. Sage was also fairly sure he had several incognito tabs full of porn that he minimized whenever they walked past, and that he was a regular partaker of pot. They recognized the smell on him, being a casual partaker themselves. They didn't care about either of those things nor did they care that the "water bottle" he brought with him every day was probably diluted vodka or moonshine. That was all penny-ante, small-town thug shtick.

No, what bothered Sage most lay deep in the swirling black pools which served as Jasper's eyes. He wasn't an average, small-town punk. He certainly presented himself as one, but something about Jasper felt . . . off. Cold. A dark aura clung to him. As if he was *pretending* to be a punk, when he was something much worse.

It was probably an overly-dramatic sentiment on their part. Sage glanced up at the back of Jasper's head again, suddenly feeling bad for assuming he was looking at something awful on incognito browser tabs. Sage had endured a fair amount of assumption and pre-judgment over the years and didn't like the realization that they were just as susceptible to it as anyone else.

To divert their attentions from these thoughts, Sage regarded the black and white composition notebook, in which they'd been writing their novel-in-progress. A novel about life as a non-binary person living in a small town with their lesbian partner.

Sage smirked at the neat, tidy script which filled the notebook's pages with meticulous precision. The story they'd been writing (ever since Grace came home from Utica) about a big-city lesbian cop coming back to her small-town to date the non-binary librarian who'd given up their dreams of teaching college literature to take care of their ailing parents was cliché. They'd shamelessly ripped most of it from their life, and the worst part about it? It didn't sound realistic, at all. Despite *literally* being their life story.

Sage shrugged. "Fuck it," they whispered as they picked up their pen and continued writing.

9.

FALL AFTERNOONS IN Pleasant Brook passed quietly, with gentle breezes rustling leaves along sidewalks as birds who hadn't yet flown South called in the distance. The occasional car or truck hummed down Main Street, usually passing through from somewhere else to somewhere else. Afternoon traffic in Pleasant Brook was always sparse, because most everyone worked in nearby towns, except for those who owned businesses in town, such as they were.

Since the quarantine of Spring 2020, however, the traffic had become even sparser. Most of the townspeople who'd been sent home to work remotely during the opening days of the quarantine chose to remain at home once the quarantine was lifted. These days, Pleasant Brook looked and felt like a ghost town in waiting.

Set in a small and shallow valley between two modest Adirondack mountains with no names, Pleasant Brook was barely a town at all, balanced on the technical edge of being called a "village" or even a "hamlet." The nearest town—Smyrna—was forty-five minutes away. Surrounded on all sides by Adirondack forest, Pleasant Brook was a tiny world unto itself. Whether it was a town, village, or hamlet with a Main Street and a collection of side streets, that meant little to everyone who lived there.

The brook the town owed its name to wound through the woods to the South. It offered decent trout fishing (for anyone willing to hike a little way and hunt for deep pools under the bank overhangs and trees), but not so good fishing that it attracted too many visitors from outside. That suited townsfolk fine, because while it would be inaccurate to say Pleasant Brook citizens shunned outsiders, it would be accurate to say they wished to avoid undue attention.

The only way to Pleasant Brook was Route 80, which ran from South Otselic through town where it turned into Main Street and continue west to Smyrna. The nearest interstate was two hours away in either direction. Consequently, Pleasant Brook didn't see much of the famed Adirondack tourism, and this was also to everyone's liking.

All the town's businesses sat on Main Street. Across from the constable's station, of course, was the library, the domain of Sage Hunter. Next to the constable's station was a small building which passed for the town hall.

West of the constable's station on Main Street was Constable Matthew's main watering hole and the town's only bar, The Tipper Inn. Across the street, Pleasant Brook's one and only diner, The Whole in the Wall. Main Street also played home to a hairdresser, travel agency, laundromat, and a privately-owned Radio Shack, one of the few left in existence.

The farthest business on Main Street was the small thrift store This and That, right before Pleasant Brook Bridge, which crossed its namesake as Main Street left town proper and became Route 80.

On the east end of town lay Martinkovic Park, a modest but well-maintained recreation park featuring a playground with swing sets, jungle gyms, two tennis courts next to a basketball court, scattered camping plots in the woods past the tree line, and picnic tables with charcoal grills next to them. It also had an overgrown but once serviceable stage set in a small hollow north of the park. In better years, it had played host to Shakespeare in the Park, band concerts, and summer movie nights. Now it only welcomed creeping vine, goldenrod, and low-lying brush.

Pleasant Brook's side streets—all four of them—were clean and tidy. The homes lining these small streets, and the homes in the immediate countryside and the small trailer park to the north of town, were mostly well-kept and respectable-looking. Pleasant Brook didn't possess the commercial glitz of Lake George or the country-side kitsch of Old Forge, but it wasn't run-down and dying, like so many other small towns dotting the Adirondacks. Its population had remained steady for over twenty years, neither growing nor shrinking to any discernible degree. It existed, from one day to the next.

Two churches called Pleasant Brook home. First Methodist, several blocks west of the library, on Main Street, and First Baptist, on 41 East Main, past Martinkovic Park. Neither church boasted much in the way of congregants. Since most of their respective congregations were still choosing to watch Sunday Services remotely from home, only a handful of die-hards came and sat in the pews Sunday mornings.

Pastor Foley—the good reverend of First Methodist—was a kindly old man in his mid-seventies. His weekly homilies were comforting, warm, and inclusive if a trifle dull and uninspired. Pastor Yorkins of First Baptist, on the other hand, was a shrill, outspoken, bullish, narrow-minded bigot who—despite his fading congregation—still believed *his* church was the only *right* church in Pleasant Brook. The only church willing to stand up to the tyranny of the town's godless, secular authorities. In other words, the progressive atheist lesbian town constable and her godless former lover, the leftist non-binary town librarian, who each year had the gall to reject Pastor Yorkins' annual bid to remove over one hundred books from the library because of their "gross immorality."

Pleasant Brook elementary and High School sat on a gentle incline to the south of town, at the end of County Road. The high school's largest graduating class was seventy-five, with its average fluctuating between fifty-five and sixty. A Class D, Section 3 school, Pleasant Brook's sports teams (football, boys and girls basketball, and track and field) performed admirably every year against schools its own size, all of which were at least an hour away. Of course, all their sports seasons had ground to a halt in light of Warren County's recent return to remote schooling.

Pleasant Brook had always been a quiet, sleepy town, even before the quarantine came and made it even sleepier. However, quarantine, remote work and schooling, virtual worship gatherings, and social distancing (and the divisions erected between those who believed COVID a real threat and those who didn't) had driven Pleasant Brook into a deep, coma-like state. A heavy sleep so pervasive, that by the time its collective nightmare reared its head . . . the town was already sleeping like the dead.

10.

IT WAS THE ugliest mask Lester McDonough had ever seen. Bulging, uneven eyes. A wide, grin-screaming mouth. Crooked rotten teeth, and stringy black hair which looked entirely too real. Also, the face's sickly gray rubber looked wrong. Too slick. Too viscous. Like it wasn't entirely solid and might dissolve at any moment.

Lester didn't like it. Not one bit. And he had no idea why his new moonshine guy had decided to wear it.

His dealer (Bobby Lee or Jesse, he couldn't tell, with that damn mask) stood under the football bleachers behind the high school. Staring. It didn't even look like he had any shine with him. That, and the mask, set Lester ill at ease. Had they been burned? Was that the reason for the weird mask? Had he talked too much when he was trashed at The Tipper last night, and the word got out, somehow . . . ?

No, he didn't think so. At least, Constable Matthews hadn't acted that way when he didn't reveal his source this morning. And besides, she wasn't the sort to hunt down backwoods stills, charging around self-righteously like as "the law." That wasn't her style. And it wasn't like she had the time, being the *only* law in Pleasant Brook.

In that case . . . where was his booze?

"Hey. What's with the mask? And where's my 'shine? I don't have time to mess around playing Halloween."

The dealer didn't answer. Only stood there, staring, hands hanging slack at his sides. Lester cursed silently. Bobby Lee always had to be "the shit." He'd been that way in high school, back when Lester was still starting out as a custodian (and had still been sober). NOW all these years later, home from the Army after he'd screwed his life up even worse than Lester's, he still acted the same way. Missing the glory days, fancying himself a hillbilly moonshine kingpin.

Granted, Bobby Lee's shine was the best Lester had ever tasted. When the memories of Holly's abandonment crowded too close, a few glasses of Bobby Lee's white lighting washed all those memories away. It did the trick better than beer ever had; fixed him right up, good and proper.

Even so, Lester didn't feel like giving in to Bobby Lee's grandiose whims today. That *fucking* mask made him feel unsettled and wary, and his day had been a slog. Cleaning an empty high school with a dull headache all day long—he didn't have time for this. He wanted more shine, so he could wash away the bad memories again tonight.

"Hello? Bobby Lee? Jesse? We doing this or not?"

The figure cocked its head, looking at him as if it didn't understand English. Not for the first time, Lester wondered if Bobby Lee's mind had finally shorted out from all the shit he'd done in the Army. Rumor was he got dishonorably discharged. Almost got court-martialed too, so the story went. Which meant he probably had half a dozen wires loose in his brain.

"Jesse, Bobby Lee . . . look. Even with the school empty cause we're on remote, I've got work to do. If you haven't got anything for me, why don't you and that weird mask take a . . . "

Hands grabbed him from behind, by each shoulder. He jerked and swore, but no matter how hard he lunged, he couldn't break their grip. He tried to look over each shoulder to see who had grabbed him, but his captors dug their fingers in and propelled him forward to Bobby Lee or Jesse or whoever the hell was wearing that mask. He tried to drag his heels, but those hands *lifted* him off the ground—like a rag doll—and carried him forward.

"What the *hell* is this?! Who the . . . "

Lester didn't get a chance to finish. His captors thrust him toward the freak wearing the mask. Lester had just enough to realize—in shock—that the mask-wearer was *naked* before he grabbed Lester by the neck and squeezed, cutting off all the custodian's air. The hands from behind released him, but the guy wearing the mask simply squeezed harder. Black spots dotted the edges of Lester's vision as he *heard* something crack in his neck. Blood flooded his throat, and he gurgled, choking on it.

The hand dropped him. He slammed onto his back, but Lester didn't feel a thing. All sensation was quickly fading. As his vision tunneled, he saw three faces peer over him. Only one of them wore clothes, but all three wore the same weird mask, which didn't make any sense . . . but what did that matter, anyway?

The mask wearer which had crushed his neck bent over until its face hovered above his. As Lester's sight died, the mask shifted, writhed, and began to melt. It *poured* over his face, seared his eyes with a burning which bore into his brain. The slime, oil, rubber, or whatever filled his mouth and poured down his throat. As he felt the strange substance tearing into his skin, his last thought was the realization that the cliché was true. There were far worse things than dying.

Logan Road
7 PM

11.

GRACE SAT ON the small porch of her modest, one-story Concord on Logan Road, down the street and around the corner from the Constable's Station. No Jack and Cokes at The Tipper tonight. Only a few beers as she unwound from another tedious day of what passed for law enforcement in Pleasant Brook before she called it a night.

She'd spent the morning returning phone calls, all of them unpleasant. Both Bob Pacione and Pastor Yorkins had blustered and petitioned to get their respective ways, both convinced Grace was "abusing her power" in order to "strip them of their constitutional right to assemble." Her patience hanging by a thread in both instances, Grace explained (as she would to children) that as constable, she was a county employee, and she was following Warren County's COVID guidelines for safe social distancing.

Pacione was partly mollified when she told him that, yes, Goodlow's Halloween Corn Maze could continue to operate so long as they observed social distancing and kept the crowd capacity and foot traffic within certain limits, and that yes, masking would be optional. She ended her call with Pacione reassuring him that, yes, children would also be allowed to Trick or Treat come Halloween night . . . so long as the infection rates across the county didn't climb any higher.

Pastor Yorkins proved to be another matter. He didn't call her a "godless liberal lesbian," but he did rant and rave about Warren County's COVID restrictions preventing First Baptist's Fall Faith Revival. Even going so far as to speculate that if they went ahead and held the revival anyway, there wasn't anything Grace could do about it.

What Grace *wanted* to do was call him and his congregation a bunch of tinfoil hat-wearing anti-vax conspiracy theorists who'd feel right at home in the deep south of the sixties, or maybe even Europe during the Middle Ages. Instead, she calmly admitted there wasn't much she could do to actually stop them from meeting, but of course, she'd then have to include that with her weekly reports to the county. And she told Pastor Yorkins she was reasonably sure the *county* police wouldn't ask nearly as politely as she was asking.

Of course, there were no weekly reports to the county, or even a monthly one. Grace felt sure Warren County politicians couldn't care less about them in the grand scheme of things. However, Pastor Yorkins didn't know that, and she didn't feel the least bit guilty about her lie, Pastor Yorkins' sputtering was worth the deception. After he gathered himself, he muttered something along the lines of "The Lord's Day is coming soon, and *then* you'll be sorry," and then, thankfully, hung up.

The call with Leslie Winter didn't go much better. Grace tried explaining there wasn't much of a sound ordinance in Pleasant Brook, and that if Winter didn't know *who* was driving past her house blasting "that godawful Five Fingered Death Punch," there wasn't much Grace could do about it. Leslie muttered something about "godless heathens with their godless rock music" before she *also* hung up on Grace.

Luckily, the rest of the day turned out to be fairly peaceful. She drove around town, walked up and down Main Street once in the morning and once in the afternoon, as was her daily routine. She didn't have to. Nothing ever happened in Pleasant Brook, and all the previous constables had spent most of their days in the station reading either *Guns and Ammo* or *Field and Stream*. She, however, liked to be out and about and interacting with people, and she'd never been much of a reader, herself.

Besides, over the past few years, Grace believed her daily interaction with the townsfolk had endeared her to them. She wasn't the "beloved small-town sheriff" of the Andy Griffith variety, but she felt reasonably sure no one hated her, either. Politics and orientation aside, she was, at the end of the day, one of them. Despite her and Sage picking fun at it last night, Grace Matthews was Pleasant Brook born and raised, and that was a fact.

She sipped from her Stella Artois and gazed at the tree line along Logan Road, at the glorious tapestry of red, orange, and brown, among the scattering of Adirondack pine. She had to admit, despite being a town with a conservative bent, no one batted an eye when she and Sage dated. She wasn't naive enough to think people hadn't talked about it behind closed doors, and she was also realistic enough to know that some of those whispers had been mean-spirited and homophobic. On the surface, though, everyone had treated Sage and Grace as equitably as always.

She grunted and took another sip of beer. Thinking about Sage and their relationship—which Grace believed had been doomed from the beginning because of the baggage she'd brought to it—was always a complicated matter. They'd enjoyed their time together, but at the same time, Grace had trust issues. Trust issues which manifested in unexpected insecurity at Sage's non-binary identity. Grace had always considered herself progressive and fairly open-minded (because she was savvy enough to realize that being gay didn't necessarily mean she was either), and people declaring themselves gender-neutral had been perfectly acceptable to her . . . in theory. But when it became personal, with all the intimate implications which went along with it?

She took a sip, swallowed, and said to the autumn air, "That isn't something I'd like to think about tonight, thanks."

Of course, that only left her thinking about her time in Utica, and the blatant misogyny and homophobia she'd endured there. It had culminated on the night she got caught alone at the station with an asshole detective who'd been harassing her for months. He cornered her in the locker room, put his hands on her shoulders and pushed her against the locker. Pressed his hips against hers and whispered whiskey-sour breath into her ear, "That's not a Glock in my pocket, baby . . . "

Oh, hell no.

Not having any of that tonight.

Grace tipped her head back and emptied the rest of her beer in one long pull. Swallowed, pushed herself out of her chair, and went inside. She'd intended on foregoing the hard stuff tonight, but now that those particular wheels in her head were turning—of that night in the Utica police barracks—she wouldn't be able to sleep without the help of good old Jack Daniels. That, of course, had been another bone of contention between Sage and Grace, which only widened the divide between them over time. That Sage wasn't enough to help Grace sleep soundly at night.

As Grace closed and locked the front door, she thought—not for the first time—that maybe Lester McDonough's plan of a slow, alcoholic dissolution wasn't such a bad idea.

Wednesday October 22nd
Carter Residence
3:00 PM

12.

SCOTT CARTER LOGGED off his last remote class of the day—Social Studies—sighed, and cracked his neck. He tried to come up with adequate words to describe how much remote schooling *sucked*—God, he'd rather be *in* school, wasn't that a kick in the head?—but he couldn't find the right word. Remote schooling sucked sweaty donkey balls, and that was all he could come up with.

He sat forward and kneaded his forehead with his fingertips, trying to massage away the dull ache which came from staring at a computer screen all day. They'd only been back remote schooling about two weeks, and he was already desperately sick of it. Every day, Monday through Friday, from 8:15 AM to 3:00 PM (with "lunch" at 12:15, and "study hall" at 10 and 1), sitting and staring at a Zoom Meeting filled with boxes of heads who stared at him with the same glassy-eyed looks he was giving them. It was enough to drive a guy crazy.

Scott shook his head and pushed away from the computer desk in the living room next to the bay window looking on the front lawn. He grabbed his empty Monster Energy can and a plate littered with sandwich crumbs and headed for the kitchen. Jasper would be waiting for him at the library (at least Jasper got to *leave* home for remote school, because they had no internet at their house), but Scott wanted to do the dishes first. Mom had worked all day at The Whole in the Wall and was working the evening shift again, too. He'd rather do the dishes now so he could chill and watch the latest streaming horror movie after he and Jasper hung out.

He was lucky he was hanging out with Jasper at all, after Scott's . . . misunderstanding last month. Jasper had threatened to never talk to him again. Even went so far as to threaten a beating from his cousin Marcus.

Not wanting to think about that right now, Scott pushed away his thoughts about him and Jasper as he entered the kitchen. He tossed his empty Monster into the almost-full recycling bin next to the fridge (almost full mostly of Mom's empty vodka and beer bottles) and headed to the kitchen sink with his plate. The sink was likewise filled with not only their breakfast plates and pans but also plates and pots from last night's dinner. Spaghetti, cooked by him, like always. He'd left the plates there deliberately, to see if Mom would do the dishes for once. She hadn't (big surprise there) which was another reason Scott wanted to do them now instead of later.

As he emptied the sink and carefully stacked the dishes on the counter, Scott thought back to what he was mentally referring to as "the good old days of quarantine."

Back then, *no one* knew what was going on. The teachers certainly hadn't. Neither had Principal Williams, nor the other students and their parents. Remote schooling was a joke. Most classes only met virtually once a week. Some didn't meet at all, and only posted their assignments online. Assignments no one did. Which didn't matter, because not only had the teachers stopped teaching, they'd stopped grading, too.

Because of this, the Spring of 2020 turned into a free-for-all. Nothing much mattered. Definitely not school. No one cared about the Rileys not having internet back then, so most of the time he and Jasper ran all over town. Hanging out at the park, shooting hoops, playing on the jungle gyms even though they were a bit too old for it, biking all the streets in town (there weren't that many), and hiking through the woods to fish for trout.

Scott smiled as he nudged the faucet into the sink's left partition and switched it to "cold" for rinsing. Back during the quarantine was when he'd first realized how close he and Jasper had gotten. They'd known each other since grade school, but their relationship had always been defined by general mischief and cutting up in class. They were the class clowns, who routinely ended up in the principal's office.

During the quarantine, however, they'd grown closer. Slowly, but over time, they'd started talking about real things. About their actual lives. About Jasper's Dad taking off—like Scott's—and how his mom was a drunk (like Scott's mom was slowly becoming) who "creeped him the fuck out when she got hammered." Scott talked about not even knowing who his dad was, and how he thought his mom might be turning into a drunk, too.

Like thousands of people, Scott and Jasper came out of that time changed. Closer. Their friendship based on things deeper than cutting school, smoking and drinking behind the Riley's barn, and stealing mom's shotgun to target practice with her empties in the woods.

As Scott washed the silverware, he couldn't help but think of those days, and how they'd talked about *deep* things which mattered. Instead of gossiping about their female classmates (who was hot, who wasn't, who had big tits, which ones were the "sluts who probably liked big dick"). Scott had gone along with Jasper's talk, but he'd always felt like he was faking. Playing a role. Saying what was expected of him, because it wasn't a good idea to admit to Jasper he didn't think about girls in those terms at all. He never had.

He'd once asked Mom about that, on the rare occasion of a day off work when she was sober. About why Jasper talked so nasty about girls all the time, and why Scott didn't see them or think of them the same way. She'd brushed the question off. Said Jasper would grow up to be just like his father, Jack Riley. *A sleazy womanizer who'll probably knock someone up before he graduates high school, and will then run out on his family someday, too.* All the Riley men were like that. Always had been that way, always would be.

When Scott asked about *his* father—something he rarely dared do—and if *he* was turning out to be like him, all Mom said was, "You're better than him in every single way" and refused to talk about it further.

Finished with the silverware, Scott started in on the cups, his thoughts turning to his absentee father, as they did these days, more and more often. He knew nothing about the man. All Mom ever said was the guy didn't have the guts to be a father, and that was it. That'd he'd skipped town when he heard she was pregnant, and disappeared.

No one in town ever talked about it. He never got any odd looks from anyone. Occasionally, Scott thought about searching the house for his birth certificate, to see if his father's name was on it. He never did, however. He wasn't sure why. Mom rarely got mad at him—tired exasperation was mostly what he felt from her—but for some reason, he thought ransacking the house for his birth certificate might cross a line.

As he finished the cups and worked on the dishes and bowls, Scott admitted the most likely scenario: despite what Mom told him, his father probably didn't even know he existed. Which, of course, meant Mom had kinda lied to him. Maybe Dad took off before he'd ever known Mom was pregnant. Maybe Mom hadn't even told anyone else who his Dad was.

As Scott washed the last dish and put it in the drying rack next to the sink, a sudden wave of loneliness hit him, and something else, as well. He'd totally gotten his signals crossed with Jasper last month, reading something in their new closeness which probably wasn't there at all. Even though Jasper eventually said it was fine, so long as it "didn't fucking happen again, ever," things had felt awkward and strange between them since. Jasper acted like everything was okay, but Scott knew better, deep down. His friend was still freaked out by what happened. By what Scott had done. And if Scott was honest with himself?

So was he.

Abruptly, Scott decided to bail on Jasper for once. Stay home and find some horror flicks on one of their streaming channels. Soon as he decided this, relief flushed through him, making him realize how uncomfortable he'd been around Jasper the past few weeks. That made Scott sad, in ways he couldn't put into words.

6:45 PM

13.

MARGRET ANN SEAVER closed the last of her ninth-grade students' poorly written essays on potential and kinetic energy. Sighing, she exited Google Classroom and her online grade book, shut down her laptop, then pushed it aside. She sat and stared numbly into space, unable to think or even move.

Since they'd returned to remote schooling a little over two weeks ago, her life had descended into a quiet hell. After the mind-bogglingly long quarantine months of Spring 2020, Margaret had hoped she'd never have to teach remotely ever again. It had been the worst experience of her teaching career. Ninth graders weren't studious to begin with, but at the least, Margaret always felt she was able to see some sort of measurable progress in them throughout the school year. By June, her students were different people because of their shared experiences. And even if they hadn't learned much about science, she believed her presence *in* the classroom had *some* sort of positive effect on their lives.

Teaching remotely during the quarantine had robbed her of all the small things which made teaching worthwhile. Interaction with her students on a personal level. Watching *their* interactions. Learning from them, and seeing how they changed over the course of the school year. Hearing their conversations with each other as she observed a world she vividly remembered but was no longer part of. Laughing with them, helping them overcome frustration and difficulty both at school and at home. All the intangible things which made teaching so rewarding, lost in the distant and impersonal nature of Google Meets. After a mostly successful (but still stressful) year of hybrid in-person learning, Margaret had thought they'd left behind distance learning for good. Or, at the least, for a long while.

However, here they were again. Students reduced to squares on her laptop's screen. Inhuman digital avatars which looked bored, exhausted, and distant. If they showed up for class at all, of course.

THE HORROR AT PLEASANT BROOK

Grading essays digitally in Google Docs instead of physically writing *on* her students' papers (which she loved to do) was fatiguing. The growing disconnection from her wild, hormone-driven chaos machines, which gave her career meaning, even more so. Juggling a dizzying array of Google Apps trying to replicate science labs which required hands-on experience proved maddening, as none of the apps worked how they were supposed to, which lead to even more confusion.

She sighed and rubbed her forehead. The most surprising thing about remote teaching? How draining it was. Morbidly, Margaret imagined her laptop literally *sucking* the energy from her body. She often (with less and less humor as the weeks dragged by) imagined her sister visiting her, concerned because Margaret hadn't called, only to find a withered husk sitting at the kitchen table, staring blindly into the laptop which had drained her life essence.

Being a widower at age fifty-five was only making things worse. Not only was she teaching remotely from home, she was *literally* alone, all the time. She didn't struggle with grief much these days. Though Steve's heart attack three years ago had been unexpected, she'd moved past it better than she'd imagined she would, especially in those first few wrenching days.

What she struggled with now was simply the lack of Steve as a sounding board. A quiet and simple man who'd worked construction, Stephen Seaver had been a marvelous listener. In those days, if she came home from school feeling as she did now, after only ten minutes of pouring it into Steve's quietly drinking ears, she felt ready to tackle another school day. Without Steve, however, she'd stewed alone in her own juices for the past three years.

She hadn't remained celibate after Steve's passing, of course. A woman had needs, no matter how old she was. She was secure enough in herself to have occasionally engaged in mutually satisfactory dalliances which scratched her itch since Steve's passing; dalliances which didn't have to turn into anything else. She'd been discrete, of course. Had to be, when—through a turn of events she still didn't quite understand—you ended up sleeping with the school custodian.

She smiled sadly, thinking about Lester. He'd been sweet, and sad, and quite frankly, much different than she'd imagined. No one in town knew why his wife had taken off with his only son; but the rumors were there, of course. That he secretly beat her. That he was sleeping around. That he was gay, even.

During her brief interlude with Lester—which had run the course of several months—Margaret learned it hadn't been any of those things. Quite simply, it had just been the bottle. Lester wasn't a mean drunk, or a dangerous one, or selfish, or even self-pitying. He was amiable, gentle, and, well, sad. But regardless, he was a drunk, and he was only going to get drunker. That was why, after several months (and, of course, after Margaret's itch had been thoroughly scratched), she quickly but gently pulled away. He didn't pursue her; which, in a way, slightly disappointed her. There was no future for them, but even so . . . it had been some time since a suitor had chased after her, and it would've been nice. Even if the suitor was a forty-five-year-old alcoholic high school custodian.

Margaret sighed. If sleeping with the custodian at your place of work wasn't a sign that something was wrong, she didn't know what was. She should call it quits. Write her resignation letter and retire. *Especially* if—God forbid—they stayed remote all year long. She'd turned eligible this year, and suspected Principal Williams would rather hire a young, motivated recent college graduate who was more conversant with distance learning methods. For a pittance, of course, rather than her 30+ years salary. It was so hard to let go. So hard to make herself believe her teaching career was over . . .

Something creaked down the hall.

Margaret looked up, unconcerned at first. It was probably Macy, her stuck-up Siamese. Or maybe Tufty, Macy's rambunctious tabby-cat roommate. They always woke her up at night. Chasing mice, their claws clicking against bare wood floors way past midnight . . .

Her thoughts trailed off, as she stared at her front door, which had somehow opened all the way. She couldn't comprehend the sight. She'd locked it. Hadn't she? How had it opened? Who had opened it? How long had it been open, while she'd sat at the table, grading essays? It occurred to her, then, with a deep cold spike to her stomach. The creaking had come from the hall leading to the bedroom, bath, the guest room . . .

Behind me!

She tried to bolt out of her chair, but she didn't even get close to straightening her legs before two hands yanked her by the shoulders and threw her like a bag of laundry to the floor. She landed hard enough to shake the walls and knock two pictures down. Their glassy shattering sounded distant and far away.

A dark form knelt over her as icy terror gripped her heart. Her lungs fluttered as she gasped for breath, and her bladder gave away completely. The man kneeling over her, the man holding what looked like a gigantic butcher knife, was wearing a mask . . . and the mask was worse than everything else. Long, stringy, real-looking hair exploded in all directions. The rubber face had a sickly gray pallor, which also looked real, though that of a terminally ill man. Eyes bulged in different directions at the same time, and a wide, black maw screamed soundlessly.

The embroidered name tag on his work shirt read *McDonough*.

Lester?

She opened her mouth, but before she could utter a sound, the masked man's arm (Lester?) pistoned back and slammed the butcher knife deep into her belly. Unimaginable pain exploded and radiated all over her abdomen. She jerked and vomited blood in a rush, arms and legs twitching.

The man wearing the mask leaned into the blade, digging it around her guts. She tried to scream, to cry, or whisper—*Why, Lester*?—but blood clogged her throat, cutting off speech and air. She gagged up more blood, but it didn't matter. Her throat remained clogged.

Quickly, her vision telescoped down a long, dark tunnel. Her eyelids fluttered. Life began to slip away. As it did, the man in the mask did the oddest thing. The last thing Margaret Seaver saw before hopefully going to join Steve. The masked man opened his mouth, and as the lights dimmed and Margaret's synapses fired their last, she realized something like liquid *rubber* was oozing out of that mask's mouth and pattering all over her face. It burned and was the last thing she felt.

Carter Residence
9:00 PM

14.

HALFWAY THROUGH HIS third horror movie of the night—a surprisingly entertaining slasher flick called *The Terrifier*—Scott realized skipping out on Jasper had been the right call. Their moment a month ago had been weighing heavier and heavier between them, and the relief he felt at ditching Jasper made him feel lighter, even though it also made him feel like a shitty friend.

Jasper hadn't called, of course. It wasn't like he had a smartphone of his own. Plus, his mom had canceled their home phone two months ago. Of course, even if Jasper had a way to call him, Scott knew he wouldn't. Being Jasper, he probably waited at the library for twenty minutes, and when Scott didn't show, headed off to whatever low-grade mischief seized his fancy. Mischief Scott would've normally been happy to join in . . .

If Scott hadn't been an asshole and kissed his friend a month ago. On the *mouth*, even.

Abruptly, Scott wasn't interested in *The Terrifier* anymore. It wasn't entertaining, or funny. It was stupid and pointless. Frustrated, Scott grabbed the TV remote and switched it off. Art the Clown's maniacally leering face disappeared, replaced by blackness. Unable to sit, Scott pushed off the couch and walked over to the den's bay window, which looked out onto the night-shrouded front lawn.

Shadows pooled and crept along, thrown by a bright moon hanging high in the sky. The trees alongside the road loomed, looking twice as tall as normal. If he let his imagination run, flickering shadows became darting figures ducking furtively out of sight. It was the perfect horror movie setting, honestly.

"What the hell," Scott whispered, "what the *hell* were you thinking?"

He didn't have an answer, because quite frankly, he hadn't been thinking at all. He'd been *feeling*. Reacting. And in the process, totally misread a cue which probably hadn't been there at all.

He kissed you back.

For a moment, he kissed you back.

They'd been hanging out at the abandoned amphitheater at Martinkovic Park. Sitting on one of the sturdier top benches, talking about whatever came to mind. How remote schooling sucked. How Jasper hated going to the library, where that weirdo librarian Sage Hunter who wanted to be called "they or them" watched him like a hawk every single day. Scott had cringed internally as Jasper slammed Sage because he'd always liked the librarian, who reserved all the newest horror novels which came in so he could have first crack.

In retrospect, Jasper's mocking of Sage's gender-neutral identity should've clued him in on how Jasper felt about such things. Love blinded people, apparently.

Love?

Really?

Then their conversation turned—as it always did—to more important things. Like fathers. Jasper's dad had recently dropped by the farm, sniffing around for money. As she usually did in such situations, Jasper's Mom ran him off with a shotgun.

When Jasper complained about his dead-beat dad who only came around for money and booze and some nookie (which he sometimes was able to get from Jasper's mom), Scott replied that he sometimes wondered if that was better than not knowing your dad at all. At least Jasper knew who his dad was. More importantly, Jasper's dad knew *Jasper* existed. Unlike Scott's.

To that, Jasper smirked and waved. "Fuck that, man. I couldn't care less if my dad never showed up ever again. Waste of space can go to hell, for all I care."

He'd turned right then and looked at Scott with an oddly *affectionate* expression, one Jasper had never shown before. "Look, Scott. If your dad can't be bothered to come around and get to know what an awesome kid he's got? Screw him. He don't deserve to know you."

Scott smiled. "Thanks. You think I'm awesome, huh?"

Jasper shrugged. "Yeah, you're okay. Not as awesome as *me*, but . . . "

They'd both laughed. Jasper threw his right arm around Scott's shoulders and pulled him into a half-hug. Then, they'd looked at each, falling silent for a few seconds. Something passed between them (at least, Scott had thought so), so he leaned in and kissed Jasper on the mouth.

For a moment—for the briefest of seconds—Jasper had responded. Scott felt sure of this. Jasper kissed him back. Something like an electrical current passed from him to Scott; something deep in Scott's gut *sang*. For that brief moment, he felt more alive than he'd ever had.

However, it ended almost as quickly as it happened. Like he was waking up from a bad dream, Jasper jerked back from Scott, sputtering and swearing. "What . . . what the *fuck*, Scott? What the fuck are you doing . . . ?"

Scott stared, mouth hanging open, his stomach dropping, Jasper staggered upright, spitting as if he'd swallowed something bad. He wiped his mouth with the back of his hand, and stuttered, "What the fuck . . . what the fuck are you . . . shit! I'm not . . . not like that . . . Jesus fuckin . . . I'm not fuckin like that!"

Scott finally came to life, standing also, hands up, apologetic and pleading with his best friend. "Shit. I'm so sorry Jasper. I don't mean . . . I shouldn't have . . . "

"No! Just . . . no. Fuck no." Jasper shook his head and stumbled over the old amphitheater bench, into the parking lot, and away.

Scott briefly debated following but ended up sinking slowly back down onto the bench. He turned and stared dully at the old stage, burying his confused emotions deep inside, until he eventually went home to eat another dinner alone in an empty house, as Mom once again worked an extra evening shift at The Whole in the Wall, which had been happening a lot lately.

Tonight, staring out over the night-shrouded front lawn, Scott shook his head. Stupid. Stupid, stupid, *stupid*. He still couldn't figure out what possessed him to kiss Jasper. Of course, that wasn't true. He knew *why* he'd kissed his best friend on the mouth. In that moment, Scott had felt closer to Jasper than he'd ever felt to anyone else. Talking about their absent dads, Jasper calling him awesome, Scott feeling something warm welling up inside at that moment. He'd acted upon that warm feeling like folks did in movies and novels all the time. The result, however . . .

"What were you expecting?" He reached out and thumped the bay window lightly with his fist. "*Jackass*."

He'd skipped out on Jasper for a few days, actually *afraid* to go near him. He couldn't imagine Jasper would actually do something to him, or hurt him, in any way. Even so. Scott couldn't forget his friend's shocked expression of *disgust*.

He kissed me back, a stubbornly hopeful part of his brain insisted. *I know he did. For a second. That's gotta mean something*.

A few days later, Jasper called from the library's payphone. Scott saw the caller ID, braced himself, and answered with a careful, "Hey. What's up?"

"*Don't ever do that again, okay*?" Jasper's voice rasped over the phone. "*I'm not . . . I'm not like that. I don't care that you are, but I'm not. Just don't ever do that again, or I'll have Marcus beat the shit out of you. Get it?*"

Deep conflict waged inside Scott right then. Part of him was relieved. Maybe he and Jasper could go back to normal. Forget it ever happened. Another part of him, however—a newly awakened part—didn't *want* things to go back to normal. Didn't want to pretend it had never happened, and that part died a little when he said, "Okay. Sure. I promise."

"*Cool.*" A pause, and then, in his trademark (though slightly forced) nonchalance, he added, "*Mom's got a few six packs of Molson in the fridge. Wanna hang*?"

They'd resumed hanging out. On the surface, everything was fine. But underneath, Scott could feel the tension. Jasper eyed him a little closer than usual. Almost as if he was waiting to fend off another kiss. For his part, Scott felt like he was working extra hard to keep things light.

The result? Not only had his "movie moment" gone awry, but he also may've lost his best friend in the process.

"Stupid," he muttered, "so fucking . . . "

His breath caught in his throat.

Something pale flickered at the lawn's edge, by the road. It looked like a figure ducking behind one of the trees. A person? Was someone lurking around the road out front?

Cold fingers played down Scott's spine as he leaned toward the window, peering closer. He couldn't see anything, now. Must've been his imagination turning moonlight into things which weren't there.

A wave of fatigue washed over him, and a warm blanket of haziness settled onto his shoulders. His cheeks became flushed and warm. He felt lightheaded. Almost as if he'd taken several hits from a joint or downed several shots of Mom's vodka. He blinked. The lawn, through the living room window, telescoped away, receding into the distance, as some indefinable force pulled him away from the window, away to . . .

His smartphone warbled his mother's ringtone.

Scott blinked again. A cold sensation washed over him as he realized he was no longer standing at the living room window. He was at the front door. His hand turning the doorknob, about to open the door, to . . .

let me in

Scott released the doorknob with a yelp as if the thing had given him a shock. Frantically, he reached up and snapped the deadbolt shut (Had he unlocked it? Why?) and stepped away from the front door.

"What the *fuck*?" His breaths came in short, hitching gasps. He felt out of breath as if he'd run a mile. Scott stared at the front door, sure something on the other side would rattle it in its frame as it tried to get in.

Nothing happened.

Silence swelled, filling the house. It felt almost like a physical thing, Pressing down upon him. Making his skin prickle and itch.

His phone rang again.

All the tension leaked away, leaving him shaky, and feeling more than a little foolish. He breathed deep, collected himself, turned away from the front door, and went to his phone where it was sitting on the side table next to the couch to answer Mom's call, already knowing (feeling a different kind of sinking dread) what it would be about.

The Whole in the Wall
Main Street
10 PM

15.

TIFFANY CARTER FROWNED as she hung up the phone. Something was wrong with Scott. He'd sounded startled. Jumpy. He'd passed it off as being so absorbed in the horror movie he was watching that his phone's ringing spooked him. Tiffany wasn't buying it. A horror movie veteran at only fifteen, Scott wasn't the type to get spooked by a ringing phone. Something else was bothering him. Tiffany felt sure of it.

Something had been bothering Scott for weeks, however, though Tiffany wasn't sure what. She hadn't been able to get it out of him, of course. It wasn't like he *told* her things. He never had. A closed book like his father, except he hid behind horror movies and novels instead of sports and a raging libido.

Thanks, Bobby Lee, wherever the fuck you are, she thought as she stuffed her phone into her jacket pocket, *thanks a whole hell of a lot.*

She shook her head as she pushed through the diner's door-to the night beyond. Thinking about Bobby Lee never did any good. The bastard had ditched her and blown town fifteen years ago. Tiffany didn't find out until she'd stopped by his house to tell him she was pregnant, and his drunken waste of a father told her Bobby Lee and his little tag-along Jesse Simpson left Pleasant Brook for the Army.

Tiffany drew her coat around her a little tighter. After she'd started to show and couldn't pretend any longer, navigating pregnancy as a single mother had been a nightmare. Ignoring the whispers and side-long glances she got in public. Enduring the stony silence at home; a silence which wouldn't thaw until both her parents held Scott for the first time.

Somehow, she'd gotten away with concealing Bobby Lee's identity as the father. She waited until several months after Bobby Lee left to tell her parents, and—in a perverse twist of luck—Scott was late, so it looked like she'd gotten pregnant after Bobby Lee left.

"Which is great," she muttered to herself as she took her car keys from the purse slung over her shoulder, walking across the parking lot. "Made me look like even more of a slut."

That didn't matter, however. None of it did. Her parents took to Scott at first sight, and eventually forgave and accepted her. Town folks did likewise, and they moved on to talking about something else much quicker than she'd imagined they would. She managed to survive on her own, and it wasn't long before she thought—no, she *knew*—that she and Scott were far better off without Bobby Lee. Hopefully he'd *stay* gone, and never come back.

She clicked her keys and unlocked her 1992 Dodge Caravan, trying to reassure herself that she and Scott had forged a life for themselves. It wasn't a great life, and she often worried about Scott. Slacking off in school and running around with white trash like Jasper Riley. If only Scott would talk to her . . .

Tiffany pushed those thoughts away as she got in her van and started it up. As she'd told Scott on the phone, she was heading to The Tipper for a "nightcap" before going home. She'd worked two shifts back-to-back and felt bone-tired. She desperately needed to relax. A few mixed drinks would do the job nicely, even if it was in a grungy dive like The Tipper.

As she drove out of the parking lot, she wondered if Scott had sounded so strained on the phone because she'd called to tell him not to wait up. She pushed that thought away, also.

16.

IT MOVED THROUGH the woods, melding with the darkness, as it slowly made its way back to the place of its birth. They were five, now, returning to the birthplace—where they'd been called from the darkness, as they had been countless times before. Its memories, as always, were shot through with holes. Fragmentary, detailing their history only in piecemeal. As they spread and made more of themselves, and took hold in this world, they would remember more about themselves, who and what they were, and how they had come to be.

Of course, as it soundlessly picked its way past trees and through brush, it knew more than the others, because it came first. It was the First. They were of one mind and one being, and yet, It was the First of them. There was always a First called forth from the darkness, a First which then called forth more.

They felt simple things. Hunger. Desire. The need to spread and consume. Fear of the Other, that the Other would reach down from its High Place and cast them back into darkness, as it had so many times before.

But as the First moved through the dark, it felt something it hadn't in a long time. It felt . . . confusion. Puzzlement. It had been watching someone. A young boy. The boy had been alone. The First could've easily taken the boy, consumed it, and made another. The First had reached inside the boy's mind, and had been drawing it outside to do that . . .

When it stopped, for some reason. And withdrew, a strange sensation coursing through it, one unfamiliar and foreign, along with . . .

Scott

Tiffany

. . . and then the foreign sensation left the First, and only the light buzz of Them remained. Even now, it couldn't recall the strange sensation, nor did it understand the significance of "Scott" and "Tiffany."

It didn't try to understand. As it slipped past trees in the darkness, the First let itself sink into the buzzing hum of Their minds, and this surging river swept its confusion away.

Thursday
October 23rd
Constable's Office
11:00 AM

17.

GRACE SAT BEHIND her desk and eyed the two teenagers sitting on the other side, enjoying their uncomfortable silence and pensive expressions. She supposed maybe she was having a bit too much fun at their expense, considering she'd once been in their shoes, about fifteen or sixteen years ago. But that was how the world turned. One minute you "fight the law" and the next became it.

"Cecilia Tiderencil. Joey McCann. Any guesses why I called your parents and had them bring you over?"

Cecilia—a wide-eyed, somewhat innocent-looking seventeen-year-old girl with short brown hair and a normally open expression—sat rigidly in her chair. Face a slightly panicked mask, lips pressed tight, cheeks pale. Joey McCann, on the other hand, slouched in his chair, arms crossed defiantly over his chest, feet splayed out before him. Kid was barely sixteen and he was already man-spreading like a seasoned pro.

Grace leaned forward, smiling gently. "C'mon, guys. Fess up. I can't do 'good cop; bad cop' because there's only me, and I'd look awfully silly playing both parts at once. Why don't we save time and cut to the chase? Get this over with, so we can put it in the rear-view."

Cecilia swallowed nervously. Grace swore she saw the poor kid's throat working, could *hear* her stomach gurgling. Joey, on the other hand, shifted in his chair as he crossed his feet at their ankles, and muttered "Whatever."

Grace spread her hands in a pleading gesture. "Don't make me go through this whole schtick. You've got remote school, and I've got more important things to do."

Cecilia sat statue-still; Joey snorted and smirked wider. Grace feigned a resigned sigh as she sat back, took her phone out of her breast pocket, and said, "Okay then. The long way around it is."

She set the phone down on the desk so it was facing Cecilia and Joey. "So, apparently you guys had quite a time on Vaughan Street last night. Going house to house, smashing every jack o'lantern you could find."

As the video clip looped, Cecilia's lip trembled slightly. Joey glanced at Grace's phone, looking worried for the first time since he'd sauntered in. Grace continued.

"I'm sure you thought you'd get away clean. What with mostly older folks living on Vaughan, and how lots of folks are spooked—and rightly so—about COVID. Here's the thing, though."

She waved at her phone, still looping the video clip. "You know those neat Ring security doorbells they have these days? The ones with fish-eye security cameras on them? Lots of folks on Vaughan have had those installed over the last two years. These things are a *marvel*, guys. They capture *really* clear video, even with how small they are. *This* is only the video from Leslie Winter's Ring."

At that—the implication there were other videos—Joey's face paled, which made Grace feel a small stab of admittedly vindictive pleasure. The tear which trickled down Cecilia's almost crumpled face blunted that satisfaction, however, as she felt a little sorry for the Honor Student who'd gotten dragged into this.

Don't kid yourself, she thought. *You've been fooled by that kind of charm before, and there's usually a healthy dose of self-deception which goes with it.*

"So, as you can see," Grace said as she gestured at her phone, "not only is there a great view of you guys smashing Leslie Winters' jack o'lanterns, there's also a very flattering view of you," Grace looked at Joey, all the fight now gone out of him, the kid finally looking a little scared, "dropping trou and pissing on what's left of her Jacks. Nice touch, by the way."

Joey said nothing as he sank into his chair, staring at his feet.

"At the end of the video, there's glimpses of you guys doing the same on the other side of the street. Guess how many *other* folks on Vaughan have the Ring, also? And how many *other* videos there are of you two jokers?"

Joey's chin snapped up, his eyes absolutely terrified now, while it was Cecilia's turn to stare into her lap, her hands clenched and unclenched. Grace continued. "Four more. *Four more videos* of you guys waging war on Vaughan Street's jack o'lanterns last night. Good, *clear* videos."

Joey blinked and finally stuttered to life. "We were . . . it was a . . . we got . . . "

Grace held up a hand.

Joey's mouth snapped shut.

"I don't want to hear it. That it was a joke, a prank, a dare, you got carried away. Don't care, because regardless, here we are."

She lowered her hand and offered what she hoped was a gentler expression. "But, this is hardly a felony. I'm also not going to lie and claim I never smashed a jack o'lantern in my day. *However*."

The faint grins which had started to tentatively form vanished. "I was an arrogant shit who didn't care about other people's property, and I had to learn my lesson. Like you're going to learn one. *Technically* vandalism is a misdemeanor, though, at the most, you'd get fines your parents would have to pay. As far as *I'm* concerned, that's the easy way out. I have a much better consequence in store. It's the same consequence Constable Ford gave *me* fifteen years ago, and I think it suits this situation perfectly."

She sat back in her chair and folded her arms. "Your parents have agreed to buy replacement pumpkins for *all* the ones you smashed on Vaughan Street. ALL OF THEM. What we're going to do is take a ride in my JEEP to Goodlow's Farm, pick those pumpkins, come back here, and you're going to spend the rest today—and tomorrow too, if need be—carving replacement jack o'lanterns for the folks on Vaughan. You will also deliver each of them *personally*. Under my supervision, of course.

"I've cleared your absence today and potential absence tomorrow with Principal Williams. Told him you'd both be assisting me with a 'special community project.' He was very impressed by your commitment to civic duty, I might add. But."

She pointed at both of them in turn. "You're still responsible for any schoolwork you miss. No excuses."

Not surprisingly, Cecilia looked thankful and relieved, probably thinking she'd just missed a future in juvie by a hair's breadth. Also unsurprisingly, Joey looked faintly disgusted, as if he'd much rather have his parents pay a fine and be done with it. "You're shitting me," he muttered in disbelief.

Grace smiled, enjoying this moment a little too much, and not feeling bad at all. "I shit you not."

Joey crossed his arms, looking sullen again, like a Dollar Store James Dean. "Well this fucking sucks."

A sniff, and then in a slightly trembling voice, "Did the cameras . . . did they get the guy in the weird mask?"

Grace frowned. "What do you mean?"

Joey smirked, looking bored already. "Some weirdo wandering around Vaughan Street wearing this ugly rubber mask. Big googly eyes, wide-open screaming mouth, stringy black hair. Don't think he actually went up on any porches, though. *She*," he nodded at Cecilia, "thought he was following us. *I* think it was probably a drunk. Maybe that McDonough guy. The school custodian? Everyone knows he's plastered half the time. Even when we were in school."

Grace shook her head. "No masked people on the Ring cameras, or at least so far as anyone's said. Only you guys. And, yeah. Lester's had some problems the past few years. But wandering around, wearing a weird mask, following kids? Not his style."

Joey shrugged again. "Whatever. I think he was drunk, is all. Definitely wasn't following us."

"He *was*," Cecilia insisted, voice tight, eyes flashing angrily at Joey. "I know it."

Grace smiled, thinking whatever charm Joey had over Cecilia was probably gone forever. "No one reported seeing anyone in a mask, and we didn't see him in the videos," she offered a reassuring glance to Cecilia, "but thanks for bringing it up. I'll keep an eye out. Now.

"We've got some pumpkins to pick up, and you've got some carving to do."

Cecilia sighed, and Joey groaned. She waved them toward the front door, and they got up and walked out of the constable's station. It made her chuckle, but her amusement was dampened by the possibility she was going to yet again have to deal with a drunk Lester McDonough. She'd like to think he took a night off after his most recent binge . . . but she knew how he got. Once he was in a drinking groove, it was hard for him to pull himself out of it without help. Even so.

Something didn't feel right about that, though. What, she wasn't sure. Stalking kids in a rubber mask? Definitely not Lester's usual routine.

Grace shook off the weird premonition and followed the two teens out to her JEEP, to take them to their just reward.

3:45 PM

18.

"**DID YOU SEE** the look on that Oakley bitch's face when I told her to get bent on Zoom today?"

Scott frowned slightly but glanced away so Jasper wouldn't see it. "Yeah. That was . . . something."

Jasper snorted and slapped his leg. "Priceless, man! She didn't know what to do! Not like she can send suspend me, can she? I bet she won't even give me a zero for not doin the damn homework, it messed with her so bad."

Scott shook his head, amazed at Jasper's self-perceived hilarity, but not in a way which would've flattered him. On the surface, Jasper Riley was a walking, talking cliché. Five-Finger Death Punch t-shirt with the sleeves torn off. Dangling skull earrings. Peroxide-blond mullet. Torn and ripped jeans, and worn but wicked-looking engineer's boots stomping down the sidewalk. Smoking cigarette in one hand, a can of Skoal in his rear pocket. He projected the textbook image of a juvie who spent the weekends sneaking into bars and strip clubs, thanks to older cousins who "knew people."

They had gotten past that image, of course. Over time, Jasper had lowered his defenses and set aside his "bad boy" gimmick as he and Scott became better friends. Jasper re-assuming his thug swagger, full force, was more fallout from Scott's mistake. Scott felt dismayed at how much it annoyed him, now.

Jasper stuck his cigarette into his mouth and took a long, slow drag. He puffed it out leisurely, and said with forced nonchalance, "You comin out this weekend?"

Scott was slow in answering, unsure if the offer was genuine. "Dunno. Mom probably won't want me to. Not with COVID getting worse again."

Using his free hand, Jasper struck Scott's shoulder with a good-natured slap. "C'mon! Don't be a fag. This COVID shit ain't nothing but a hoax, man. My uncle works for the government. He knows this stuff."

Scott cringed at Jasper's slur and said, "Your uncle is a postman in Smyrna."

"Still, man! He hears shit, all the time! Like how he always sees these weird black SUVs with tinted windows at all the COVID vaccine centers, deliverin the vaccines, cept they're not vaccines but really . . . "

Scott grunted, in no mood to debunk Jasper's wild stories. Jasper swatted him on the shoulder again. "Well, c'mon. Are you comin out this weekend, or not?"

Scott shrugged. Maybe Jasper's invite was genuine, and if so, he didn't see why not. Even if Mom didn't want him going out, it wasn't like she could stop him. She was working all weekend at the diner, and would probably go out to The Tipper after work for a "nightcap" both nights. Last night she hadn't gotten home until 3. He could stay out until two, both Friday and Saturday night, and still get home before Mom. He could get away with it, easy.

He'd felt weird all day, though. He kept thinking about that odd shape he'd seen out by the road, and the weird way he'd sleepwalked to the front door and almost opened it still unnerved him. It made him feel unsettled and off balance, for some reason.

Remote schooling wasn't helping, of course. Rumors were going around by text that the custodian, Lester McDonough, skipped work yesterday morning. Some kids were saying he'd gone on a drinking binge, because why not? He didn't have to be at school for anything. Wilder stories were saying he'd been a perv and got fired for having kiddie porn in his office.

Even weirder, Mrs. Seaver hadn't shown up for science class this afternoon. He'd clicked the Google Meets Link in his email, but she never logged on. According to the flurry of text messages between his classmates, no one knew why.

Not that he cared one way or another. Mrs. Seaver's absence meant he could bail and leave his house early to meet up with Jasper outside the library on Main Street. Even if Constable Matthews saw him, it's not like she knew his school schedule, or could do anything to stop him.

"Well? C'mon. My older cousin is one of the bouncers at The Hot Pot in Utica. He'll get us in. We can get wasted and watch real live naked girls dance! See their titties and everything!"

Scott hated the way he felt inside. It had been *months* since Jasper had pulled this Alpha Male shit. Talking about getting into the strip clubs in Utica, seeing "pussy and titties." But the Bro-Dog Act was in full effect. Even worse—more than anything—this convinced him that Jasper *had* felt something when they kissed, and he was playing the sex-crazed bad boy to cover up. It made him sad, in a way he couldn't articulate.

Of course, he couldn't say any of that to Jasper.

"Right. I'm sure it'll go over great when I get COVID and tell Mom I probably got it from a lap dance . . . "

He looked away, across Pleasant Brook Bridge, his voice dying mid-word. He coughed, a strange anxiety clawing at his throat. "What the hell is up with *that*?"

Jasper followed his gaze and frowned. Standing on the other side of the bridge were two people. Hard to tell from their distance, but though they were shaped differently—one of them taller and lankier, the other shorter and stouter—something about their faces looked similar. Almost the same. Like they were related, or . . .

"Fuck me," Jasper spat. "Are they wearin fuckin *masks*?"

Scott narrowed his eyes. The strangers on the other side of the bridge had to be at least a hundred yards away, so he couldn't make out specifics about their faces, but something in his gut said Jasper was right. The general shape of the faces, the long stringy black hair. The mouths hanging open as if they were screaming silently.

They were both wearing masks.

"What the hell is this, Jasper? Your older cousins get all dressed up, trying to freak me out?"

Jasper didn't say anything. Scott glanced at him, expecting a wide grin, followed by another one of Jasper's laughs.

What he saw instead unnerved him. Jasper was growling, like a threatened dog. Apparently, Jasper was as spooked by the masked duo as he was.

"No way," Jasper finally muttered through clenched teeth. "I ain't got nothin to do with this. Motherfuckers better not be thinkin of messin with me, 'cause . . . "

In perfect synchronization, the masked duo stepped onto the bridge and started walking toward them. Their gait stiff-legged, arms hanging slackly by their sides.

Jasper's bravado fled at the sight. "Fuck this, man."

He glanced at Scott. "I'm headin home," he pointed right, up Kovac Road, and was already moving in that direction, "going the back way. You wanna come?"

Scott shook his head. One of the few cool places in Pleasant Brook was a little junk store called This and That, across the street, only a few steps away. "I'm good," he tossed over his shoulder, pointedly not looking at the weirdos in masks crossing the bridge, "I'm gonna duck into the junk shop. Kill a few minutes there."

Scott expected a sneer at that, but Jasper must've been spooked bad because he nodded and turned down Kovac Road in a jog. "See you tomorrow after school!" he called out over his shoulder.

"Yeah! Sure." Scott turned and trotted across Main Street. When he hit the opposite sidewalk, he dared look back at Pleasant Brook Bridge, his stomach tightening. He didn't know what he'd do if he turned and saw them striding toward him, those rubbery masks (he felt sure they were made of rubber) leering idiotically . . .

The bridge and street were empty.

Scott sighed, not realizing how frightened he'd actually been until now. He turned around and saw nothing. Only empty street that way, also.

He was alone.

Still. He was three steps away from This and That. He'd go hang out in there for a few minutes, then go home. He may hang out with an idiot, but that didn't mean he *was* one.

19.

BY THE TIME Jasper had reached the small bicycle bridge which branched off Kovac Road, his spiteful and arrogant facade had reasserted itself. He sneered, forgetting his pants-pissing fear (which he'd never would've shown to Scott, even before that fucked-up thing that happened a few weeks ago). Of course, he didn't like thinking about that fucked up thing which almost happened between him and Scott, because even *thinking* about that day . . .

but you liked it

you know you did

. . . pissed him off, which at least made him feel less jumpy.

jumpy, hell

more like scared shitless

"Whatever," Jasper muttered. Fucking loonies in this town, anyway. Running around playing Halloween dress-up in fucking weird masks. They were lucky his cousin Marcus from Utica wasn't in town. Marcus would've fucked those crazy assholes *up*. They'd *need* to wear masks after Marcus got done with them.

Jasper stuck his hands into his pockets and kicked a small rock, sending it skittering down Kovac Road. In a year he'd turn sixteen. Soon as that happened, he was quitting school and moving to Utica to live the good life with Marcus. Get fucking high and wasted whenever he wanted. Marcus was always promising to get him into the Utica strip clubs—the *nice* ones, not like that shit hole The Couger's Den—and they'd party nonstop, smoking pot, getting laid . . .

But Scott wouldn't be there—no way he had the stones to quit school and ditch home—and a part of Jasper hated that. A part that whispered whatever "party" life he found in Utica would be empty and meaningless without Scott. They'd gotten close over the years—damn near inseparable during the 2020 quarantine—and the thought of leaving Scott bothered Jasper in ways he couldn't define.

"But he ruined it," Jasper snarled softly. "He fucking *kissed* me. Why'd he fucking *kiss* me?"

you know why

you kissed him back

"I'm not like that, though. I'm not a fucking . . . "

Something scraped behind him.

A boot on asphalt.

Something sharp and hard slammed into his back, right near his spine. It punched through clothes, flesh, and muscle. Pain worse than anything he'd ever felt exploded through him. Blood rushed up his throat and shot out his mouth in a deep red fountain.

A burning cold spread through Jasper. He felt the object (a knife, his brain thought dully) pull out, and then slam into another part of his back. This time, it hardly hurt. Just felt colder, and the knife sawing against his insides felt strangely distant. Like a dentist tugging on a numbed tooth.

The knife pulled out again. Hands roughly spun him around and pushed him. He flopped onto his back, arms and legs twitching uselessly against the ground. A form bent over him, its face hovering mere inches from Jasper's, and his eyes—the light fading from them—registered two things before everything went dark for good.

One, a breast pocket nametag which read *McDonough*.

Two, the figure was indeed wearing a rubber mask. A mask which was bubbling, stretching, melting, and dripping onto his face. As his skin burned, Jasper was able to muster one final mewl, before gouts of molten rubber fell from the mask into his mouth, and pushed down his throat.

Friday, October 24th
Constable's Office
Main Street
9:00 AM

20.

GRACE MATTHEWS HUNG UP her smartphone and set it on her desk. With a sigh, she pushed her chair back and tried to sort through her jumbled thoughts. She hadn't had much to drink last evening, but even so, she didn't sleep well. Strange dreams haunted her all night. Dreams of that fucking detective in Utica morphing into nonsensical dreams of being pursued across shadowed, surreal nightscapes. Of course, by a person wearing a mask, like Cecilia and Joey had described yesterday.

She folded her hands behind her head, closed her eyes, and sighed. Unusual things had happened the past few days. Things which bothered her, though she couldn't put her finger on why. These occurrences weren't bizarre by any means, or too terribly strange. They struck her as . . . odd. Like an uneasy intuition lingering in the back of her mind was tapping out an unknowable message in alien Morse code.

She opened her eyes, grabbed the notepad she'd been jotting on, and tapped the first item on the list. The day after he'd sobered up in her only cell, Lester hadn't shown up at the school. He hadn't called in. No one noticed him missing until partway through the morning when Principal Williams called Lester's office phone, and the custodian never answered. Thursday, calls to his small house on Reynolds Road hadn't been returned, despite threats of firing him.

Principal Williams finally called Grace this morning, asking her to check on McDonough, because she was the only one in town who bothered to take care of him after a binge. Despite his drinking problems, Lester McDonough hadn't ever been the type to ditch work and not answer his phone.

Around eight-thirty she'd hopped into her JEEP and headed to Lester's house. Everything looked in order, his car in the driveway. She knocked on the door, to no answer. Best as she could tell by peering through the front windows into the den, nothing seemed amiss. Without probable cause or anything else to go on, she didn't have a reason to break into Lester's house.

Not yet, anyway.

Grace moved her finger down to the second item, part of the same call from the beleaguered Principal Williams. Margaret Seaver, widowed fifty-five-year-old ninth-grade science teacher. She'd missed two days of remote school in a row without calling or emailing. This, too, was highly out of character. Calls to her home had also gone unanswered.

Grace had gone to Seaver's house after Lester's. When Grace knocked on Seaver's door, no one came. When she looked into the window, everything appeared fine. No signs of struggle, or anything out of place.

Two people who worked at the high school had vanished. Neither of them had family in the area, or even in the state. No one to miss them any time soon. Though it was a little dramatic, the last bit bothered Grace more than she wanted to admit.

Grace was hooked into most of the town scuttlebutt, so she knew both Lester and Margaret had shared a thing several months ago. Of course, when she'd suggested to Williams that maybe Lester and Margaret had run off together, the principal sputtered indigently, as if the thought was offensive.

He asked Grace what she planned to do. Grace told him nothing until something else happened, and Williams got even huffier. However, at the moment, all Grace had were two adults who had left town without telling anyone, and she had absolutely no reason to force entry into either of their homes.

Grace sighed and moved her index finger to the last item on the list. The one which bothered her the most. Jasper Riley had never come home Thursday evening. Joan Riley calling Grace, worried about Jasper, was odd, also, something Grace wasn't exactly used to. Usually, other people called *her* about one of the Rileys, not Mrs. Riley calling because she was worried her son had gone missing.

Joan's hand-wringing fear about Jasper's whereabouts was even odder. He hadn't been caught doing anything illegal *yet*, but Jasper was a Riley. Which meant he mostly likely spent his free time hell-raising all hours of the night, drinking, and smoking pot. Grace would expect Joan Riley to be accustomed to Jasper keeping whatever hours he felt like.

She'd been frantic, however. Claiming Jasper never spent the night out. That she had an "awful bad feeling somethin's happened to my boy." Grace promised to look into the matter.

A quick call to Sage had offered Grace her only lead regarding Jasper's whereabouts. Sage had often seen Jasper meet Scott Carter on the front steps and then head off down Main Street. They hadn't seen who Jasper left with yesterday afternoon, as they were in the back sorting new library purchases. But it was a fair bet Jasper had met up with Scott again.

Grace tapped the notepad, thinking. She'd visit Joan Riley in person. Then pay a visit to Tiffany Carter and talk to Scott. Thinking about Scott made her think of what Sage had said about seeing Jesse Simpson, and hoping he and Bobby weren't squatting around somewhere outside Pleasant Brook. That bothered her, also.

Burns Hill Road
1:00 PM

21.

MARTY CRENSHAW HITCHED his old Army rucksack higher up on his shoulder as he turned onto Burns Hill Road. The road inclined, and the rucksack was tightly packed with a small pup tent, along with fishing and camping gear. Though he was in good shape because he walked everywhere, his burden would've still weighed him down if the rucksack wasn't settled on his shoulders right, especially with the cooler full of fish in his left hand.

His destination was the barn at the top of Burns Hill Road. Formerly known as old Hathaway barn, it now belonged to him. Though it was over fifty years old, its roof and structure still held solid, as well as its flooring. There were no holes or gaps in its walls because Marty patched them regularly every August. Every Spring, he also applied a fresh coat of weather-resistant paint on all four walls, inside and out.

The barn didn't have electricity, of course, but Marty was able to keep his living space fairly well-lit with a combination of the battery-operated and propane-fueled lanterns he'd collected over time. Several years ago—with the help of some men in town—he'd installed a cast-iron fireplace which vented its smoke through a tin chimney. It still got cold occasionally, especially in the Adirondack winters, but Marty had always been somewhat hot-blooded, and more comfortable in cold weather than most.

Through hard work, the barn had come to possess some of the comforts of home. Because it *was* Marty's home. The only one he'd known for the past fifteen years.

Marty's story was rather pedestrian. He'd started his drinking career soon as he was old enough to nick his Dad's beers without the old man noticing, but it wasn't a problem. Not at first. Gradually, however, it consumed him from the inside out.

No sad or tragic event was the cause. For whatever reasons Marty—who'd taken a job as a linesman at the lumber mill in Pleasant Brook soon as he'd graduated high school—kept drinking a little harder every year. To quote a phrase used often by Pleasant Brook old timers, "Marty usta to hold the bottle, but now the bottle holds him."

No horrific accident caused by on-the-job intoxication led to Marty's firing. His boss, Sheldon Temple, simply got tired of Marty coming into work late on Monday mornings with a hangover, or not coming in on Mondays at all. When he did fire Marty, he did so through an apologetic phone call. One which Marty received amicably, understanding Sheldon's reasons perfectly.

Bills went unpaid. The bank repossessed his truck. Finally came eviction from his small apartment over the Napa Auto Parts Store on Main Street, after not paying rent for five months straight. He'd started bedding down in the old Hathaway barn after his eviction. At the time, all he cared about was the temporary (and back then, barely adequate) shelter it offered from harsh weather.

However, somewhere along the line, Marty sobered up and stopped drinking. No one knew how, or could pinpoint exactly when. Regulars at The Tipper Inn simply saw less and less of him over an indefinable period.

Eventually, they realized with a start they hadn't seen him drunk and leaning against the bar in months. Word spread gradually. When people encountered Marty around the town, they started noticing his generally cleaner and sober appearance.

Then, after he was three months sober, Marty officially started attending Pleasant Brook's small A. A. chapter, which met in the basement of First Methodist. He was officially on the wagon, and the trajectory of his life changed dramatically afterward.

Marty never chose to find another steady job. During the summer and spring, he managed almost daily employment bailing hay and doing odd jobs for three different farmers outside town. Every Saturday, he cleared brush and dead-fall around Gerhart Trailer Park. When the carnival came every year, for a week, Marty cleaned the grounds before opening and after closing.

In the fall, he parked cars for the pumpkin maze and also helped Goodlow harvest their pumpkins. During the winter, he shoveled the front walks of several older Pleasant Brook residents. Handy with small engines, he fixed lawnmowers, tractors, and other small engine vehicles out of the barn for a decent fee.

He fished and learned to hunt by bow and arrow. Though only in season, and every year he bought a proper hunting and fishing license. Saturday nights he splurged and bought dinner at The Whole in the Wall on Main Street, while his funds allowed for a moderate biweekly grocery budget of nonperishable goods, seeing as how he didn't have access to long-term refrigeration.

THE HORROR AT PLEASANT BROOK

Marty never again bothered to pay for lodging. No one knew or understood why, but no one questioned it, either. The old Hathaway barn simply became "Marty's place" in the minds of townsfolk (the Hathaways didn't mind; being dead and gone over twenty years). Marty's quiet and simplistic existence simply became part of the fabric of life in Pleasant Brook.

Cars and trucks honked as they passed him on Burns Hill Road, and he offered his usual spare nod as he thought about the day ahead. Several things needed to be done. He'd taken a few days off his odd jobs to camp one last time deep in the woods along Pleasant Brook. The result was the cooler full of rainbow trout which needed to be salted and smoked. Also, he'd been meaning to clean out the furnace and its flue before cold weather hit.

So consumed by these thoughts, he didn't register the strange sounds behind him until he was about ten feet from the barn. It was a soft, sucking sound. Like someone trying to pull a booted foot out of muck. He paused, almost *afraid* to look behind him. The sounds turned his stomach and sent an instinctual shiver through him. Whatever made that sound was *wrong*. Something not right. Something unnatural.

Marty stood there for several seconds. The sounds died out soon as he stopped, but even so . . . he *felt* something behind him.

Deep conflict waged inside. He didn't back away from things easily. Marty had lived in the rough for the past fifteen years, and he was still alive simply because he'd learned to heed his instincts. Instinct told him that to look back would be his end. It didn't make any kind of rational sense. What could possibly be following him up Burns Hill Road that could harm him? This was Pleasant Brook. Barely enough people lived here to call it a town. There wasn't much in the way of dangerous animals living in these woods. Why was he so scared of something which sounded like someone walking around in water (or mud) filled boots?

Keep walking.

Or look over his shoulder.

He was about thirty feet away from the barn, so Marty took a deep breath. Slipped his hand into his right pants pocket and pulled out the key for the heavy padlock on the barn's front door. Flexed his shoulders, making sure his rucksack was balanced and started walking toward the barn in long, even strides.

Immediately, the sounds started up again in the same measured pace he'd heard before. It sounded like someone walking barefoot in mud, making a wet and viscous squelching sound, which of course didn't make sense, because the roadside was completely dry.

Pursuit. That was the word, without a doubt. Something was pursuing him up Burns Hill Road.

Marty lengthened his stride, resisting the urge to break into a run, as he was only about ten feet away from relative safety.

He didn't like the sound of that, of course.

Relative safety.

Three feet away. The oozing muck-footfalls continued, and though he couldn't tell for sure, he didn't think they'd sped up or closed the distance. Even so, a weird *panic* had actually set in, nestling like a cold serpent in his guts. He lengthened his stride even more and finally gave in to a lumbering sort of jog the last few feet.

`Finally, as he somehow had known they would all along, the liquid-mud footsteps behind him finally increased their pace. A bolt of cold *fear* lanced through Marty, as he reached the barn's front door. In a smooth, practiced motion, he slipped the key into the padlock, swiped the heavy lock off its latch, and nudged the door open a crack. He barely managed to slip everything through the crack before spinning and slamming the door closed. With slightly shaking hands, he slapped the padlock on the inside latch and snapped it shut.

He stood there, staring. There was enough of a gap for him to peer through, so he could see a sliver of Burns Hill Road through it. If the thing (why did he call it thing?) kept coming, he'd see it, in another minute . . .

A shadow fell across the gap between the doors. A body was standing outside. The wet footsteps fell silent. Despite the strange wave of revulsion which washed over him, Marty held his ground, panting slightly not only from his exertion . . . but also because of *fear*.

The shadow in front of the gap didn't move. An oppressive silence filled the barn. And . . . a *smell*. Something wet, rubbery, and rotten.

Marty's eyes slowly adjusted. He was able to make out more of the form standing outside the barn. Peering closely, he saw the form—which looked human—wasn't much bigger than a teenager. He saw jeans, ripped at the knees. Scuffed boots. A dingy black t-shirt of some modern rock band he didn't recognize, with the sleeves torn off. "Five-finger Death," or something. And, as his gaze traveled upward . . .

A mask.

Part of him desperately seized on an explanation. It was almost Halloween. Obviously, this was some bored punk who wanted to mess with the local vagrant by wearing a mask and following him alongside the lonely countryside road. With all the schools on remote, there were more idle kids and teens in town than ever before. Marty had seen proof of that firsthand.

Still.

Something didn't feel right. Especially that *mask*. It was hideous. The rubbery skin looked mottled and sick with disease. The stringy black hair, greasy and patchy. The eyes bulged wetly and they looked so *real*. Though he couldn't tell for sure, peering through the gap in the barn doors, the gaping mouth looked dark and wet like it actually led down to a cavernous throat.

"Go away," Marty rasped, his throat tight and dry. "You've got no business being here. Go bother someone else. Go *away.*"

Then, on instinct, Marty did something he hadn't done since long before he started drinking. Now, however, something surged inside him. The words poured out of him like water from a gushing faucet, as he closed his eyes and prayed.

"Hail Mary, full of Grace," he whispered, "the Lord is with thee. Blessed art thou among women and blessed is the fruit of thy womb, Jesus. Holy Mary, Mother of God, pray for us sinners, now in the hour of our death . . . Amen."

Silence.

After a heartbeat, Marty swallowed with some difficulty and opened his eyes. Nothing but light streamed through the gap between the barn doors. Whatever punk kid who'd been standing there, staring him down with that awful mask, had gone.

not a punk kid

not a mask

Marty took a deep, cleansing breath. Stared at the gap between the barn doors—safely padlocked—for another moment. Then, he turned on one heel and walked away. He had a lot to do, and he had to get his fish smoked and packed with salt before he started his other chores. Slowly, the fear faded from his mind, as he clung (rather desperately) to the explanation of a punk kid having fun with too much time on his hands. Routine took over.

Even so, he couldn't quite banish the image of those wet, rolling eyes and gaping black mouth for the rest of the day.

Friday Night
The Cougar's Den
Route 180
10:00 PM

22.

JULIE LOMAX WAS only halfway through her first routine of the night when she first saw them, standing inside the club's foyer. Wrexx-N-Effect's "Rump Shaker" was blasting from the Den's cheap, tinny speakers, and she was trying her best to do exactly that as she butt-strutted her way across the tiny stage in the middle of the club.

She swayed her hips back and forth, twirling her bikini top around her right index finger. Smiling as big and as brightly as she could, despite the usual stomach-twisting worry that she might trip while walking in the most ridiculous pair of high-heels ever conceived. Not for the first time since she'd gotten sober, Julie wondered *how* long this gig could go on. Time to grow the hell up, get her ass out of Dodge, and get a real job. Even if it meant bagging groceries at a supermarket in Utica, or even Smyrna.

All those thoughts fled the instant she saw them, standing there, past the foyer. Arms hanging slack at their sides, and their faces . . .

Shit. What the hell?

Cold revulsion and shock rippled through Julie so badly she nearly faltered in her routine as she approached the tiny stage's edge. For a minute, she wondered if she *would* fall. Right into the lap of the Den's most stalwart customer, eighty-year-old Skip Bernstein. She'd at *least* end up straining a muscle if she did, so Julie awkwardly—smiling and twirling her bikini top the whole time—pulled up short, cocked her hips, and pretended it was all part of the show, except inside . . .

What the fuck are those guys wearing on their faces?

Masks. Had to be. The two guys standing at the edge of the club (now being approached by Conroy, the lead bouncer, thank *God*) were wearing the most grotesque masks she'd ever seen. They hung off their faces like the rubber was melting, or even rotting. Both masks had stringy black hair hanging from diseased-looking scalps, and oddly wet, bulging eyes which looked in opposite directions at once. And the mouths . . . God, they were *disgusting*. They looked real, and . . . did they have *tongues*? How could rubber masks have tongues?

For a heartbeat, Julie forgot about her routine and the avid attention of the Den's five patrons. The two men in masks *stood* there, staring at her, and for a moment she thought they were going to simply walk into the club and make a beeline for the stage, and *her* . . .

"Hey! No masks in here. Get them off, or get out."

Relief flushed through Julie as Conroy Ortega headed straight for the two guys in masks. He protected the dancers here like they were his daughters. In fact, so confident was she of Conroy's protection as he advanced on the two guys in masks, (who were oddly backpedaling away), Julie resumed her routine, flashing the five old men in attendance her brightest smile yet. She turned her back on the audience (and those two freaks), casually tossed her top away, slipped her thumbs under the straps of her g-string, and slowly, teasingly shimmied them all the way down and off.

When she kicked them aside and pivoted to continue her routine, she saw that, indeed, the two freaks were gone. In their place stood Conroy, his broad shoulders tensed and thick arms crossed as he faced the club's entrance.

Even so, for the rest of the routine—and the rest of her shift—Julie couldn't quite forget the *look* of those masks and how strange they'd made her feel deep inside.

Saturday, October 25th
Taylor Residence
8:30 AM

23.

CONSTABLE MATTHEWS SMILED at Scott. “Morning, Scott. Now listen. You’re not in any kind of trouble. I have a few questions I hope you can help me clear up. None of them involve you directly.”

Scott shifted uncomfortably on the couch, hands clasped tightly before him. His shenanigans over the past few years were limited to not doing schoolwork, cutting class, and sneaking cigarettes and booze, so he knew he hadn’t done anything bad enough to warrant a visit from the constable. He was sure you couldn’t get arrested for underage smoking, and the only time he drank was sneaking beers when his mother wasn’t home, or out behind Jasper’s ramshackle barn.

No, Scott knew he wasn’t in trouble. That’s not why Constable Matthews had come to visit him on a Saturday morning.

It had something to do with Jasper. Scott knew it. Even felt it, deep down. Jasper hadn’t been at the library Friday afternoon. That in itself wasn’t strange. Jasper regularly cut school on Fridays.

But Jasper usually called him Thursday night if Marcus was going to be in town. Jasper certainly mentioned it Thursday afternoon, but when he didn’t call Scott Thursday night, Scott assumed his intuition had been correct. Jasper’s invitation hadn’t been genuine, and he still felt weirded out by what happened between them.

Even though Sage told him Jasper hadn’t shown up at all Friday, Scott waited around the library for about half an hour before he gave up and set off toward Jasper’s house. It was unlikely, but maybe Jasper had *actually* gotten sick and wasn’t able to do remote schooling. Maybe something happened to him or his mother. Maybe he had a legitimate excuse for missing school.

Scott’s nerve gave out right around This and That, however. He ducked in there again, instead. The shopkeeper had recently gotten a whole box of horror comics from the eighties, and Scott wanted to look through them.

That served as a handy excuse for not going out to the Riley farm to look for Jasper, because as much as he hated to admit it, he still felt creeped out by those freaks in masks they saw Thursday afternoon.

Of course, a part of him still thought maybe Jasper had been pranking him after all. Another part, however, remembered too clearly the look of real fear in Jasper's eyes. When he stopped near Pleasant Brook Bridge, he'd half-expected to see those masked figures again. Waiting for him there, like Thursday.

"Jasper's missing," Scott blurted out, "isn't he?"

Constable Matthews only tipped her head. Her eyes widened slightly, however. Scott knew he'd not only scored a hit; he'd also surprised or impressed the constable. For some reason, he hoped it was the latter. "Why would you say that?"

Scott shrugged. "Didn't see him at all yesterday. Librarian said he never showed up. When he's gonna skip school, he usually tells me first, so we can skip together."

"When was the last time you saw Jasper? And where were you?"

Scott thought. "I think . . . 3:30, 4:00 Thursday? We were heading out to his place to hang out . . . "

"To smoke and drink, no doubt," Mom muttered, managing to look disgusted and sad, all at once. Which was a joke, considering *her* drinking.

Constable Matthews held up a hand, and Mom fell silent. "You ever get there? His mother called yesterday morning. Said he never came home Thursday night."

"No. We split up. He went the back way to his house. Down Kovac Road to the bike bridge over the brook. I decided to check out the thrift shop."

Constable Matthews nodded. "Why'd you go there instead of with Jasper?"

Scott opened his mouth, but for some reason, paused. He wasn't sure about telling Constable Matthews about the two people in masks. The thing was so bizarre, *he* wouldn't believe it if someone told him.

But the timing of events was impossibly coincidental. Jasper and him run into two weirdos wearing masks. The weirdos start walking toward them. They split up, the weirdos disappear, and Jasper doesn't come home that night. It didn't take a genius to connect the dots.

Also, Scott was an avid horror fan. He spent his evenings and weekends watching them, and he'd been reading grown-up horror novels for years. He knew this moment too well. This was when the kid who doesn't trust adults because he's been burned and hurt and blah blah blah doesn't tell the authorities a crucial piece of information, and that omission only leads to a lot more people getting killed.

Fuck that noise, he thought. "It was because of the weirdos in masks."

Riley Residence
10 AM

24.

JOAN RILEY SAT on the front porch of her decaying old farmhouse, sipping homemade moonshine from a Mason jar. She'd been drinking since she rolled out of bed around nine. Normally she waited at least until noon, but when she'd called for Jasper to get his ass out of bed and get started on his chores, only to hear silence in return, reality came crashing down on her. She started drinking earlier than usual.

The world knew thousands of women like Joan. At one time, she'd possessed a body and face all the boys (and a good number of the men) in Pleasant Brook wanted. Even a teacher or two. She remembered this one Math teacher in eleventh grade. A short, wiry middle-aged man with a bushy mustache and receding hairline. She didn't have to do any homework that entire year, because of their "extra credit" sessions after school.

All the boys wanted her. All the girls hated her because of it. Yet, at the same time, they hung around Joan, hoping to catch scraps from her table. All she had to do was find the right guy who had enough money and didn't treat her too bad, and she would've had it made.

Unfortunately, that never quite happened. The "right guy" either pissed his money away, or started beating her, or pissed his money away *and* started beating her, or ended up doing something stupid and getting sent to Warren County jail. Suddenly, she was in her mid-thirties, married to a farmer and "self-employed mechanic" (Jack Riley had been a wizard with anything mechanical, when he wasn't drunk, high, or whoring around), with three kids, and one on the way.

Jack took off after her last, Jasper. Why, she never figured out. In all fairness, after a while, she didn't care. When she discovered that as a single unemployed mother with no job skills, she could cobble together an existence out of food stamps, food banks, and welfare (and whatever she could get from Pleasant Brook men who'd gotten tired of their wives), she settled into the half-life she still lingered in today. She'd found that with the right amount of whiskey and moonshine, almost anything could be tolerated.

Which was why she felt so confused about her reaction to Jasper's disappearance. More than likely, Jasper was off drinking, smoking, or raising hell. Took after his father, sure enough. The thing was, he usually did that with Marcus. Marcus hadn't come around this weekend. Where was Jasper, then?

She gulped down the rest of her shine. Wincing slightly at the fire which burned down the back of her throat. Steadied her grip on the arms of her chair, to push up so she could stand, go inside and get more of the hill-brewed hooch she got in "payment" for her "company . . . ."

She stopped. Arrested in place at what she saw standing in the driveway, not five feet from her front steps.

It was Jasper.

It had to be. She recognized his worn jeans, his scuffed engineer boots, and that rock t-shirt with the sleeves torn off. She knew it was Jasper. It had to be, but she didn't run down the steps toward him. She didn't call out his name. Didn't move, because of . . . of the mask he wore.

It looked hideous. Long stringy black hair which appeared disturbingly real. Bulging eyes which poked out in opposite directions. Gray rubbery skin which looked diseased. And worst of all, a gaping black mouth which looked wide enough to swallow her head whole.

"Jasper? What . . . where have you been? Why are you wearing that . . . that horrible thing?"

Her son said nothing. He stood there, the mask's idiot bulging eyes staring. Hands hanging slack, next to his sides. The longer she stared at the mask's yawning black mouth, the more certain she felt that, if he could, Jasper would be screaming.

"Jasper? H-honey? Where have you been? Is . . . is that a mask you got for Halloween?"

No answer.

No sound. Save her own rasping, wheezing breaths. Her heartbeat thudding against her rib-cage. A slight wind rustling the trees.

She forced a smile, faking good cheer. "Well, if it's for Halloween, it's certainly horrible enough. Makes my heart pound to look at it."

Jasper remained silent. For a moment, Joan wondered if perhaps Jasper was laughing behind that hideous mask, barely holding in his usual horse-like guffaws at her fright. Any moment, he might lose it and start braying like a donkey. Whip that mask off, crowing over the way he was making her piss her pants. In fact, a part of her felt desperate for this. Was willing to endure any indignity from him, should that happen.

Seconds passed. Minutes.

It didn't. He continued to stare at her silently. Only, was he now swaying? Back and forth, like goldenrod in the wind?

Her fear escalated to near-panic levels. She stoked her anger to try and bury it. She stood straight, scowled, and spoke in what she hoped was a firm voice. "All right, Jasper. You've had your fun. You get that damn fool thing off and get yer ass in here. I oughta beat it black and blue for the worry you caused me. Had to call that Matthews bitch. Had to beg her to come out here last night and poke around a little, her giving me the stink-eye all the while, like I was a horrible mother. That's all 'causa of you, hear me?"

Nothing.

Jasper stood motionless, the mask's bulging eyes staring, its gaping mouth howling silently. Fear clamored inside and clawed at her heart, so she let her anger loose, to try and push the fear aside. She dropped her empty Mason jar, bawled her hands into fists, and let the fire burn white inside her, so she wouldn't feel so damn scared of a stupid dollar-store rubber mask.

She took a step forward, growling, "Don't you be thinkin I'm scared of you with that mask on, or that you're too big for me to give a whipping to, Jasper Lowell Riley." Her hands moved to unfasten her belt, which she'd used on all her boys, at one time or another. "When I git done with you, won't be able to walk straight for a . . . ."

It happened so fast, her eyes couldn't follow. Something silver flashed into her vision from behind her. She felt little, at first, past a stinging line across her throat. Then, the stinging turned to burning. And she couldn't breathe. No matter how hard she gasped, she couldn't get any air.

She tasted blood in the back of her throat.

A hand grabbed her by the hair and yanked her head back. Something cracked dully. Her neck and her chest felt warm and wet, while her fingers and toes got cold. Still, she tried to breathe. She only gurgled, spitting bloody bubbles from her lips.

Her bowels let go about the same time as her bladder. While the one hand held her head back, the other grabbed her shoulder and pushed her down. She thudded onto her knees, boneless, only those hands keeping her from falling over, face-first, into the dirt.

Jasper loomed over her, bending close. He gently took her face into his hands. So gently, so lovingly, in a way none of her sons had. Not even Jack had, back in the good days. She saw that, indeed, she had been right. The mask's mouth was opening. Wider and wider, its stretching blackness filling her world.

She felt no fear, however. Oddly, a sense of peace. As that black mouth stretched impossibly wide and oozed over her head, even as she felt her skin burning and maybe even dissolving, she didn't fear, or hurt, at all. She felt herself joining something inconceivably vast and all-encompassing, becoming part of an All. As the mask consumed her, as her being became one with it, she rejoiced in the pain, and the burning, and the dissolution.

Saturday
3:00 PM
Goodlow's Farm
Corn Maze

25.

A STRANGE KIND OF nervousness—one he didn't understand and couldn't pin down—played along the edges of Marty's thoughts as he walked along one of the main corridors of the corn maze at Goodlow's Farm. A few folks had complained of being harassed and followed by "people wearing weird masks," so Roger Goodlow—a sixty-five-year-old bachelor farmer who'd been running the corn maze since time out of mind—had told him to go "flush out them sumbitchin asshole kids."

Of course, this wasn't the first time he'd had to kick out rambunctious kids and prank-minded teens, and he figured it wouldn't be the last. He felt oddly unsettled, however, and of course—even though he didn't want to admit it—he knew why. His odd encounter with the teenager who'd followed him up Burns Hill Road the other day. A teenager wearing what looked like a weird rubber Halloween mask. A mask which bore an eerie resemblance to the ones described this afternoon.

Marty had been parking cars at Goodlow's Halloween Corn Maze for the past ten years. Old Man Goodlow had come to rely on him so much he wouldn't hire a single seasonal employee until Marty checked in first to confirm he was working. He'd proved far more dependable than the bored teenagers who usually worked with him. He took the job seriously and followed Goodlow's annual instructions to the letter.

Because of this, it wasn't long before Old Man Goodlow put him in charge of the other parking lot attendants. Given Marty's well-known nomadic existence, at first, the younger attendants took offense at working for a "homeless guy." It hadn't taken long, however, for them to warm to Marty's leadership. He wasn't the town drunk like Lester McDonough, or strange hill folk. Slowly but surely, Marty won over his fellow parking lot attendants the same way he did everyone else in town: With hard work, honesty, patience, and his generally affable nature.

That affable nature, however, was on edge as he walked down the seemingly endless branch of the corn maze. Even if it *was* just teens fooling around, having some pre-Halloween fun, that wasn't necessarily a comforting thought. Of course, because Marty hadn't ever been married and never had any kids, his interaction with them was limited to seeing them around town, and through the course of his odd jobs. Even so, it seemed—from his admittedly narrow perspective—that kids and especially teenagers had hardened the past few years. Gotten more caustic. Cruel, even.

He'd no theories why. It just seemed, from his experience, that their jeers had gotten sharper, their stares colder, more intrusive. Suffice to say, reassuring himself the "people in weird masks" were only teens wasn't reassuring at all . . .

Something rustled in the rows of corn stalks to his right.

Marty stopped and turned casually, peering into the stalks, trying to remain nonchalant. Maybe if the teens (if it was teenagers, but who else could it be?) saw he wasn't impressed, they'd ditch, with only a little encouraging.

Nothing.

Nothing but corn stalks, dry and withered and past their prime, gently rustling in the slight breeze.

More rustling. What sounded like *wet* footsteps. Corn stalks to his left parted and shook, as if something was moving *away* from him, farther into the corn.

Marty's instinct was to peer deeper, maybe even shout a good-natured warning to clear out. He didn't do that, for some reason. Instead, he held his ground, staring at the inscrutable wall of dry and crackling cornstalks as they swayed gently back and forth in the breeze.

It was probably nothing.

The breeze, or an animal or something. Maybe the folks who complained had gotten jumpy and imagined one of the maze's badly dressed-up mannequins was an actual person. Easy enough to do if you put yourself into the right state of mind. Marty almost convinced himself of this and was turning to leave, when something rustled in the cornstalks *behind* him, on the other side of the corridor.

This time he made no pretense and spun quickly, shouting "Hey!" He turned fast enough to catch a glimpse of a dark form retreating deeper into the cornstalks, wearing what most *definitely* looked like a mask. A mask with a gaping black mouth and stringy black hair. The cornstalks shook and parted as the form darted away, into the field.

Someone *was* stalking around in the cornstalks. Was it the same teenager who'd followed him home the other day? Or someone else? If someone else . . . why the same mask? Maybe a bunch of kids were running around town wearing similar masks, like that clown prank local kids—and people across the country—pulled a few years ago?

Marty stared into the cornstalks, which had largely gone still, save for the occasional hiss of wind rustling through them. He thought there might be two, maybe even three people hiding out in the corn (though he couldn't be sure), and he wasn't about to go looking for them. He'd head back to Goodlow's home, get the old man's shotgun, and call Constable Matthews. It had been a while since he'd owned a television, much less watched it, but he'd seen how *that* movie ended. Clutching his hands into fists, Marty turned and walked quickly back to the farmhouse, forcing himself to stay at a brisk stride instead of breaking out into a jog.

Cougar's Den
Route 180
10:00 PM

26.

CONROY ORTEGA APPROACHED the two punks standing past the foyer, clenching and unclenching his hands at his sides. This was the second time in as many days these guys had tried to start trouble in his club, and he wasn't having it. Last night they'd fled as soon as he'd advanced on them, but tonight it looked like they were going to try and stand their ground.

Conroy didn't want to get physical with these idiots. He avoided it these days, especially since getting sober. However, sometimes you had to take a more hands-on approach to solve problems, and he had no issues busting heads, should the need arise.

"*Hey,*" Conroy snapped as he jabbed a finger at the mask-wearing duo, "I told you guys last night. Lose the masks and pay the cover, or you can get the hell out of here."

Unlike last night, the two men—wearing dirty jeans, scuffed Timberland boots, one with a white t-shirt, the other red—simply stared at him through their ugly masks. Heads cocked, like curious dogs who didn't quite understand what they were being told. Their shoulders were slightly hunched, hands hanging from limp arms, and they stood there and stared through the wet, rolling eyes of their *fucking* weird masks.

(How can their eyes look like that? They look real. Same with their mouths and tongues. How do fucking masks have *fucking* tongues?)

Not wanting to look at those disgusting masks one minute longer, Conroy inventoried them, looking for anything which might identify them. In minutes, Conroy saw it. One of them wore a gaudy silver skull ring on their right hand. The one wearing the white t-shirt. Conroy knew who that ring belonged to, sure enough . . . because that fucker was *banned* from the Den for threatening to work over one of his dancers with that same ring.

Conroy stepped forward, hands tightening into fists. "Jimmy Riley, you'd best get yourself out of my club. Told you the last time I saw you, I was gonna beat your white-trash ass black and blue, *then* call Constable Matthews. You know she won't say boo about it. She'll see it as me performing my civic duty in kicking the ever-living shit out of you."

The figure to the left, with the stained white t-shirt and silver skull ring, didn't move. It simply stared at Conroy, its hands hanging limply at its sides. For the life of him, Conroy thought Jimmy Riley was giving him a "fuck around and find out" look.

What Jimmy should know better, of course, was that Conroy Ortega was *much* more than happy to oblige.

"Okay. Let's do this." Conroy unzipped the black hoodie he always wore and took it off. He draped it on the back of a nearby chair. He hadn't gotten into too many scraps since sobering up, but he still preferred to do so in a tank-top, to keep his arms as free and as loose as possible. He flexed those heavily muscled arms, which were covered in tattoos of crosses in all shapes and sizes, and advanced on the two mask-wearers.

To his surprise, the masked assholes performed abrupt about-faces and retreated from Conroy's advance. *Fleeing* him, like scared animals afraid of a much larger predator. Exactly like the night before. Oddly enough, he'd been wearing a tank top that night as well, exposing his cross-tattooed arms. That felt important, somehow, though Conroy didn't understand why.

Bel Biv Davoe's "Poison" ended, and in the sudden lull, a smattering of applause from the den's slightly larger weekend crowd signaled the end of the current dancer's performance. Conroy glanced over his shoulder and saw that—also like last night when the two weirdos first tried to get in—Julie Lomax was waving to the crowd and walking off-stage.

Julie's gaze found his. For a moment, her brilliant, white-toothed perma-smiled slipped, and she offered Conroy a flickering, grateful smile. Conroy nodded—protecting the girls wasn't just his job; it was his calling—and Julie's true smile faded behind her practiced grin as she blew the crowd kisses, then disappeared backstage.

Conroy turned away to watch the Den's entrance, troubled in a way he couldn't put his finger on.

Sunday, October 26h
Pleasant Brook Cemetery
11:00 AM

27.

CONSTABLE MATTHEWS SAT in her JEEP, which was idling on the side of the road, out front of Pleasant Brook Cemetery, at the east end of town. It was a little colder than normal, so she had the heat on, but even though it felt warm in the car, she couldn't shake a chill deep inside.

It was because of the weirdos in masks.

Whatever she'd been expecting Scott Carter to say yesterday morning, *that* hadn't been it. She'd expected Scott to say he and Jasper had gotten into a fight and went their separate ways. Or, Scott would evade the matter, like most teens in similar situations. Quite honestly, it was refreshing to hear someone speak so bluntly.

She also hadn't been expecting that the people Scott had seen would vaguely match the descriptions of Lester McDonough and Margaret Seaver. Scott admitted he wasn't sure because he'd been too far away, but when Grace related the descriptions of the missing people, she'd seen the light of recognition in Scott's eyes. Though she lacked any real proof, Matthews felt sure that on Thursday afternoon, Scott Carter and Jasper Riley had seen Lester McDonough and Margaret Seaver standing on the other side of Pleasant Brook Bridge, both wearing weird, identical rubber masks.

Scott hadn't been able to tell her much else. Spooked by the two strangers wearing masks, he and Jasper split up. Jasper went home the back way to hopefully avoid the "weirdos." Scott visited This and That to wait them out. However, Scott said right after Jasper left, he turned to look for the two strangers, only to find them gone.

Grace had felt a peculiar chill cling to her since. It seemed dreadfully clear what happened to Jasper Riley. The problem, of course, was lack of any real evidence.

After talking to Scott, Grace had gone to Pleasant Brook Bridge and walked up Kovac Road to the bike bridge over Pleasant Brook. She'd found precious little. Nothing on the bridge. The only thing which looked mildly suspicious was a small blob of rubber on Kovac Road. It looked like it had melted, then hardened again. She thought of the rubber masks, though she didn't know why.

She'd then returned to what remained of the Riley farm. It hadn't been the picture of health when Jack Riley had been around, but after he'd disappeared, it had fallen into complete disrepair. The only things living in the barns these days were rats and stray cats. The house looked like it was barely standing. The door was wide open, the house empty.

Grace spent the rest of the morning driving aimlessly around Pleasant Brook. Looking for anything strange or out of place, though she had no idea what to look for. She stopped to eat lunch at The Whole in the Wall, and then afterward, again visited both Lester McDonough and Margaret Seaver's homes.

Based on the build-up in their mailboxes, they still hadn't returned. She walked around both properties. Checked their backyards, jiggled the front and back doorknobs, to no avail. Frustrated, she returned to her JEEP and was about to head back to the station when she got a call from Marty Crenshaw, out at Goodlow's farm. Something about guys in masks lurking around the corn maze and spooking patrons.

guys in masks

When Grace arrived there, she found the usually taciturn and nonplussed Marty Crensaw visibly agitated. He related to her in oddly clipped tones how several corn maze patrons had complained that morning of people lurking around the corn maze in weird rubbers masks, stalking them. When he walked through the maze himself, he himself thought he'd heard and seen someone moving around in the corn, though he hadn't seen enough to be sure.

"I'm wondering if it's some sort of viral prank like that
clown thing a few years ago."

Standing beside her JEEP, Grace crossed her arms and frowned. "Why? Have you seen other people wearing masks?"

Marty nodded, and again, Grace noted how the normally calm and unruffled man looked nervous. "Someone in a mask followed me up Burns Hill Road Friday afternoon. Figured it was a kid pulling a Halloween prank."

When Grace asked for a description of the kid, Marty offered one which vaguely resembled the now-missing Jasper Riley. She didn't share this with Marty, however, as she toured the corn maze with him. Predictably, they found and heard nothing. She told Marty to call her if he saw anything else weird, got back into her JEEP, and drove around Pleasant Brook some more.

Grace eventually went home to a microwavable Mexican dinner, a few beers, and then she went to bed early. That didn't help. She tossed and turned through a thin sleep, plagued by confusing dreams of people lurking in the shadows, wearing odd rubber masks.

Early the next morning, two calls woke her. The first, Jud Collins, practically *demanding* she meet him at the cemetery. The second, a far politer Conroy Ortega, from The Cougar's Den.

Never liking the ornery and cranky Jud Collins—even on a good day—Grace chose to meet Conroy first. When she got to the station and invited the man in, Conroy calmly related the story of "two punks in masks" trying to sneak into the club, two nights in a row. When she asked if Conroy recognized them, the bouncer swore one of them was Jimmy Riley, Jasper's older brother, because he recognized the silver skull ring the elder Riley was wearing.

Grace put on a poker face (not wanting to appear upset at the mention of masks) and told Conroy she'd pay a visit to the Den tonight, to make sure everything was all right.

guys in masks

weirdos in masks

"What the *fuck* is going on?" Grace whispered. She zipped her coat up and shut the JEEP's engine off. Reluctantly (preferring to be home watching an old movie sipping from a mug of coffee spiced liberally with Bailey's), she got out and headed for the entrance of the tiny Pleasant Cemetery, where caretaker Jud Collins waited impatiently.

Grace tried not to feel annoyed at Jud. The retired engineer had, for the most part, done a capable job the past ten years as cemetery caretaker. Even so, as she drew near the short, wiry man (who practically vibrated with impatience), Grace couldn't help but feel she'd much rather deal with Pastor Yorkins.

"All right, Jud. I'm here instead of on my couch, watching reruns and sipping a nice, hot, Irish coffee. Who painted their initials on gravestones this time?"

Jud Collins shook his head, bouncing on his toes. So far as Grace knew, Collins had always been an engineer, spending most his adult life working behind a desk. Despite that, the man possessed a powerful vitality and force of will which he expressed in emotion and body. The way he bounced on his toes, shoulders always squared, chin thrust out, eyes defiant, made him look like a bantam-weight boxer willing to take on all comers, even those twice his size.

"No way, Constable. This isn't something like that. I wouldn't call you at home to handle graffiti."

Grace came to a stop before Collins and rubbed her hands to keep them warm. She didn't like Collins' expression. Didn't like that chill she felt inside, which had nothing to do with the weather. Didn't like where this was headed, at all. "And you're sure this couldn't have waited until Monday?"

"No ma'am. I hate to disturb your Sunday morning; I truly do, but I need you to see this, now."

Grace sighed, her stomach twisting into greasy knots. She'd been hoping this would be a trivial matter completely unconnected to the weird mystery she felt brewing in the air, but there was little hope of that now. She gestured up the hill. "Lead the way."

***

"Now you see what I'm talking about, Constable? What the hell does something like this?"

Grace stared at the sight before her, momentarily speechless. Collins hadn't been overreacting. This *was* above and beyond tagging headstones with initials.

"When I found the first one Friday morning, I thought some animal had been digging at it. Was only one grave disturbed, and that happens sometimes. Badgers get into graves now and again. Then, Saturday morning, when I found a few more, then I thought maybe someone was playing a mean-spirited Halloween prank. But this morning, when there were *more*, I looked closer . . . and damn it all, Sheriff. That dirt doesn't look spaded or shoveled up or dug at by something small like a badger. It looks like they were dug up with . . . "

Collins trailed off. Grace finished the caretaker's sentence with, "Hands. It looks like someone dug this up with their hands."

They stood facing an open grave. As Collins had said, and as Grace now agreed, it didn't look as if someone had shoveled the grave out. It also didn't look like something the size of a badger has been at it. It looked like someone—or something, or something*s*—had dug the grave open with *hands*. And the casket?

The latches had been broken off. The casket opened. And its corpse? Dragged from its resting place and torn apart. Its graveclothes shredded to bits, bones scattered in the mounded dirt.

Grace glanced at the dates on the grave's headstone. "Jud. This . . . body was buried only two weeks ago. Stan Greely. Died of a heart attack after getting COVID."

She met the caretaker's deeply troubled expression. "I don't know much about this sort of thing . . . but shouldn't there be . . . something of the body left? Some flesh and muscle, even if it was starting to rot?"

Even though she didn't want to, Grace turned away, knelt, and examined the mounds of dirt. "All I see is bone. Could animals have done this before you found it?"

Jud stepped forward and knelt next to Grace. "Maybe. Depends on when it happened last night. But here's another thing. Take a closer look at those bones. You know how a ham bone looks like after a dog's been after it? All jagged and gnawed to hell? Take a close look at those marks, Constable. What do those look like to you?"

Grace squinted. Bent closer, looked at the marks . . . and then sucked in a sharp breath. "Shit. Are those . . . ?"

Jud Collins nodded. "I think so. Like you, I'm no expert, but those are *people* teeth marks, Constable. I'd bet my life on it."

Taylor Residence
10 PM

28.

DESPITE HIS BEST EFFORTS, Scott hadn't been able to go about his weekend like always after Constable Matthews's visit yesterday morning. Up until the moment Matthews had showed up, and until the moment he'd told her about the strangers wearing masks, he'd been able to pretend, at least, that the world wasn't getting weird.

Now, it proved almost impossible. Especially the way Constable Matthews had questioned him about the weirdos' appearance; coming near the mark when she'd asked if one of them looked tall and "lanky," as Matthews had put it; the other shorter and stouter. Scott had answered honestly that even though it had been hard to tell from a distance, he thought so. The look in Matthews's eyes at his answer made Scott wonder if the constable knew, or at least thought she knew, who those weirdos were.

Mom hovered around him all Saturday afternoon, making matters worse, not letting him out of sight. Then this morning she dragged him to Pleasant Brook Baptist, which they'd started attending five years ago. She was acting as if he'd been targeted by serial killers and was forbidding him to go anywhere. Also demanded he stay home while she worked the evening shift Saturday and Sunday.

Normally he didn't really care what Mom demanded, but truth be told, (though he hated to admit it), he still felt spooked by the whole thing. Of course, the only person he hung out with was Jasper, so there was no point in going out anyway.

The worst part was, he couldn't work up any desire to watch horror movies like he normally did on the weekends. Either every movie he'd tried on Netflix last night had been lame, too corny, or too intense (which was out of character for him, and further evidence of how spooked he was). He'd tried and bailed on four movies before he went to bed at 10, a personal record in early bedtimes.

All Sunday afternoon after she came home from church, Mom kept him hopping with chores. When she'd left for work again, she'd levied the same demand about him staying home. He'd pretended he didn't care. Acted as if he'd go out if he wanted, but honestly? He didn't have any more desire to go out tonight than last night.

After Mom left, he'd settled down and tried to watch a DVD movie he'd ordered from a Pennsylvania-based indie horror production company called Reelsplatter. A post-apocalyptic Christmas tale titled *Dreaming of a White Doomsday*. However, despite having great production values and suspense for an indie film, Scott still had a hard time paying attention.

That annoyed him. He thought he would've enjoyed the film if the circumstances had been different. The whole thing with the weirdos wearing masks and Jasper disappearing had ruined it. Though he felt like a shit for thinking that, he couldn't stop feeling angry at Jasper for disappearing. Even after the movie was over, and he was in the shower. Of course, considering that the distance between them the past few weeks was *his* fault, this made Scott feel even worse.

As he toweled off, a glint in the bathroom mirror caught his eye. It was the necklace he'd been wearing the past few weeks, a really Gothic-looking cross. He'd bought at This and That on a whim. Mom hated it. He couldn't help goading her about it, especially because it was, after all, a cross. Shouldn't a holy roller like her appreciate it? (A holy roller who drank like a fish, of course). She'd merely scowled and changed the topic to her favorite and reoccurring tune, his poor grades and poorer choice of friends.

The flash of spitefulness he felt toward his mother soured his stomach. He didn't want to think about any of this. He didn't care how distracted he was. He'd hit the couch and try to watch at least one more horror movie, and dammit, he'd enjoy it. He'd nick one of Mom's beers to try and relax.

He pulled his boxers on. Thought about taking his cross necklace off. Then decided to hell with it, he'd leave it on.

***

He was having a weird dream. He and Jasper were in the living room, which was weird because Jasper never came over to his house. Ever. Also, they weren't doing anything. Scott was laying on the couch. The television showed nothing but hissing white static, while Jasper stood in the front doorway. Hands hanging to his sides, not saying a word.

He asked Jasper, *Where you been, dumbass*? (at least he thought he did, though he hadn't felt his mouth move). *Your vanishing act ruined the whole weekend. Even brought the constable to my house. You been hanging out with Marcus in Utica? Smoking pot and getting lap dances from those stripper-whores you're always dreaming about*?

Jasper didn't say anything.

He stood in the front doorway. Something else weird? In Scott's dream, there was light in the living room. The TV was still on also, throwing ghostly white flickers. But the shadows fell on Jasper's face so Scott couldn't see it. The way Jasper stood so still, without saying anything, made Scott think he was talking to a mannequin.

Then, a whisper.

Not a voice, exactly.

Not Jasper's voice. But a whisper. A feeling, coming from Jasper to him.

Your fault. It's your fault. You left me.

What the hell do you mean? It was your *idea to split up*!

Again, Scott thought this. He didn't speak it. Couldn't speak, only think. Also, in his dream, he couldn't move. He lay pinned to the couch.

Jasper's whole body twitched. Then, it (why it?) took one halting step forward. Then another, and another. While Jasper (it?) staggered toward the couch, the accusatory feelings of betrayal intensified.

No, no, I'm sorry, Scott whined, without using his mouth or any words. *I didn't mean to leave you behind, you said you wanted to go home the back way, I didn't leave you, I didn't . . .*

His vision flickered like a filmstrip jumping its track. Jasper abruptly stood above Scott. Bizarrely enough, though he could see everything else of Jasper, his friend's face was still cloaked in shadow.

Jasper leaned down. Scott squirmed on the couch but still couldn't move. The television's glow behind Jasper threw even more darkness onto his face, but as Jasper leaned closer, Scott thought he could hear something liquid shifting. Like mud or slime sloughing off Jasper's face.

A terrible, chemical-burning smell filled his nostrils. Similar to the smell when he once accidentally threw an old pair of rubber wading boots into a garbage fire. Melting, burning rubber.

A rubber mask.

With a Herculean effort, Scott thrashed upward. He bumped chests with Jasper, pinning the metal Gothic cross between them. Something *screamed*. Not aloud, but in his head. It didn't sound human. He heard sizzling, and now the sickly-sweet smell of burnt flesh made him want to vomit. The scream in his head ululated, ranging up and down in strange pitches which made him want to clap his hands to his head and scream also . . .

***

Scott woke from his dream when he thumped off the couch and onto the floor. He jerked upright and threw his hands out, to push Jasper off him . . .

Nothing.

He scrambled to his feet and turned in a quick circle. Alone. He was alone. Jasper wasn't here. He'd never been here. Scott had been having a bad dream, that's all. Served him right for having two of Mom's Miller Lights and watching *Ghoul*, based on the much better novel by Brian Keene.

Even so. "A fucking dream," he muttered. "That's all. Just a . . . "

The skin on his forearms prickled into cold bumps. He turned slowly. Gaped at the open front door, through which wafted a chill October breeze . . .

Monday, October 27th
Gerhart Trailer Park
11:00 AM

29.

"**JULIE. JULIE?** Hey, Jules! Wake, up girl! C'mon, sleepyhead. Let's go."

Julie Lomax opened her eyes. Everything looked blurry and smeared. For a moment, she didn't know where she was. The ceiling didn't look like her bedroom's, even though it did look familiar, somehow. She closed her eyes, rubbed her face, and mumbled behind her hand, "Gimmaminute."

She rubbed her face hard once more. Opened her eyes again. This time, she recognized a series of blotchy water stains in the far right corner of the ceiling. In the living room. She'd fallen asleep on the futon in her trailer's living room.

For a brief moment, cold panic gripped Julie's heart. She didn't remember falling asleep on the futon. She'd been tired. It'd been a rough few nights at work, especially because those weirdos kept showing up, but even so. She remembered sitting down with a Sprite, intending to unwind before bed . . .

Nothing.

She remembered nothing else.

"Jules?" The voice sounded concerned. "You okay?"

For another breathless second, she didn't answer. The trailer was dry, contained no alcohol of any kind. It had been dry for almost a year now. She'd come straight home from work. Hadn't stopped at the Sip and Save; she knew she hadn't. Yet, when she glanced fearfully at the old, dinged coffee table before the futon, she fully expected to see a glass of moonshine, a bottle of vodka or whiskey, a few of those little economy packs of Fireball or Southern Comfort the gas stations sold, or even several beers . . .

Nothing except the Sprite can.

"C'mon, kiddo." The locked door to her trailer rattled. "You're freaking me out a little."

Julie reached out a trembling hand. Picked up the Sprite, and, terror clutching her heart, brought the can's mouth to her nose. She sniffed, certain she'd catch the sweet whiff of schnapps, or the stinging scent of whiskey or moonshine . . .

Nothing but Sprite.

"Julie!"

"Yeah," she called as she rose off the futon on slightly shaking legs, her voice cracking with relief. "Hold on. I'm fine, Sage. I'm fine."

Of course, maybe she should've said sober instead. She certainly *was* sober. Fine, however? She wasn't sure about that, at all. She hadn't been fine for a while. She wasn't sure when she would be fine, if ever. After the strangeness of the last few nights, *fine* was a long way off. For now, sober would have to do.

***

"I swear to God, Sage. Thought I'd fallen off the wagon for a minute. Totally expected to see bottles of booze on the coffee table."

They both sat in Adirondack chairs on the small porch attached to Julie's trailer. Sage Hunter wore jeans and a red and black-checkered flannel over a white t-shirt. Julie, a pair of sweatpants and an oversized sweatshirt. Mugs of coffee steamed in their hands.

It was noon. Sage normally took Mondays at the library off to visit with Julie, but since the schools had went back on remote learning, a student needed to use the library every day because they didn't have internet at home. Julie hadn't been expecting Sage because of this. The student in question, however, had skipped out since Friday so Sage came over to check in.

Sage offered a small, knowing smile. "It happens. You're only a year into your recovery. Besides," their cheeks reddened slightly, and they looked sheepish, almost embarrassed, "I got a little carried away myself last Monday. Had a *little* too much Crown Royal, drunk-dialed Grace, quoted her Emily Dickinson, and tried to get her to come over."

Sage sipped from her coffee, expression turning somber. "Some sponsor I am." They offered Julie a cracked smile. "Can't be choosy in a small town like this, I guess."

Julie felt a flash of sympathy. She reached out, took Sage's free hand, and squeezed. "Nothing could be further from the truth. I've made it this far partly because of you. *Besides*."

She squeezed Sage's hand again and said, "You have a little too much to drink and you drunk dial your ex and read them poetry. *I* blackout, sleep with strangers, and forget their faces the next day. Big difference."

Sage shrugged. “Even so. Probably not the best role model.”

Julie gave Sage an arch look. “Not true. At all.”

Until a year ago, she and Sage had only been casual acquaintances. They’d shared a few mutual friends, saw each around town occasionally, and that was it. She wasn’t sure when she first realized they both lived in the small trailer park off Route 180, but they’d seen each other coming and going, occasionally said hello, nothing more.

A year ago, Julie tossed back one too many shots of whiskey and moonshine at a “private party” she’d been dancing for. The rest of the night ended in an indistinguishable blur. To this day, she had no idea what happened. No idea what she’d done, who she’d done it with, or even worse, how many folks she’d done it with. The next day Sage found her face down in her own vomit on the ground outside her trailer.

She didn’t remember much of what happened next. Sage got her cleaned up, inside, and into bed. Somehow they managed—despite working full-time at the library—to take care of her for the next two weeks. They took her to a Dr. Fitzgerald at Utica General and got her checked into the detox unit. When she was released, Sage hooked her up with the AA group which met at Pleasant Brook First Methodist every Thursday morning.

Sage had never shared much about their own personal battle with alcohol. Only that they’d walked the same road, and even though they weren’t exactly “dry,” they knew what Julie was going through. They pledged to walk through it with her. Julie didn’t care that Sage was a little secretive about their own struggles. Far as she was concerned, if it hadn’t been for Sage, Julie probably would’ve drunk herself to death by now.

“So,” Sage said with no preamble, “how was last night? What did you have to drink?”

Julie sipped her coffee and swallowed again. “Water and Gatorade. That’s all.”

Sage nodded “Did you want to drink last night?”

Julie also nodded. “Hell yes. Bad. Worse than usual. Probably why I crashed so hard when I came home last night. I never thought wanting to drink so badly and saying no to myself over and over could be so . . . exhausting.”

Sage tipped their head. “It can be. It’s a mental and spiritual exhaustion which eats away at your resources. I know this is a touchy subject, but that’s why you need to consider different employment. Staying sober doesn’t happen through white-knuckling in the face of temptation on a daily basis. A strip club serving alcohol where you’re dancing doesn’t have the healthiest of boundaries.”

Julie sighed. “You’re right. I know. It’s just . . . ” she waved at the rows of trailers lined up in their regimented plots, and their poor excuses for lawns. "You know, all the time I danced at The Den, I never once saved the money I made. I've been doing that for a year now, and I've almost got enough money to move out of this town."

She looked at Sage. "I've got no job skills. I'm twenty-two. I know staying at The Den puts my sobriety at risk, especially because that creep who owns the place, Lancing, would rather see me drunk all the time and open to 'freebies' for him and his buddies. But where else can I make this kind of money? Especially in *this* town?"

Sage nodded as if deciding to table the discussion for a later date. "Why were you triggered last night? What set you off?"

Julie shivered at the memories and cupped the coffee mug closer to her body as if she could draw warmth from it. "Friday and Saturday night, these two guys have been trying to get into the club without paying. They were wearing these creepy masks, but I think one of them might have been Jimmy Riley. I recognized the big skull ring on his finger. Threatened to beat up one of the girls with it, once. That's why Conroy banned him in the first place." She shivered again. "They didn't show up last night, but I was on edge the whole time, expecting them to."

Sage frowned. "What did they do?"

"That's the thing. Nothing. Both nights, they stood in the foyer at the front desk where you pay cover. Stood there, staring, all limp and everything. Like they were puppets, and their strings had been cut, or something. Anyway, that wasn't the worst part."

"What was?"

Julie clutched her mug even tighter. "Their masks. With stringy black hair, big bulging eyes, and huge, gaping mouths." She shivered again at the memory. "God. It looked like they could bite a person's face off, those things."

"All they did was stand there? That's it?"

Julie shook her head. "You don't understand, Sage. You couldn't see their eyes, but it was like you *knew* they were staring at you. Knew their real mouths were open and drooling behind those masks."

"How'd they get in?"

"They didn't get in all the way, not really. They came through the open door and stood there, staring, and I think Lydia—it was her turn to collect cover, both nights—was so spooked both times she didn't say anything."

Sage grunted. "What stopped them from coming in?"

Julie took another sip of her coffee, found it had cooled, and set it on the arm of her chair. "Conroy. Thank God for him, as always."

Sage smiled knowingly. "Isn't he the big guy with crosses tattooed all over him?"

"Yep. A cross on each shoulder, on his forearms, on the back of his hands, on the inside of each wrist, and I think one on his chest and his back. Not to mention the big gold cross necklace he wears around his neck."

"I love it that your lead bouncer is a 'born again Christian, looking after his girls' spiritual welfare.'"

"Honestly? He doesn't drink either. He's the perfect gentleman, he won't let the other bouncers touch us, *he* never touches us, and he'll be the first one to toss a rowdy customer out. And I mean literally toss. That's the kind of Christian I can get behind."

Sage glanced at Julie coyly over the top of their mug, eyes glittering. "Or on top of."

Julie slapped Sage's knee playfully. "Stop."

"So what happened?"

Julie shrugged. "It was weird. Both times, soon as they saw Conroy coming toward them, they turned and almost ran out the door. And I don't think it was because they were afraid of Conroy. It was almost like . . . like they didn't want him to touch him. Like he had something they didn't want to catch? I dunno. It was weird."

"How long were they there? Sounds like only ten to fifteen minutes."

Julie shook her head. "Yeah, but it stayed with me. All I've been able to think of since was how they looked at me and the other girls. Like . . . like . . . "

Julie drew her knees up to her chest, feeling colder than ever as she remembered those bulging eyes and wide, gaping mouths. "Like they were hungry," she whispered. "Like they were hungry, and they wanted to eat us."

Riley Farm
1:00 PM

30.

GRACE STOOD BY the front of her JEEP, staring at the ramshackle remains of the Riley farm, which somehow looked even more decayed than when she'd been there only a few days prior. The air felt dense, oppressive, and even though she figured it must be her imagination, she swore a *weight* bore down on her shoulders. It made her skin crawl and her guts twitch.

The Riley farm hadn't ever been a decent place to visit. Its refuse-littered, overgrown lawn and dilapidated buildings were the antithesis of Pleasant Brook's clean and orderly (though rather mundane) existence. However, it felt even worse this afternoon, if that were even possible. An indefinable aura lingered about the place. Grace's skin felt oily, soiled, and tainted, standing this close to the old house.

Something happened here, she thought, as she had the first time she visited. *Something bad. But what? And where are the Rileys? Where the hell are those other folks?*

Her right hand dropped instinctively to the butt of her holstered Glock. A Glock, she realized ironically, she'd decided to strap on this morning, for the first time in over five years. With good reason, she thought, because she still felt a tense anticipation sure hadn't felt since her brief tenure at Utica PD.

What the fuck. Why not?

She smoothly drew the Glock and held it down, at her side, trigger finger along the barrel. She cracked her neck, swallowed, and called out, "Hello? Mrs. Riley? Jimmy? It's Constable Matthews. Had a few more questions to ask."

Only an eerie silence answered her. No birds called in the trees, no frogs or crickets, and something else was missing, too. It took her a moment, and then she realized—she didn't see any signs of the stray cats which usually populated the Riley's lawn.

"Hello?"

Still nothing.

Flexing her grip on the Glock, Grace stepped forward, slowly. She'd come here on a whim, after talking to Conroy Ortega on the phone this morning. When she'd visited the Den last night, Conroy said the masked men hadn't shown. That morning when he'd called to inform her that no, the two hadn't come back, he reiterated his suspicion that the one wearing the gaudy silver skull ring was probably Jimmy Riley, and that maybe the other one had been his younger sibling, the middle child, Jody. Grace told Conroy she'd stop by the farm, and after conducting her usual morning drive about, (was she imagining things, or did the streets look emptier this morning, even given the current COVID worries?) and here she was.

She regarded the leaning, gray and mottled Riley farmhouse. At one time, she supposed it had looked better. Maybe even *stately*. Now, all the paint was peeling and the wood underneath looked black and diseased. Its roof sagged in several places, its front porch was tilted, its railing crooked and also sagging. The windows were smeared and crusted with grime, and most likely hadn't been cleaned in ages.

Slowly, the back of her neck tingling as if the weight of unseen eyes burned into her, Grace circled the old house, Glock down at her side. She picked her way carefully through the debris strewn about the lawn; a lawn which had long since gone to weed.

Around back, she considered the dilapidated barn, which was in even worse shape than the house. For a moment, she thought about exploring it but rejected the idea almost immediately. She didn't like the look of that inky darkness and figured the barn was crammed with all sorts of sharp, rusted equipment. The last thing she wanted to do was trip over something in the dark, even with her flashlight.

Grace was completing her circuit around the old house when she finally heard something. A faint, rhythmic squelching. Like someone walking around in mud-filled boots. As soon as she stopped, it vanished. Like something was following her and had stopped also, to avoid detection.

Grace flexed her grip on the Glock and scanned the tree line. She didn't see anything. But something could be hiding behind the house, out of sight around the corner. Or, something was tracking her movements past the tree line.

She glanced at the Riley's front door and saw, with a start, that it now stood wide open. It had been closed when she'd arrived. She felt sure of this.

She didn't waste any more time. She turned to her JEEP. Walked to it at a crisp pace, and didn't re-holster her Glock until she was inside, behind the wheel, with the doors locked.

Trace Avenue
3:00 PM

31.

CONNIE BETH WILLIAMS (only sibling to Margaret Ann Seaver, formerly Margaret Ann Williams) hated Pleasant Brook more than any other place in the world. And here she was, back in town, driving toward her sister's house. It was the last place she wanted to be; yet it was a place she *had* to be, right now.

Margaret hadn't called Saturday night, which she'd been doing every Saturday since her husband died. Connie had called Margaret multiple times since, with no answer. Last night, she decided to drive back to her hometown and find out what the hell was going on. Margaret rarely missed her Saturday call, and when she did, she always returned Connie's calls. Always.

Something was wrong.

Connie and Margaret were the only children of John and Hester Williams, both long passed on in a retirement community down in Florida. Connie had never seen fit to marry (she'd dated several nice men she'd liked over the years, none of them, however, worthy of giving up her independence). Margaret had found Stephen's extended family amiable in a distant sort of way, and—as she'd always predicted to Connie—following Stephen's death, after the heartfelt condolences and pies and covered-dish meals, the Seaver clan simply didn't have much to do with her anymore. Hence the Saturday night calls. They were all either woman had left.

Connie cursed Pleasant Brook as she drove. Far as she was concerned, anyone with an ounce of common sense got the hell out of this piss-ant town soon as possible. When she graduated, Connie left for college in Utica, then graduate school in Philadelphia, and then settled in Pittsburgh. Soon as her parents retired, they moved South. First to Tennessee, then eventually to Florida.

Margaret, however, attended two years at Webb Community College, living at home those two years. She finished out her Education Degree at

Utica College . . . but still lived in Pleasant Brook, commuting back and forth. She landed a job almost immediately at Pleasant Brook Junior High. Soon as she did that, she said "Yes" to Stephen's marriage proposal. She completed her master's degree online and settled into life as a ninth-grade science teacher with her construction-working husband.

Even worse, she'd acted happy. Content. She and Stephen never had kids. Because of that, Connie was always after Margaret to move near her. Whenever she heard of openings in the Pittsburgh school districts, she routinely emailed the details to Margaret.

Margaret, of course, would thank Connie and promise to consider it. After a while, however, Connie understood that was a reflex reaction, nothing more. Though she couldn't fathom anyone enjoying life in such a small, claustrophobic town where nothing ever happened, Margaret enjoyed it fine.

Though Connie had liked Stephen well enough because he'd treated Margaret well and Margaret had loved him, Connie had also (secretly) felt a perverse kind of joy in the wake of Stephen's unexpected passing. She'd hoped that, at last, she could convince her sister to move.

No such luck. Margaret said, like always, she'd consider it. In the end, it never went past that.

As she finally approached 456 Trace Road, the ranch home Margaret and Stephen had lived in their entire marriage, Connie's heart sped up. Despite the lawn looking a bit overgrown, and the curtains being drawn, everything seemed normal. Margaret's car sat in the driveway.

She pulled in, parked her car, and shut it off. Thought for a moment about calling the town constable, but instantly dismissed the idea. Margaret had given her a key at Stephen's funeral, so she didn't need anyone to let her in. She'd wait to see what she found inside. Then, if she had to, she'd call the county or state police. Someone who knew what the hell they were doing, instead of a backwoods town constable. A dyke one, at that. Probably didn't even carry a gun.

Fearing the worst, Margaret got out of the car.

***

Her fears were confirmed the instant the front door swung closed behind her. The air tasted stale. As if no one had lived in there for days, the windows closed the entire time. Everything was in place, except for at the kitchen table, where she found a closed laptop next to an empty tumbler and a half-empty bottle of Johnny Walker.

Her worry deepened. She felt a powerful urge to leave the house and dial 911 immediately. Went so far as to pull out her smartphone, though she didn't dial the numbers.

Connie moved slowly down the hallway leading to the bathroom,

Margaret's bedroom, and the guest room. Something smelled bad in that direction. Got worse the farther she got. Something rotten, certainly. Something . . . dead.

She stopped before the bathroom door. It was open a crack. She sniffed experimentally. Jerked back and gagged as her stomach curdled. Something was dead, in the bathroom.

Stop now, a voice clamored in her head. *Call the police, even the dyke town constable, it doesn't matter! Right, no one knows you're here, and if something happens . . .*

She didn't call. Instead, she placed her hand flat against the bathroom door and, bracing herself and holding her breath, pushed it open. She stepped inside, turned slightly right, saw what lay in the bathroom sink . . .

She stared. Her mouth opened and closed, but the only sounds she made were tiny squeaks. Her throat clenched, and she couldn't breathe. Her hands started shaking, and her phone fell from nerveless fingers. She knew she had to bend over and pick it up, call the constable, right now, but she couldn't. The shaking had spread from her hands, up through her arms, and into her whole body. It took every scrap of willpower to keep herself standing, and to keep from screaming.

What lay in the bathroom sink defied description. At least, that's what her conscious mind clamored. It looked like ground meat. Like hamburger, but the flesh was the wrong hue. That, and though she wasn't sure, the matter lying clumped in the sink looked regurgitated. Thrown up. And the clumps of hair, which looked like they were striped white and orange . . .

Bile burned the back of her throat. She covered her mouth with a fluttering hand and moaned. She didn't want to recognize the pulped mass in the bathroom sink, but she knew . . . she knew . . .

Tufty.

One of Margaret's cats.

The bathroom door creaked open.

Connie spun and shrieked when she saw what stood in the doorway. The stout body—wearing a dress which was torn and soiled—was Margaret's. She knew because they shared the same figure. But the face.

Connie gazed in horror at the rubber mask her sister was wearing. Wild stringy black hair, bulging eyes, and a wide, gaping black mouth. She didn't know why Margaret would be wearing it, and when she looked down that wide black mouth it didn't look like a mask, because she thought she saw an oily, slick tongue wriggling back there . . .

"Margaret? What . . . what the hell . . . "

The thing tipped its head. Regarded her for a moment. Then sprang forward with a quickness and agility Margaret had never possessed. Margaret's right hand darted out, closed around Connie's neck, and slammed her back into the wall hard enough to shake several pictures off their hooks, sending them crashing to the floor.

Connie clawed frantically at Margaret's grip, digging her nails in and raking them across flesh, but it didn't feel like flesh, exactly. It felt like she dug into rubber which didn't tear, but gave, and then sprung back.

She didn't think about that anymore, however, as Margaret's fist plunged into her gut, tearing past muscle and flesh, cracking against her ribcage. Agony worse than anything she'd ever felt exploded inside. She tried to scream, but Margaret's hand on her neck squeezed tighter, causing something in there to crackle.

Margaret's other hand dug around Connie's wet insides. Grabbed hold of something and yanked. Had Margaret not been crushing her trachea, Connie would've vomited blood and viscera everywhere. As it was, it clogged her throat and flooded her nasal passages. She felt the blood leaking out her nostrils, down over her lip . . .

Everything dimmed, the light fading with the pain. But before she went away completely, she saw the thing hold up a handful of long, glistening, shiny ropes of flesh, which had been pulled from her guts. It stuffed them down the yawning black gullet of what *couldn't* be a mask. It was chewing and swallowing as Connie's lights winked out for good.

Constable's Office
4:00 PM

32.

AFTER LEAVING THE abandoned Riley farm and driving a circuit around town once more (the streets and sidewalks looked even emptier if that were possible), Grace returned to the station to think. A few hours later, she'd added to her yellow pad of notes. Sipping from a Jack Daniel's, neat (she kept the bottle in the lower right drawer of her desk). No matter how long she stared at her notes, she couldn't piece them together in a way which made sense. Even so, she re-read them once more.

There had been another incident at Pleasant Brook Cemetery like the one Jud had shown her Sunday afternoon. Corpses disinterred, and—as best as Jud could tell—the remains devoured by something (they still didn't want to admit the human-like teeth marks found on all the bones). Jud was getting hot, demanding Matthews deputize men from town and post them as guards at the cemetery, because if not, he'd sit up all night with a shotgun and take care of matters himself. Somehow, she'd talked him down.

The second notation was her visit to the Riley farm a few hours ago. She'd found no one, even though she was *convinced* someone had been watching her from the tree line, making those mud-squelching footsteps.

The Riley family's absence complicated matters. She'd been toying with the idea of calling both county and state police and officially listing Jasper Riley as a missing minor. But now, with the whole family gone, she knew neither the staties nor the county boys would go for it. They'd point out the whole family being gone, suggested they were on a trip, or maybe even skipping out on their various debts, which, of course, was plausible.

This morning, she'd finally tried calling Margaret Seaver's only living relative, Connie Williams. No answer on her home phone and her cellphone went straight to voicemail. Until she heard back from Ms. Williams, that was now a dead end, also.

Grace tapped the notepad and exhaled noisily. Her head was starting to ache, she was tired, and sipping Jack Daniels the last few hours wasn't helping. She should call it a night, for sure. Go home, get something to eat, and get to bed early.

She didn't move, however. She picked up her glass of Jack, sat back in her chair, sipped from it some more, and wondered what the hell was going on in her town, also fearing that whatever it was, she was too late to get ahead of it.

Night

33.

THEY WERE ONE, and they were growing, spreading, consuming. They were always hungry, and they always needed to feed, take everything into them, make everything them, until nothing remained but them.

They didn't remember where they came from. Long ago, they'd woken from sleep, hungry. They fed, spread, and made more until something made them sleep again until it was time to wake once more.

Sleep in darkness.

Wake and feed.

Go back into the darkness and sleep, until it was time to wake and feed again. This was the cycle of their being. They were summoned from the dark by the First, and then they served the First. They would feed, spread, and become more until something made them go back to sleep once more. As always, there was the hope and the hunger that perhaps this time they wouldn't have to go back to sleep. They could continue to eat and spread, eat spread . . .

But part of them had been hurt recently. Hurt by a thing which had hurt them before. They didn't know what it was or what it represented. They only recognized the burning agony when it touched them. Whatever it meant, it was opposite of them. It was Other. Always, wherever they'd been before, that Other eventually helped drive them back into the darkness, until they slept again.

Twice they'd been hurt by it, here. They knew by instinct, by seething fluid images which weren't memories but thousands of sensations and feelings which pulsed and swirled through them all, that while they couldn't touch what hurt them and couldn't feed on the bearers of what hurt them or make the bearers part of them, they could find ways to end the bearers of Other.

They seethed, pulsed, and flowed together without number, without end. In this place where the First had called them, they joined with each other, melting into each other, becoming one with another, pulsing, throbbing, being. Soon it would be time to feed. They would separate and hunt, so they could return to this place and become one again.

They had much to feed on. Things which lived, and things which did not. It preferred things which lived, but could still feed on things that did not.

However, they wouldn't only feed. While some of them went out and fed, others would find the things which bore the Other which hurt them and would end them. *After* they hurt them.

They didn't feel happiness, delight, or joy. They felt hunger, satiation, and the burning agony when they touched the Other. But what pulsed through them now, as they thought about feeding, and thought about ending the bearers of what hurt them, was the closest they came to happiness, delight, and joy.

They would feed.

They would end those who hurt them.

But for now.

They were one.

Tuesday, October 28th
The Cougar's Den
10 AM

34.

CONROY ORTEGA FINALLY got right with God and his son Jesus ten years ago, as he lay recovering from a two-car accident in Utica General Hospital. A bouncer who'd been working for The Golden Kitty in Clifton Heights for about five years, three days prior he'd been driving to work in the middle of a rainstorm when the accident happened.

Twenty-four hours before that, he'd been stink-ass drunk as he'd driven home from The Kitty (a lithe and playful stripper named Candy along for the ride) with the slow, exaggerated care of an experienced alcoholic. That night, he'd made it home to his apartment in Booneville without incident. Candy spent the rest of the night "entertaining" him in varied and wildly diverse ways.

On the night of the accident, Conroy had been—through a stroke of good luck, or, as he came to think of it later, God's Will—sober as a Puritan minister in a Nathaniel Hawthorne short story. He'd been late, was all, having overslept from his and Candy's torrid exertions the night before.

Also, as he sped through the storm, driving too fast on rain-slicked roads, he'd been arguing with Candy about their "relationship." Ironically enough, he'd wanted something formal and official. He wanted to be her "guy." Candy was more of a "flavor of the month" kind of girl. That month the flavor had been anything vaguely Hispanic. He knew she was already jonesing for something new.

He'd never seen the little Escort drift off the ramp from the Route 20 East overpass. One minute he was calling Candy a "bitch-ass hoe who'd played him," the next looking up and jamming the brakes as Candy screamed and the Escort filled his vision.

He'd T-boned the little car. Despite his seatbelt, the impact jerked him forward and slammed his forehead against the wheel. Everything went black. When he woke up, he was in Utica General, and according to a stern but compassionate Dr. Fitzgerald, he'd suffered a Grade 3 concussion. Candy had suffered a dislocated shoulder from where the seatbelt jerked her on impact.

Miraculously enough, the driver of the Escort survived the accident with a mild concussion and a sprained wrist. Her son hadn't been so fortunate. He'd somehow been ejected from the vehicle and had died on impact.

Conroy spent three weeks recovering from his concussion. He suffered persistent headaches and eye aches. Periodic memory loss, mild speech lapses, and slippery emotional control. He would break down into soul-wrenching sobs or rage uncontrollably, at any given moment.

Toward the end of his three weeks at Utica General, his headaches subsided, his emotions smoothed out, and Dr. Fitzgerald decided he hadn't sustained any lasting injuries. He was eventually discharged, with certain concussion protocols he had to follow (no television, no reading, plenty of rest and sleep) for a few more weeks.

He was also discharged a changed man with a rejuvenated belief in God and the saving power of his son, Jesus. Raised in a moderately Catholic home, Conroy was familiar with the trappings of faith. But over time he'd fallen away. A subtle drift, one thing leading to another, until he felt sure that faith was a con, and if God did exist, he didn't give a damn about humans.

Over the course of his hospital stay, Father Ward—a priest who liked to volunteer in the chapel at Utica General—met him almost daily. He didn't talk with Conroy about God or Jesus or the Bible for almost about a week. He simply got to know Conroy. It was Conroy who finally asked Father Ward how he could believe in a God who allowed terrible things to happen.

Ten years later, relocated to an even smaller town in Pleasant Brook, and working as a bouncer at the much smaller Cougar's Den, Conroy Ortega no longer drank or smoked. He read his Bible every day. He attended Sunday morning mass at St. Mary's in nearby Smyrna. Every Thursday morning, he attended an AA chapter also in Smyrna.

He no longer mingled intimately with the girls under his charge, but instead, he'd gotten to know them as the real people they were. To other Christians, strippers and those who associated with them were the lowest of the low. The dirtiest of all sinners. Conroy, however, saw in every single one of them sparks of what made up the best of humanity. As far as he understood the Bible, God's grace was for everyone.

Though during recuperation Conroy briefly considered changing career paths, he eventually decided to take the advice Father Ward had given him. Bloom where you were planted. For better or worse, he'd been planted as a strip club bouncer. At The Kitty—and, eventually, at The Cougar's Den—he'd seen both the best and worst humanity could offer. Far as he was concerned, faith wasn't supposed to paint everything in black and white. It was supposed to help people better navigate the gray.

So, even though he decided a change of locale would help him avoid old temptations (most particularly in a stripper named Candy), he looked for work in the same venue. When he was hired ten years ago as head bouncer at The Cougar's Den, he made lots of changes. Declared the girls off-limits to bouncers. Petitioned the owner (an out-of-town sleazeball by the name of Peter Lancing) for better changing facilities for the girls, and a higher cut from their tips. And, he wouldn't tolerate grabby customers on his watch.

Quite simply, the girls and the other bouncers at The Cougar's Den had become like family. Contrary to popular media, he didn't believe religion and faith should make everyone in the family the same, or make them pursue their lives the same. It should pull them closer together, because once you decided God wants to love you, how can you not, in turn, want to love others?

Conroy knew most Christians didn't share his views. Most Christians—even those he encountered at mass, or at AA—were more concerned with controlling others' lives. Telling others how to live. Putting their efforts behind elected officials who would then try to legislate how others should live, while living any way they pleased.

Conroy wanted no part in that circus. He wanted to keep studying his Bible and growing in his relationship with God, so he could grow in his love of others. To the best of his ability, he would serve others and wash their feet, as Jesus did to his disciples.

His only radical move upon his return to faith were his cross tattoos. Almost immediately upon his release from the hospital, he'd gotten two cross tattoos, one on each shoulder. Every week after that, he got another. On each wrist, forearm, and anywhere else he could fit one. At the time he couldn't have said why he heeded the compulsion to get them. He'd felt driven to have the instrument of Christ's torture and the symbol of his triumph over Death tattooed on him in as many places as possible, that was all.

Never once did he think that instead of serving as protection, his tattoos might serve as bulls-eyes, instead.

***

Soon as Conroy stepped out of his truck into The Cougar Den's empty parking lot, he felt something off. He'd come from his AA meeting in Smyrna, feeling the usual peace and determination he always felt after his weekly connection with those who had walked similar paths as he. That peace fled, however, soon as he stepped onto the asphalt parking lot, replaced by a crawling sense of malign unease.

Something felt wrong in the air. He turned and looked over his shoulder, at the tree line bordering the far edge of the parking lot. He saw nothing in its shadowed depths, yet he felt something lurking in there, regardless. Watching him. Waiting.

Without wanting to, Conroy's thoughts returned to the two punks wearing masks, (one of which he was sure was Jimmy Riley) who'd tried to sneak into The Den without paying Friday and Saturday night. He thought how they'd fled him, almost as if they hadn't wanted to touch him. Especially the night he took his hoodie off.

The tattoos, a part of him thought, *for some reason, they didn't like my tattoos.*

The worst part about those weirdos was their masks. It was close to Halloween, and they certainly weren't the first patrons who thought it'd be fun (or maybe simply safer) to visit The Cougar's Den wearing a "Halloween" mask. But usually, those folks acted with good-natured chagrin when Conroy told them to unmask, and also? Folks who wore Halloween masks into the Den around Halloween wore masks *clearly* bought at the store. They were *Halloween* masks, and impossible to mistake as anything else.

The masks those weirdos wore, though. With their bulging wet eyes, sagging gray skin, and gaping black mouths? Conroy had been hard-pressed not to believe they were faces *actually* skinned off dead bodies. Especially in the Den's dim lighting.

Conroy stared at the tree line, cracked his neck, and tried to push away the feeling of being watched. He had work to do. The Cougar's Den opened at two in the afternoon. Girls started arriving around noon. The club's "manager," Rob Kittering (Lancing's lazy nephew), would show up anywhere from 12 to 2, depending on how bad his hangover was from the night before. Which meant it was up to Conroy to get the club open and everything ready.

He scanned the tree line once more. Nothing moved there. Even so, he felt sure something was lurking beyond the trees, in the darkness. He stared for a few more minutes.

Nothing.

He gave himself a shake and turned away, muttering a prayer as he did so. He didn't have time to get the willies. He had to get The Den ready for business.

First Methodist Church
11:00 AM

35.

"**IT'S BEEN A** rough few days. Not gonna lie; I've been tempted to drink a couple times. Especially last week. Something happened at work . . . "

Julie paused and shook her head. She tried not to think about those two weirdos wearing masks who'd tried to get into The Cougars Den. Sage was right. They'd been weirdos in masks. Maybe the Riley boys. Still, the unease they spawned had clung to Julie. Even though they hadn't shown up since Saturday night, she kept expecting them to, right to the end of her shift. If she was dancing, waiting on tables, even giving a private dance out back. Every single minute she expected to see one of those masks looming above her. Its mouth unhinging and spreading wide enough to swallow her whole face.

With a start, Julie came back to herself. Sitting in a metal folding chair with others in a circle, in one of First Methodist's Sunday School classrooms. Her AA meeting. Her weekly lifeline to sanity. She'd needed it more than ever, today.

She brushed hair out of her eyes and flashed a bright, fake smile. "Sorry. Like I said, it's been a rough few days. Some jerks showed up at work a few nights last week. Didn't do anything because security threw them out. But it spooked me, bad. Don't know why. I've been on edge since then."

She shrugged. "It doesn't help that booze is available where I work. I know I should find another job somewhere else because of that. But I don't know where I can make the same kind of money, so for now . . . "

She spread her hands, and looked at everyone in the group, offering another fake smile. "Anyway, that's my story for this week. Thanks for listening."

Thank you, Julie, the group murmured. The group's leader, Jeffery Kimall, said, "Thank you for your honesty as always, Julie. Now. Let's start talking about next week's food bank. I've got Constable Matthews' permission to hold it, but I'm going to need some volunteers to help us achieve proper social distancing and to minimize direct contact . . . "

Jeffery's voice faded as Julie caught the gaze of the man across from her. Weathered face, in worn but clean clothes, with shaggy but combed salt-and-paper black hair. Marty. Marty Crenshaw. She smiled at him and nodded. He nodded back.

However, she could see it in his eyes and the set of his jaw. While everyone else had bought her sunny smile, he hadn't. Had seen right through it. Knew, somehow, how terrified she still felt. She wasn't sure if that made her feel better, or worse.

***

She wasn't consciously avoiding Marty, but even so, she cringed inwardly when he approached her as she was helping herself to the donuts and cider provided for this week's meeting. She'd sensed he'd been able to look past her cheery exterior. Seeing as how her shift at The Den began in two hours, she didn't want to think about those two in the masks, at all.

With no preamble, he stuck out his hand and said, "Don't think we've talked since you started coming. Marty."

She accepted his handshake and was pleasantly surprised to find it firm and confident, though not aggressive or overbearing, like some men's handshakes were. Despite the group's confidentiality pledge, she'd never shared her employment at The Den, for obvious reasons. However, she sensed in Marty's handshake the kind of man who wouldn't treat her any differently if he knew what kind of "work" she did.

"No, I don't think we have. Julie." She pumped his hand once, squeezing it for good measure before releasing it. As she did, something occurred to her, and she blurted out without thinking, "You live in the old Hathaway barn on Burns Hill Road."

She immediately covered her mouth, kicking herself for being so bold. "Omigod. I'm so sorry. That was too personal, wasn't it? I remember you talking about that at one of our last meetings."

He smiled. In his eyes, she saw good-natured humor. "It's fine. I *was* talking about it at the last meeting. About how I was getting the barn ready for winter like I always do this time of year."

She noticed a shadow pass over his expression, there one moment and gone the next. As if he'd thought about something he'd been trying to keep at bay. Like her and the weirdos in masks. "It work out okay? You're all settled for winter?"

That shadow passed over his face again. It stayed a bit longer, even when he nodded. "Uh. Yeah. Some routine patching. So the walls hold in as much heat as possible. Waiting on hay bales I ordered from the local farms. Lining the walls with them helps keep heat in."

She saw it then, flickering in his gaze. The same thing he'd probably seen hiding behind her fake smile. Fear. An unreasoning, cloying fear. "Oh. That's good." Then, before she could stop herself, she also blurted out, "If you ever need a couch to sleep on, somewhere warmer . . . I mean, I don't want to sound too forward, but I've got room, and . . . "

She stammered and trailed off, cheeks glowing hot. She sounded like an idiot! Even worse, she sounded like a desperate woman trying to con a man into her bed, which she wasn't doing. At all.

All Marty did was smile, however. Though she thought his cheeks might've reddened slightly, too. "Thanks for the offer. I'll manage, though. I always do. Plus, I like my space."

"Right," she nodded too hard, hard enough to sprain her neck if she wasn't careful. "Right, because you've got that whole free-living, independent thing going on. Right. I get it."

She clammed up, feeling foolish, or even worse, stupid. Silence fell between them. Abruptly, there was nothing left to say. Whatever impulse had brought him over had obviously faded. She certainly didn't want to make any more of an ass of herself than she already had.

He took a cup of cider and a doughnut. Nodded at her and said, "See you next week." She nodded back and felt relieved (also a little disappointed) as he turned and walked away.

Tuesday
Goodlow's Farm
Halloween Corn Maze
8:00 PM

36.

JASPER HAD BEEN missing for about a week. The one time Scott *had* forced himself to walk over to the Riley farm—yesterday afternoon—he'd found the place abandoned. Though it had felt like something had watched him from the woods the brief time he'd circled the house, and he'd heard wet, mud-sucking sounds in the swamp behind the barn, he hadn't seen a thing or heard any other sounds.

None of his classmates had mentioned anything about Jasper's absence from remote classes or seemed to care. Of course, with *everyone* remote and mostly staying home, it didn't seem like many of the kids Scott knew cared much about anything these days. Mrs. Seaver was still absent and not signing onto her Google Meets, and no one was saying or doing anything about it. His Mom had called school, but she'd only been told they were still "looking for a replacement."

Everyone remembered the long quarantine months of Spring 2020, of course. Even though Warren County's recent remote schooling mandate was only supposed to be temporary, most of Scott's classmates were acting as if the situation was permanent. Why leave the house when classes were remote? Most of the kids had good Wi-Fi, and over a hundred channels of television to watch. Plus, smartphones, tablets, Nintendo Switch, and every other gadget imaginable. Gadgets Scott himself didn't have, and probably never would.

Also, Scott knew many of his friends liked to raid their parents' liquor cabinet even worse than he did. No doubt with all of Pleasant Brook's high school students "remote learning" and most of their parents away working, (because the county itself wasn't quite back in quarantine; not yet), a fair amount of them were probably spending their days buzzed on their parents' booze. When Scott called Terry, one of Jasper's other friends, asking if he knew where Jasper had gotten to, the fourteen-year-old malcontent slurred, "HellsifIknow," sounding as if he were trashed.

Constable Matthews had visited their house once more. Monday evening, asking Scott if he'd seen Jasper, or heard from him. He'd said no. The constable mentioned she'd visited the farm twice, and it didn't seem as if anyone was there now. She wondered if the whole family had gone somewhere. That's what sent Scott there the next day.

He didn't tell Constable Matthews the weird dream he'd had of Jasper Sunday night. Of him wearing that weird mask, and sneaking into his house. He didn't tell Matthews about waking up to find the front door open or feeling his cross necklace warm to the touch for some reason. Or, the small blob of what felt like hardened plastic he'd found stuck to the sofa. The constable was okay for an adult, but Scott still thought she'd wave those things off as a kid's overactive imagination and nothing more.

There hadn't been any more dreams of Jasper, though another weird thing had happened. Despite his strange dream Sunday night, Scott had once again fallen asleep on the couch Monday night, watching a stupid horror movie on the Sy Fy channel about a psychotic entomologist who had discovered how to mind-control fire ants. He hadn't dreamed of Jasper again, but he had jerked awake, once again convinced someone had been standing over him.

No one was there, but when Scott rolled over, he discovered his cross necklace lying on the floor, the chain broken. He told himself it was because it had gotten twisted up in his sleep. Of course, the thing would break so easy. He'd bought it at a pawnshop, after all. He'd managed to believe that.

Mostly.

Scott drifted through Tuesday. He attended some of his remote classes, skipped others (Science and especially PE, because how the hell could you do remote gym class?), leaving his mic on mute and flipping through various channels on the television, not even bothering to answer when teachers pinged him in their forced, half-assed virtual discussions. It was obvious his teachers remembered the 2020 quarantine also because they'd quickly sunken back into their own blasé and numb indifference to their students performance, or lack thereof.

After remote school ended the past two days, Scott mostly stayed near home (except his one foray to the Riley farm). Without Jasper around, he simply didn't feel like doing anything or going anywhere. He'd fallen into a sort of "sleep mode," without the catalyst of Jasper's mayhem. The reality Scott didn't want to face, of course? That he felt *incomplete* without Japer. Even though Jasper had rejected Scott's advances, a part of Scott felt empty without Jasper around. Empty, and even . . . dead.

Mom, of course, was delighted. She hadn't said anything. Probably afraid she'd jinx it. But, she hadn't hassled him about his homework (even though he still wasn't doing it) or his after-school activities, because of course, he wasn't doing anything or going anywhere. In fact, that's what had led him here tonight. Mom had suggested maybe he'd like to visit Goodlow's annual Haunted Corn Maze (which hadn't been shut down by Constable Matthews, so long as everyone observed social distancing rules) and have some fun while she worked *another* late shift.

Normally, Scott would've scoffed at the suggestion. He'd heard his classmates talking about the Haunted Halloween Corn Maze in the days before they'd been sent home on "temporary remote learning." The girls squealing in glee about how "spooky" it was. The boys snorting and calling it a "lame maze with stupid mannequins that didn't look real at all." But for some reason, when Mom had suggested it at breakfast this morning, Scott shrugged and said, "Sure. Sounds cool."

So here he was, at Goodlows's Farm, wandering through the corn maze as little kids ran by screaming behind their masks, tired and annoyed-amused parents staggering behind, trying to keep up. He'd been walking around for about twenty minutes, and he had to admit—while not frightening in the slightest—the maze was kind of cool. Whoever had carved it out of the massive cornfield on Hitchens Road had mapped an intricate network of intersections, switchbacks, and dead ends. After about ten minutes of apathetic wandering, he'd found himself far more engaged than he'd thought he'd be.

He'd passed some classmates from school. Kids he hadn't seen in person for over two weeks. A few clusters of junior high girls clinging to each other, shaking with exaggerated giggles of fear. A handful of high school students slouching through the maze, pretending they were bored with it all. He'd ignored them, as they'd ignored him. He didn't need their company.

But as he turned a corner to see nothing but a long stretch of corn maze, he found himself thinking how empty it felt. Quiet, also. One moment, he'd heard little kids screeching and parents lecturing them to *slow down you'll fall*; junior high girls yelping as they scared themselves, and the general background noise of everyone else in the corn maze.

Now, nothing. An almost deafening silence, with the exception of cornstalks rustling in a mild night breeze. The moon hung high in the night, casting the path ahead in a silvery glow. Scott suddenly felt unsure of progressing any further down this stretch. All the other passages hadn't gone long before they'd turned or split into intersections. This stretch went on forever. It also led away from the farm and the road, deeper into the corn field. Away from *people*.

He didn't like that, at all. Abruptly, he wanted to go back, hop onto his bike, and head home.

He stuck his hand into his pocket and pulled out his smartphone. He thumbed it on, typed in his pin, and brought up Google Maps. Some part of him complained he was cheating. That he should find his way back through the maze on his own. Another part wanted to get the hell out of there.

Google Maps loaded for several more seconds until finally, it flashed the message: "Check connection." He looked and, sure enough, he didn't have any bars.

Fine. He'd turn around. He activated the flashlight app on his phone (for some reason, it was a lot darker than it had been moments before), stepped back the way he came . . .

And saw him. Standing at the corner. A kid about his height. Wearing a dingy and ripped Five Finger Death Punch t-shirt with the sleeves torn off, and that damn mask.

The figure didn't move. It stood there, arms hanging slack. Though it was only a mask (it had to be, right?) he couldn't help but feel like those bulging rubber eyes were staring at him. Measuring him. Judging him. Taking him in.

Instinctively, he stuck his free hand into his other pocket and grabbed hold of his broken cross necklace. He couldn't say why he'd felt compelled to grab it before he'd left home, just that he had. Also, instinct whispered to keep it in his pocket, and not pull it out yet. It was like . . . he didn't want Jasper, or whoever the hell that was, to know he had it. It didn't make sense, but he obeyed the whisper, regardless.

Another instinct sparked. He thumbed open his phone's camera app, held it up, tapped zoom once, and snapped a picture of the figure. The flash illuminated them for a brief instant. In that glow, Scott realized with horror that the mask didn't lay still on the figure's face. It pulsed, writhed, and moved.

Like it was alive.

The figure in the mask twitched in the camera's flash. Tipped its head, as if curious. Then, it started walking toward him in big strides short of a run.

Again, for some reason, Scott didn't pull the cross out. He muttered, "Fuck it," and instead of turning around and running down the long stretch of maze, turned left and plunged into the corn, thrashing his way back toward where he thought the farm and road must be.

Fear spiked through as he heard something dive into the corn and thrash its way after him.

37.

"GOTCHA!"

Julie mock-screamed when Sage jabbed her in the side. They rounded a corner at Goodlow's Corn Maze and were confronted by a mannequin lurking half-out of the corn, dressed up to look like Michael Myers from the *Halloween* movies. Though she knew it wasn't real and the knife was mostly likely plastic or rubber, Julie still couldn't repress an instinctual shiver at that iconic, blank face.

"Stop!" She playfully slapped Sage's hands away and shoved her friend back a few steps. "I swear to God, you don't stop, I'll ditch you. You can hang out with Mikey here all by yourself."

Sage snorted, waving off Julie's threat. "Naw. Serial killers are lame. I'm more of a 'He Who Walks Behind the Rows' kinda girl, myself. Cosmic entities who thrive on ritual sacrifice are *dope*."

"Dope? What is this . . . the late nineties?" Julie shook her head, laughing, feeling good for perhaps the first time in a week. Yesterday Sage convinced her to take tonight off. Put some distance between her and The Den, and her anxiety about the guys in masks. Kittering had balked at first, but Conroy ran the show. He'd acquiesced easily, with a soft smile and a gentle look in his eyes which made her wonder if Sage was on to something about the potential between them.

It had been a wonderful idea. Sage suggested they visit Goodlow's annual corn maze for some good old-fashioned Halloween fun. It would offer some safe shivers, and take Julie's mind off the weirdos in masks.

At first, Julie balked. She tended to go out as little as possible. Not so much because of the COVID resurgence. She'd gotten her initial shots and her booster shot; and besides, she danced on a pole and in people's laps for a living. If she hadn't caught COVID by now, she probably never would.

No, the bigger reason was The Den itself. She'd never once recognized a club patron around town or felt as if anyone recognized her. Even so, she sometimes felt as if, the rare times she ventured out, a fluorescent light blazed over her head reading: *Hi, I'm a Stripper, and I Take My Clothes Off in Front of Strangers for Money*!

But Sage's will proved irresistible. It wasn't long until they were squealing through Goodlow's corn maze, clutching at each other like silly fools when they encountered mannequins dressed like Freddy Krueger, Jason Vorhees, mummies, Frankenstein, and even one Julie thought might've been Pumpkinhead.

The night turned out perfect. They'd bought warm cider and donuts before entering the maze. While slightly chilly, it wasn't too cold at all. The maze's corridors were lined with intricately carved pumpkins lit with small LED lanterns. Some little kids had even dressed up in Halloween costumes early, so every few minutes pint-sized witches, mummies, and goblins pranced by, pulling their beleaguered but bemused parents in tow.

"Y'know," Julie linked arms with Sage, "this was a great idea. Thanks for talking me into it."

Sage nodded, smiling. "Of course, it was a great idea. It was mine. I always have great ideas. And, hey—not a single person has come up and offered to slip a dollar under your belt. I told you there was nothing to worry about."

Even though they were alone in this particular stretch of maze, Julie shushed Sage with a hiss. Sage laughed and nudged her with their shoulder. Julie was about to jab Sage's with a playful smack, when the cornstalks rustled from their right, and exploded as a form burst from the corn and hurtled toward them.

38.

BLINDING FEAR PROPELLED Scott through walls of cornstalks as the figure wearing the mask thrashed behind him. Breath roared in his ears. His heart pounded against his chest. He wanted to scream for help. For someone, anyone, but for some reason, he couldn't gather enough breath to make anything more than weak, mewling rasps.

The thing behind him pursued silently. It said nothing. Didn't even grunt or breathe hard. It just kept coming.

Scott burst free from the cornstalks into an abandoned stretch of maze. He turned right, but his foot caught on a rut and he tumbled face-first into the ground.

The figure burst from the corn. It reached for him, its mask melting, pulsing, and oozing. It loomed over him. Scott felt he only had moments left.

Now, a voice whispered in his head.

He pulled the cross out of his pocket and slammed it against the thing's mask. His fingers touched its slickness, and revulsion pulsed through him. It didn't feel like rubber at all. It felt like the hide of a reptile, but it pulsed with an oozing warmth that made him want to throw up.

The thing reacted instantly. Its black mouth opened much wider than it should. Scott had to force down his gorge as its serpentine tongue writhed deep in its throat. Its eyes bulged to the point of popping out, and—like in his dream—Scott *felt* the thing's scream of pain in his head, rather than heard it.

The smell of burning rubber and flesh filled his nostrils. Smoke rose from where he pressed the cross into its mask. The rubber (skin?) blackened, bubbled, and cracked in an outline around the cross.

Scott heaved a knee into its stomach and threw it off. Rolled onto his hands and knees, set to propel himself forward . . .

It grabbed his ankle.

He looked over his shoulder as it yanked him backward. Desperate fear giving him strength, he flipped onto his back and swung his other foot as hard as he could. His sneaker connected at the thing's temple with a wet thud. Rubber, flesh, or something else splattered like an over-ripe pumpkin under a sledgehammer.

He rolled back over onto his hands and knees. Not sparing another glance, he dove into the corn, running as fast as he could. He didn't stop, until he plunged into another corridor, tripped, and fell at the feet of two people not as old as his mother, but much older than high school seniors.

He sat up, barely registering either of them. All he worried about was the hole in the corn he'd plunged through, and if the thing was following him.

39.

THE BOY—probably in ninth or tenth grade, Julie thought—sat and stared at where he'd come through the corn, panting, face white and sweating. His eyes were wide with terror. His free hand grabbed at the soil, spasming in fear.

For some reason, Julie didn't think he'd gotten spooked by the corn maze, or that he'd been running from bullies. His terror was too large to have come from upperclassmen punks. For some reason, she thought instantly of the weirdos in masks, though she didn't know why.

"Hey," she crouched next to him, checking him over for any obvious injuries, and finding none. "You okay?"

He panted, eyes flicking from the hole in the corn to her, back to the corn.

"I . . . uh . . . some . . . something . . . uh, someone was chasing me, and . . . and . . . "

"Julie, look at this," Sage muttered. Julie turned and saw her friend bending over a smartphone lying in the dirt, which the boy had obviously dropped. As Sage picked it up, an image—a picture the boy had taken—resolved into clearer view. It was a figure standing in the corn maze, and its face . . .

"What . . . " Julie swallowed, then rasped, "What's on its face? Is that . . . "

She looked at the boy. "Was that . . . was that chasing you?"

The boy offered her a spare glance, nodded, his gaze darting right back to the corn.

"Jules."

Julie turned back to the phone Sage held. They'd enlarged the picture, to see the figure's face clearly. It was wearing a mask. The same exact mask the weirdos had been wearing when they'd tried to get into The Cougars Den.

"Holy shit," she breathed.

40.

MARTY WALKED SLOWLY through Goodlow's parking lot. Only a handful of cars remained, and no new cars had arrived the past thirty minutes. He wasn't surprised. It was only 9:30, but it was also a Tuesday. Even with remote classes, still a "school night." He expected the lot to empty by 10.

As Marty paced along a row of parked cars near the maze's entrance/exit, he casually flicked his flashlight through back windows. Occasionally amorous teenagers or college students got a little too grabby and a quick tap of his flashlight on the passenger side window was usually enough to peacefully convince couples to take their extra-curricular affairs elsewhere. Not that Marty had anything against backseat romances, but Old Man Goodlow was firm in that he "didn't want no hanky panky in my parking lots 'cause this here's a family 'establishment," and Marty always followed Old Man Goodlow's rules.

Luckily he'd never come across a guy trying to take advantage of his female company. If he ever did, his flashlight was heavy and long-handled. He supposed it'd prove enough encouragement for said young man to keep his hands to himself, if a little less peacefully.

This particular night, however, every high school student in Warren County could've been making out in the back of their cars and the usually attentive Marty would've failed to notice. His mind wrangled with the recent unexpected complications to his life. He didn't like complications. He liked simplicity. He knew it was a bit legalistic, but simplicity had kept him sober all these years. Conflict and complications paved the road to stress, which in the past he'd self-medicated with booze. He didn't want to travel that road ever again.

The problem was, he didn't know what to do about one of the recent complications, the weirdoes in masks. What *was* there to do about them? He'd seen the one kid outside his barn, and since Saturday, there had been two more reports about people wearing masks and stalking people in the corn maze. *He* hadn't seen them Saturday night, (rustling corn didn't count), or Sunday and Monday.

The two additional times Constable Matthews had stopped by, she hadn't seen anything, either.

And it wasn't like the constable had time to patrol the corn maze every single night. She was the only thing passing for law in this town, and even as small as Pleasant Brook was, she was only one person. She must have more important things to worry about than punks messing around the local corn maze. Especially with Warren County once again teetering on the verge of full-blown COVID quarantine.

His other complication? Truth be told, he *did* have some measure of control over that. He'd had every intention of not letting it become something that would seriously impact his life. However, it had become harder and harder to avoid thinking about Julie from AA. Especially since he'd worked up the nerve to talk to her the other day.

She was too pretty by far for the likes of him. Much younger, also. But he saw a kindness in her eyes, and distant hurt, too. She had the look of someone battling guilt and regret. Battling also that insidious little voice which whispered to her every hour of every day that she had no self-worth. That she wasn't *good* enough for recovery. That her alcoholism was destined to haunt her forever. Marty could relate.

Of course, anything past casual friendships was discouraged within the group, especially if one partner or both were less than a year sober. For good reason. Mixed signals and hurt feelings easily lead to depression and a downward spiral which often ended at the bottom of a bottle. Even for members further along in their recovery, romantic relationships within the group were discouraged.

Which made his growing attraction to Julie a complication. One he worried could be troublesome. Either for him, her, or both of them. It was important he nipped it in the bud right away. Attraction, though distracting enough, could be managed and eventually dismissed. If he developed *feelings* for her, however, that was a whole other issue.

During his drinking years, Marty spent countless nights with women he hadn't known. Most he didn't even remember. Since drying up he'd avoided all entanglements with women, telling himself he didn't need the complication. He'd enjoyed (suffered?) enough of that particular complication to last him a lifetime. But the more he thought about Julie—casual thoughts about getting lunch or coffee—the more his resistance was buckling.

He was so absorbed by these thoughts he didn't hear the young woman saying, "Excuse me? Sir? Do you work here?" until she was almost on top of him.

His head jerked up and he felt annoyed at letting his attention drift. His annoyance quickly changed to confused pleasure, however, when he saw it was none other than Julie. With her stood another person with short brown hair and bright green eyes. Sage Hunter, Marty recognized immediately. The town librarian. Marty mowed the library's small back lawn every summer. The teenage boy with the shaggy black hair standing between them, he didn't recognize.

Julie's eyes widened. "Oh. Marty! I didn't know you worked here."

He nodded, hoping his smile didn't look as idiotic as it felt. "Every Halloween the last fifteen years. Decent pay for easy work. Can't beat it."

He sobered, noticing all three of them looked upset, the boy more so than Sage and Julie. "Everything okay? You guys don't look so hot."

Sage and Julie exchanged a worried glance. "Well," Julie began, "we're not sure, but you might want to call Constable Matthews. Someone's running around the corn maze, harassing . . . "

The boy lifted his head and met Marty's gaze head-on without flinching. The boy had some steel in his spine, Marty could tell. "He was after me," the boy said tonelessly, jaw firm. "He was trying to get me."

Marty crossed his arms and regarded the boy closely. Anyone else would try to kneel so they were at the boy's eye level, to put him at ease, make him feel more comfortable and relaxed. Based on the fierce glint he saw in the boy's eyes, Marty figured such a manipulative tactic wouldn't be well-received, so he simply asked, "Who was trying to get you? Why?"

All three exchanged glances. This time, when the boy spoke, his voice sounded uncertain. "At first I thought it was my friend Jasper. Pulling a prank on me. He was . . . was wearing this weird mask . . . "

Marty frowned, cold fingers playing along the back of his neck. "Mask?"

Sage touched the boy's shoulder gently. "Show him."

The boy nodded, not looking defiant at all, now. Only scared. He pulled his smartphone from his pocket, unlocked it, and handed it over.

Marty grunted. The picture was a bit blurry, but he could see, all the same. It was the same mask worn by the teen who'd followed (chased?) him up Burns Hill Road the other day. It might even be the same *person*, because the rock t-shirt looked familiar. Also, he was willing to bet—based on their descriptions—that it was the same mask corn maze patrons claimed those stalkers were wearing.

Julie must've seen the recognition in his eyes. "You've seen it," she said. "You've seen that mask."

Marty nodded and handed the phone back. "Yes," he admitted. To the teen, he said, "At first you *thought* it was your friend playing a prank. But now you're not sure."

The boy shook his head, face stiffening as he rallied his tough exterior. "No. At least . . . I don't think it's Jasper anymore. Maybe it *was* him. But it's not now."

Marty frowned. "What do you mean?"

The boy took a deep breath. Looked down at his shoes for a heartbeat. Looked back up, eyes shining with an odd mix of anger and fear. "I don't know. But I don't think . . . don't think he's Jasper anymore. Or *human*, either."

Gerhart Trailer Park
Midnight

41.

JULIE HANDED MARTY a Pepsi. He settled onto her futon, cracked it open, and took a long, satisfied drink. After he swallowed, he said with a wan smile, "Y'know, it's funny. I don't miss the taste of booze. Haven't missed it for a while. But I don't think I could go a week without a Pepsi."

Julie returned his smile as she sat in the old thrift store recliner next to the futon. She cracked her own soda—a diet Sprite—and admitted, "If I don't get a least one diet Sprite a day, I'm an unhappy girl, that's for sure.

He took another sip, swallowed, and snorted. "Aren't we textbook? We haven't gotten over our addictions. Only traded them. Me, booze for caffeine. You, booze for artificial sweetener."

They chuckled at the irony, and, of course, their mutual understanding. They may've traded addictions, but the happy reality was they'd at least traded the destructive for the benign. There was relief and gratitude in that.

They lapsed into silence. He took another sip and stared into nothing. She stared, unashamedly, at him. Marty was certainly older than her. He wasn't much of a "looker," either. In fact, Conroy was more "handsome" when it came down to it. Sage had hit near to the mark when she'd teased Julie about being attracted to him.

There was something in Marty's eyes, however. A forthrightness. A strength. Also, his face had a kindness to it. Julie knew Conroy had grappled with a drinking problem of his own and suffered the consequences for it, but she also sensed he'd pulled up before hitting bottom. In Marty, she sensed not only a man who'd hit bottom, but who'd also plunged *through* that bottom to even deeper levels before slowly, achingly climbing back up. All by himself, somehow.

Her attraction to Conroy came from a more basic, surface instinct. Her growing attraction to Marty (which she'd decided to simply admit) came from a deeper place. Though she didn't know why, she wanted to know exactly what kind of man he was. She was surprisingly willing (even eager) to tell him about *her*. Everything about her, holding nothing back.

She was about to lecture herself about the dangers of two recovering alcoholics getting involved emotionally when he cleared his throat and dashed her warm feelings with the equivalent of a bucket of cold water. "So. What the *hell* did we talk about tonight?"

Julie leaned forward and cupped her can of diet Sprite in both hands, grateful (and slightly regretful) for the distraction. "I have absolutely no idea. Nothing which makes any kind of sense, that's for sure."

After Scott Carter's pronouncement that whatever chased him in the corn maze wasn't human anymore, everyone stared silently at each other until Scott mumbled, sounding embarrassed, "I gotta go. Mom'll be home from work soon." Sage offered Scott a ride home, saying his bike would fit in the back of their old Chevy Blazer easily enough.

Scott reluctantly accepted, and then the surprising happened. Marty asked for a ride also. If they didn't mind waiting twenty minutes for the maze to close. Sage glanced at Julie and must've seen something in *her* eyes because she smiled and said she'd loved to.

On the way here, Marty asked Scott more about the masked person chasing him in the corn maze. Under the guise of safety concerns, but Julie thought he was probing for a personal reason. Scott told Marty his story in detail, though he recanted his claim that the person "wasn't human anymore." Said he was stressed because his friend Jasper and his family had left town without explaining, and Constable Matthews was looking for them. Julie thought he was deflecting but wisely held her tongue. So did everyone else.

After dropping Scott off at his house, making sure he got inside safely, and locked the door, Sage drove them back to Gerhart Trailer Park, leading off with a typically unflinching question to Marty. "So. What's the deal with these masks?"

Marty recounted in simple terms his encounter with a youth wearing a similar mask outside his barn, and the reports of people wearing masks bothering people at the corn maze. He also mentioned that neither him nor Constable Matthews had seen them, however.

After his story, Sage glanced at Julie with a raised eyebrow, and *she* proceeded to tell Marty about the two masked weirdos who'd tried several nights in a row to get into her "place of work." When he asked where she worked, he hadn't batted an eye when she hesitantly said The Cougars Den.

Sage dropped them off at Julie's trailer, saying they were tired and were calling it a night. With a smile, they'd admonished Julie and Marty not to "stay up too late," then drove to the other end of the trailer park, to their home.

And here she and Marty were.

"Do you think the masks are the same?"

Marty shrugged and sipped his Pepsi. "Far as I could tell. What about you?"

She nodded. "I think so. I mean, the lights were in my eyes because I was . . . uh . . . on stage . . . and they were standing in the shadows. But I'm sure they're the same."

He nodded, looking nonplussed at her mention of being "on stage." Suddenly, she felt a swell of gratitude deeper than she'd ever known.

"What do you think Scott meant by 'not human anymore'?"

Julie shook her head. "No idea." She paused, then said, "Do you think he was lying when he said he'd imagined all that stuff?"

Marty finished his Pepsi. Set it on the rickety coffee table in front of the futon. Looked at the ceiling, (not seeing the water stains, Julie desperately hoped), cracked his neck, then met Julie's gaze. "Yes. He's definitely holding something back."

"You think he's lying about Jasper and his family being gone, and Constable Matthews looking for them?"

"No. He was telling the truth about that, I think. In fact, that part of his story worries me the most. The whole family missing. I know the Rileys. I don't have anything to be proud of especially, but the Rileys are no-account, low-down trash with no moral compasses. They're thieves, grifters, and lowlifes. But they'd never leave. Not if the whole town was on fire."

Marty shook his head. "I think Scott is a scared kid who doesn't think adults will believe him. Something *definitely* happened in that corn maze he's not telling us."

They fell into silence again. She finished her diet Sprite while he laced his fingers behind his head and stared at the ceiling again, apparently deep in thought. After a few minutes passed, she broke the quiet with, "What should we do? Call Constable Matthews again?"

He sat forward, elbows on thighs, and shook his head. "No. Not right now, at least. She's already been out to the maze a few times, and she didn't find anything each time. I have a feeling it would be the same tonight. Plus, it's late, and we both need sleep. We'll think a lot better in the morning, so I'll call Constable Matthews then. See where a good night's sleep leaves us."

He looked at her. "Past that, I have no idea."

She nodded, and then, without thinking, blurted out, "You're welcome to sleep here tonight. Instead of in a barn. If you want."

Marty didn't answer right away. He opened his mouth, closed it, then finally said, "I can walk. It's no problem."

Julie frowned slightly, confused. "At this time of night? No way. *Stay*. Marty. It's fine."

He sighed, looking embarrassed, of all things. "Honestly, I don't want you to . . . "

"Marty. Listen." Something in her tone must've struck him, because he fell silent instantly, and didn't try to protest further. "Don't mean to be blunt, but here it is. I am *not* trying to get into your pants. Seriously. I know the AA thing about relationships so early in recovery. I like you. Honestly, I do. There's a quiet strength about you. A kindness I haven't seen in most of the men I've known. But I'm only a little over a year sober. I'm not about to complicate things for me *or* you with a fling. *Stay*. I've got a spare bedroom, or you can sleep out here on the futon if you prefer."

She grinned, hoping to put him at ease. "Your virtue is safe. I promise not to lure you into my bed with my seductive wiles or ravage you in the middle of the night. On my AA honor."

Marty smiled, and Julie saw him visibly relax. It was at that moment she realized that whatever pull she felt toward him, he felt something similar. This made her feel pleasantly warm inside. Not enough for her to go back on her word, however. At least . . . not at the moment.

Marty chuckled and sat wearily on the futon. "That's good. I'm exhausted talking about all this. About ready to drop off sitting here. And you're right. I'd rather not walk home in the dark. Not after talking about all . . . this."

He gave her a sincere smile of gratitude, which also held a hint of something else she couldn't quite decipher. "Thanks, Julie. I appreciate it."

She nodded and smiled in return. "My pleasure."

She hustled off to get some blankets and pillows before he could get even more charming, and inch her closer to going back on her word.

Pleasant Brook Cemetery
Midnight

42.

JUD COLLINS SAT on the cot in the cemetery caretaker's shed, smoking his third cherry-flavored, plastic-tipped cheroot of the night. Staring out the small, square window above the cot, his .30 aught Springfield Winchester lying across his lap, oiled, loaded, and ready for use.

There'd been three more grave desecrations since he'd last spoken to Constable Matthews. Little Jimmy Thompson, the seven-year-old who'd drowned in the Thompson's pool last summer. Bob Cozenback, who'd died of a stroke at the ripe old age of forty-six in August, and Fran Jenkins, the poor girl who'd gotten lost snow-shoeing last December. When they finally found her in the woods, she was stone-cold frozen, all the way through.

Decent people who deserved decent Christian burials. Decent people whose remains had been dug up by something worse than animals. Every bit of flesh stripped, nothing left but gnawed bones. Even the brains had been eaten, and Jud only knew that because the skulls had been cracked in two and discarded like peanut shells.

Thinking about it made his stomach turn, but not because seeing dead things made him queasy. If it did, he never would've taken over the caretaker position. No, the thought of what had been done to those people's remains made him sick to his stomach with rage. He hated to think of the uproar should folks discover how their beloved dead had been disinterred by some foul and unclean thing. He'd spent the whole week re-burying folks in their shattered coffins and putting their resting places back to rights, hoping all the while no one would decide to visit their dearly departed while he was doing so. He was plain fed up with it and *done.*

So he was sitting here in the caretaker's shed past midnight, smoking like a chimney and clutching his rifle instead of home sleeping with his wife Lida. He aimed to find out *what* the hell was digging up his graveyard, and put a stop to it. Much as he liked Constable Matthews and thought her a fine officer of the law, she was only one person.

No, Jud was alone on this. That suited him fine. He'd been a project manager at Falvo Manufacturing in Utica for thirty-five years before retiring five years ago. He was used to calling the shots. That's what he was prepared to do now. Call the shots and sort this shit out. Cemetery caretaker may be his retirement gig, but he took it seriously. This graveyard was *his* house, dammit. Nobody was going to fuck with it on his watch.

Still, even as he made such a bold declaration in his head, his heart shivered as he wondered *what* was digging up the graves and *eating* the decayed flesh of Pleasant Brook's corpses. He'd never heard or seen anything like it, except maybe on the Shock Theater Horror marathons when he'd been a kid. This was real life, though. Not a horror flick. There had to be a rational explanation.

He sat up straighter, hands clenching his Winchester. He leaned closer to the window, peering into the dark. He thought he'd seen something flickering around the Lassiter Mausoleum, the only above-ground burial plot in all of Pleasant Brook. If those fuckers thought they were messing around with *that*, they had another thought coming.

James Lassiter the Third founded Pleasant Brook back in the 1700s. There'd been Lassiters living here long as anyone could remember, though the latest generation was all girls, and unmarried. Corinne Lassiter died last Spring from that fucking coronavirus. An elementary school teacher, she'd caught that shit from a snot-nosed brat in her class because the state (in Jud's opinion) gave the go-ahead for in-person learning too damn quickly.

She'd been buried last *May*. She wouldn't necessarily be rotted all the way down to the bone, and she'd been a *big* woman. Prime candidate for whatever the hell was ripping up his graveyard.

"Oh, hell no," Jud whispered as he stood, clutching his Winchester tightly. "This shit stops tonight."

43.

THEY WERE HUNGRY. They were always hungry and always needed to feed. They'd been biding their time. Careful so they wouldn't draw the attention of the Other, but the more quickly they spread through this place and tasted its darkness, the more they thought maybe the Other didn't exist here or didn't have as much power as it did elsewhere. If that were true, by the time the walls thinned on the night of Sowin, their strength would be at its peak, and they would change everything in this town into them, and make every face theirs.

Until then, however, they would move slowly and build their numbers carefully. Pick off strays so as not to attract the Other's notice, should it exist in this place in some form. The First dictated it, and so they ate the dead, as they had for untold centuries.

As always, they'd been slow in remembering what they were. Where they came from, and who made them, and why. Slowly, however, as they spread and made more of themselves, their memory returned. The first thing they remembered: They always woke in darkness. And, they always woke during *this* season, when the walls between worlds thinned. The season of Sawin. Sowin. Saihwin.

Sauhein.

As they'd spread through this place—a place filled with such lovely, strange darkness, where the Other wasn't so strong—they'd slowly remembered who made them and why. They and their totem had been made in the image of Sauhein Himself. The chief bringer of Darkness. They'd been made in the image of Sauhein, to spread his image everywhere during His season. They would make everyone over into His image, and when His night came, they would number enough to open the door and usher Him into this world, so He could walk among them—those who wore His face—once more.

It hadn't happened since the Days of Old. As they grew strong in this dark place and spread, they remembered. So many times they'd been called out of the darkness and they'd spread, only to be checked by the Other and cast back into darkness. Sauhein had not walked among them for uncounted years.

But this place was darker than most. A special kind of dark. The Other wasn't strong here, and not many of the herd walked with the Other. They'd only encountered a handful so far. A young one, who'd merely burned one of them with Other's sigil, apparently ignorant of its meaning. Another had covered itself in the Other's sigil, writ on its flesh, making it untouchable. A third had spoken words of power which had hurt them. Words of the Other.

The young one was no threat. He didn't walk with the Other; merely possessed its sigil. The one with the Other's sigil in its flesh would be dealt with tonight.

But for now, some of them would feed. They'd come here to this feeding ground again, looking for more. They'd fed well here, but much of the dead had been in the ground too long and didn't offer much meat. The only substantial flesh they sensed was behind hard rock walls in a building surrounded by metal. They used their taken hands to pull and strain at the metal, and it was groaning apart slowly, but they would have to deal with the stone building next, and they didn't know if they would be able to break past it. Flesh was in there, however. They needed to feed, to grow stronger . . .

"Hey! You sumbitches get the *hell* away from there!"

Something roared. Heat and fire exploded their flesh. They felt pain and anger, and most of all . . .

Hate.

Hate, stoked by the fires of *need.*

44.

JUD COLLINS HAD never considered himself trigger-happy. He'd never pointed a gun at a human being so he didn't know for sure, but he'd always thought deep inside he simply didn't have enough guts to take a human life. He'd hesitate, he felt sure.

When he neared the figures—three of them—pulling at the wrought-iron gate around Lassiter Mausoleum, however, he didn't feel an ounce of hesitation. He jammed the Winchester's stock into his shoulder, shouted, drew a bead on the closest, and pulled the trigger, aiming at the back of its head.

Because these things *weren't* human. He didn't know why he thought that. They just weren't. They had two arms and walked upright on two legs and had a head each. But they weren't human, he instinctively knew, and didn't have a "life" to take.

His shot struck the closest thing in the back of its head. He'd never once in his life thought of what a 30-aught would do to a man's head, but even if he had, he doubted very much his poor imagination could *ever* have conjured such a sight.

The thing's head *exploded.* Not only exploded but damn near disintegrated into an expanding geyser of gristle which splattered all over its shoulders and ruined neck, leaving nothing behind. Even stranger, somehow that hurt the *other* things. Like they *felt* its head getting blown off. They clamped hands on the side of their heads and stumbled to their knees, shaking and quivering . . .

But they didn't make a sound. Not a scream, a cry, or even the slightest groan. They huddled there. On their knees, quivering, holding their shaking heads. As for the third one, the one whose head he'd destroyed . . .

Something cold and greasy curdled in Jud's stomach. The Winchester grew impossibly heavy. His heart pounded, and his mouth opened and closed wordlessly for several seconds before he could finally utter in a terribly old, raspy voice, "What . . . What. The. *Fuck?*"

The one with no head was *not* on its knees. It still stood, clutching the wrought-iron fence tightly, shoulders and arms shaking. At first, Jud thought in death spasms, but then the headless thing *pushed* off the fence. Lurched around and *faced* him. Took a shambling step toward him. Then another, and another. Hands outstretched and reaching.

Jud ratcheted the Winchester's lever and pulled the trigger. The rifle bucked against his shoulder and the blast hit the headless thing square in its chest. It shuddered as its guts blew open. Blackish-green gore and chunks of rotted flesh splattered wetly, but though the thing staggered, it didn't go down. The other things reacted again, jerking as if they'd felt the rifle blast in *their* guts.

Jud didn't think. He pumped the rifle and pulled the trigger, blowing a massive chunk of rotting flesh from the thing's right shoulder. Worked the lever again, pulled the trigger, and blew out its right knee. It stumbled and fell onto its other knee. Jud worked the lever again and blasted away at its guts some more. More blackish-green guts splashed and sickly-looking intestines spilled to the ground. To his horror, the intestines *wriggled* where they fell. Writhing, twitching, *crawling toward him.*

Clenching his rifle and swallowing an acidic taste in the back of his mouth, Jud fired again, this time blowing away a significant portion of the thing's upper chest. Its torso was a mangled mess of shredded black flesh. Viscera and fluids leaked down its body. Bits and pieces fell from the gaping wounds with soft *thumps*, like wet clay dropping onto the ground.

And still, the headless, tattered, and rotten thing reached for him.

Jud blew out the thing's right knee. It flopped onto its belly with a wet, meaty thump, thrashed for several minutes, and then lay still. A widening pool of something black and oily spread under its body. Not blood, but something else.

A hand twitched once, flopping in the spreading pool of black gore, then fell still. A rasping breath of relief exploded from Jud . . . until a terrible thought struck him. He swung his Winchester back up and pointed it toward Lassiter Mausoleum . . .

They were gone.

The other things trying to get into the mausoleum had disappeared while he'd been so focused on shooting this one to hell. Icy horror flushed through him. "Shit," Jud mumbled, swinging his Winchester around, "shitfire, damn it all to hell, where the *fuck* are they . . . "

Something crackled behind him. Crisp and brittle autumn leaves underfoot. Heart pounding, lungs spasming, Jud spun awkwardly around . . .

Two silhouettes stood still about ten feet away. Hands at their sides, heads cocked at an angle. How they'd moved so fast and so quickly he'd no idea. One minute they'd been kneeling and shivering in pain every time he put a bullet into the headless thing; the next, they'd somehow snuck around him, and now they didn't look like they were hurting at all . . .

Something shifted behind him. Not wanting to take his eyes off the two shadows before him, but fear pounding his heart, Jud spun, aiming his Winchester wildly. What he saw brought his mind to a shattering halt, as the gears in his head froze and locked up, all at once.

The thing he'd shot six times had somehow pushed itself back up onto its knees. Tattered holes in its clothing bore witness to the shots he'd fired, but he could see the knotting, twisting flesh *filling back in*. As for its head . . .

The gore pooling under the body was shrinking. Defying gratify and flowing back *into* the thing, which was growing a new head from its ragged neck. Almost as if it was drinking up its own guts.

"Fuck that," Jud rasped as he brought his Winchester to bear. "I'll blow it right the hell back off!"

He ratcheted the Winchester's lever.

Pulled the trigger.

Heard nothing but a soul-emptying *click*.

He cried out. One hand darted to his pocket where he'd stuffed more shells. The other clumsily held the Winchester with one hand. Even as his nerveless fingers dug around his pocket for a shell that he'd never hold, the thing—now with a new head—launched itself at him. Its face was a swirling mass of liquid, surging black flesh.

Jud's finger grazed a shell's brass casing as the thing hit him in the chest, slamming him backwards onto the ground. Jud's breath exploded out in a great *whoosh* and electric pain raced down his spine from the back of his head. His rifle flew from his hand. Blind hysteria filled Jud's mind.

The thing grasped both sides of his head and *squeezed*. Pressure unlike anything he'd ever known filled his head, replacing his panic with a high ringing which canceled out everything else.

He *felt* the spiderweb cracks ripple across his skull. For a moment, the bone breaking crashed even louder than the ringing. Distantly, Jud felt his heels drum the wet grass spasmodically. He heard one last soul-splintering *crunch*, and then nothing.

***

They applied more pressure on the old one's head. His mouth opened wide, eyes bugged out in terror. They flexed and squeezed once more, sensing the end was near. The old one's head made several crackling sounds. Blood geysered from his mouth and both eyeballs popped and splattered onto the old one's face.

They released the old one's head—now a flattened, oblong shape—and sat back, regarding the ruined face. Contemplating if they should leave it, eat it, or remake it into His image. There was the matter of the dead inside the stone building, which they couldn't reach. The old one had taken offense to their trespass, because he was a guardian of the dead, like many they'd encountered in their murky past. Instinctively, they sensed he would possess knowledge about this burial ground, and its dead.

They bent over and felt the totem of His visage—their face—bubble, shift, and melt. *His* flesh poured off them onto the old one's ruined face and quickly began remaking it into His image. *His* flesh seeped into the old one's cracks and tears, filling them up, re-knitting mangled flesh and shattered bone. From them, *His* flesh poured and made another face in His image.

The old one's body jerked and twitched. Sat up. Stared at them with His face, and was immediately part of them. Instantly they all knew what the old one had known. Everything about this burial ground. Including where the freshest dead were buried. The unwanted attention the disturbed graves were bringing them. And also, the location of the "key" to the "door" of the "Lassiter Mausoleum."

The newly made visage stood, turned, and walked away. They followed, for there was much to do.

Carter Residence
2:00 AM

45.

SCOTT SAT ON the front porch of their small home, staring at the little patch of their driveway illuminated by the security light mounted on their small garage. He could see about ten feet down the driveway, no further. Everything past the arc of yellow faded into darkness.

Scott drank from the mug of coffee he'd made after Mom went to bed. No sneaking sips of her booze tonight. He needed to stay sharp and ready. Jasper . . . or *whatever* that thing in the corn maze had been . . . was coming for him.

He'd be ready. Across his lap lay his grandfather's hunting rifle, a Remington 760, taken quietly out of the rifle case when he'd felt sure Mom had fallen asleep. Because he'd never openly shown an interest in guns, she never kept it locked. What she didn't know was that he and Jasper had been sneaking it out and shooting beer cans and bottles off low-hanging tree branches in the woods behind their home for the past three years. He had half a box of shells from their last practice session four weeks ago, from before school went remote. Where Jasper got the shells Scott didn't know and hadn't asked.

In his other hand, he held a large wooden cross he'd screwed together with pieces of scrap wood—two broken broom handles—he'd found in the garage before Mom came home. He remembered what his cross necklace had done to that . . . *thing* tonight, and what it'd done in that dream he'd had a few nights ago, though he wasn't sure anymore that had only been a dream.

Regardless, he needed to test his theory. Needed to verify it. See if it was true. He thought for sure he'd seen that thing's face melt when he touched it with his cross. He didn't think he'd imagined it. Even though that's what he'd told that girl Julie, the librarian, Sage, and that guy Marty; that he'd imagined everything. But also, maybe it hadn't been the cross itself. Maybe jamming it into that thing's face so hard had done it.

He had to be sure.

He shifted in his chair, glad he'd dressed warmly, as the cold was definitely seeping into his bones. Part of him strongly argued giving up his vigil and retreating to the warm comfort of his bed, reasoning that locking his door would be good enough. Another part of him, an instinctual part, argued as strongly that Jasper or whatever he was now would return tonight, and a stand had to be made. A declaration that this house was under his protection. Such as it was.

Scott snorted, amused at how cliché the sentiment was, and how derivative of the horror movies he loved. The smart thing to do was lock the doors and windows and go to bed. *Another* smart thing would've been to come clean to everyone about what happened in the corn maze. How the rubber "skin" of that thing's mask had bubbled, sizzled, and melted when he'd touched it with his cross pendant. Or how he'd kicked its jaw *off* when it grabbed his foot.

He'd backed down, however. Told them he'd probably been "imagining things." He didn't know why, exactly, and he was kicking himself for it, now. Julie seemed trustworthy enough, he *knew* he could trust Sage, and he felt the same about Marty.

He and Jasper had seen him a few times, of course. Walking along Main Street with his backpack, and Jasper had called him a "homeless bum." After only one meeting, however, Scott knew Marty wasn't a bum, regardless of his living situation. He radiated a kind of quiet strength. The same kind Scott felt from Constable Matthews. He thought if he told Marty what he'd seen, the guy would've come home with him, and would probably be sitting next to him.

Scott sipped from his coffee again, realizing in dismay it was probably the sense of Marty's resolve which had kept him from telling the man everything. Deep down, he felt awful for all the shit he'd put his mother through the past few years. He'd acted like a little punk ass. A miniature version of his unknown father. After he'd told an edited version of his story, all he'd wanted to do was get home before Mom did, make sure the house was clean and make it look like he'd been home the whole time, and pretend everything was chill. He didn't want to make his mother's already long day worse.

Somehow he'd pulled it off. Sage got him home before Mom. He'd managed to not only clean the house and microwave a frozen dinner for good measure, but he also slipped into bed as Mom pulled into the driveway.

Mom crashed hard soon as she went to bed. She always did after working second shift, because not only did she go to The Tipper for a "nightcap" (which was happening more and more frequently these days), she also came home and routinely downed several glasses of vodka and Sprite before stumbling to bed.

She also used noise-canceling headphones and played white noise on her phone so she could sleep in late after an evening shift (and her "nightcaps" at The Tipper). These used to be the best nights for him to sneak out and meet Jasper.

Of course, in a way, he was still sneaking out to meet Jasper, wasn't he? Only with his grandfather's rifle and a half-ass homemade cross instead of a six-pack he'd liberated from Mom's stash in the garage. Also, the Jasper he was expecting wasn't exactly Jasper anymore.

Which begged the question, of course . . . what the hell was he?

Scott drew in a deep, fluttering breath as he stared into the darkness past the spill of yellow light from the lamp in the garage. He was scared. No question about it. Though it didn't make sense, maybe that was another reason why he hadn't told the truth about the corn maze. He felt like he could trust Julia, Sage, and Marty enough to admit his fears. That scared him almost worse, in a way. Opening the door and letting fear all the way in, admitting he *was* scared to others? What good could that do?

He grunted. "Yeah. So, because you can't admit to being scared, now you're sitting here by yourself, practically shitting your pants, instead of sitting here with help. Genius, Scott. Absofuckinglutely genius."

He thought about taking another sip of coffee but realized he was wired enough as it was, and unlikely to fall asleep anytime soon. That, and if he had much more to drink, he'd have to piss, and he didn't want to abandon his watch, or drop his guard by pissing off the porch. That would be an inconvenient time for Jasper—or whatever the hell he was now—to arrive.

Deep down, Scott didn't believe Jasper was alive anymore. Neither was Jasper's mom or his brothers. They weren't exactly dead either. What they were, he didn't know. Undead Zombies? George Romero Zombies, Brian Keene Zombies, or *Serpent and the Rainbow* zombies?

Ignoring the insanity of these questions, Scott turned his horror-brain on and thought about it. Definitely not Romero Zombies or *Resident Evil* zombies. These things had purpose. More like Brian Keene zombies. "Jasper" had sought him out twice now. Regardless, whatever was happening to "Jasper" was rotting him from the inside out. When he'd kicked "Jasper" in the jaw, its mouth had exploded like a rotten pumpkin.

"Jasper's" reaction to the cross made it seem like a vampire, but considering it further, made it even more like Brian Keene's zombies from *The Rising*. Those things had been foul spirits banished from this world. He didn't remember if the zombies in *The Rising* were afraid of crosses, exactly. But he did remember them hating the Christian God.

Was Jasper possessed? Like in *The Exorcist*? Of course, in lots of movies and books people got possessed when they messed around with occult shit, and Jasper had never been into that. He didn't even claim to "read the articles" in Playboy, so reading about the occult or learning Latin incantations seemed unlikely. Then again, what had Regan done to get possessed in *The Exorcist*? Nothing. It was tough shit for her. Maybe the same thing had happened to Jasper? But how?

Of course, there were these fucking masks. They all looked the same. That made Scott think of cults and shit. But Jasper join a cult? Also, the mask had *become* Jasper's skin, somehow. When he'd kicked Jasper in the face, the mask hadn't flown off or slipped. It had ripped and spewed fluids. Like rotten skin. When he'd touched it with his cross, it had burned and melted, too.

An idea teased the edge of his thoughts. Was it something like zombies and vampires mixed together? Both horror monsters spread by biting victims. Maybe these things didn't have to bite, however. All the masks looked the same. Maybe the *mask* is how they spread. But more like vampires. Spreading on purpose, not mindlessly like zombies (the George Romero kind, anyway). Did they have a plan?

Scott snorted and ran his hand through his hair. It sounded ridiculous. Almost as ridiculous as a kid who'd watched way too many horror movies sitting on his front porch past midnight, rifle in one hand, homemade cross in the other. He'd seen all the classic old-school horror movies, and all those new "meta" ones too. The *Scream* movies, *Cabin in the Woods*, and a bunch of others. Horror movies that tried to analyze horror movies. Not only was it stupidly cliché for him to hold a nighttime vigil against the forces of evil, it was stupidly cliché to be thinking how cliché it all was, which was as cliché as wondering if his current situation was more "old-school horror" or something that "broke the rules." The worst part was it didn't matter how many horror movies he'd seen or how much he thought about it, he was still going to be taken by surprise by whatever happened, no matter *how* stupid or cliché it was . . .

Something scraped against the gravel driveway, out in the darkness. All Scott's clever and self-informed thoughts about the horror genre fled in the face of the adrenaline flushing through him. He sat up straight. Hand clutching the cross tighter, his other hand adjusting his grip on the rifle. He peered into the darkness and saw nothing.

At first.

He heard another scrape. And another. Now footsteps on the gravel, approaching him. Slowly, steadily—not like a mindless zombie at all—a figure walked into the swathe of light thrown by the lamp in the garage.

Scott stood on suddenly rubbery legs. Cross in one hand, rifle in the other. Standing two feet from the porch was the thing he'd dreamed about . . .

that wasn't a dream

. . . and the thing which had chased him in the maze tonight. The thing wearing Jasper's *Five-Finger Death Punch* t-shirt. The thing which he thought used to be Jasper and was now something else.

not human anymore

Staring at the figure wearing that same disgusting mask (a mask, or its face?), a cold chill crept through him. When he'd pressed the cross pendant against the mask, he'd burned it. He'd smelled it burning. When he'd kicked its lower jaw it exploded like rotten fruit. But there the figure stood, its mask—or face—completely whole. Those wet and bulging eyes staring at him. Strands of slick black hair hanging loosely from its peeling scalp. Its slimy black tongue wriggling in its wide-open mouth . . .

masks don't have tongues, do they?

. . . while the thing stood there. Staring at him. Silently. Hands hanging at its sides. For perhaps the first time, Scott sensed what it was on a primitive level. It was a hunter. A predator. Scott was its prey. It had tracked him here, and it wasn't afraid of him, at all. Not in the slightest.

It frightened Scott, but oddly enough, it also pissed him off. He couldn't say why for sure. Only that it made him feel like he was at the mercy of high school bullies. They knew they were bigger and stronger, and there was no help for you, and they knew *you* knew it, too. You were about to get the shit kicked out of you, there was nothing you could do to prevent it, and there wasn't anyone around to stop it.

It eventually pissed you off enough to fight back. Maybe that only made things worse. But in the end, if you were able to bloody the bully's lip or blacken his eye before you got beaten down, it was worth it.

That was how Scott felt. He was all alone with no help. He knew that, and IT knew that. Despite the rifle and cross he held, that thing felt like it could do whatever it wanted. Scott could see that in its stance. That pissed him off, badly.

The only problem?

The stakes were more fatal than simply getting beat down.

He took a deep breath, and somehow, in a steady voice, he said, "Get the fuck out of here. You don't have permission to be here. I won't let you in."

It was a bluff, straight and simple. Pulled from a dozen different vampire novels, movies, and TV shows. He had no idea if it applied or even worked. This *thing* had been in his house the other night, (if that indeed wasn't a dream), so it obviously didn't need an invitation. Even so, something in Scott compelled him to say it. If only to bolster his own courage, or because he took comfort in the scene's familiarity.

Feeling ridiculous and empowered all at once, Scott raised the cross, held it out in front of him, and walked forward. Somehow he made it down the porch's two steps without stumbling and falling flat on his face. He stopped five feet away from the thing and thrust the cross out in front of him.

Up close, the mask looked even more hideous. The bulging eyes rolled and twitched, gazing in two different directions. Its hair hung limply to the thing's shoulders. Its thick, rubbery lips were slicked with mucus and drool, as the mouth quivered with wet, wheezing breaths.

"Go away," Scott said. This time his voice broke, and he felt ashamed at its wavering tone.

The thing looked at him.

Cocked its head, as if confused.

Then it grinned. Its horrific yet somehow cartoonish, rubbery mouth opening wide, revealing jagged teeth and a writhing, oily black tongue. It was *smiling* at him. Grinning and drooling everywhere. Maybe crosses did hurt these things somehow, but that didn't matter because Scott could see the truth in the thing's madly rolling eyes. *It didn't care.*

Scott's stomach sank. "Oh, *shit*."

Faster than anything should be able to move, the thing launched at Scott, reaching with hands which instantly morphed into grotesque claws. Heeding an instinct he still didn't understand, Scott thrust the cross into it. The thing slammed into the cross. Somehow, Scott kept his arm locked. The bulk of the cross slammed into the thing's chest.

The reaction was instant, and the same as before. Where the cross touched it, "flesh" hissed, melting and burning. A horrible stench filled Scott's nostrils. The thing jerked and flailed its arms in obvious pain as if the cross was jolting it with thousands of volts of electricity. Smoke actually began to rise from beneath its tattered sleeveless shirt.

Unlike the other time, however, the thing didn't relent. It thrashed in pain as Scott pressed the cross against it, hideous mouth opening wide in a silent scream, eyes bulging sickeningly, but it refused to retreat. As if it somehow knew the pain wasn't enough to kill it. As if it was gaining a *tolerance* to it. Even as the sizzling sound intensified and the smell of burnt rubber worsened, the thing pushed *back* against the cross.

Scott's feet slid back several inches. The cross wasn't going to work. The thing would shove him onto his ass, especially with one hand on the cross, the other hand holding the . . .

Pump-action shotgun.

Loaded-pump action shotgun.

Fucking idiot!

With a yell, Scott lowered his right shoulder and threw everything he had behind a shove which sent the thing reeling back several steps. He released the cross but saw it *stuck* to the thing's sizzling and melting skin. It thrashed against it, but couldn't throw it away.

Scott pumped the shotgun and took aim.

With a lurch, the thing finally dashed the cross to the ground and faced him.

Scott braced the shotgun against his shoulder. Took a breath—preparing for a kick which would probably leave a bruise—and pulled the trigger.

The shotgun's blast roared in the night's silence. The kick knocked Scott's breath out of him but somehow—even though he'd rocked slightly on his toes—he kept his aim steady and true. The thing's face exploded and dissolved in a spray of oily wet matter and flying chunks of greenish-black tissue. Whatever passed for its brain flew out the back of its head and splattered onto the ground.

But it didn't fall down.

It stumbled sideways. Claws morphing back into hands, which flailed at its shredded, ruined face. Its shoulders twitched. It took several steps to the right and then to the left, weaving drunkenly side-to-side. Scott choked up on the shotgun. Pumped another shell into the chamber, pressed his finger on the trigger . . .

Cold and heavy fear filled his guts. The thing had staggered to the edge of the light, so it was hard to see completely, but he could see enough. In the ravaged mess of its face, thick black liquid—like melted rubber—oozed and filled the destruction. Smoothing and evening out. Expanding and molding into something resembling a face. *Growing* a fucking face, right before him.

For a moment he couldn't move, paralyzed with fear. Couldn't even depress the shotgun's trigger. It couldn't be. He'd shot it in the fucking face. Didn't matter what it was, he'd shot it in the *fucking face*.

Two bulging eyes popped out of the black tarry mass and glared madly at him. A slit opened into a mouth and grinned, exposing those jagged, shard-like teeth pushing out of slick gums. A wriggling, tattered tongue *grew* out of its mouth.

"Shit!" Scott braced the shotgun against his sore shoulder and pulled the trigger. His bruised muscles throbbed wildly, however, sending arcs of pain shooting down his arm and across his chest, so his aim wavered. The shotgun roared again, but Scott's shot flew wide, hitting the thing's shoulder. The blast knocked it sideways and ripped a sizable hunk of flesh away, leaving a gaping hole which leaked black fluid, but again, it didn't fall down.

It straightened. Glanced calmly at its cratered shoulder, which was already filling with black rubber liquid and reforming. It looked back at

Scott, its face—not a mask, its *face*—reformed. It walked forward, its stride resolute and inevitable.

Scott pumped another shell into the chamber, backpedaling frantically. He raised the shotgun to his shoulder, but in his haste, his feet tangled and he fell backward, finger spasming against the trigger and sending a useless blast into the sky.

Scott landed on his back, the wind knocked out of him. Gasping, he dug into his pocket for more shells, but fear made his fingers clumsy, and he couldn't tug them free.

He heard it push off the gravel and jump. A dark form descended upon him, its rubbery mouth wide, with that slick black tongue wriggling inside.

A booming roar shook the night.

The thing flew sideways and crashed to the ground.

46.

CONSTABLE MATTHEWS WAS about done in for the night. She felt frustrated, tired, annoyed, and a free-floating tension crawled along her shoulders, making her feel twitchy and nervous. She'd driven through town multiple times; eyes open for people wearing masks. Of course, that hadn't turned up any results, as she'd figured it wouldn't. What was she hoping to find? Mask-wearers lurking on street corners, rubbing their hands together maniacally, acting "lurky?"

She'd driven out to The Cougars Den before it opened and chatted further with Conroy Ortega, and then afterward interviewed some of the girls. Most of them could only relate the same story Conroy told her this morning, about two men trying to sneak into the strip club without paying. They'd both been wearing the same ugly masks. They'd also acted—weirdly enough—afraid of touching Conroy, retreating and leaving the club as soon as he neared them. They hadn't returned to the club since.

She'd thought about driving over to the Goodlow's to talk with Marty some more. See if they'd had any more trouble. Instead, she spent the early evening cruising the side roads around Pleasant Brook. Not thinking consciously, letting her instincts guide her to places where folks might want to hide. She didn't ask herself *why* they'd be hiding. She simply looked for places which might offer adequate hiding space. Every ramshackle and unused barn she could think of. The abandoned houses she knew in the surrounding areas, which, of course, led her to the old Owen house.

Sitting in its driveway, she thought of the gruesome violence enacted there three years ago. Getting out to walk around it hadn't helped her feel any better. Especially when the tire tracks she'd found (probably from a truck) made her think of Sage seeing Jesse Simmons, and wondering if Bobby Lee Haskel had come home with him.

By happenstance or blind fate, the route back to her home passed Scott Carter's house. As she neared the edge of their property, she heard the distinctive *boom* of a shotgun going off. The report came from directly ahead, and then . . .

A second blast.

Grace hit the gas, speeding the rest of the way to Scott's house. Jerked the wheel to the left and made a hard turn into the driveway. She slammed on the brakes, threw the JEEP in park, reached down with one hand, and unlatched the riot gun from under the dash. The riot gun she *always* kept in the JEEP, despite the unlikelihood of ever needing it in such a small town. She pulled the riot gun out, shouldered open the driver door, and stepped out of the JEEP, bringing the gun to bear.

In the Jeep's headlights, Scott Carter lay on the ground, pump-action shotgun in his right hand. A figure in a dingy white sleeveless t-shirt was advancing upon him, stiff gait already speeding into a run. Instinctively—without a word of warning—Grace swung the riot gun to her shoulder, flipped the safety off, and placed her finger on the trigger.

The figure leaped, hands outstretched. Grace pulled the trigger and the riot gun roared. Her shot caught the figure dead center in its back, jerking it sideways, away from Scott. It slammed into the ground, next to what looked like a couple pieces of wood nailed or screwed together to form a . . .

Cross.

Scott scrambled from his position faster than Grace would've given a kid credit for. Before she could even open her mouth to shout, Scott swooped toward the figure lying on the ground. Grabbed the pieces of wood lying next to it—which definitely was a cross—and with a yell jammed the one jagged end straight down onto the figure's chest. It plunged into its flesh like a hot fork through soft butter, impaling it into the ground itself.

Grace stared in disbelief. It had all happened so fast, and now the *thing* (it wasn't a person; not at all) was thrashing and flailing. Kicking its legs, heels drumming the gravel, trying to free itself. Its hands grabbed weakly at the wood lodged through its body and pinning it into the ground, and it threw its shoulders back and forth, trying to wrench itself free.

But it couldn't. It thrashed, jerked, pulled at the wood—not making a sound the entire time—but it couldn't free itself.

Grace looked at Scott, standing out of arm's distance, glaring at the spasming thing with an intensity she wouldn't have thought possible in someone so young. Grace shook herself mentally, raised the riot gun, and slowly approached the thing, finger on the trigger, stomach clenching tightly.

As she neared it, however, its desperate movements slowed. Its hands clutched weakly at the wooden pole—a broken broom handle, Grace now saw—then slipped off to lay limply at its sides. Its kicking stopped. Its shoulders stilled. To Grace's utter amazement and disgust, it started to *melt*.

Literally.

The thing's exposed skin sagged, going soft, then began sloughing off onto the ground in great wads of rubbery sludge. Its hideous face collapsed in on itself. Bulging eyeballs turned into an unnatural yellow pus and oozed down its sinking cheeks, which deflated like a punctured balloon. Chunks of soggy flesh the consistency of cottage cheese gone rancid plopped to the ground in a steady liquid patter.

A stomach-turning odor of burnt flesh and rubber, and something oddly chemical, made Grace wince. Wisps of smoke trailed up from its body, accompanied by an acidic hissing.

Though it was hardly possible, within moments nothing remained but stained clothing lying in congealed puddles of a blackish-green oily substance. Jammed into the mess, at an angle, was indeed a homemade cross.

Grace released an explosive breath. "Fuck *me.*"

47.

SCOTT BARELY NOTICED Constable Matthews approaching. He stared at the puddled remains of black gore slicking his driveway, wondering at the instinct to impale the thing in the chest with his homemade wooden cross.

Its heart. He didn't know how he knew, but that's what had done it. On instinct (probably informed by countless vampire movies) he'd grabbed the cross while the thing was down and jammed it where he thought its heart might be.

Was it the cross itself? The wood? Or because he'd managed to plunge the wood into its heart? Maybe that's where the legend of killing vampires with a stake came from.

A gentle but firm hand on his shoulder interrupted his thoughts. He looked up and saw Constable Matthew's concerned gaze. "Scott. You okay?"

"I think I got its heart," Scott said distantly, having a hard time pulling his scattered thoughts together. "Not because it's a cross. Crosses hurt them but don't kill them. I think it's the heart. I don't know if it has to be wood, or if it can be metal. But I . . . I think I got its heart. I think that's what killed it."

He trailed off when Matthews squeezed his shoulder. "Scott. Are you *okay*?"

Scott rubbed his face and took a deep breath. Little by little, he felt more connected to his surroundings. He actually felt *here*. "Yeah." He looked at Constable Matthews. "I'm okay."

Matthews nodded at the cross jutting crookedly from the gore-soaked ground. "That was impressive. Quick thinking. How did you know to . . . ?"

Scott shrugged. "I dunno. Felt like the right thing to do."

"What about your mom?"

Scott nodded. "She's fine. Asleep. She always has a few drinks after a night shift and wears headphones with white noise. Probably didn't hear a thing."

The constable nodded, looking relieved. Maybe because she was happy his mother hadn't seen what happened; maybe because she wouldn't have to try and *explain* what happened. Scott didn't much care either way.

Matthews squeezed his shoulder again, then waved at the mess on the driveway. "Scott. Is that the same t-shirt you said Jasper was wearing?"

Scott sighed. "Yeah. Or, at least, it *was* Jasper. Not anymore though. Don't know what it was. Or how he got that way. But he wasn't . . . wasn't *human* anymore."

He looked up at the constable. "Just like I told the guy working at the corn maze."

Constable Matthews looked back at him, expression curious. "What guy?"

Scott shrugged. "Marty Something? Homeless guy who works odd jobs all over town. Jasper . . . "

He forced down an odd lump in his throat and continued. "Jasper used to rag on him for being homeless. Called him a scumbag and stuff. He's an okay guy, though. Better than Jasper and his whole family."

The constable smiled in recognition. "Yes, he is. I know Marty Crenshaw well. He's a good man." Her smile faded slightly. "You saw him at Goodlow's tonight? He runs the parking lot there. There've been some problems with guys in masks bothering customers. Did something happen tonight? Has anything happened since the last time you and I spoke?"

Scott opened his mouth but had no idea what to say.

Matthews did something then which Scott would've found condescending from any other adult, but from the constable, it felt like a genuine gesture. She dropped her gun, faced Scott, and gripped his shoulders with both hands. "I need the truth, Scott. Something strange is going on, and I don't know *what* the hell to do. Whatever you tell me, I *will* believe you."

Scott looked into Constable Matthew's eyes for a heartbeat. It didn't take any longer for him to make his decision. "I think it's time for 'the talk.' Like in horror movies."

The constable's smile looked confused. "How do you mean?"

Scott shrugged. "Well, at some point in almost every small town horror story—cause *that's* what this is—after a bunch of weird shit happens the people who *haven't* been killed get together, admit weird shit is happening, and then try to figure out what's causing the weird shit, and if they can stop it. So that's what we need to do. Talk. And figure out what the fuck is going on."

"We do at that." Constable Matthews sobered. "Killing, huh? Well, that tracks, unfortunately. Some folks have gone missing lately." She paused, then added, "You said 'we.' I'm guessing more than you, Marty, and I?"

"Yeah. Sage and Julie. They were at the corn maze tonight."

"Sage Hunter and Julie Lomax. Sage and I are . . . old friends. Julie's . . . manager recently reported some trouble they've had with two guys in masks trying to get into her place of work."

Constable Baker nodded toward Scott's house. "Okay. You need to go inside, make sure your Mom's okay, lock *all* the doors and windows, and try to get some sleep. I'll clean up here."

Scott nodded and turned back toward his home when a thought occurred to him. "Wait," he said, turning back to face Constable Matthews, "aren't you going to like . . . " he waved at the smoking mess that used to be something that wasn't Jasper, or human, "report this to someone?"

The constable smiled tiredly. "There's only me, Scott. No one to report it to. I mean . . . technically, Warren County I guess, but . . . what would I even say?"

She waved, shooing him toward the house. "Get to bed. We'll talk about this tomorrow."

Suddenly tired—and sad for Constable Matthews, though he wasn't sure why—Scott gave up and trudged for the front door. He thought it would be *impossible* for him to sleep after everything that happened, but forty-five minutes later, he slipped quickly into a deep and bottomless slumber.

The Cougar's Den
1:30 AM

48.

THE STRANGE FEELING of being watched swept over Conroy again. He was on his final round closing The Cougar's Den for the night. Making sure the doors were locked, the cash box secured; and the lights turned off in the restrooms, the girls' changing room, and the back office. He tugged on the door to the backroom where the booze was stored, found it locked solid, and turned to examine the empty club.

It had been a slow night. On a superficial level, that was a good thing. Fewer customers hungry for lap dances and private sessions meant less trouble. That had certainly been the case tonight. No one had gotten grabby or complained, which meant an easy night for the girls and the other bouncers.

But something intangible had bothered Conroy all night. A feeling in the air. A dampening presence, for lack of a better term, which brought with it a cloying sense of unease. It was the same thing he'd felt in the parking lot the other night, only subtler.

The same thing he'd felt when those weirdos with masks had tried to get into the club.

The patrons had sensed it also. They bought fewer drinks than usual and acted only semi-interested in the girls. Conroy could tell the girls sensed it, too. Usually energetic and maybe sometimes overzealous in their endeavors, they'd acted lethargic and nervous all night. Their hearts clearly weren't in their lackluster performances. Which, of course, hadn't encouraged the patrons any, either.

For some reason, Conroy felt good Julie had asked for the night off. She'd been the most affected by those masked weirdos who'd tried to gang-rush the club. He didn't like seeing her so uncomfortable and on edge. He didn't know too much about her past, (he'd never asked), but he knew her sobriety was fresh. He'd hate to see her relapse.

Which, of course, only brought up the conflict he felt whenever he thought about Julie. He knew firsthand how hard it was to maintain his own sobriety surrounded by booze almost nightly. However, as a bouncer, he *had* to stay clear-headed as part of the job. Made it easier for him to resist temptation.

Julie, on the other hand—like lots of the girls still did at The Den—used to get buzzed before hitting the stage as a matter of course. Needed a shot (or several) of their favorite brand of "liquid courage." For Julie to stay sober, she had to abstain from something all the other girls did every night as part of their routine.

She had to get out of here. If she wanted a chance at staying sober and living a normal life, she had to leave The Cougars Den and stop stripping. Which, of course, meant he wouldn't be able to see her anymore.

He snorted. He was ten years older than Julie, at the least. No way she'd be interested in a grizzled old horse like him, and besides. He wasn't going down that road again with one of the girls under his charge. Even with both of them sober, and at better places in their lives. He'd drawn a line in the sand regarding that. One he wasn't willing to cross.

He shook his head, stepped forward to turn out the lights, and lock up for the night.

Something scraped quietly behind him.

A shoe on the floor.

Conroy spun, throwing his hands up, balled into fists, leaving his gut completely unprotected from the metal shaft thrust at him. Its jagged end punched into his stomach with a force which wasn't human, tearing through muscle and ribs, ripping through his back muscles, scraping past his spine.

He doubled over with a gurgling gasp. Hands clutching futilely at the blood-slicked metal, and slipping off. It wouldn't have mattered if he could've gotten a grip, however. He couldn't straighten. His torn and ruined insides were twisted around the metal shaft. Strength left his legs, and he sank to his knees.

He looked down at the shaft blearily, drooling blood. An old road signpost. They always got knocked down and sheared off by snowplows in the winter. Plenty of them laying around. But who would . . . who could . . .

Something pulled the post out of his guts. A spasm rippled through him as his muscles tore even more, and he coughed up clots of blood. The broken signpost rang against the floor, thrown there by . . .

Slowly he raised his head to look at who'd done this, though his view tilted as he leaned slowly to one side and crumpled to the floor, hands fluttering uselessly around his shredded guts.

He saw them, each standing about five feet away. *More* freaks in masks. The same masks as the other night. Instinctively, he knew they hadn't wanted to touch him, for some reason. Couldn't touch him. That's why one of them had used a shorn road signpost. They couldn't touch him, because . . .

The crosses.

His cross tattoos.

Sure, his dying brain thought, as his eyelids fluttered. That made sense. He didn't know what those fucking things were, but they were *evil*. He knew that. *Felt* that. And evil things wouldn't be able to touch the cross of the Savior. No way in hell.

He actually chuckled a little at that. Which forced more blood up his throat and out his mouth, and sent another icy wave of pain crashing through him. This one felt more distant, which probably meant he wasn't long for this world. That was good, so he wouldn't feel any more pain.

Something wet splashed on his face and ran into his eyes. Something which burned. He recognized the smell because it was similar to what he smelled mowing the lawn during summer.

"No," he croaked through blood-slicked lips as he felt more gasoline being poured on him, all over. "No, no . . . "

The fumes made him choke and gag. He tried to roll over onto his back, but that tore his guts even more. He cried out in pain, finally.

He'd gotten a glimpse, though. Of a burning match thrown at him. It lit in the vapors wafting before his face. The world exploded into heat, light, and mind-scrambling pain as his gasoline-soaked cheeks and forehead exploded.

For a moment—the briefest of moments, which felt like an eternity—he felt his skin bubble, crackle, and ooze off his face. Something happened, however. A blessed coolness spread over him. He fell into a darkness which comforted and eased and did not terrify. His final thought before moving on from this world to the next was that, if God were merciful, the entire club would go up in flames, so Julie Lomax could have that chance at a normal life she so desperately needed.

Friday morning, October 29th
Collins' Residence
5:00 AM

49.

WHEN JUD HADN'T woken Lida up at 5 AM with his customary early-morning trip to the bathroom, the sixty-five-year-old retired elementary school teacher instantly woke on her own, sure something was wrong. Jud woke up at 5 every morning to empty his bladder, like clockwork. Regardless of whether or not he felt like he had to go. The only times in the last forty years Lida *hadn't* woken up for her husband's 5 AM constitutional was on the rare occasions when one of them was sick. Which begged the question: Where was he?

Lida sat up, entertaining the feeble hope that Jud had overslept and somehow she'd missed it. That hope deflated, however, when she saw his side of the bed still made, and not slept in.

Something was wrong. Lida knew that, deep in her gut. Jud had been complaining all week about vandalism at the cemetery, that he was going to camp out in the caretaker shed with his 30-aught and handle the problem himself. Last night, despite her vocal protests—usually enough to stay Jud's hand—he'd left around 8 PM with his rifle to do that. She hadn't been able to reason with him. He was determined to stop the "thing desecrating good folks' graves."

At first, she hadn't felt terribly worried. Pleasant Brook had its fair share of malcontent vandals. This wasn't the first time the cemetery had been vandalized. It wouldn't be the last.

Even so, as Lida watched Jud's pickup rattle down the road, a vague uneasiness nagged her. She didn't know why. There'd been a strange feeling in the air for the past several days. People walking the sidewalks quicker, talking more tersely than usual, treating each other more curtly. And of course, with the county issuing warnings about COVID spikes in the area, more and more people were staying indoors, as more and more events were canceled, or changed to remote status.

Her Wednesday Book Discussion Group—7 PM, usually at the library, but through Zoom the past few weeks—had been canceled because of "extenuating circumstances." One of the group members, Mrs. Margaret Seaver, a ninth-grade science teacher at the high school, had left town without saying a word to anyone. She hadn't been answering her smartphone, which was strange. She *always* answered her smartphone.

Also, Lida had heard that Lester McDonough, the school custodian, had also mysteriously skipped town. It was odd, and she couldn't bring herself to believe the rumors that Margaret and Lester had run off together. Margaret had *some* taste, after all.

Despite her reservations and strange sense of ill-portent, Lida had gone to bed at her usual time around 9 PM and slept soundly. She must've dreamed, however, because at some point she hazily remembered rolling over and seeing Jud (at least, she thought it was him), standing on her side of the bed, staring down at her. However, though the shadow had been roughly Jud's size and shape, she hadn't seen much of his face. What little bit she'd seen looked different, somehow. Though now she couldn't remember much about it at all. It had to have been a dream.

Had to have been.

Lida sat against the bed's headboard, staring at Jud's untouched side of the bed. The strange foreboding she'd felt last night returned with frightening intensity. Something had gone wrong. She knew it. *Felt* it. Something had happened to Jud. Either the vandals had gotten violent and hurt him, or if some animal was digging up graves (which she'd never heard of, though of course, she wasn't an animal expert), maybe *it* attacked Jud last night. Maybe he was lying insensate in a pool of his own blood at the cemetery. Maybe *worse*.

Unable to sit still any longer, Lida Collins slipped out from under her covers, stuck her feet into her slippers, and moved stiffly across the room to the closet, where her bathrobe hung. She'd pulled it on over her nightgown and was cinching the belt tight when she heard the bedroom door creak open behind her, followed by a familiar tread into the room.

Weak-kneed with exasperated relief, she said, "Judson Henry Collins! What the *hell* do you have to say for yourself . . . "

She turned, and her breath died mid-sentence, taking her words with it. What stood in the doorway wasn't her husband. It wore his clothes, yes. Clothes, she registered with dim horror, stained by dirt, a black and oily substance, and what appeared to be coagulated blood. It held Jud's rifle by the barrel.

The face wasn't Jud's. Her stomach turned over in revulsion and nausea looking at it. It looked so hideous—with wet and drooping eyes which bugged in opposite directions, sickly gray flesh and a wide, gaping mouth. She'd thought at first it was a mask, but what mask would have an oily green tongue wriggling inside its mouth?

"P . . . Please," she rasped, her mind spinning with words like *rapist* and *burglar* but somehow knowing neither was right. The truth was far worse. "Please don't . . . "

The thing raised Jud's rifle by the barrel—holding it like a club—and stepped toward her.

Lida's mind broke. She screamed and tried to flee, with the vague notion of scrambling over the bed and somehow making it to their bathroom. The bathroom of course had no lock, but that thought never occurred to her as she jumped for the bed, away from the thing wearing her husband's stained clothes.

She got as far as one knee on the edge of the bed before a clammy wetness snagged her ankle and dragged her off, kicking and screaming, to the floor. She grasped wildly at the bed's comforter, trying to gain enough leverage to pull her ankle free, but all she did was yank the blankets off the bed.

She heard a whistling sound, of something swinging through the air, and her vision exploded into fireworks of pain. Her head suddenly felt twice as big. Her right temple throbbed to the tune of her heartbeat. She reached a trembling hand to touch where it hurt most and felt something warm, wet, and sticky.

Her husband's rifle. Swung by the thing. That was the only hazy thought she could muster (her head feeling heavier and heavier) before she heard the whistling sound again.

This blow struck her in the back of her head, with twice as much force. It drove her face into the ground and she felt something snap in her nose. The good thing was, she'd been hit so hard the second time her whole head was turning numb, so she couldn't feel any pain. The bad thing was, she was suffocating on the blood clogging her nose and filling her mouth.

The air whistled again. She felt a dull *crackling*, and then nothing more.

Gerhart Trailer Park
6:00 AM

50.

WHEN JULIE SHUFFLED into her trailer's living room, smelled cooking bacon and freshly brewing coffee, and saw a man in the kitchen, cooking and whistling a light tune, her first thought was: *Oh God. I fell off the wagon. Blacked out and brought a customer home. Shit, shit, shit*!

But when she glanced at the futon and saw neatly folded blankets on a pillow, last night came rushing back, and she remembered *everything*.

Masks. A friend who "wasn't human anymore." And an attraction to man which (ill-advised as it was) she couldn't deny. She found herself staring at this man as he moved economically around her cramped kitchen, not only cooking bacon but also scrambling eggs. She was shocked to find that such a mundane sight only made him more attractive.

To stop these thoughts before they ran away with her, she cleared her throat. When he glanced over his shoulder and smiled, she said, "Smells delicious. You certainly know your way around a kitchen."

Marty shrugged and turned back to the bacon sizzling in a frying pan. "It's nothing. Easy for anyone to look like an amazing chef when there's bacon frying in a pan."

She laughed at this, putting her hands into her bathrobe pockets. "Bullshit. You move like a short order cook. No offense, but how does a homeless guy get this good in the kitchen?"

The words had barely left her mouth before she clamped her hands over it. She mumbled through her fingers, "Oh my God. That was awful. I'm *so* sorry."

Marty smiled and waved it off. "No worries. It's a fair question, actually." With tongs she hadn't used once since buying them over a year ago, he plucked cooked bacon from the pan and onto a plate loaded with scrambled eggs. He picked up the plate and faced her. "Before I . . . uh . . . came to my current state, I loved to cook. On all my dates—back when I was sober enough to still have them—most of the time, I cooked, instead of taking a girl out to eat."

He gestured at the small kitchen table separating the kitchen from the den. Julie sat, and he continued. "I'm sure you've heard the spiel before, but one of the most important parts of maintaining your sobriety is finding a purpose. Something to dedicate yourself to."

Marty set the plate before her and turned back to the kitchen. "I found mine quickly. Or, at least, one purpose. I not only attend AA at First Methodist but also another program called Celebrate Recovery at First Baptist, Wednesday nights. It's like AA but addresses addictions across the spectrum. It also leans more strongly into the spiritual nature of addiction recovery."

He returned from the kitchen with two cups of coffee. He handed one to her and sat on the opposite side of the table. She raised an eyebrow. "You eating?"

He sipped from his coffee and smiled. "I've been up for a while. Already ate." He gestured at her plate. "Dig in."

She did and he continued. "Anyway, meals are a big part of CR. We have one for every meeting, and they have a monthly Saturday morning breakfast." He sipped his coffee again. "Didn't take long for me to realize they didn't have a cook. Ordered pizza from The Whole in the Wall and bought wagon loads of donuts and jugs of orange juice for the monthly breakfasts. So, I offered to take over. That was about six years ago. I've been cooking for the Wednesday night meetings and the monthly Saturday breakfasts ever since."

Julie chewed and swallowed her last bit of bacon—fatty, greasy, and wonderful—and said, "Well, you're welcome to cook breakfast for me, any time. I mean . . . "

She felt her cheeks warm, her throat tightening. "Not that you'll ever be here for breakfast again. I just mean that breakfast for me is usually . . . well," she shrugged, "donuts and orange juice."

He opened his mouth to reply, but she rushed on. "So. You said you were up early. Couldn't sleep? Still thinking about last night?"

Marty's face sobered as the reality of their circumstances blunted whatever good feelings he'd had. Julie felt bad about ruining his good mood, and also felt guilty for doing it purposely to dampen the increasing chemistry she felt building between them.

He sipped his coffee, set the mug down, and nodded. "I tried to sleep, but I couldn't get my mind to settle down. Thoughts were racing all night. There's too many puzzle pieces that don't fit together."

He ran a hand through his hair and fell quiet for a moment as if collecting his thoughts. He sipped his coffee again. "The kid following me up Burns Hill Road was one thing. Kids are kids. Hassling the local homeless guy? Par for the course.

"But then there's the guys in masks bothering customers at the corn maze the last few nights. *You* saw two guys wearing similar masks trying to cause trouble at The Cougar's Den, two nights in a row. And then there's Scott's story—though I *know* he's holding something back—about his friend Jasper wearing a similar mask, playing a prank on him, last night."

He sighed, leaned back in his chair, and laced his fingers behind his head. "Something awfully strange is happening."

A ludicrous (but oddly chilling) thought occurred to Julie, and she spoke without considering how it would sound. "It's spreading. Like a sickness. A virus. Like . . . vampires, or zombies."

He met her gaze head-on, without flinching. An even colder thought: He was taking what she'd said at face value, considering it seriously, and not laughing it off. "Huh," he said quietly.

Julie opened her mouth to respond. To say what, she wasn't sure, but a knock on the door interrupted her. And even though her guard was certainly up, she didn't think these things wearing masks (why things, not people?) would politely knock before breaking in.

Even so, when she cleared her throat and called out, "Who is it?" she had to force her voice not to waver.

"Julie? Julie Lomax? It's Constable Matthews."

For some reason, even though no one had mentioned the mask-wearers ever talking, this didn't put her at ease. At least, not as much as she would've preferred. Marty must've felt the same because he looked tense and alert, eyes narrowed slightly.

"What can I do for you, Constable?" Her voice sounded much steadier than she felt inside. "It's awfully early."

"Sorry about that. But there's been . . . .an accident at The Cougar's Den. I need to talk to you."

Julie's heartbeat sped up. She bolted from the chair, grabbed the doorknob, and flung the door open, her throat tight with worry, also expecting to not see the constable, but instead fall under the horror of something with bulging eyes and a wide, black mouth with a tongue wriggling inside . . .

She went limp with relief and sagged against the door frame when she saw Constable Matthews. She swallowed and managed, "Accident? What kind?"

If possible, Matthews looked even more worried. "We probably should sit down. May I?"

She nodded and moved aside, revealing Marty, who'd stood from his chair. Matthews took in the man's presence with aplomb, not acting surprised at all. In fact, it was almost like she'd been looking for Marty, also. She confirmed this by nodding at Marty and saying, "Well. This kills two birds with one stone."

Carter Residence
7:00 AM

51.

SCOTT PULLED THE living room shades aside and peeked out the window, watching his mother pull out of the driveway for her day stint at the diner. As he'd predicted to Constable Matthews, Mom slept like a rock all night, last night's insanity not penetrating her booze-fueled sleep and white noise machine. She'd woken at 6:00 AM ready for her day shift, completely oblivious.

For Scott's part, he felt like a wrung-out dishrag. Even after crashing last night when the adrenaline finally wore off, he'd struggled to fall asleep. He kept jerking awake at every little creak and shift of the house. Clutching a piece of the broken broom handle as if his life depended on it. Which, considering last night's revelations, wasn't far off the mark.

Mom hadn't noticed his unease as she'd puttered around the house getting ready for work. More than likely she thought he was being his usual sullen and sour self. Or, maybe she thought he was still depressed over Jasper's disappearance. Even though Scott knew he wasn't being fair to her, he assumed she wasn't that upset about Jasper being gone.

She'd never liked Jasper. If Scott asked her why, Mom would probably say something about Jasper's destructive behavior (he did like to vandalize), his habit of cutting class, and the general state of his family.

Sometimes, however . . . Scott wondered if Mom had sensed his growing feelings for Jasper. Had somehow known Scott had started to view Jasper as more than a friend, and *that's* why she didn't like them spending so much time together.

Mom and him never talked about that sort of thing, of course. They'd never talked about puberty, or how things were changing in mind and life, or girls, or any of those things. He didn't think (at least he hoped) Mom would hate him for what he was. If he had to guess, he supposed she didn't understand it, and everyone was scared of things they didn't understand. Easier for her to call Jasper a "bad influence" and be done with it.

When Mom pulled out of the driveway and left for work, an immense blanket of fatigue settled over Scott. He toyed with the idea of getting some more sleep. But, tired as he was . . . he was also now alone in his house. Alone, and unguarded. He figured if he tried to lay down, he'd struggle to sleep as much as he had last night.

Instead, he went back into his room (after making sure all the doors and windows were locked), and got on his Chromebook (which had been bought used on Amazon and was at least two years behind his classmates' models). He booted it up and opened his email. He then got out his smartphone and emailed the picture he'd taken of the Jasper-thing last night to himself. When the email came through, he downloaded it. Opened it, and gazed at it for several seconds.

It *looked* like nothing more than a hideous rubber mask. Bulging, unnatural eyes. Lank, stringy black hair. Gaping mouth. It especially looked like a mask rendered in digital. He could almost make out its edges on the neck.

But that's not how it had looked in real life. In person, the mask looked like a real face. Skin glistening with an unnatural dew. Bulging eyeballs wet and rolling. In the gaping mouth, a greenish-black tongue which writhed like a twisting worm.

Scott cropped the photo, opened Google, and uploaded it into Google's Image Search, which would scan the internet for similar images. He didn't hold out much hope. He'd only received mixed results with Google's Reverse Image Search in the past.

As predicted, most of the initial results were rubber masks on sale at costume stores, both online and in real life. All of them only vaguely resembled the mask in the photo. Some of the image results were from social media posts of people wearing them at Halloween parties. He scrolled past them. None struck a chord.

After scrolling past more images, growing frustrated and tired, Scott teetered on the verge of giving up. Maybe now he would fall asleep if he tried. No one would miss him if he skipped his remote classes today (more and more kids had been skipping lately, something which now made him uneasy), and his eyes and head certainly felt heavy enough. In fact, he was already moving the cursor to close out Google when an image caught his eye. Bottom-most to the right. The last image on the screen. He maximized it. When it filled the screen his heartbeat triple-timed. A flush of fear-laced adrenaline washed his fatigue away.

It was the mask.

It looked like it was made from a different kind of material, however. It looked wooden, of all things. But the features were unmistakable. Stringy black hair. Bulging eyes and gaping black mouth.

Scott zoomed in on the image, his breath hitching. It was clearly the same mask, though it indeed looked wooden rather than rubber. It also didn't look like the kind of mask you pulled over the head. Rather, it looked like leather straps were tied behind the head, to hold the mask on the wearer's face.

Even so, a chill played along his spine as he regarded it. Despite the different material, this was it. This was the mask the Jasper-thing had worn before dissolving into a pile of slime. Slime which looked like melted rubber.

Scott clicked on the link under the image. It led to a basic website which looked homemade. It was titled DRUIDIC LORE. Embedded on the page was the same picture of the mask. Underneath, a paragraph read:

> "The Masg na Samhna
> , or masg de dhìochuimhneachadh
> —loosely
> translated as Mask of Samhain, or Mask of Forgetting -
> finds its roots in ancient Celtic and Druidic lore.
> According to legend, the Druid priests wore the mask
> at the halfway point between the autumn equinox and winter solstice, when conducting sacrifices to Samhain, Lord
> of Death, believing the mask would transform them into
> Samhain's image. It was also called the Mask of Forgetting
> because those in great pain could wear the mask and offer
> up the source of that pain to Samhain, which would give the offeree—the First—the aspect of Samhain so they could consume their pain and suffering, leaving nothing but the hunger of Samhain in its wake, a hunger which spreads uncontrollably, until nothing is left.

Scott re-read the paragraph. Glanced back at the grainy black and white picture, thinking now it looked even *more* like the rubber masks he'd seen. That, and several phrases stood out to him, ringing an alarm in his mind. Narrowing his eyes, he re-read the part which struck him most.

"'The mask would transform them into Samhain's image,'" he said softly, "'the mask will give them the aspect of Samhain . . . '" he skipped a few lines, "' . . . leaving nothing behind but the hunger of Samhain.'"

The web page didn't say anything else. Nothing about what the "aspect of Samhain" looked like, acted like, or how to kill it. When he returned to his search results, after scrolling through dozens of additional images, he found nothing else. He returned to the website, copied the image, then pasted that image into Google's Reverse Image Search. The only result was that website, *Druidic Lore.*

Scott returned to that page and clicked 'print' from the browser's drop-down menu. As he heard his mother's wireless printer creak to life across the living room, (it was also used, and who knew how much longer it would work), he sat back in his chair, closed his eyes and rubbed his face, thoughts whirling.

According to the paragraph, under the right conditions, when people wore the "mask of Samhain" or the "mask of Forgetting" they became an "aspect" of Samhain. Nothing remained of who they were, only the "hunger of Samhain."

Scott uncovered his face and opened his eyes, sighing noisily. "Vampires," he muttered. "Fucking vampires."

Of a sort, anyway. The cross irritated and annoyed them, but they adapted to it. He had no way of knowing, but he supposed the same theory might apply to Holy Water, too. Although where he'd get some, he'd no idea. He didn't suppose he could walk into St. Mary's over in Smyrna and ask them if he could fill up a Super Soaker full of it. Although that image rang a bell. From a movie he'd seen, no doubt.

The wood through the heart had certainly done the trick last night, but Scott wondered if the wood was the most important part of that equation, or if the heart was. Again, he'd no way of knowing, but he thought *anything* through the heart might do the trick. Killing off the last bit of the original body. The host dies, so does the parasite, as they'd learned in science class. Before Mrs. Seaver disappeared, most likely possessed by the mask herself. *If* that had been her he and Jasper had seen crossing Pleasant Brook Bridge, what seemed like years ago.

The mask—*masks*—were more than parasites, however. They weren't only feeding on people. They were *changing* them. Making them into something else. Something not human. Something able to survive a lot of physical damage, including a shotgun blast to the face. Scott idly wondered how they'd react to fire, which served as a weapon in lots of horror movies.

Also, the mask was making more of itself. The article spoke of one mask, and also something called "The First," but it also ended with: " . . . a hunger which spreads uncontrollably, until nothing is left." Normally, Scott would've thought that was a figure of speech, but in this case, it was literal. The mask *itself* and its hunger was spreading. Multiplying. Making more of itself.

until nothing is left

The printer fell silent. Scott shut his Chromebook off and got up to get the printout. He plucked it from the printer and tried to read it again. The words blurred and swam in his tired vision.

He'd heard of Samhain, of course. Countless movies and novels featured different versions of the Lord of Death. In most stories, Samhain was always trying to break into the human world, or cults were always trying to summon Him.

He didn't have any time to sift through his movie and book collection for information, however. He'd no idea how badly this had spread through town, how many masks or "aspects of Samhain" there were now. And besides, he figured movies and stories only ever got it half-right, anyway.

He had to do something. Even though Constable Matthews said to sit tight and wait for her. She wasn't the only person who knew about these things. Julie, Sage, and Marty knew more than they'd told him. He felt sure of it. Which was fair, because he hadn't been completely honest with them, either.

He folded the printout, stuck it into his back pocket, and headed for his bike. Gerhart Trailer Park was on the other side of town, but the way his heart was racing and his nerves were humming over his discovery, he figured it wouldn't take long to get there.

Gerhart Trailer Park
8:15 AM

52.

MARTY STOOD QUIETLY by as Julie sat on her futon, sniffing and wiping her eyes with a sodden napkin. He felt sorry for her (or maybe it was more) but even though he found himself keeping his distance emotionally, he found it hard to resist the urge to go to her, sit next to her, and put his arm around her shoulders.

He'd no doubt she wouldn't resist such a gesture and would probably even welcome it, (unless he'd misread the signs between them completely), but she'd just heard that a dear friend died violently in a fire which had destroyed her workplace. She was extremely vulnerable, and—mindful of her newfound sobriety—he didn't want to take advantage of that, even unintentionally.

She sniffed, swallowed back a sob, and said in a shaky voice, "Was . . . was anyone else there?"

Constable Matthews, sitting in an old recliner facing her, with the coffee table between them, shook her head, face somber. "No. At least, I don't think so. Warren County Fire and Police will need to examine the remains, but at the moment, I think we'll only find Conroy. His truck was the only vehicle in the parking lot."

Julie sniffed. Looked down into the tissue she was wringing to bits. "Do you think he was . . . murdered?"

"We won't know what caused the fire until Warren County's departments conduct their investigation, so there's no way to tell officially. Any remains will go to the county Coroner's office, and an autopsy will be performed. Until then, there won't be an official cause of death. But . . . "

Julie finally looked up, her wide (and beautiful, Marty admitted reluctantly) eyes shining with tears, but something else, also. Rage. Burning rage. Marty wondered anew over the hidden layers in this young woman. "You think he was. Don't you?"

Constable Matthews clasped her hands tightly. "Normally I wouldn't make such a leap. Not until we had official reports. But based on recent events, especially last night . . . "

Julie sniffed and shook her head as if refusing to believe Conroy was dead. Sorrow filled her eyes, dimming the rage Marty had seen burning there only moments ago. "He was kind," she whispered. "To all of us. He took care of us. Watched over us. He was a good man."

Julie snorted, actually laughing slightly. "A God-fearing man. A deeply spiritual man, if you can believe it."

Matthews smiled. "That he was. Quite frankly, a truer Christian man I've never met."

Her smile faded and her expression resumed its serious cast. "Conroy visited me yesterday morning and told me about the two men in strange masks trying to get into the club without paying. Though it could get me into a lot of trouble, I withheld this information when I was talking with Warren County PD and Fire this morning."

Julie glanced at Marty, and he nodded. Sharp as always, Constable Matthews didn't miss their exchange. "Can you describe the masks?"

Julie nodded, and as she did so, Matthews' face tightened even more, becoming pensive. "Could you tell who was wearing them?"

She shrugged. "One of them might've been Jimmy Riley. Used to be a regular, until Conroy banned him. Thought I recognized a skull ring on his finger. Can't say for sure, though."

"Constable," Marty said quietly, "do you think that . . . "

Someone knocking on the trailer door interrupted him. "Sorry," Julie called out, "I'm kinda busy right now. Can you come back later?"

There was a pause, and then a voice Marty and Julie recognized—as did Matthews, based on her surprised expression—said, "Julie? Please. It's Scott Carter. Think I learned something. About the masks."

Matthews didn't waste time. She stood and opened the door. Scott's eyes grew wide when he saw the constable, as Matthews said in her usual dry, nonplussed tone, "Scott. Your timing is perfect."

Mid-morning

53.

SOMETHING HAD HAPPENED. Something both bad and good. Many of them died last night, and their number—the faces of Sauhein—was diminished. Some of them died serving Sauhein. They'd gone after the one marked with Talismans of the Other, which burned them if they touched it. They'd killed him, and set fire to him.

However, in their long sleep, they'd forgotten that fire killed them also. It was one of the few things which could. Last night's fire spread too fast and many of them were consumed by the flames. The growing heat made them sluggish, made the aspect of Sauhein melt, then made their hosts melt. They felt their number burn, die, and descend back into the Darkness from which they'd so recently woken from.

They died serving the aspect of Sauhein. With their deaths, they eliminated a potential threat. One of their number, however, died in an unexpected way last night. Unexpected because they'd forgotten about this method of death during their long sleep, also.

However, it was unexpected also because somehow one of them had broken away from their will to pursue its *own* desires. Or rather, the desires of its host. It had sought out the young one who wore the Other's talisman around its neck. Even more alarming, they'd been so focused on destroying the one who wore the Other's mark all over, they hadn't even *noticed* one of them sneaking off . . . until its shriek of agony rippled through them.

Even now, as they communed where they'd been born into this world, their essence rippled as they shivered together in memory of the cry's sharp, excruciating pain. They felt not only shadows of pain, but also anger. They would make more of them to overwhelm this place and make the way clear for Sauhein Himself.

But even as they sent a portion of themselves to make more, they wondered how a host's obsessions could make one of them break off from their will. They wondered this, as they communed and quivered as one.

Columbia Residence
Slater Road
10:00 AM

54.

AS MARY BETH COLUMBIA, organizer of Pleasant Brook's only book appreciation society, (Book Love), tidied up her kitchen and set about getting ready for her day, a dull kind of worry nagged the back of her brain. Something was bothering her. What, she couldn't put her finger on.

As she finished washing her breakfast dishes and the dinner plates she'd neglected last night, she turned it over in her mind, humming aimlessly all the while. She supposed part of it was the news of COVID cases spiking in Warren County, and the possibility of their small town—already extremely isolated from more populated areas—descending into quarantine and lock-down again. She'd certainly agreed with all the measures taken last time. She was *not* a COVID denier or anti-masker. She was vaccinated, boosted, and wore her mask out in public, regardless of what the "current" mandate was.

Even so, she desperately didn't want to return to quarantine life. All last Spring and this past summer, despite talks of infection rates rising across the county and the nation, she and others had entertained the fantasy that life was mostly back to normal. There'd be no returning to the slow, numb, crawling existence of remaining home all day, every day, for months on end. By no means did she think she'd endured a worse experience than anyone else, but even so. Despite believing COVID was a real threat, she didn't think she could be stuck at home for two or three months, again.

However, three weeks ago, Warren County ordered all schools to return to remote learning. Local events—like the annual Halloween Festival and First Baptist's Tent Revival—were canceled. Normally in-person events—like Book Love—reverted to Zoom and Google Meets. A curfew hadn't been leveled yet, and they weren't quite in quarantine. Still, Mary Beth had felt a growing disquiet in her stomach the past week.

She thought her friends had felt it, too. That's why she'd canceled this past week's Zoom meeting of Book Love. So many members had called to say they wouldn't be online for one reason or another (all fabricated, she felt, but she couldn't blame them, herself *loathing* Zoom with all of her heart), so there was little point in meeting.

Also troubling was the rumor that one of their number, high school science teacher Margaret Seaver, had skipped town with the school custodian, Lester McDonough. She knew Margaret better than most. Knew she'd enjoyed her fair share of casual lovers since her husband died, and knew also that, for a time, Lester had been one of them.

But Margaret was devoted to her students, heart and soul. At the most, she was capable of going away for a "dirty weekend" in Utica, and that was it. So far, she'd missed a whole week of school. Hadn't logged on to any of her remote classes, and hadn't answered the phone when anyone tried to call. This was highly out of character for Margaret. Even stranger, her car still sat in the driveway.

Mary Beth racked the last dish. Dried her hands on a towel, and dropped the towel onto the dishes to dry. Also troubling, she'd been feeling the inexplicable urge to ring up Lida Collins to see what she was doing today. She'd called once around nine, to no answer.

Which was also odd. Jud kept his own hours at the cemetery. Unless something specific came up or he had a body to inter, he didn't begin work there until eleven in the morning. Lida, a retiree, liked to spend her mornings reading (she was the most avid member of Book Love). Neither of them answering the phone troubled Mary Beth, though she didn't know why.

Pushing these thoughts away, Mary Beth was about ready to grab her keys and head out the door—maybe to drive over to Smyrna, even if only to get out of town for the day—when she heard a metallic *click* in the living room. Her blood cooled as icy spiders scrambled up her spine. She stood still, listening, but heard nothing more.

Every instinct screamed for her to leave. There was a back door in the kitchen. She could leave that way. However, her car keys were hanging on a peg by the front door. Slater Road was on the outskirts of town. The nearest place was the trailer park, a good three miles away. Though she'd kept in shape over the years, it'd be a long walk, and even longer run for someone her age.

She listened closely. Heard nothing more. She breathed out deeply. Mary Beth Columbia hadn't survived spinsterhood to the ripe old age of fifty-five by being afraid of strange sounds. It must've been her imagination. The windows were open because this morning had been unseasonably warm. Most likely, a breeze knocked something over. That was all.

It had to be.

Even so, she found it hard to take the first step. Though the living room sounded still, it sounded . . . *too* still. As if expectant. Waiting, for her.

Which was ridiculous, of course. This was Pleasant Brook. Not Syracuse or Utica, or Lake George, even. She refused to believe hoods lurked around every corner, hungry to break into homes and rape middle-aged spinsters. Those things didn't happen, here.

And yet. Everyone was staying home more and more. Working from home if they could, withdrawing slowly from public life, and she imagined a good number of the more troublesome high school students didn't bother to attend remote school at all. They were probably skulking about town, getting up to all sorts of mischief. Maybe even daring each other to break into people's homes to steal things, or to scare those who lived alone . . .

"That's it," she muttered, forcing herself to lift one foot, then the other, toward the living room. "This is *stupid.*"

She walked through the doorway into the living room and came to a skittering halt at what she saw. At first, her mind couldn't quite comprehend the sight. Wasn't able to assemble all the pieces together. Someone—some*thing*—stood next to the fireplace. It held the general shape and form of a human, but its face . . . its *face* . . .

Was wrong. It couldn't be real. Had to be a mask. Its oily hair, strands falling to its shoulders, looked plastic. Its grotesque, bulging wet eyes rolled mindlessly and pointed in opposite directions. Its *mouth* gaped wide in a silent scream.

Unable to look at the thing's face any longer for fear she might vomit, Mary Beth looked at what it held. One of the fire pokers, (completely ornamental, because the fireplace was one of those gas ones with fake logs) which must've made the metallic *clinking* sound. Ornamental or not, the poker was cast iron, all the same.

When she glanced up again—keeping her gaze away from the thing's face—she finally registered the clothes. A dingy bathrobe splattered with what looked like blood and a greenish-black fluid, over a likewise stained nightie. Mary Beth's stomach twisted as she recognized the pink floral pattern on the stained nightie, which matched the bathrobe's pink fringe. Lida Collins had worn this last year when she'd had the flu (not Coronavirus, thank God), and Mary Beth brought over several containers of her home-cooked stews.

She forced herself to stare disbelievingly at the hideous mask. "L-Lida? Is . . . is that you?"

Lida—or whatever it was—merely cocked its head and stared at her. Such a small action, but it filled Mary Beth with a hysterical kind of fear. It wasn't the action of a human. Rather, that of an animal. A predator, evaluating its prey.

"Lida. Please. What *is* this? Are you all right? Speak to me!"

Lida—the thing—remained silent. Head cocked. Bulging wet eyes rolling, distended and glistening pupils still looking madly in opposite directions.

Then, slowly, its maw opened even wider. Out of it wafted a rotten odor of stagnant mud and wet leaves. An oily tongue twisted, writhed, and dripped mucus.

Mary Beth's mind shattered, sending frenzied signals to her legs to *run*, but those signals fizzled, overshadowed by the cold hysteria in her heart. She stood there, trembling, as she felt (with great shame, as well as an odd relief) her bladder release, soaking her crotch and inner thighs. This wetness broke through her gridlock, the signal to flee finally reaching her legs, but it was too late.

As she pivoted on one foot, the thing leaped forward before she could turn fully, covering more ground than was possible. One hand grabbed her shoulder, while the other—still clutching the poker—pistoned back and plunged the cast iron into her belly. She dimly felt it tear out through her back, but as she was puking gouts of blood down her front, it wasn't much of a concern.

A cold, paralyzing weakness filled her. The thing (not Lida, she distantly understood), pulled her close, face-to-face with its ridiculous yet hideously oozing visage. She tried to say something (what, she had no idea) but all she managed was a hiss between her teeth because she was suddenly cold. So cold.

The thing twisted the fire poker. The cast iron scraped against her spinal cord. Electric fire pulsed up and down her back as her legs buckled and she fell to her knees.

The thing yanked the poker back. It came free with a soft, sucking *plop*. With it came a thick, knotted, gray tube of flesh Lida could only assume was one of her intestines.

The thing dropped the poker, grabbed the slick gray rope looping from her belly, and tugged. Something came loose inside her, and she felt as if her entire insides had fallen out. Which they had. They were laid before her in a wet, glistening, steaming pile.

Mary Beth Columbia slumped over onto her side. Facing the wet, mounded pile of her intestines. As her vision dimmed into darkness, her last image was of the thing falling to its knees, bending over, its mouth opening impossibly wide as it stuffed its gullet with her steaming guts. The sounds of it chewing on her rubbery insides was the last thing she heard. And a soft sucking, slurping, and what could only be considered a mewl of pleasure.

Constable's Station
11:00 AM

55.

"**YOU'RE KIDDING.** I've got a burned-out building at the edge of town, with at least *one* fatality, and you can't even be sure if you'll be here tomorrow, or the next day? Are you freaking *kidding* me?"

"*Look, I don't know what to tell you,*" said Warren County Fire Marshal Pete Simmons. "*I'm shorthanded as hell. Got four people out with confirmed cases of COVID. Four more in quarantine for exposure. That, and I've got at least six or seven folks who won't come in until the COVID spikes level off, and three more who quit because they refused to get the vaccine. I can't spare anyone.*"

How many fires could you possibly *have in Warren County*? Aloud, Grace sighed and said, "Whatever. Do I at *least* have your permission to sift through the remains myself?"

"*Have at it. Just try not to disturb too much.*"

"What about the fatality?"

Simmons' shrug was evident in his tone. "*You can call Warren County Coroner, but they're as shorthanded as we are.*"

"What am I supposed to do? Put the body in a fucking freezer?"

"*I guess. If you even have freezers that big.*"

Grace sighed. "Okay. Whatever. If you can scrounge anyone up before tomorrow, give me a ring."

"*Sure. Have a good one.*"

Simmons hung up.

Grace did also, fighting the urge to chuck her smartphone across the station. Instead, she set it down on her desk, closed her eyes, covered her face with her hands, and massaged her temples with her fingertips.

Fuck.

Fuckity fuck fuck fuck.

Grace rubbed her face once more, blinked, and opened her eyes. She pulled her laptop closer to her, signed on, and opened her email browser. She'd asked Scott to email the picture he'd taken at the corn maze. She opened that email, downloaded the photo, cropped it to show the mask only, then composed an email to one of the few people from Utica PD she still talked to, Monica Hagert, a crime scene forensics investigator she'd dated briefly. She typed a quick message which said, *Could you run this for me, see if you get any hits*? and clicked *send*. Grace then picked up her phone, opened her contacts, found Monica's number, and hit *dial*.

Monica answered on the second ring. "*Hey, you. Been a minute. To what do I owe the pleasure*?"

Grace smiled instinctively at the sound of Monica's voice—with its slight lilt, which sounded vaguely British or Irish, even though Monica was USA-born and raised—and tried to speak amiably, but neutrally. They'd been dating when that asshole detective assaulted Grace, and even though they'd parted badly (Grace accusing Monica of choosing her career in Utica over her), Grace still missed Monica and knew Monica missed her. In many ways, the lingering ghost of their relationship was one of the many reasons why she and Sage hadn't worked out.

"Hey yourself. I sent you an email. A picture taken on a smartphone. We've got something . . . weird going on. Remember that clown thing back in 2016? The viral thing where people dressed up as clowns in a bunch of small towns?"

"*Ugh.* That *was delightful.*"

"Yeah, I think something similar might be happening here in Pleasant Brook. Folks have been running around wearing these weird, ugly-ass masks. Probably a Halloween prank, but something feels off. Wondering if maybe the same thing is happening in other towns. If you could run that picture, see if it sets off any web alerts, that would be great."

"*Sure. Hold on.*" Monica paused. In the background, Grace heard light typing, and then, "*Wow. That* is *ugly. Anyway, yeah. I'll run it.*" Another pause, and then, in a mischievous tone of voice, "*But it's gonna cost you.*"

Grace snorted, amused in spite of the circumstances. Monica always had been a bargainer. Grace knew what the forensics specialist was going to charge. "Cost me what, exactly?"

"*Dinner and drinks next time you're in Utica. No hinky stuff, I promise. Just two old friends catching up. Deal*?"

Grace smiled, knowing Monica's promise of "no hinky stuff" was a bald-faced lie. *What the hell? We get through this alive, I'll let Monica have her way with me for the whole weekend.* Which, of course, wouldn't be much of a sacrifice at all. "Deal."

Grace heard the satisfied grin in Monica's voice. "*Great. Call you back in a bit.*"

Monica hung up. Grace pulled up her call list, found Julie's number, and hit *dial*. Marty answered instead of Julie, which was exactly what she'd been hoping for. "*Hello?*"

"Marty, it's Grace." Not *Constable Matthews* anymore, just Grace. How quickly odd circumstances brought people together. "Can you meet me at what's left of The Cougar's Den? I might . . . need some help with something kind of . . . distasteful."

"*Sure. What're we talking about?*"

Grace told him. Marty agreed instantly, with no change in tone. "*Absolutely. I'll take Julie's car; be there in ten minutes or so. Soon as Sage comes over to sit with her.*"

"Good. See you then."

They both hung up. Grace pushed away from her desk and stood, grimly aware that she was about to go look at what was most likely the first crime scene in Pleasant Brook since she started ten years ago. Ironic, how she'd once almost wanted a crime to happen to break up the boredom. But now?

She forced those thoughts aside and pushed through the door.

Gerhart Trailer Park

56.

SCOTT SHIFTED UNEASILY on the futon in Sage Hunter's trailer. None of what was happening felt real. It felt like they were all play-acting scenes from horror movies. This, of course, being the classic parlay scene when all the main characters who'd encountered the movie's threat on their own finally came together to compare notes and plan for action. Figure out how to kill or stop whatever evil was threatening their hometown. It was happening right now, before his eyes. Almost as if it were scripted. It didn't feel *real*.

And yet, here he sat in Sage's trailer. Lukewarm, half-finished can of Pepsi in his hand. Folded printer paper about the "aspect of Samhain" in his back pocket. Watching and waiting for the muttering adults—Julie, Marty, Sage, and Constable Matthews—to start the clichéd meeting.

Mom was working another late shift at The Whole in the Wall and had already informed Scott she was "meeting a friend at The Tipper" after. Which meant she probably wouldn't get home until near midnight. At this point, he no longer worried about skipping remote classes, or about Principal Williams calling Mom to say he hadn't shown up. After showing up at Julie's trailer this morning, he'd hiked around town, killing time until they met up at Sage's trailer. All the time, walking along dead and empty streets, (emptier than usual), Scott couldn't help but replay, over and over, the Jasper-thing melting into goo in his driveway last night . . .

"All right," Matthews said in a casual but no-nonsense tone as she entered the small but immaculate den from the equally small and spotless kitchen, with Marty following. "Let's start. Before anything else, I need everyone to share a *full* account of your experiences over the past two weeks. Hold nothing back. Tell us *everything*. No matter how bizarre or unbelievable."

Each person did so. As they told their stories, the constable's expression grew more solemn. When everyone finished, she shared the grisly story of the desecrated graves at Hillside, and she backed up Scott's nightmarish experience last night.

After he fell silent, they stared at each other. Unmoving, saying nothing, until Julia blurted out, "What the *fuck* is going on? This is . . . like a fucking horror movie."

"This isn't a movie, though. It's happening, here, in our town." Matthews crossed her arms and addressed the group. "So if we're all on the same page that this is something . . . abnormal, I may've come across a lead. It's thin, but it's all we have. On a hunch," she nodded at Scott, "I took the picture you forwarded to me, cropped it, and ran it through some channels I have at the Utica PD. She has access to the kind of records I don't."

Sage smirked. "And by friend, she means an ex-booty call desperate for a second go."

Scott wasn't sure, but he thought the constable was working hard not to smile. "ANYWAY," she said, ignoring Sage's comment, "I got back some interesting hits."

"Such as?" This from Marty, his expression intrigued.

Constable Matthew's expression grew somber. "Scott, you were probably a little young, but does everyone else remember the Owen murder/suicide two years ago?"

Julie looked confused, obviously not remembering. Sage's face grew sad, however, and Marty grunted. "How is *that* connected to this?"

Scott cleared his throat, and—feeling nervous speaking up among adults—asked, "What happened?"

The constable paused for a moment, looking uncertain. She obviously thought it was important, but also looked like she was worried about sharing the gory details with a teenager. "It's okay," Scott reassured her, "I've seen all the *Saw* and *Hostel* movies. I can handle it."

Matthews chuckled and nodded. "Okay. Well, it was nasty business. The short version: a troubled marriage exploded two years ago when county police arrived at the Owen residence—just outside Pleasant Brook—to find Mr. and Mrs. Owen dead. The wife apparently attacked the husband and gutted him with a butcher knife, and the case files reported that it looked like she was killing him *sacrificially*. In some sort of ritual. She'd administered fatal cuts across her own abdomen, intent on going out with him. *She* ultimately died from a knife wound in her neck, which severed her jugular. Probably from the same knife, which she must've dropped at some point when she was disemboweling her husband."

Julie's hand fluttered to her mouth. "Oh. Oh my god . . . "

Constable Matthews continued. "Police found the knife clutched in her dead husband's right hand. Best they can figure, when she dropped her butcher knife to finish whatever ritual she was performing, he mustered his last bit of strength to end her first."

"Wow." Scott noticed with surprise the usually stoic Marty looked shocked, eyes wide. "That's a lot more than what the news reported. Were you on the scene?"

"No. The Owen house is just slightly outside my jurisdiction. *But*, I also have friends in Warren County PD who keep me updated on their goings-on."

Sage winked at Scott and mouthed, *booty call*. Scott smiled, somehow relieved at the librarian's ability to find humor in anything.

"How is *that* connected to this?" Julie's voice came out as a soft, husky rasp.

"After I sent my friend the picture Scott took, she got a close match to the Owen case file. Lisa Owen was a curator at the Munson-Williams-Proctor Arts Institute in Utica. At the Owen residence, county police found crating and an invoice for what was later discovered to be an artifact Owen had *illegally* shipped to her, using her museum credentials, and the entirety of the trust they'd set aside for their children. Children they were never able to conceive, unfortunately. The artifact wasn't found on the premises. The museum wanted to avoid a scandal, so they kept it quiet."

A knowing look crossed Marty's face. "What was the artifact?"

"It was The Mask of Samhain . . . .wasn't it?" Scott blurted out, embarrassed, but unable to stop himself. "The Mask of Forgetting."

Constable Matthews looked at him with open amazement. "Okay. Way to steal my thunder. Where'd you learn about that?"

Fingers shaking slightly, somehow knowing he wasn't in trouble but still afraid he might be for upstanding an adult (he'd learned in school the consequences of this, the hard way), he fumbled the print-out from his pocket, unfolded it, and read in a slightly cracking voice what he'd read himself earlier that morning. When he finished, he looked up and saw something in Constable Matthews' and Marty's faces he wasn't accustomed to seeing in adults: unabashed pride.

"Wow," Matthews said, undisguised admiration in her voice. "You accomplished in a twenty-minute Google search what took me an hour of wrangling on the phone with the museum in Utica. Well done."

Marty folded his arms and gazed thoughtfully at the ceiling. "The aspect of Samhain. And apparently, it can spread. Transfer to others." He looked back down at them. "It certainly makes a disturbing sort of sense."

Matthews nodded, face taking on a more somber expression. "Yes. We also know, now, what kind of ritual Lisa Owen was likely trying to perform. For someone whose marriage was buckling under the weight of depression, infertility, and her husband's reputed infidelity, the Ritual of Forgetting—enacted by the offering of the 'source of your pain'—makes sense, also."

Julie finally spoke in a horrified voice tinged with disbelief. "Where's the mask been this whole time?"

Matthews shrugged. "Who knows? Say the mask was at the Owen

residence, but the police weren't able to find it for some reason. Then two years later, kids or squatters messing around break into the old Owen place and came across it."

Marty sat up straighter. "Whoever may've found it—if they started messing around with it? Who knows? And now . . . this *aspect* of Samhain is spreading through town."

"Question is," Sage said, voice low and serious, "what do we *do* about it? What *can* we do about it?"

Constable Matthews held up a hand. "Before we begin rolling out plans, you all need to hear this: You can walk away. Right now. You don't need to be part of this if you don't think you can. And you," he pointed directly at Scott, "have already faced more than the rest of us, so you're staying out of this next part. Or, at the least, as far away as possible."

Surprisingly—and to his slight shame—all the protests Scott had planned in anticipation of this mandate wilted. He realized that, honestly, he'd had more than enough. The thing that had been Jasper was dead. He felt relieved, which also made him feel like a coward as he nodded and accepted the constable's word without protest.

Julie raised her hand timidly, looking as ashamed as Scott felt. "I'm sorry. I want to help. I do. But not against those things. I can't. This is all too much. Y'know?"

Sage, who sat next to Julie on the futon, put their arm around Julie's shoulders and hugged her. "It's okay," they whispered.

Marty looked at Constable Matthews, his expression thoughtful. "So you think this whole thing started at the old Owen house?"

The constable shrugged, looking uncharacteristically (as far as Scott knew her) uncertain. "That's where the artifact—this mask of forgetting—was at one point. Far as I know it's been empty since the Owens. No one ever tried to sell it. But."

She paused. Shook her head, sighed, and continued. "I drove back and forth through town last night, and along the side roads. Without even knowing what I was looking for, but thinking of places people could hide, or looking for . . . "

"A nest," Scott whispered, without even thinking. "In movies, these things *always* have a nest."

Constable Matthew shrugged, her expression one of grudging assent. "I guess. Anyway, I did stop by the Owen place last night. Don't know why. Felt . . . drawn to it, for some reason." She shifted from foot to foot, looking distinctly uncomfortable. "The place felt *bad*. Different from the other places I checked out. And there are tire tracks there. Decently fresh, as in the last three weeks or so. Probably a truck. I think the Owen place would be a good place to start looking for these things."

"If that's where they were summoned," Scott said, "that's probably where they are."

The constable offered him a flickering smile. "More horror movie logic?"

Scott shrugged, not knowing what else to say.

"When will you go?" This from a nonplussed, calm-looking Sage.

"As soon as possible." Constable Matthews looked at all of them in turn. "I'm not sure what I think about all this. But it's spreading fast. We need to move."

Matthews looked at Scott. "I can't believe I'm even saying this . . . but did you find anything in your research about times of day when they were strongest or weakest? I hate to admit it, but when I think of those things, I think 'vampire,' for some reason."

Scott shook his head. "No. Jasper . . . " he swallowed, felt his throat tighten with unexpected emotion, and then he plunged on. "Jasper and I first saw them around 4 in the early evening. Then I saw . . . saw what Jasper became, at night."

"It was early morning when the one—I think it was probably Jasper, too, because it had the same t-shirt—followed me up Burns Hill Road," Marty added. "People at the corn maze saw them at night."

Julie shrugged limply. "I only saw them at night, when they tried to get into the club."

Constable Matthews shook her head. "Okay. No rules, then, about when to go after them. So far as we know, anyway. Still. I don't want to be at the old Owen place any later than I have to be." She looked at them all again. "I should probably go now."

Marty offered a small, resolute smile. "Not alone, that's for sure."

"You don't have to go, Marty. I'm the constable. It's my job."

Marty's smile spread into a grin. "Like I've got anything better to do." His smile faded, however, as he added with less humor than he probably wanted, "Besides, Scott'll tell you. Splitting up in a horror movie is a BAD idea."

"Okay," Sage interjected, their tone business-like. "If you two are going, Julie and I are staying at Scott's house." They offered Scott an arched eyebrow and mischievous grin. "I'm sure your Mom wouldn't mind some help 'keeping you in line.' She's working the evening and late shift again tonight?"

Scott nodded eagerly, not upset at the notion of a 'babysitter' at all, ironically. He was glad for the company.

"Good," Marty said. He looked at Constable Matthews. "So. What kills them?"

Matthews sighed. "Shotgun blasts to the face don't work, but wood through the heart does. Don't know why. Maybe the heart is the only organ those masks can't reform, or something."

Feeling like he was now part of them—like he actually *belonged*—Scott surprised himself by piping up. "I've been thinking about that. We learned in school that parasites can live off a host, but the most successful and longest-lasting parasites can live off a host longer if it leaves more of the host's systems intact. Maybe the heart *has* to be left alone, while the parasite—the masks—change everything else. That's why you can kill it by stabbing it through the heart." He paused, then added, "Maybe that's also where the myth about killing vampires comes from. Vampires are basically parasites. Maybe these things have been around forever, and the stories turned them into vampires. Through . . . whaddya call it . . . oral tradition."

Everyone looked at him with mute amazement.

"Guess we better make some stakes." Constable Matthews chuckled and shook her head. "I can't believe I just said that."

Marty shook his head, brow wrinkled, looking troubled. "We can't take these things one on one."

"You're right." Matthews nodded. "I'm not suggesting we try. Stakes would be a desperate measure if we get pinned down. No, I'm thinking . . . fire."

She looked at all of them before continuing. "Warren County Fire Marshall let Marty and I poke around the wreckage of The Cougar's Den this morning. Well, actually," Grace smirked, "they told me they were too shorthanded to deal with it right now, and they had no idea *when* they could get here, so I asked them if I could look around, and their response was: 'Sure, why not?' Anyway."

She sighed and continued. "I found a strange substance there. A charred, burnt resin. If those things killed Conroy—and I can't imagine who else would—I think the fire caught them by surprise and they couldn't get out. It looked similar to the blob of material I found near the bike bridge, though burnt. I'm willing to bet fire kills them."

Julie sniffed and looked on the verge of crying, though she somehow held it together. Her voice shook slightly as she spoke. "I still don't understand why those . . . things would kill Conroy like that."

Matthews hooked her thumbs on her gun belt. "From what you said, Conroy wouldn't let them into the club both nights. Based on what Scott said about the cross being an irritant, I wonder if it had something to do with Conroy's faith and his cross tattoos. I mean, he had them all over his body. Maybe those two things made him more of a threat."

Marty shook his head. "Where's a priest or a pastor when you need one?"

Matthews flickered a faint smile. "I don't think Pastor Foley would be up for this. He's pushing eighty. And honestly? Push came to shove, I'd probably let Pastor Yorkins get eaten."

"Did . . . did you find Conroy's body?" Julie's voice was soft and wavering, though Scott thought he sensed a hard undercurrent to it, of repressed anger. "Marty said that's why you called him along."

Matthews looked troubled as she shook her head. "No. At least, no obvious signs, but of course, we didn't know what we were looking for, and all joking aside, Warren County did ask us to be careful poking around. There wasn't much left. No way to be sure if Conroy's remains were burnt up, or if those things . . . "

"Took him," Julie rasped, eyes flashing. "You think they came and took his body."

Matthews shrugged, still looking troubled. "Maybe. I don't know."

"So," Sage said, looking eager to distract everyone's attention from the subject of Conroy, "you're going to burn down the old Owen house?"

Shock registered on Julie's face. At the suggestion itself, or Sage's calm delivery, Scott wasn't sure. "You're . . . kidding. You're going to set an old house on *fire*? Just like that? Without telling anyone?"

"Who would we tell?" Marty's voice sounded quiet and sympathetic, yet firm. "The county police? State police?"

Matthews shrugged. Even Scott could tell she wasn't happy about what she was going to say. "Marty's right. No one would believe this. Until it was too late."

"The legend I found," Scott said softly, "on the printout. It says their hunger grows and grows, and they spread . . . until nothing's left." A thought struck in its terrifying simplicity. "Geez. We could end up like Roanoke. Or Salem's Lot."

Sage tilted their head. "You'll never be able to get them all in there at once."

Matthews nodded. "Some will likely escape. Others might not be there at all. But I still think our best play is to kick apart their 'nest.' Try to get as many of them as we can in one stroke. It's all we can do."

She pointed at Scott, Sage, and Julie. "You guys take care at Scott's. All doors and windows locked. I know this sounds crazy but make some stakes. Make some crosses."

"Even if you can burn their nest down . . . you know that won't be the end of it, right?"

Everyone turned to look at Scott. Once again, he couldn't believe his boldness. He cleared his throat and continued in a less confident voice. "I mean . . . in the horror movies, when the good guys make their move, lots of times it goes well, but one of the monsters always escapes, and one of the good guys always dies in the process."

He shrugged limply. "It's just . . . even if you kill a lot of them tonight, even if *no one* dies . . . it's not over."

Constable Matthews nodded, expression grim. "I know, Scott. But what else can we do?"

Constable's Station
5:00 PM

57.

WHEN GRACE OPENED her gun locker, Marty whistled in amazement. "Wow. That's quite an arsenal. Especially for a small town like this."

Grace smiled ruefully as she withdrew a Glock 19 from a shelf in the cabinet, which held ten of the squat, black handguns. "What can I say? I'm a progressive lesbian who likes her guns." She popped the magazine out, saw it was full, slapped it back in, and handed it to Marty, butt-first. He accepted it tentatively, as if were a live grenade.

"To be honest," she said as pulled out another Glock and proceeded to check its magazine, "I never thought I'd need all of these, of course. I have friends on the gun show circuit, and they always send me emails about discounts and deals, or when a new model is coming out, and I . . . uh . . . " she handed this Glock to Marty, also, feeling slightly embarrassed, as if someone had learned about her secret collection of ceramic Hummel figurines. "It turned into a hobby, I guess."

She reached into the locker and pulled out a gun belt with two holsters, and handed that to Marty. He set the guns down on the table next to the locker and accepted the leather belt in his hands, a bemused expression on his face. "It's what's in fashion this year, I guess." He wrapped the belt around his waist, buckled it, and tried to adjust it to hang right.

Grace reached into the cabinet and pulled out a riot gun similar to the one in her JEEP. She worked its breech, made sure it slid smoothly out, then reached into the cabinet, grabbed a box of shells, and carefully began loading it. When she finished, she pumped it once and laid it on the table.

"I gotta ask—not that I care one way or the other—but did the county pay for all these?"

Grace's laughter barked sharply. "Hell no. Bought all of these out of pocket, over the past ten years. Like I said. It's kinda my hobby."

"Good for us, I guess." He paused, then said, "What's next?"
"We stop at the Sip and Save, fill some five-gallon containers with gas, and go commit some arson."

Clinton Road
Carter Residence
6:00 PM

58.

"**SO," SAGE SAID** as they plopped next to Scott and Julie on the couch, bowl of popcorn in one hand, Roku remote in the other, "where do we hunt for horror movies? Vudu has lots of good cheesy ones if you're in the mood. So does Tubi. Shudder, Netflix, and Amazon Prime have a mix of good *and* cheesy movies."

Sage tilted their head and offered a quirky grin. "What's your poison, young sir?"

Scott stared at Sage, struck mute in amazement at their calm. They were acting as if nothing was wrong. As if everything was normal, and they hadn't spent the afternoon talking about monsters. Actual *fucking* monsters, and how to kill them with fire. How was Sage so . . . chill?

They weren't putting on a brave face for him, either. He saw through those. Had gotten great practice with his mom over the years. He could see right through Julie's brave face. Her smiles were stiff and forced, eyes wide and jittery, and she kept bouncing one foot on the floor. Her laughter had a splintering sound to it. Like it was about to crack. Julie was terrified, Scott could tell.

Not Sage. Since they'd parted ways with Marty and Constable Matthews earlier in the day, Sage had acted as if it was another day. And they weren't *acting* that way. Scott thought they believed it. Believed everything was fine, and eventually would be.

Sage mock-scowled, gesturing at him with the remote. "What? Something on my face? Snot on my nose?"

He flickered a nervous smile, and before he could stop, said, "Why aren't you scared?"

Sage looked at him for a moment, then offered a kindly smile which made them look much older. "I'm scared, Scott. I'd be crazy *not* to be."

"But you don't look scared. Or act like it, and you're not faking. *I'm* scared shitless." He glanced at Julie, "and so are you. You're pretending you're not, but I can tell." Julie smiled nervously but said nothing.

He looked back at Sage. "But you're not acting scared, and you're not pretending, either. How are you doing that?"

Sage's smile faded, their face becoming somber. They set the remote on the coffee table and shifted to face Scott more directly. Their eyes looked wide and expressive. "It's hard to explain. Part of it is probably because I've lived here my entire life, and I figure I'll probably die here, too. Could happen any time."

This confused Scott. "Don't you want to leave? Go somewhere else?"

"Wanted to, once. Had plans to attend college, like everyone else." They shrugged. "It didn't work out. Stuff happened, and I stayed here. Made me mad at first, but eventually, I accepted that it was meant to be. Once I did that," they shrugged again. "Things fell into place. Sure, I'm scared. About what might happen tonight, tomorrow, or the next day. Next week, next year. But I guess I'm more scared about what might happen to you guys, or your mom, Scott, or Marty. I don't want to see any of you hurt.

"Me? Whatever happens to me is supposed to happen. I accepted that a long time ago. I guess that makes it easier to process my fear."

"Sounds fatalistic," Julie said flatly. "Like you're giving up and don't care if you live or die."

Sage shook their head. "Oh, I *definitely* want to live. Trust me. I've got lots left to do. But I also believe everyone has a purpose. Maybe I'm supposed to die tonight. Or in a few weeks, or in twenty years. But my death won't be random. It'll be my time."

They picked up the Roku remote and settled back into the couch. "Also, I don't think this life is it. I think we go somewhere after."

Julie snorted. Scott couldn't tell if she was annoyed or acting sarcastic to mask her fear. "Please. You're not gonna preach, are you?"

Sage smiled. "No preaching, promise. I just believe there's something better than this world, afterward."

"What about Constable Matthews?"

They looked at him with raised eyebrows. "What about her?"

"Aren't you scared for her, too?"

Sage tilted their head. "I am. I definitely don't want her to get hurt. We've got . . . " a slow smile spread, one Scott couldn't quite interpret, "history. But she's like me, I think. She's accepted this is where she's meant to be, and whatever happens to her is supposed to happen. Does that make any sense?"

Scott wasn't sure if it did, but he still said, "I guess."

"All right then." They gestured at the TV with the Roku remote again. "Where to?"

He decided in a heartbeat. "Tubi. That's where all the low-budget horror movies are."

Sage grinned, and he instantly felt better. "Tubi it is."

They proceeded to scroll through the cheesiest horror movie offerings Scott had ever seen, eventually selecting one called *The Barn*. As the opening credits rolled, Scott was able to momentarily forget the last few days . . . so long as he didn't glance at the shotgun, loaded and ready, leaning against the couch, or at the wooden stake made out of an old broom handle, tucked under Sage's belt.

Owen House
6:45 PM

59.

THEY SAT IN Grace's JEEP, which idled in the overgrown and cracked driveway of the old Owen house. Dark was falling quickly. Faster than Grace had anticipated, which made her more nervous than she liked to admit. She didn't want to search through this house at dark, but at the same time, felt it was imperative to make a move, now.

The JEEP's headlights cast the old house's front door in an eerie, ghostly-yellow glow. The house's front windows—the glass long since broken—peered out at them like bottomless, empty eye sockets.

"This is insane," Marty said with perfect aplomb. "You know that, right?"

"Most certainly is."

Silent communication passed between Grace and Marty. Leaving the JEEP running, they both got out and closed the doors quietly behind them, for the moment leaving the containers of gasoline and flares in the back of the JEEP. Even though her riot gun wasn't effective last night, she brought her Glock, holding it at the ready in her right hand, braced over her left hand, which trained her flashlight in front of her.

They made a rough circuit around the old house, careful not to trip over deadfall lying in the weeds and grass. They took special care to press close to the siding when they neared the windows, and then the backdoor. In about ten minutes, they circled back around to the front door, where they stopped and conferred.

"I hate to say this," Grace said, "but we have to go inside. If this *isn't* the place and we burn it down, it's gonna be a waste."

"I was thinking the same thing." Marty paused, then asked, "Warren County Fire is going to wonder why you've had two buildings burn down in the space of two days. They'll be thinking a serial arsonist is running around."

Grace shrugged. "We get rid of these things, they can think what they like, and ask as many questions as they want." She nodded at the front door. "Shall we?"

"After you, Constable."

"All right. Let's go.

They crept forward, as the falling night hung silent and expectant around them.

***

The instant she and Marty stepped through the front door of Owen House, an awful, rotting chemical stench assaulted her nostrils. It was the smell of burning rubber, of meat gone over, of spoiled milk, all mixed together. Based on Marty's quick intake of breath and sharp cough, she guessed he smelled it, too. That, and . . .

They stopped and stood in what must've once been the dining area. Someone, in the past two years, had dragged the sofa (now lumpy, sagging, with springs poking through the cushions, and spilling its innards) into the den. Grace shined her flashlight on it. The tattered couch was littered with old cigarette butts. Also, dotted with patches of what looked like hardened rubber.

She gestured at the substance with her flashlight's beam. "I'm not touching it, but I'd bet my last dollar that's the same stuff I found on Kovac Street, and at The Den."

Marty nodded, lips pressed together tightly. "Looks like it."

Grace shined the flashlight around the remains of the house's dining room and kitchen. The wallpaper was yellowed, cracked, and peeling. The floor, covered with natural debris. Twigs, leaves, gravel. Also, beer cans and bottles. The floorboards heaved and creaked under their feet, and the walls looked swollen. Pregnant, almost. The comparison made Grace shiver.

An air of deep neglect pressed down upon Grace. That, and the sense of something . . . wrong. Foul. Unnatural. She'd never considered herself much of a spiritual person, but this house felt all *wrong*. Unclean of spirit. If she hadn't already known of the house's bloody history, she wouldn't have been surprised to learn it, after spending only a few minutes in the place. She had no doubt those things had been called to life here, and probably bedded down here at one point. Now, however . . .

"I dunno," she muttered as she continued to pan her flashlight around the ruined house. "This place feels all sorts of wrong, and not just because it smells. It feels . . . warped. Like the place should be burnt to the ground, and the earth salted. But it also feels . . . "

"Empty," Marty finished for her. "This place feels empty. Whatever was here is gone."

Grace turned and shined her flashlight up the flight of steps leading to the second floor. The beam barely flickered in the murk swirling up there. Where the Owens killed each other, of course.

Where they had to go.

She nodded at the stairs disappearing into the inky darkness. “I don’t want to go up there,” she whispered, “but I guess we have to.”

Marty sighed heavily. “I suppose so. After you, constable.”

“Thanks,” she said dryly as she slowly approached the stairwell, unsure if she was glad he hadn’t tried to pull a macho “I’ll go first,” or slightly annoyed that he hadn’t “Thanks a *lot*.”

As she moved toward the dark stairway, with Marty behind, she realized such concerns mattered little in the face of her lurking fear.

Carter Residence
7:30

60.

THEY MADE IT halfway through *The Barn* until the middle act got bogged down with an odd side trip which made no sense. After abandoning the low-budget Halloween horror movie, they searched for something else and came up with a ridiculous-looking flick called *Thankskilling*. A fine piece of work about a demonic murderous turkey who goes on a bloody rampage right before Thanksgiving. Against all odds, it had proven to be a better choice, so far. It couldn't be taken seriously on any level, which was what they needed at the moment. Julie, especially.

Because not only was she having a much harder time forgetting their circumstances than Sage and Scott, she also couldn't stop thinking about Sage's belief in everyone and everything serving a purpose. That what happened to her and everyone else was *meant* to happen, and that they'd accepted that. Julie wasn't sure what bothered her more. The concept of some larger purpose defining everyone's lives, or *accepting* it without protest.

About forty minutes into the movie, she asked Sage and Scott if either of them wanted a drink. Neither did, (thankfully), so she went for one as an excuse to get away and clear her head.

To have something in her hand when she returned, she opened the fridge for a can of Sprite from the case they'd bought on the way over. On the fridge's bottom shelf, several six-packs of beer sat next to a bottle of Smirnoff. Her hand wavered the slightest bit before she grabbed a Sprite from the top shelf. She closed the fridge door, taking care not to slam it like she was tempted to.

A flush of shameful guilt filled her as she turned away from the fridge, (too slowly for her own liking), making her stomach feel cold and heavy, drawing her breaths out in short gasps. She felt slightly feverish, also. Signs she knew well.

She knew the drill, of course. Feeling the thirst wasn't a relapse. She hadn't done anything wrong. She'd likely feel the thirst for the rest of her life, though hopefully it would decrease as it receded further into her rear-view mirror. Wanting to take a drink wasn't relapsing. *Taking* the drink, hiding it, and rationalizing it *and* her deception *was*. She hadn't done that. There wasn't anything to feel ashamed about. She'd grabbed the Sprite, closed the fridge door, and turned away. She'd done what she was supposed to do.

Even so, the guilt and shame still simmered inside. She cracked her Sprite and took a sip as she approached the sliding glass doors leading to the Carter's back porch, in a weak escape attempt she knew was fruitless. She sipped again and looked out into the growing darkness, (which looked much deeper than forty minutes ago), thinking about purpose and things "meant to be," and giving into that purpose.

Julie supposed believing that everything had meaning brought a certain measure of peace. Thinking nothing in life was random, that behind all the chaos, a certain kind of order and harmony existed. She understood how that might inspire peace. Was something a person could believe in. Sage was the type. The kind of individual who drew comfort and strength from a belief in a "Grand Plan."

But if that were true . . . Conroy had been *meant* to die. All these others who'd disappeared were doomed to die also, and anyone else who died next . . . that was their fate. Their destiny. There wasn't any escaping it. Horrible deaths *destined* to happen for some unknowable, ephemeral reason. Awful, bloody, disgusting deaths. Where was the meaning in that? The purpose? How could *any* good come from such horrible things?

What about *her* broken home? A mother who beat her, and a father who slept with any woman with a heartbeat? The drugs and booze which dominated her life from high school to a year ago. The abortion her senior year of high school, which she'd never told anyone about, not even Sage. What about all the horrible things she'd seen done to the girls at The Den, and the horrible things she'd seen them do? The horrible things *she'd* done? Marty's own alcoholism, and whatever dark things hiding in his past. How could any of these things happen on purpose? Because they'd been planned? What did that say about whatever did the planning?

As she sipped from her Sprite and gazed into the still-deepening night, a voice whispered, *You met Marty because of all this. Both his choices and yours brought you to AA. Whatever Marty did during his addiction led to a life which was simple and peaceful, a life he's content with. And these terrible things had led all of you together. If Scott's father had stuck around, that might've been better . . . or maybe not. Because he took off, he's become who he is, and is now facing these things with all of you.*

She took another sip, scoffing at her inner voice. This wasn't some fairy tale in which a group of hearty travelers banded together in some mystical number to face down an epic evil. They were all cattle, while things out in the dark moved in for the slaughter. It wouldn't be long before one of them—or all of them—ended up dead, like Conroy.

Julie's breath hitched with a partial suppressed sob. She set down her Sprite on the counter and covered her eyes with shaking hands as a deep well of sadness gaped inside her. She'd had no time to process Conroy's death, none at all. Conroy was *dead.* Dear sweet Conroy. A devout Christian man faithfully serving in a decidedly unchristian place, their protector and big brother, dead. Set on *fucking* fire.

Horrific images of fire and destruction invaded her brain. Hitting her so hard she felt dizzy and she wobbled. The ground felt unsteady beneath her feet. Visions of Conroy's blazing death flooded her mind. She felt as if she was literally standing in The Den as it burned to the ground. She could *feel* the heat. Smell the smoke, as she coughed on its caustic bite. She could hear Conroy screaming in agony, screaming her name . . .

It didn't make sense.

A small part of her mind understood this. Even so, a black tide of grief and despair washed over her, as well as something *else.* A tickle in the back of her mind. A belief she could save Conroy and make it right, if only . . .

"Conroy? Are . . . " she coughed on acrid smoke. Tears sprang from her eyes, making it hard to see. The flames leaped higher and higher, lighting up the night sky . . .

night sky

how can I see the night sky inside a burning building?

She stumbled toward Conroy's voice, hands reaching blindly out in front of her, hacking and coughing on smoke and something . . . else. The sickly-sweet smell of meat and *rubber*, burning. "C . . . Conroy! Are you there?? I'm here! Come . . . "

A coughing fit seized her and she bent double and kneeled in the grass, hacking and wheezing . . .

grass?

She straightened and peered through smoke at a shadowy figure crouched about ten feet away. Conroy's screams intensified, and he was screaming *her* name. The figure—a charred, burning corpse—reached ashen and crumbling fingers and screamed from a ruined, collapsing mouth, "*Julie! Help me! Julie, help meeeee . . .* !"

"Julie?"

Vertigo washed over her, making her dizzy, unsteady on her feet. Julie blinked several times, confused because there were no flames. No smoke, but she still couldn't see well because it was dark. Had the power gone out, or . . .

"Julie, what are you doing?"

The night's chill air pimpled her flesh. She hugged herself and shivered, glancing around, still confused and disoriented, because she wasn't in the Carter's kitchen anymore, she was . . .

"Ohmigod. Julie! Get in here, *now*!"

Julie turned slowly, feeling drugged. She hadn't felt this way in over a year, and this wasn't the pleasant high at the start of the night, or at its peak. This was the "end of the night and too far over the edge" stupor, when nothing was fun, it was too hard to move or think, your legs and thighs were weak as jelly, mouth filled with saliva, and stomach gurgling . . .

"JULIE!"

When Julie faced the Carter's back porch she blinked again, still confused. She wasn't standing in the kitchen. She wasn't even on the back porch, and she certainly wasn't in The Cougar's Den. She stood in the backyard, the night thick and chilly around her.

Sage stood on the deck, staring wildly over Julie's shoulder, gesturing for her to come, come *now*, their face wearing an uncharacteristic expression of terror. Behind them, Scott stood, eyes wide, gaping at something over her shoulder, where Julie heard something rustling in the grass toward her . . .

A heavy, wet, acid-burning weight slammed into her back and drove her face-first to the ground, screaming.

Owen House

61.

THEY CLIMBED THE dark stairway leading to the second floor in a tense silence. Grace led the way, flashlight gripped in her left hand, pointed up the stairway, braced on her right wrist, her Glock in her right hand aimed along the flashlight's beam. Marty followed (finally having pulled out one of the Glocks Grace had given him), and they proceeded up the steps slowly, trying to be quiet, but the stairs creaked under the slightest footfall, betraying their ascent.

Grace's nerves were drawn tight. She expected *something* to happen with each groaning footstep. A rubbery, melting face leering out of the darkness at the top of the stairs. Marty's muffled gasp as something grabbed him from behind.

Nothing happened. They reached the top without incident, and before them stretched a short, ordinary hallway. It felt as empty as the rest of the house, and looked anti-climactic, especially after such a tense climb.

Even so, Grace sensed a *wrongness* about the place. She *felt* it, like the frigid waft of a breeze from an open window. From down the hall, from the only open door at its end to the right.

Without looking back, Grace gestured at the open door. "There," she whispered. "I think we have to go in there."

"That's where the Owens killed themselves. Isn't it?"

She nodded as she proceeded down the hall slowly, both Glock and flashlight still up, hands crossed at the wrist. "Yep. Sure is."

"That's somewhere you want to go?"

She shook her head. "Don't want to at all. But for some reason, I think we need to."

"All right then," Marty said, sounding as if he was shoring up his resolve, "let's get to it."

Their trip down the hall proved as tense as up the stairs. The floorboards creaked and groaned louder than the steps. Grit crunched under their shoes. Even worse, every time they passed one of the closed doors, Grace felt sure one would fly open, admitting a pack of masks upon them, their melting hands reaching for her and Marty.

Like their trip up the stairs, however, the journey down the hallway proved uneventful. They found themselves before the open door at the end of the hallway faster than she'd thought possible.

Grace turned the corner, stepped into the room, shined her flashlight back and forth . . . and came to a halt, muttering, "What the *fuck*."

"What is it . . . what do you . . . "

Marty trailed off, as he bumped into her shoulder from behind, and said, "Oh."

Grace panned the flashlight back and forth across the room, her hand shaking slightly, making the circle of light jitter and bounce. What she saw in the flashlight's beam weakened her legs and turned her calves to jelly.

"God," Marty whispered. "What . . . what is that stuff?"

Grace only shook her head, unable to speak, as she gazed at a room coated with what looked like a translucent gel. It clung like a second skin, a sheen of rubbery putrescence which covered every inch of the walls, the floor, the ceiling, and even the old mattress in the middle of the room.

"I have no fucking idea," Grace whispered. She panned the flashlight back and forth and saw strands of the rubbery stuff hanging from the ceiling, dripping slowly onto the floor, where it oozed into rubbery piles. "But I think Scott was right to use the word *nest*. I think this was it."

She directed the flashlight at the old mattress in the middle of the room. Next to the mattress were piles of clothing, covered with the same slime, and on the floor next to the clothes, she saw . . .

She entered the room and walked slowly toward the old mattress and stained clothes. She thought her footsteps would've crackled in the discharge, sticking and squelching, but they were eerily silent, and her shoes didn't stick at all.

"Constable, what are you doing?"

Grace didn't answer as she neared the humped piles of clothes in several careful steps. She aimed her flashlight on the object she'd seen. A wallet, lying open on the floor. Kneeling carefully, trying not to actually put her knee in the muck, Grace reached out with her Glock (not wanting to touch this shit at all) and used its barrel to pry the wallet up from the floor. After some prodding, it came free with a slight *ripping* sound, and flipped over to reveal its inside and the driver's license in its plastic sleeve.

She saw the picture, read the name, and felt her insides twist.

"*Shit*. Goddammit to hell, *fuck* me."

Marty, having carefully followed her, leaned over her shoulder. “Who is it?”

Grace stared at the driver’s license, her stomach sinking. “It’s Bobby Lee Haskel. Fucking Bobby Lee Haskel.

“Scott Carter’s father.”

62.

"JULIE!"

Standing behind Sage, the gears in Scott's mind jammed. He couldn't comprehend what he was seeing. Despite everything that had happened, when Julie had taken to so long to return from the kitchen, Scott hadn't expected . . . *this*. He'd expected *anything* but this.

He'd figured she was probably still upset about her friend dying in that fire. That she needed some quiet time alone. He didn't even think twice when Sage took the pump action shotgun with them to check on Julie, figuring it was a precaution.

When he'd heard Sage's panicked "Julie?", he'd known *something* was wrong and immediately darted into the kitchen, but he'd been expecting to see Julie had maybe fainted, or maybe . . . worse. Maybe she'd . . . done something to herself because she was so upset.

He *hadn't* expected to see Sage step through the open sliding glass doors, out onto the back porch, raise the shotgun, and frantically call to Julie, who was wandering dreamily in the backyard, *definitely* acting as if she'd taken several hits from mom's Smirnoff.

Then *they* advanced upon Julie. From out of the shadowy tree line. Three of them, from different angles. Julie continued to wander blindly, acting as if she couldn't see, *coughing*—on what?—calling out someone's name. *Conroy*. Wasn't he the guy who died in the fire?

Sage screamed Julie's name. This snapped her awake, as she turned (way too slowly) toward the back porch. Blinking and shaking her head, looking disoriented and unsure of her surroundings, as Sage kept screaming her name and waving her toward the porch.

One of them struck. Leaping with unnatural speed and strength, it pounced onto Julie's back, pushing her face-first into the ground. Scott's mind reacted in horror as he saw the thing's horrible mask shift, ripple, melt, and begin to drip thick gouts of *something* over the back of Julie's neck.

Julie wailed, high and shrill. A keening, despairing sound of unbearable pain. Scott went cold all over. He couldn't breathe, and for the first time in a long time, he felt his bladder twitch. He wondered dully if he was going to piss his pants.

"Fuck!"

Sage moved so fast he could barely comprehend it. Despite the other things advancing from opposite corners of the backyard, Sage leaped from the porch and sprinted toward Julie. Apparently with no clear shot, Sage deftly flipped their grip to the shotgun's muzzle, wound up, and swing the shotgun's stock at the thing riding Julie's back. Scott could hear Sage's enraged scream and the *whoosh* of the stock whipping through the air.

The shotgun's stock smashed into the thing's face, caving it in completely as if it had the consistency of a rotten pumpkin. Pulped matter exploded everywhere as Sage's blow obliterated the thing's twisted and melting features. Its arms flailed as it sagged off Julie's back and crashed sideways onto the ground.

Sage wasted no time. They bent over, looped their arm under Julie's shoulder, and dragged the shivering, hoarsely shrieking young woman to her feet. Julie staggered for several steps, then her feet caught traction as she stumble-ran alongside Sage toward the back porch.

But it was already reforming its face. Like the Jasper-thing when Constable Matthews shot it. The liquid flesh was already filling in the hole Sage made with the shotgun's stock, it was already rising to its feet and taking several staggering steps after Sage and Julie, the other two things trailing behind.

Scott finally found his voice as he screamed, "Sage! HURRY!"

Sage was already running, but one of the things coming in from the right suddenly increased its speed, blasting past the other two as it loped toward Sage. Its shoulder slammed into the librarian's midriff, and the thing and Sage toppled to the ground.

The rifle flew from Sage's grasp.

Sage wasted no time in going after it, however, rolling over and managing to wedge a knee against its chest, arresting its lunge. As its face started to shift and melt, as the other two things advanced, Sage smoothly drew the broom-handle stake from their belt and slammed it into the thing's chest. They kicked it off, rolled to their knees, and shouted, "Shoot the other one!"

Later on, Scott would look back on this moment in amazement, marveling at his unthinking reaction. He leaped off the porch and darted to where the shotgun lay on the grass. He scooped it up, swung it around, balanced the stock against his shoulder, and was pulling the trigger even as he aimed.

The shotgun's kick knocked him back several feet and almost cost him his balance, but it actually worked in his favor, tilting the shotgun's aim a bit higher at the last moment. The blast caught the onrushing thing full in its face.

Its head exploded, raining clots of blackish-green matter and slime everywhere, leaving nothing but a ragged, oozing neck stump. It toppled to one side and crashed onto its shoulder into the ground, hands grasping at the place where its head used to be.

On their feet and running past him, Sage ripped the shotgun from Scott's hands, pumped it, and aimed it at the last one, about five feet away. They pulled the trigger and blew a fist-shaped hole into its breast, where the heart should be.

Apparently, it had to be wood in the heart. The thing staggered and fell backwards, but its arms and legs were already thrashing in the grass, trying to get itself upright.

Sage grabbed Scott's hand and tugged him toward the house. As he stumbled after, he cast a glance sideways and saw the thing Sage stabbed was almost gone, nothing more than a mass of hissing, steaming black and green slime on the lawn.

But the last two were still alive. One's head was reforming, and it was already lurching to its feet. The other would soon follow.

Sage yanked Scott up the porch steps and toward the sliding glass doors. Julie stood inside, screaming inarticulately, pointing at the thing whose head was almost back and was gaining on them.

They were almost there. Four steps away, three steps, two, one, but *other* feet pounded on the deck behind them. They weren't going to make it; they weren't going to . . .

They plunged through the open sliding glass doors into the kitchen. Sage spun, grabbed the doors' wooden handles, and heaved it closed with a cry.

It stuck a hand through.

Sage slammed the door on its fingers, but no matter how hard they leaned into the door, it wouldn't close the door all the way. The thing's fingers wriggled and gripped the edge of the door, as it tried to get its other hand into the gap.

Exploding in a spasm of violent motion Scott would never have guessed her capable of, Julie flew forward, brandishing a butcher knife she must've pulled from the knife block on the nearby counter. Screaming in a high, shrill, rasping wail, she slammed the knife onto the thing's fingers over and over, hacking away. Green ichor and white mucus spurted in tiny jets, coating the glass, Julie's arm, and her face, but she kept hacking and screaming until, with one last blow, she sliced the thing's fingers off.

Sage heaved and slammed the sliding glass door shut, and snapped the lock. They stepped back, raised the shotgun, and chambered a round . . .

The things were gone. Both of them vanished.

"What the *fuck*?" Sage glared at the empty deck as if daring the things to reappear. As the seconds ticked away into minutes, however, the deck remained empty. Silence fell, punctuated only by Sage's rasping breaths and Julie's hitching sobs as she sat on the floor and rocked back and forth, knees clutched to her chest.

63.

"**SCOTT DOESN'T KNOW** Bobby Lee is his father. Does he?"

Grace shrugged as she drove, her mind spinning. "No, but honestly, most likely *Bobby Lee* doesn't know. Didn't know. Whichever." She shook her head and continued. "He skipped town and enlisted before anyone knew Tiffany Carter was pregnant. From what I've heard, she decided never to tell Bobby Lee. Figured she and Scott were better off that way, and she was probably right. Bobby Lee hasn't ever been anything but trouble."

Marty grunted. "Did Tiffany know Bobby Lee was back in town?"

Grace shook her head. The dark trees passed by outside, looking like Gothic sentinels in the night. "I doubt it. *I* wasn't even sure he was back. Sage said they thought they'd seen Bobby Lee's tag-along, Jesse Simpson, at the Sip and Save, but that was it."

"So more than likely, Scott's mom never knew Bobby Lee was back, and Bobby Lee never knew he had a son."

"We can hope he didn't find out, that's for sure."

"Why?"

Grace turned onto Route 180, which would eventually turn into Main Street. "Well, it bothers me. That maybe Bobby Lee found that damn mask. That he's this 'First' referenced in the myth. And if he somehow knows, or even *senses* Scott is his son . . . "

In its hands-free harness on the JEEP's dash, Grace's smartphone rang. She glanced down, saw the number, and tapped the blinking green 'answer' icon. "Sage. Is everything . . . "

Her good friend and former lover rasped breathlessly over the phone. "*Grace, we need you here, now.*"

Carter Residence
Saturday, October 30th
6:00 AM

64.

AFTER TOSSING AND turning for five hours, Tiffany Carter finally gave up and dragged herself out of bed. She'd slept fitfully, despite her "night cap" at The Tipper, (which had been strangely empty, the only other person was the bartender Jim, and he'd acted oddly quiet and withdrawn), her nightly glasses of vodka and Sprite when she got home, and white-noise headphones. She was restless the whole night, as sleep refused to come all the way.

Something was wrong. Something had *gone* wrong last night, and she felt that, deep inside. She couldn't stop wondering what it was.

She sat on the edge of the bed and rubbed her face, a slight headache throbbing in her temples, either from the nightcaps, the vodka, or lack of sleep. Her stomach felt acidic and uneasy. She probably needed to eat, even though she didn't want to.

Regardless, she was working another long shift at The Whole today, which started in two hours. Had to get herself around. Besides, Scott had school. Remote school, of course, but still school. Even though he was more than capable of getting ready by himself and making breakfast, she felt gripped by the sudden need to play mother for once. To make him something more than a bowl of cereal and two pieces of toast for breakfast. Maybe pancakes, or waffles, using the waffle maker she'd bought herself last Christmas.

She rubbed her face once more, fingertips massaging her temples. She grunted, gathered her tattered reserves, and forced herself to stand and shuffle out of her bedroom, toward the bathroom for a shower. On the way, as an afterthought, she grabbed her bathrobe off the bedroom doorknob and clumsily put it on.

A good thing, because when she reached the bathroom she saw Scott was already up, showered and dressed, and eating a bowl of cereal at the kitchen table (so much for making him pancakes or waffles), reading a folded piece of paper. Something he'd printed off the internet. Maybe about those horror movies he liked so much?

"Hey," she said, voice sounding raspier than she liked, "look who's already awake."

Scott's head jerked up, eyes widening slightly. He looked nervous, almost as if he'd been caught doing something he shouldn't. The idle thought passed that maybe he was looking at porn he'd printed off the internet, but the paper didn't look like it had much in the way of pictures. Mostly text and what looked like some weird symbols.

His expression quickly relaxed into something more natural. "Hey mom. Yeah, I couldn't sleep. My mind was kinda . . . running all over the place."

A dull kind of grief swelled inside Tiffany as she walked to stand next to Scott. Life hadn't been great for them; for Scott,in particular. He didn't say much, and acted like it didn't bother him, but growing up without a father . . . without even knowing who he was? She thought it must eat at him terribly.

He'd never fit in with his classmates, growing up here in this small town. He didn't play sports, didn't excel in school, (though she knew he was smarter than most kids his age,) and didn't play social games like his peers, to jockey his way higher up some nebulous and mercurial teenage social ladder. She hadn't liked Jasper much—actually, she'd gotten concerned, for some reason, how *close* they'd gotten the last two years—but he'd been one of Scott's only friends.

And now he was gone, along with his whole family. Disappeared without a trace. While it was likely the Rileys had finally skipped out on their various outstanding bills, their vanishing act still caused Tiffany's guts to curdle with an unfocused worry.

She tousled his hair. Surprisingly, he grinned without his usual protest, which had become commonplace since he'd turned ten. "I'm sorry, Scott. Got a lot on your mind, huh?"

He shrugged and returned his attention to the creased piece of paper before him, and his cereal. "Yeah. I guess."

She put her hands in her bathrobe's pockets and glanced down at the paper he was reading, though she couldn't make heads or tails of it, her glasses still on the nightstand next to her bed. "I suppose it's asking too much that you're studying for a test, huh?"

Scott snorted and glanced at her, smiling slightly. "No tests lately. Too easy for us to cheat, being remote and all." He looked back to the paper. "It's some myths and legends about Halloween. I was thinking of writing a story—maybe a Halloween story—for English extra credit."

She searched his eyes and thought he was telling the truth. The truth, at least, about what was on that paper. About working on a Halloween story for extra credit, she wasn't sure. "Neat. What's it called?"

He shrugged again as he kept reading. "No title yet. Haven't written it."

"Cool." She withdrew her hand from her bathrobe, patted him on the shoulder, and wandered over to the coffee maker, which was percolating away. "I'd love to read it when you're done. If that's okay with you, that is."

"Sure."

She sensed the slightest hesitation in his voice but decided to let it go without a comment as she got herself a coffee mug from the rack next to the coffee maker, and opened the fridge for the creamer. She'd always figured Scott would write stories or make movies someday, (scary ones, of course), and maybe even make a living doing it. Or try to, at least. It was what he loved, after all.

Even so.

She thought he might be lying about writing a story right now, and lying about why he was reading Halloween myths. It was a hunch. A gut feeling. Also, she couldn't understand *why* he'd lie to her. Maybe he was *actually* studying, and didn't want to admit it?

She set her mug on the coffee maker's pressure plate, and as the mug filled, she said over her shoulder, "I was thinking of grabbing a pizza from the diner tonight. Sound good?"

"Sure."

Her coffee mug full, Tiffany poured a bit of creamer into it. She thought—for a moment—of sneaking some Bailey's crème liquor into it, making it a nice, bracing "Irish coffee," but decided against it. Just this once, she could do without. Where the thought came from, and why she felt it with such conviction, she didn't know. She heeded it, without wondering why.

She lifted the mug to her lips and blew on it before taking a sip. Finding it at a satisfactory temperature, she walked back toward her bedroom, saying, "Think you can rustle up some eggs for me?"

"Sure. Scrambled or fried?"

She paused, thinking for a moment before saying, "Fried. Over-easy, with cheese on them."

He nodded, gaze never leaving the creased paper he was still reading. "Will do."

Tiffany nodded at him, even though he wasn't looking at her. She took a deeper sip of her coffee and left the kitchen, nagged by a vague and indistinct worry.

65.

SHOWERED, DRESSED, AND FED (thanks to her thirteen-year-old son's deft skill with a frying pan, something she felt proud of and shamed by, at the same time), Tiffany Carter was in her Toyota Corolla and on her way to The Whole in the Wall by 7:30. She'd get there in time for the start of her 8 AM shift.

As she drove, Tiffany couldn't help but notice the empty sidewalks and streets. It was early, so both foot traffic and car traffic was normally light this time of morning. Even so, she usually saw at least one or two other vehicles on their way to their own early morning shifts, as well as a jogger, and Bob Ketch, a sixty-five-year-old retiree who walked his dog like clockwork every morning. The streets were completely empty, however. Her car was the only one on the road. She didn't see a pedestrian anywhere.

It reminded her of a short story she'd read for English class in high school. Called "The Pedestrian," or maybe "The Walker;" she couldn't remember. And she didn't recall much about the story, either. Only that it took place in the future and was about this lonely guy who walked at night, in a world where no one went outside at all anymore. She couldn't remember how the story ended, but the comparison between it and the barren streets of Pleasant Brook made her shiver.

If she were honest with herself, she'd admit to having seen fewer people around town the last week or so. Fewer around the shops or outside their homes, and foot traffic at The Whole had dropped off drastically. Especially among the elderly regulars who never missed their morning cups of coffee or their lunches. Their customary booths and tables remained eerily empty as the days passed.

Maybe people were alarmed by the spikes in COVID? The last time she'd seen Pleasant Brook this quiet was during the quarantine months of Spring 2020. Their small hamlet had become a ghost town overnight. All business shut down with most employees sent home on remote, and The Whole open for take-out business only.

But she'd also remembered seeing more teens and adolescents roaming town. Loitering on street corners, hanging out at the park, gleefully skipping remote schooling the teachers were powerless to enforce. She hadn't seen *any* kids around town the past few days, which was doubly strange, considering Halloween was on the way.

Even stranger? Life hadn't seemed to change at all in nearby Smyrna when she'd gone there on errands a week or so ago. Their school was remote also, and while its streets and stores certainly looked less busy than usual, she'd still seen people out and about.

She supposed that contributed to her sense of unease. The empty sidewalks and streets, which felt ghostly, abandoned. There was last night to consider, also. When she'd returned home from The Tipper around midnight, something had felt *off* in her own home. Sage Hunter, who'd graciously (and randomly) offered to watch Scott while she worked, had been all smiles when Tiffany came home, but she'd sensed a tension beneath the librarian's calm surface. She smiled and chatted amiably, but never quite met Tiffany's gaze directly.

Also, Scott had been in bed already. That had set off Tiffany's alarms, too. Scott was a night owl. Always had been, even on school nights. Especially during October, this close to Halloween, and even more so because he didn't have to actually "go" to school in the morning. It was extremely odd for him to have gone to bed before she came home. After Sage and Julie left, she'd peeked into Scott's bedroom. The lights were off and he lay still beneath his blankets, but she'd felt *sure* he was faking. She didn't check, however, and let him lie.

As she approached The Whole, she grappled with the usual despair, (which had been increasing, over the past few years), of being a single parent. More and more, Scott was turning into a stranger. And not because he liked horror movies, or liked to write, and liked to read strange things like Halloween myths over breakfast. She didn't care about those things at all. He liked what he liked, and that was fine by her.

No, what bothered her far more was Scott's increasing reticence to confide in her about . . . anything. He'd become guarded as the years passed. Increasingly a closed book she had less and less access to. Not so much that he hid things from her, (though she knew he did), or that he lied to her, (she suspected this also), but that she had no idea what he was thinking anymore, what went through his head, or what he wanted out of life.

Take Jasper, for example. Forget his grungy background, questionable family life, (as if hers had been any better), his budding juvenile delinquency, or his destiny as a high school dropout. What bothered Tiffany the last few years or so was how *close* he and Scott had gotten. They'd spent almost every waking moment together. Granted, that was easier with the school's bouts of remote instruction, and the fact Scott didn't fit in with anyone else in town. Jasper was—had been—his only friend.

Even so, Tiffany hadn't been able to shake the premonition that something *more* than friendship had grown between Scott and Jasper. Something maybe even . . . intimate. Her unease made her feel guilty, of course. Tiffany liked to think she was as open-minded as anyone else. Hopefully more so than other folks in this town, more so than Bobby Lee had ever been, certainly. If he'd stuck around and raised Scott, (what a nightmare that would've been), and, like her, suspected Scott was gay . . . it would've been a disaster. She hadn't seen Bobby Lee in over fifteen years, but she was fairly certain her old boyfriend's parenting policy in this situation would be to "beat the gay out" of his son.

She didn't know if Scott was gay, and in most ways, Tiffany supposed she didn't care. But did he have to be gay with someone like Jasper Riley? And it wasn't like Scott would ever ask her for advice or answer her straightly if she asked him.

Tiffany pushed these thoughts away as she turned into The Whole's parking lot, not surprised in the slightest to see she was the first to arrive. She honestly didn't know why the hell Henry Dearling (The Whole's owner) was still staffing the cafe as if they were experiencing peak business. Denial, she supposed. Even though she was happy to receive the extra pay, it also meant she and three other waitresses would spend the whole day sitting around, scrolling through their phones.

A paycheck's a paycheck, she thought as she parked her car and shut it off. *If Dearling wants to pay me to scroll through Facebook all day, that's his deal.*

As she got out of her car and headed toward the diner, Tiffany was struck by the unexpected wish that Bobby Lee *had* stuck around. Though she was fairly certain he'd botch the gay part, (if Scott indeed was gay), she wished he'd known about Scott, so he could've at least *tried* being a father, so Scott would know *who* his father was.

Another part of her, however, a deeper, sadder part, knew Bobby Lee hadn't a fatherly bone in his body. Scott was far better off not ever knowing who his father was.

So consumed by these thoughts, she barely registered the scrape of footsteps on the asphalt behind her. By the time the cold, slick, and rubbery hands closed around her neck, it was too late. She would never feel conflicted thoughts about Bobby Lee Haskel—or feel *anything*, for that matter—ever again.

66.

THE FIRST GAZED down at the broken body lying on the ground at its feet. Thoughts from the Hive gurgled and bubbled through It. As it gazed at the body—whose head now lay parallel to the shoulders, neck bent ninety degrees—It felt something strange. Foreign. Unnatural. It felt . . .

Glee.

A word which held no meaning. Merely an echo of its former self, before it became the First, before it helped wake the Hive from its long dark sleep. Even so, despite the inhuman buzz thrumming through all of them, something inside the First *gloried* over the meat at its feet. It was *happy*. *Joyful*. Even . . . *triumphant*.

Stupid bitch, a ghost of a voice—a *human* voice—whispered in its mind. *Got what you deserve. Never loved you anyway.*

The First felt confused. It was . . . *happy* it had killed her. *Happy* she was dead.

The First cocked its head. *Her*. *She*. It did not understand these words. In the Hive, there was no gender. There was All. No distinction, no individuality, no differences. They were the Aspect of Sowein, and they were All. Yet, as the First gazed upon the form lying at its feet, it thought of the thing as . . . *her*.

Tiffany.

Stupid whore.

Still confused by the ghost-whisper, the First hesitated another minute, before the Hive's imperative—to consume, spread, make more—took over. It banished the ghost whispering faintly against the buzz, knelt, and positioned itself over it . . . *her*. The buzz inside its head sharpened in pitch, buzzed higher and higher until all their voices merged into one humming crescendo.

Its face—the aspect of Sowein—softened. Rippled. Oozed. Slowly at first, but faster and faster and more and more sloughed off it, and down onto its face. *Hers*. As the First's face turned to liquid and poured all over the broken thing lying at its feet . . .

Tiffany

. . . the chorus of voices sang. They were one, they were all, and they were making more.

The First's face hardened.

It rocked back on its heels.

Gazed down at the other they'd made, and watched with great satisfaction as the neck snapped back into place, and its face became the aspect of Sowein.

Another voice joined the chorus.

The thing with long blonde hair (Tiffany) sat up stiffly and turned its aspect upon the First. They gazed at each other and into each other, they were one and all, and the First knew all it knew, and along with that, came a whisper . . .

Scott.

My son.

Carter Residence
7:30 AM

67.

AFTER SCOTT WATCHED his Mom pull out of the driveway, he sat in one of the recliners in the living room to think. Hehad no intention of attending remote school today. It wasn't like anyone would notice, or care. More and more kids were skipping, and now two teachers—Mr. Phillips in History, and Mrs. Perry in Math—had stopped signing into *their* remote classes.

So he sat in an old recliner in the corner of the living room, knees drawn up to his chest, chin on knees, running last night's insane, terrifying events through his mind *again*. Mom was correct in assuming he hadn't slept much, though not for the reasons she thought. No, Scott had spent the night tossing and turning because, quite frankly, they'd almost *died* last night.

But not *died*. Turned into something *else*. "The Aspect of Samhain," whatever the hell that meant. And the way the Jasper thing had kept coming after him made Scott wonder. If he was turned into one of those things, who would *he* come after? Sage or Julie?

Mom?

He still couldn't believe they'd been able to sort things out before Mom got home last night. After ten minutes of Julie sobbing hysterically, sitting on the floor hugging her knees to her chest, while he and Sage stared out the kitchen sliding glass door, they finally got moving. Sage helped Julie to her feet, talking to her in a soft, reassuring voice, and gently led her to the bathroom. Without being told to, Scott got cleaning spray and paper towels out and started mopping up the blackish-green slime splattered on the glass doors and walls, from where Julie had slashed the thing's fingers off. Heeding some instinctual knowledge, Scott made sure he grabbed a pair of rubber gloves also and was careful not to get any of the residue on him.

As for the fingers Julie cut off, they'd hardened into lumps of weird rubber. After cleaning the glass doors, the wall, and the kitchen floor, Scott scooped up the lumps, quickly opened the sliding glass door, and threw them as hard as he could, underhand, into the darkness. He slammed the door shut and locked it as fast as he could, but despite the fear pounding in his head, the night remained deathly still.

Julie's shirt was a total loss. Rather than risk making the washing machine a mess, Sage borrowed one of Scott's plain t-shirts. Scott knew Mom would never miss it. Especially since he did the laundry most of the time while Mom was working. Sage got Julie into the shower first, however, and washed off the slime which had splattered all over her when she'd slashed the thing's fingers off. Her skin wasn't broken, just red, and she seemed fine, though complaining the places she'd gotten ooze on her—the back of her neck and forearm—itched and burned, like a bad case of poison ivy. Afterward, they led Julie to the couch, where she curled up under a comforter and lay there, shivering, staring into nowhere.

Sage called Constable Matthews. Somehow she and Marty got there before Mom. Marty carefully helped Julie into the constable's JEEP, while Sage and Scott broke down the night's attack to Constable Matthews. Scott felt sure the constable would insist Scott tell his mother everything, but to his surprise, she merely reiterated to Sage that they lock down the house tight as possible, and to call if anything more happened. They managed to pull out of Scott's driveway and get down the road before Mom pulled in, as Sage and Scott were putting everything in order, and returning the shotgun to the gun cabinet.

Rather than try to pretend to Mom nothing had happened, Scott hustled into bed to fake sleeping. Sage must've made a convincing show, because Mom didn't talk to them long, and they left not long after Mom came home. When he heard his bedroom door creak open as she checked on him, he realized his mistake: he never went to bed before Mom came home from the late shift. She was going to wonder about that, for sure.

This morning, he could tell she *was* worried. With her questions about how he'd slept, and how he was feeling. Far as he could tell, however, Mom wasn't worried about anything specific.

That was good. He wanted to keep her far from all of this. As far as he could, anyway. Last night had struck too close, and he was suddenly, dreadfully aware of how much danger they were all in, even more than before.

Before Mom got up, he'd fixed himself a bowl of cereal and poured over his well-worn printout, looking for something he might've missed. He didn't come up with anything. Of course, he wasn't even sure what he was looking for. He could watch all the horror movies in the world and know every kind of plot, but in reality, he was a kid. How the hell could he do anything?

He covered his face with his hands and rubbed his forehead with his fingertips. His head throbbed from not sleeping well. He was tempted to go back to bed and see if he could rest a few more hours. Thing was, he knew that after last night, there'd be no way he could lay still long enough to fall asleep. No, he had to get out. He wasn't sure *where* he was going—Sage said they'd be at the library as always, so maybe there. Maybe Julie's too, but he guessed that after last night, she and Marty probably wanted to be alone. More than likely, she was having an even rougher time shaking off their close call than he was.

"Fuck," he muttered. "What the fuck are we going to do?"

There was no answer, of course. He sat there for several more minutes before he slowly got out of the recliner to head out, though he had no clear idea where he was going.

Constable's office
9:00 AM

68.

GRACE SIPPED FROM her coffee—home-brewed this time and not from the Sip and Save, which was good, because it looked like it was closed when she drove by—wishing for a shot of Bailey's in it, or something even stronger. She wasn't a morning drinker by habit (was strictly an "after six in the evening" kind of gal) but after last night's events and an impromptu circuit of Pleasant Brook this morning, she felt close to making an exception, because, quite simply?

The town felt dead. Dead, or at the least, dying an alarmingly quick and silent death.

Instead of coming directly to work, Grace toured all the residential streets. She stopped at several houses and shops, knocking on doors and ringing doorbells on the pretense of asking if anyone had seen the missing Jasper Riley. To her dismay, few people answered. Those who did acted curiously disinterested, unfocused, short, and abrupt with her. They hadn't seen him, or didn't even know him, and would contact her if they did, thank you and have a good day. Folks didn't exactly shut the door in her face, but they also weren't inviting her in for coffee, either.

Also, it wasn't like she'd found abandoned homes with doors wide open, signs of struggle strewn throughout. The houses no one answered were locked, tidy, and ordinary-looking. Either indicating folks at work, (plausible, seeing as how a complete COVID lockdown hadn't been issued as of yet), remote students who simply didn't want to answer the door, or a handful of remote workers who didn't want to answer either, for various possible reasons.

She stopped by Jud Collin's house and found it locked up also, with no one answering the doorbell, which didn't make sense. Jud's wife didn't work, (she was retired, too), and Jud didn't usually get to the cemetery until 10 AM, at the earliest.

Jud's pickup was gone, so at first, Grace supposed *maybe* they'd gone somewhere for the day. That idea evaporated when she eventually found Jud's pickup at the cemetery, parked in front of the caretaker's shed. Jud was nowhere to be found. Though the cemetery felt empty, and no graves were disturbed like the ones Jud had shown her, Grace felt uncomfortable and vulnerable the entire time she was there. As if dozens of eyes watched her from the shadowed tree line at the cemetery's edge.

Grace sighed, sipped from her coffee again, (wishing even more strongly she'd spiked it), and thought about the wallet she and Marty found at the Owen house last night. Bobby Lee Haskel's wallet. Tiffany Carter's ex, and Scott Carter's father.

Important as the discovery seemed last night, she didn't know what it meant now, if anything. It certainly indicated that at one point, Bobby Lee, (and most likely his side-kick Jesse), had been hunkering down in the Owen house. How long ago, Grace had no way of knowing. That it had been coated in the weird slime they'd found throughout the house indicated it had been before the things started nesting there. Before they'd been . . . born. Maybe Bobby Lee had fallen afoul of them. Or . . .

He'd put on the Mask of Samhain and somehow brought them forth.

She didn't like the idea of Bobby Lee—Scott's father—being one of those things, or even worse, being the *First*. Far as she knew, what she'd told Marty was true. Tiffany never told Bobby Lee about Scott. Maybe she'd broken down and told Bobby Lee recently? Maybe Bobby Lee had called her, and Tiffany let it slip? Maybe that's why he and Jesse had come back to Pleasant Brook after all these years?

Suddenly possessed with the need to get up and move, Grace pushed away from her desk, stood, and walked toward the front door. She crossed her arms and looked out on Main Street, which was eerily empty and silent, even for this early hour. Though she didn't want to, she couldn't help but imagine the same scenario which occurred at Scott's house last evening happening all over town, in the dead of night.

Sage's report of Julie being somehow *enticed* outside with visions of Conroy Ortega put an even more disturbing spin on her imagined scenarios. It also made her think of Scott's story that he'd "dreamed" Jasper had come into his living room one night. If these things had that kind of power—some awful form of telepathy—they were all sincerely *fucked*. That's why she'd insisted last night that Sage take a gun, and that's why the normally pacifist Sage had taken it.

Mercifully, her smartphone rang right about then. Still looking up and down a chillingly empty Main Street, Grace pulled her smartphone from her pocket and answered without looking at the number. "Constable Mathews."

"Grace. It's Sage. Did you drive around town this morning?

How was it?"

"Quiet. *Too* quiet. Lots of locked doors and the people who answered weren't interested in talking. Almost like they were afraid to open their doors. Anyone at the library?"

"*No. Which isn't unusual this early in the morning. No one usually comes in before ten. Even so, there's a feeling in the air. One I haven't felt before today.*" They paused, then added, "*Makes me wonder if what happened at Scott's house last night . . .* "

"Happened around town at other homes," Grace said "I was thinking the same thing." She turned from the front door and headed back to her desk. Picked up her coffee, took a sip, then added, "Stopped by Jud's place. No one's home. His truck wasn't there, so at first, I thought—I *hoped*—they'd gone out of town. Found the truck at the cemetery, though. No Jud."

Sage grunted. "*On a whim, I called Mary Beth Columbia, who runs the town book club. They canceled their Zoom meeting Wednesday night . . .* "

Grace couldn't help but grin, even though Sage wasn't there. "You go to the Book Club? *Fancy.*"

"*Fuck off. I'm the town librarian. Need to know what people are reading, right? Anyway, thought I'd call to see if they were meeting next Wednesday. No answer at home or on her smartphone. Which is odd. She's one of those folks obsessed with answering her phone, no matter what she's doing.*"

"Great. One more thing to worry about." Another sip, and then, "Any word on Julie and Marty?"

"*They're at Julie's trailer. Marty said she crashed as soon as they got there. She was shaken up, bad. I mean, so was I, but . . . Julie almost bought it last night. I'm worried that might've pushed her right up to the edge.*"

"Hopefully not over it. Though you can hardly blame her. Scott's mom working today? I forgot to ask last night, in all the bustle."

"*Yeah. All day.*"

"In retrospect, we should've told Scott to do remote schooling at the library, with you, so you could keep an eye on him. Tiffany could've dropped him off. I don't like the idea of him home, alone. Worried he might get bored and decide to venture out. You'd think he'd be too spooked, after last night, but . . . "

"*Kids are flexible. They bounce back quicker than we do.*"

"Ain't that the truth." Grace sipped from her coffee again and grimaced; it was starting to cool. This tasted better than the swill from the Sip and Save, however, so she walked over to the microwave on the table at the back wall, stuck it in, and punched the "coffee warm" button to nuke it for 45 seconds. "Probably will hop in the JEEP and drive around town again. Knock on a few doors, maybe stop by Scott's, see how he's doing. Then head over to Julie's and see how they're faring."

"Are you going to tell Scott and Tiffany about Bobby Lee Haskel? And finding his ID at Owen House?"

The microwave dinged. Grace popped the door open, tapped the mug to test its heat—not bad—carefully removed it, and took a tentative sip. Finding it much improved, she took a deeper sip, swallowed, and said, "No. I don't think Tiffany's ever told Scott about Bobby Lee, and I don't even know if Tiffany was aware Bobby Lee was back. I'm not sure what good it would do."

"If this Jasper thing was seeking out Scott because some remnant of Jasper remained . . . if Bobby Lee knew he had a kid . . . "

Another sip. "You're right. I'd better ring him up, and if he's not home, go out looking for him."

"What the fuck are we going to do, Grace? Should we call someone, at this point? County police? State police? Fucking National Guard?"

"What would we tell them? There are monsters in town? Serial killers? These things are leaving no traces. People are disappearing. No bodies. No bloodshed. Cars left in their driveways. And if we lied and said there was a massive outbreak of COVID here, they'd probably just send supplies. I honestly don't know what to do, except find this nest Scott was talking about, and burn the damn thing to the ground."

"This town is dead. Isn't it? There's no saving it."

Another sip. "I don't think so," Grace said quietly after she swallowed. "I think it'll be a miracle if any of us . . . "

She didn't finish her sentence. Instead, she took a much bigger swallow of her coffee, set the mug next to the microwave, and said, "When you get off work, meet me at Julie's trailer. I'm going to drive around, knock on a few more doors, and go get Scott. Or find him, if he's gone out. We'll meet you there. Say around 4:30?"

"Okay. See you then."

They hung up. Grace Matthews pocketed her phone and left the office to make another tour of the town, trying not to dwell on Sage's death pronouncement, and failing utterly.

This town is dead.

Isn't it?

69.

DESPITE HIS CERTAINTY that he didn't want to stay home and had to be out and about, Scott couldn't figure out where to go once he left home. At first, he thought maybe he should go to Constable Matthews' office and see if she'd learned anything new, or ask her if she and Marty found anything last night. His interaction with the constable last night had been brief; the town's peace officer was more concerned with the attack than anything else.

But he figured the constable would be busy. Constable Matthews hadn't treated Scott like a little kid; she didn't talk down to him, and she respected him. Still, she had more important things to do right now than listen to the theories of a kid who loved horror movies.

Scott considered visiting Julie and Marty, or Sage at the library. Doubt assailed him once again. Julie he dismissed immediately. She'd been a mess after those things almost got her. Could barely talk at all. He felt sure she wouldn't want any company after what happened. Plus, Marty was probably still with her. While Scott didn't think they were a "thing" quite yet, he figured it wouldn't be long. Marty and Julie probably wanted to be alone right now.

He strongly considered visiting Sage at the library. Most likely the place would be empty, and Sage wouldn't be busy. But he imagined sitting in the quiet, empty library, him and Sage basically staring at each other, with nothing much to say. He supposed maybe he could ask for books on Samhain and masks, see if there was anything else to learn. But it was morning. He couldn't see spending the entire day there. He also couldn't imagine that the small library of Pleasant Brook would have many books on the occult. He supposed Sage would let him use the computers to get onto the internet, but even so, Scott decided if he was going to the library, he'd walk around town first to kill time.

It took him a good twenty minutes to get into town. As he walked, no cars passed. It made the road feel empty and desolate. It wasn't like Pleasant Brook had lots of traffic to begin with, but even so. The place was starting to feel like a ghost town.

This of course made him think of all the weird stories he'd read over the years of small American towns mysteriously drying up and disappearing across the country. Especially small towns disappearing in the Adirondacks; Tahawus and Frontier Town, in particular. Which led to all the horror stories and movies he'd read and watched which had used that same plot device. He shivered, wondering if Pleasant Brook was going to become another unexplained mystery.

Once in town, he wandered aimlessly, with no firm idea how he was going to spend his time before he finally headed over to the library. He thought about the "Mask of Samhain," and, oddly enough, (as he occasionally did) about the absentee father he'd never met.

As he passed Stuart's, a small pharmacy on Brown Street, he wondered why he thought about the man at all, and why now. Mom never mentioned him. The few times he'd asked about his father when he was younger—when he started realizing his family lacked something most other Pleasant Brook families had—Mom only told him his father was a man poor in spirit and character, with no integrity, unable to take responsibility for himself, much less anyone else, much less a *son*. According to Mom, his father wasn't worth knowing or talking about. That was the only answer Scott ever got.

It didn't stop him from wondering, however. Who his father was, what type of man he was . . . and *where* he was.

Scott turned onto Pleasant Brook Drive. Up ahead was Martinkovic Park. It had a playground, two basketball courts right next to two tennis courts enclosed by chain-link fencing, a picnic area with scattered picnic tables and charcoal grills, ten campsites back in the woods and, his favorite place to sit and think, the old outdoor amphitheater. Scott realized as he turned into the park it had been his unconscious destination the whole time.

He crossed the parking lot and veered left, away from the courts, the playground, and the picnic tables toward the old amphitheater. He stepped over a crumbling railing, picked his way through the weeds, and gingerly sat down on one of the topmost stadium benches in the old amphitheater (you never knew which one was too rotten to support your weight). Guilt nagged him about Jasper. Even though Jasper had claimed he wasn't scared and didn't want to duck into This or That, Scott still felt responsible for his friend's fate.

He'd left Jasper. One of those things *got* him. Turned him into a monster. Scott could've done something. Cajoled Jasper into going with him. Headed back into town with him. *Anything*. Instead, he'd let Jasper go off on his own, and that was the last Scott saw of him.

The worst part was Scott couldn't banish the guilty thought that if only he hadn't misread the signals and tried to kiss Jasper a few weeks ago, that uncomfortable awkwardness would've never sprung up between them, and maybe—*maybe* Jasper would've gone into This and That with him, to wait those things out. Maybe that awkwardness had sent Jasper to his death. An awkwardness Scott had created.

Scott knew, in some way, that didn't make any sense. Jasper had always been the most stubborn son of a bitch he'd ever known. There was no talking him into doing something he didn't want to do, mistaken kiss or not. Even so, regret stung Scott deeply.

Scott looked out over the abandoned outdoor amphitheater and tried to focus. He'd discovered this place a few years ago one summer when he and Jasper had gotten bored on the playground. They were in the parking lot, unchaining their bikes, (which they hadn't ridden in forever because Jasper had decided it wasn't 'cool' anymore) when Scott saw what looked like an old wooden railing in the weeds at the parking lot's far edge. As usual, Jasper hadn't wanted to bother exploring, more interested in going back home to drink beers behind the barn.

Usually, Scott gave in when Jasper got like that, but that time, he'd resisted. *Jasper* was the one who gave in as Scott ignored him and walked to the edge of the parking lot to explore. Bitching the whole time, of course, as was his usual response to anything he didn't want to do.

They'd found the old amphitheater on the hill sloping down from the parking lot into the woods. The stadium benches were in a rough arc on the hill, and a warped and uneven wooden stage sat at the bottom, in a hollow. It looked like something from a Discovery Channel show about abandoned ruins.

When Scott researched the place at the library, he learned band concerts and plays were held there about twenty years ago. Over the years, these events drew fewer and fewer people, until the stage finally fell into absent-minded neglect.

Since discovering the amphitheater, Scott often came here to think through things important and heavy matters. Like why he didn't care about school anymore, and why it bothered him so much that he didn't care. About how Mom drank a little more every year, to "relax" or "sleep better." His growing feelings for Jasper, and how girls didn't interest him in the slightest—at least, not in the way he'd been interested in Jasper. And also, the things Jasper himself hinted about his own home life. Especially his mother, and how . . . when she got drunk, she touched him on the arm or the shoulder, with this look in her eye . . .

Scott shivered at that part, as he always did.

Of course, Scott had also spent many hours here, sitting on one of these benches, gazing at the empty and weathered wooden stage, wondering who his father was. He'd conjured up countless scenarios over the years. Mentally playing them out on the old stage, in the theater of his mind. A theater for one, and the scenes were always different.

Maybe his father had gotten caught up in drugs and alcohol and rambled all over the country, high and drunk, living a nomadic life working odd jobs for booze money, but maybe he'd also missed his son, and wanted to change. Maybe one day he stumbled into a small roadside church, found Jesus, got clean and sober, and finally came home, dry as the desert, sober as a judge, full of mournful regret for leaving his only son behind, and determined to make up for lost time.

Another recurring fantasy was his father returning from the Army, Navy, or whatever, and this story played out in several different ways. Maybe his father was returning from a top-secret, covert mission to save the world (this had been his favorite when he was younger). Or, maybe he'd returned from years of mundane and dutiful service, doing his part to make the world a safer place. Maybe he'd only learned about Scott recently. Maybe Mom had finally broken down and written a letter about him, and his father was finally coming home to a new duty, as a father.

Scott entertained other, less glamorous and dramatic scenarios, also. Maybe his dad had left because he'd been scared of being a dad. Maybe *his* dad left too, and that was all he'd ever known. Maybe he was coming back—late, but better than never—to finally break a generational cycle of abandonment. In these fantasies, Scott even acknowledged the fact his father might have married someone else and started another family elsewhere. So long as his dad wanted to be a part of his life, Scott was open to any scenario.

With a sigh, Scott ran his hand through his hair and gazed at the old stage below, where he'd played these scenarios out, over and over. With an aching suddenness which made him feel small (and stupid) Scott desperately wished his dream would come true, right now. That his father would come home right that instant. Literally step out from behind the trees in the hollow below. Eagerly but tentatively begging his forgiveness and asking for a chance to make it all up to Scott.

Holy shit, a scornful voice said inside. *What the fuck? How old are you? Five? Your Dad's gone. Who knows why he split? It probably had nothing to do with you at all. Probably didn't even know he'd knocked mom up. He was a shit person who bailed, and that's it. He's gone, he's not coming back, and that's all there is to it.*

Grow the fuck up.

"Geez," he muttered aloud, "what the hell is my problem? Of all the times to turn into a baby whining for his daddy, now is not the time. Not with this shit going on."

Usually, his self-recrimination would be enough to keep maudlin thoughts at bay, but for some reason, the childish wish for the return of his long-lost father persisted. The desire that he step out onto the stage below *right now* blossomed. It was nonsensical. It was the stuff of childhood fairy tales, but at that moment, a part of Scott didn't care. If fucking zombies made by a fucking wish existed, then why couldn't his father magically appear, too?

Scott snorted and stood, annoyed. This was pointless. He'd walked into town to think and kill time but instead wandered to Martinkovic Park and the old amphitheater on some unconscious wish-fulfillment quest. He had more important shit to do than moon over a father he didn't know, and never would know.

He turned, about to leave, when he heard it. The sound of footsteps on the weathered old planks below. And, like a sigh on the wind, "Scott?"

He froze.

He didn't turn. Fear and unbelievably intense longing waged a pitched war in his heart. This was his dream come true, wasn't it? The thing he'd been wishing, right this moment. It *couldn't* be real; it *had* to be real.

Last night, a voice frantically clamored in his head, *remember what happened last night with Julie! Don't turn around*!

Don't!

And yet, despite this shrill and panicked warning, Scott felt himself doing exactly that. Even though it went against all he felt and *knew* to be true, Scott turned in the direction of that soft voice calling his name from the old stage below.

If his glamorous dream of a father returning home from the military had stood there, or the touching Hallmark caricature of the recovered alcoholic or addict held out his hand, Scott's mind might've snapped free and he would've recognized the figure for what it was. Instead, the phantom standing on the old, weathered stage below presented itself as the most likely (yet still unlikely) version of his dream.

A regular guy. Dressed in jeans, and an unzipped gray hoodie over a light-blue t-shirt. A pleasant, unremarkable face smiling tentatively, features painted with the perfect mix of hope and regret.

"Scott?"

The image whispered his name humbly. With the perfect inflection of that same hope and regret. "It's me. I'm . . . I'm your dad. I . . . talked to your Mom a bit ago. She's worried, Scott. She's wondering where you are."

Even though a part of his brain screamed, Scott stepped forward, his legs acting of their own accord. "D-ad? Is it . . . are you really here?"

The figure nodded, blue eyes (as Scott had always imagined) wide and happy, yet shining with the right amount of unshed tears. "It's me, son. It's me."

A trembling sense of unreality washed over Scott, as he felt himself irrevocably drawn toward the figure . . .

It's dad! My father!

No, it's not!

. . . standing on the old stage below. Confusion warred against that pull, however, and he paused. "How . . . how did you know I'd be here?"

The figure . . .

Dad!

Not Dad!

. . . flickered a smile. As if feeling shy, or worried he might have overstepped his bounds. "Your mother's worried, Scott. She called home and you didn't answer. She's called your phone and you didn't answer that, either. She called me. I got into town a few months ago and we've been . . . reconnecting. Waiting for the right time for her to introduce us. But she's worried about where you are, so she called me, and asked me to come here because she knows this is your special place."

The figure's words, (odd he kept referring to it that way), acted as a bucket of cold water splashing into his face. He stared at the figure . . . the *thing* . . . standing on the old stage in the hollow below. Cold fingers played down his spine as the figure's face *wavered*. Almost as if the flesh itself rippled . . .

she knows this is your special place

He'd never told Mom about the old amphitheater. Wasn't sure why. He'd wanted to keep it to himself. Whenever he returned from spending a few quiet hours here, Scott would only tell her was out walking. Only Jasper knew about this place.

Cold fear pulsed through him. Tightening his guts, locking up his joints. He squeezed his hands into fists, fighting against the trembling which threatened to overtake him. The figure dropped its outstretched hand limply to its side. Its face indeed rippled, its perfect expression of regret and hope melting into a plastic, emotionless mask.

Behind him, Scott heard tires roll to a crunching stop near the parking lot's edge. A car door opened and shut, and footsteps scuffed blacktop. "Hey! What the *hell* is going on, here . . . Shit! Scott . . . get up here, now!"

The figure—now naked, glistening, wearing the oozing and silently screaming face Scott had gotten to know too well—leaped forward from the stage and loped up the hill toward him.

70.

RORY JABLONOWKSI HAD only ever wanted one thing: to serve and protect his community. His father, Patrick Jablonowksi, had served Warren County as a sheriff's deputy for over twenty years before retiring. His uncle, Brian Smith, had served as a state trooper for thirty years. Rory grew up in a cop's home, and his all-consuming desire for as long as he could remember was to be a cop, too.

As a kid, he'd consumed cop movies and stories like they were candy. Even though he'd known, (or at least suspected on some level), they were all made up by writers and directors who had no idea what it meant to be a cop, it didn't matter. If it had to do with law enforcement in any way, shape, or form, Rory loved it.

During his teenage years, his dad and uncle spoke at Smyrna Public High School every year on Career Day. When his dad took over Warren County's DARE program, he always dropped Rory off at school in the DARE squad car. He'd spent his formative years listening to his dad and uncle swap stories, and his dream was to someday swap his own stories with them.

Of course, he didn't want to be a three-time divorcee like his uncle, and he didn't want to drink as much as his father did. Nor did he want to bicker about his drinking with his future wife, like Dad did with Mom. Somehow, he never considered these things as the potential hazards of a law-enforcement career. He figured his uncle couldn't stay married, and his dad had a bad drinking habit. Just because he wanted to be a cop didn't mean those things would happen to him.

After Rory graduated from Smyrna High, (not at the top of his class but not at the bottom either; solidly in the *middle*, which was as a good a summation of his life as anything else), he attended Adirondack Community College, enrolled in their Criminal Justice program. Like in high school, he finished his two years there with solid but not flashy grades. Solid Bs, right down the line. With his criminal justice degree in hand, Rory started applying to local police departments, as well as the Warren County police. He even applied for the State Police.

Two years later, and the only thing he'd found?

Park security in the smallest town he'd ever lived in, Pleasant Brook. Even worse, Pleasant Brook was so small, it didn't have a police department. It had a constable who spent most of her days driving around town and walking the sidewalks talking to people because *nothing* ever happened in this town.

He didn't begrudge Constable Matthews anything. He'd gotten to know her fairly well the past two years, working with her to deal with the usual kind of vandalism and mischief teenagers got up to in parks all over the country, regardless how small the town was. She was capable and hard-working. From the few conversations they'd shared, he learned she'd worked in Utica as a cop, and came home to be constable about ten years prior. Not having grown up in Pleasant Brook himself, he didn't know why anyone would want to come back to such a small town, but there it was, regardless.

In fact, probably the only thing he had against her, (and it wasn't much), was the fact the town would probably never have cause to get rid of her. What little her job required of her she did well and approached it with the kind of meticulous attention to detail you'd expect of someone who'd worked as a city cop. Unless Matthews left Pleasant Brook on her own, the town constable position wasn't opening anytime soon.

Even so, for some reason Rory stayed on as park security, if only because Martinkovic Park was a *county* park, which meant park security was a county position, with county pay and benefits. Though he wasn't living his dream of working in law enforcement, he viewed it as a resume builder (*not* a resume *killer*, as he sometimes feared, deep inside).

As the only security officer, Rory conducted regular patrols day and night in his green 1999 JEEP Cherokee, (an older model similar to the constable's), with the Warren County crest on the doors, and the words PARK SECURITY stenciled in white underneath it. When he wasn't driving around the park, he sat in the security booth at the park's entrance, nodding to people who entered, alternating between reading the Joe Lansdale *Hap and Leonard* novels, and, (in clumsy but still-enthusiastic fashion), writing his own crime novel in black and white marble-covered notebooks.

He wore a green uniform which looked vaguely official, with a top-of-the-line police officer's utilities and gunbelt he'd purchased off Amazon. It carried all the items a police officer would need: flashlight, batteries, gloves, pens, pencils, keys, a multi-tool, and an easily accessible pouch for his smartphone. He of course didn't carry a taser, pepper spray, baton, or a gun. He hadn't been able to convince the county or Constable Matthews to let him. Not for lack of trying, of course.

In the last two years, he'd gotten valuable, (or so he told himself), experience filling out reports regarding vandalism and mischief, as well as helping Constable Matthews manage special town functions at the park. He liked to think that overnight teenage drinking had lessened since he took over the position and actually conducted night patrols when folks camped at the sites. He prided his reports as being meticulous, neat, and detailed, and always delivered on-time—weekly to Constable Matthews, monthly to Warren County—and even though he had no idea if his reports were actually read, he liked to think if they were, valuable information could be found therein. At the very least, clear and organized information.

He had no allusions. He wasn't even a rent-a-cop. But the folks of Pleasant Brook were good people. They treated him well and respected him, and so did Constable Matthews. Sure, maybe when he'd a little too much to drink at The Tipper Inn, he privately mourned unrealized dreams, but for the most part? He considered himself decently satisfied with his current situation, if not completely fulfilled.

Rory had been on one of his routine drives around the park when he'd seen the Carter kid, (who liked to come and sit at the old amphitheater; Rory had shared several conversations with him over the past few years), standing above the old amphitheater, staring down at the stage.

It occurred to Rory that Scott was skipping out on remote school, but that didn't bother him, much. Rory had skipped his own share of school. He also couldn't blame the kid for wanting to ditch a whole day of staring at a computer screen, pretending to pay attention. He'd attended his own share of Zoom county meetings the past two years, and he'd had to fight the urge not to drink himself into a stupor each time.

Something didn't look right, however, as Rory stopped his JEEP and put it into park. He shivered unconsciously. Scott was standing, not sitting, staring at something down on the old stage. From his vantage point, Rory couldn't see what. But the kid hadn't heard him drive up. Plus, he held himself rigidly, but he also looked poised on the verge of flight. Like a field mouse frozen under the eye of a hawk, Rory thought.

He hopped out of the JEEP, leaving it running, (he didn't know why), and rounded the front to the parking lot's edge, right above the amphitheater. Scott's name was poised on his tongue, but when he saw what Scott stared at on the stage, Rory slid to a stuttering halt, momentarily at a loss for words.

A naked man stood on the old amphitheater stage, and he didn't look . . . right. His skin had a wet sheen to it. Like he was covered in a translucent, viscous oil, or something. Also, it was *melting*, for lack of a better word. The naked "man" had two arms, two legs, a human torso, a head, and something vaguely resembling genitalia hanging between its legs . . .

(its?)

. . . but it didn't *look* right. Didn't look like a real human being at all, more like something a kid might form out of lumpy, wet clay, with humps and bulges along the chest, arms, and legs where there shouldn't be any . . . and it was wearing a fucking weird mask of some sort. At least, Rory *hoped* it was a weird mask, because if it wasn't . . .

It *had* to be a mask. Its face drooped, long and sagging, and looked like it was melting too. The hair was black and stringy and hung limply from a spotted and flaking scalp which looked diseased. The eyes rolled wetly and bulged in opposite directions. A fat, oily tongue, like an enormous slug . . .

how does a mask have a tongue?

. . . flopped out of its mouth and twitched in the air. Almost like it was tasting the boy's scent.

Scott Carter slowly stepped downward, toward the thing standing on the amphitheater's old stage.

A hysterical kind of fear pulsed through Rory, flushing his system with adrenaline. "Hey! You! What the hell . . . Shit! Scott . . . get up here, now!"

With the speed of a striking snake, the glistening, melting thing exploded into motion and bounded up the hill toward the still-paralyzed Scott Carter. With absolutely no thought—not even a sense of pride that he was finally getting a chance to serve *and* protect—Rory leaped forward, down the hill, at the thing.

71.

PANICKED DISMAY FLASHED through Scott even as he jerked awake and scrambled away from the thing bounding fluidly up the old amphitheater's benches toward him. He'd fallen for it, like Julie last night. The thing had gotten inside his head, made him see what he wanted, and now he was going to die.

That dismay turned to terror as his toe caught the bench he'd been sitting on. His foot twisted, throwing him off balance. He tilted sideways, and no amount of frenzied arm-flapping could balance him. He crashed to the hard ground on his side. He was dead, he was *dead*, even worse, he was going to become one of *them*, and then he'd come after Sage, Marty, Julie and Constable Matthews . . .

A figure in green ran by. Rory Jablonowksi, the park security guard. A good guy who never hassled him, even if he knew Scott was skipping school to hang out at the park. Rory had always made it a point to stop and chat with him, and even though Scott didn't know him well enough to like him, he thought of him warmly. Rory was a lot like Marty.

And now he was probably going to die because he had *no* idea what he was running at. Scott scrambled to his feet, about to shout "Wait!" as loud as he could, but his throat closed up in fear. He could only stand and helplessly watch what happened next.

Rory slammed into the thing with a shoulder to its gut, hitting it with a fairly respectable football tackle. Hard enough Scott heard the security guard's grunt from where he stood. The thing didn't make a sound as they both crashed among the old amphitheater benches, legs thrashing and hands and fists flailing.

They rolled down to the old stage, where they landed with a *thump*. They fought and wrestled, until finally Rory somehow managed to roll on top, knees on the thing's chest, pinning it to the stage. The well-intentioned security guard must've finally realized how much danger he was in because when he looked up at Scott, fear twisted his face as he shouted, "Get out of here! Keys in the JEEP! Go! Get Constable . . . "

Rory's voice choked off in a gurgle as the thing's hand wriggled free and clasped onto his throat. Rory's face reddened immediately. He flailed and clawed at the thing's grip, to no avail.

Despite the security guard's command to run, Scott couldn't move. His legs had turned to quivering jelly. He could barely even stand, as he watched it all happen in what felt like agonizing slow motion.

The thing effortlessly lifted Rory up, and it slid out from under the security guard and to its feet. It held Rory high in the air, and cocked its head, regarding the kicking and flailing figure curiously with its bulging wet eyes.

With one fluid motion, the thing grabbed Rory's right thigh, raised him higher with both hands, then brought the security guard viciously down on its knee. Rory's back *snapped* with a wet-sounding crunch Scott could hear. The thing didn't stop, however. It kept thrusting down, *literally* folding Rory's twitching body in half.

Something white and spiny tore through the front of Rory's uniform, along with a spray of blood and also curling intestines which splattered onto the old wooden stage. *His spine*, Scott thought dully. *That's his spine*.

The thing grasped the end of Rory's spine, and with a mighty tug, yanked it free from the security guard's body. It tore out of Rory with the sound of a wet sack of meat splitting open. More gouts of blood and viscera splattered onto the weathered and slightly warped planks of the old stage.

It dropped the rubbery, spineless mess of Rory's body at its feet, where it landed in a strangely formless pile. It then turned its blank gaze upon Scott. The spine in its hand, dripping fluids onto the wood with an insistent pattering sound.

Its thick, oily, muscled tongue oozed out of its mouth and flicked the air as if tasting the scent of Scott's fear.

Scott's paralysis finally broke. He wanted to scream but he couldn't, only rasped soundlessly as he spun and stumbled toward Rory's JEEP, which was still running, the driver's side door hanging open. He knew how to drive; had done it plenty of times in one of the old trucks Jasper's brothers were always tinkering with, doing donuts in the field behind their old barn.

He didn't know if the thing was following him. He didn't take the time to look. He jumped into the JEEP, slammed the door shut, threw it into gear without hooking his seatbelt, and slammed on the gas. The JEEP sped away, Scott's heart hammering in his chest, guts twisting, his vision darkening slightly at the edges, and he thought for sure he was going to pass out, or puke and *then* pass out.

He did neither. He sped out of the park, turned left, and drove into town, the frantic thought in his mind to find Constable Matthews, and find her *now*.

72.

THE FIRST WATCHED the green car drive jerkily away, bearing the boy . . .

Scott

. . . away with it. It stood still for several seconds, gripped by a strange uncertainty and conflict. Since coming into being, The First had made more of its kind. Those, in turn, had made more. Their time was drawing near. The Great Feast. They would feed and make as many of themselves as possible until there was nothing left. It knew what it should do, now.

The boy . . .

Scott

. . . was out of reach. They usually moved quietly, carefully, in isolation or the darkness, to try and escape the notice of the Other, lest the Other burn them back into the darkness, which They did not want (though the Other had done this many times before over millennia). If they could feed their fill, they would enjoy a good sleep. A quiet sleep. One of contentment and peace, suffused in the glory of scorning the Other.

If, however, they were sent into the dark before they'd eaten their fill, their sleep would be uneasy. Full of groaning and misery. Because of this, the First knew what it had to do. It must drag away the tattered thing at its feet into the dark, feed, and make it over into an aspect of Sowhein.

But the First wanted to chase the boy, instead. This brought confusion, because chasing the boy among its people was not moving in the dark, or creeping silently. It was sure to make itself known, and yet the First wanted to do it anyway. In a sudden flash of emotion alien to its mind, the First realized that it . . . *knew* the boy. Since making the . . . *woman* with the blond hair into Sowhein's aspect, it had known this boy, who he was, and now it wanted to take him, feed on him, turn him, and make him into the aspect of Samhain.

Scott

my

The First cocked its head, listening. It heard something. A whisper. A fragment. Something left over from the body it now held. This wasn't uncommon. It had heard the whispers of the taken before, but always as echoes of former selves which no longer existed. When they came forth from the darkness and fed, nothing remained but those echoes. Whatever they consumed and made over into the aspect of Sowhein was nothing but a wisp of an afterthought.

Except . . .

Scott

my

The First reached down and grabbed the leg of the thing in green clothes. It turned and dragged the limp, jelly-like body off into the woods. It had already remained in the open too long. It must feed, and remake another into the aspect of Sowhein. It didn't know why it wanted the boy, but no matter. The time of the final feast was at hand. It would retreat and feed and make more of them.

During the final feast, It would find the boy, and take him. It wouldn't matter then if they were seen, because it would be the night of the final feast. They would spread and consume until nothing remained. Then they would retreat into the dark and sleep once more until they were called forth again.

73.

SCOTT. MY . . . *The final feast . . .*

". . . Julie?"

"Hmm?"

Julie turned from whatever she'd been staring at, (she couldn't remember), and met Marty's concerned gaze. For maybe the fifth or sixth time that day, (had it been longer?), she wasn't sure of her surroundings. She *thought* they were at her trailer, in the living room, where they'd been all . . .

day?

night?

afternoon?

. . . and she thought they were alone, but ever since last night at Scott's house . . .

my

Scott

. . . she'd struggled to keep her thoughts in order. At first, she figured it was the after-effect of last night's terror. When those *things* had somehow made her think Conroy, (poor, sweet, dead Conroy), was calling for help. She'd almost *died.* That would be more than enough to throw anyone out of sorts. It made sense she'd had a hard time sleeping. Suffering terrible nightmares all night of not only being chased by those things but also strange, disorienting dreams of *being* them. It was probably PTSD or something.

She'd also expect to feel groggy and tired all morning, given how little she'd slept last night. Even so, she found her lethargy alarming. All morning she'd drifted in and out of focus. Coming to after staring off in space as Marty said things she didn't really hear and couldn't remember. It was a good thing he'd spent the night, (on the futon again, and a vague disappointment flickered inside at that), because she never would've bothered to get up or eat, if he hadn't been there to make her breakfast.

She felt numb. Her skin tingled all over. She'd fumbled a steaming mug of coffee Marty handed to her and hadn't felt a thing when some of it splashed on her wrist. She'd only eaten at Marty's insistence; the food tasted bland and stale. Her forearm and the back of her neck—where she'd been splashed by those things' blood or guts or whatever—itched and burned, like she'd gotten into poison ivy or something. The skin on her forearm was red and starting to blister. Her neck felt the same.

Even worse?

She was hearing things. Voices. In her head. Lots of them. Muttering completely unintelligible words over and over. At first, it had been something of a background whisper. A soft, fuzzy sound she could easily explain away as her imagination. As the morning (day?) crept by, however, the voices rose to a humming buzz. As if her trailer was crowded with invisible, muttering people.

"Julie? Hey. That's the third time in the last half hour you've spaced out on me."

Julie blinked slowly. It was on the tip of her tongue to say, "No, you just said my name now" when she realized Marty was right. She'd been staring blankly at him this whole time. Seeing nothing, her thoughts buried deep inside . . .

them, she was with them and one with them

surging in one mass, one thought, one mind

She smiled weakly, tamping down the hysterical fear cresting inside as she scratched her forearm through her thin, long-sleeved shirt. She'd been scratching it and the back of her neck ever since last night. Sage had helped her to the shower at Scott's, and she'd washed the guts off, but for some reason, her forearm and the back of her neck kept burning and itching.

She said faintly, "Sorry. I'm tired. From last night."

A shadow passed over Marty's face. Julie felt sorry for saying that because she knew Marty felt guilty for going with Constable Matthews and leaving her and Sage alone with Scott. What happened wasn't his fault, of course. She wouldn't have wanted to be the reason why he stayed behind and let Constable Matthews explore Owen House alone. Even so, he was the kind of man . . .

like Conroy

. . . who would always feel responsible for things he couldn't control.

"I'm sorry," he said, tone heavy with regret, "I should've stayed with you guys last night. As it turned out, Owen House was empty. We didn't find anything, so I should've . . . "

Warm affection pulsed through her, momentarily piercing the weird fog which weighed down her mind, giving her a burst of clarity (though she couldn't stop itching her forearm). "You couldn't have known that," she insisted, "it was the smart thing to do. There was no way you could've let Constable Matthews go alone."

"Even so. *You* shouldn't have had to face that alone, last night."

She shook her head. "We managed. Thanks to Scott and Sage. *No* thanks to me. I was *worthless*."

He leaned closer to her on the futon where they sat, right arm behind her, not exactly around her shoulders and holding her, but close enough, so *close*. "No. Don't think that. We didn't know those things could get inside our heads like that. You've been under terrible stress, especially because of Conroy's death. Any one of us could've fallen victim to the same thing."

For a moment, Julie couldn't speak or think, but for different reasons. The empathy in Marty's voice cut straight inside. His expression of concern, his kind eyes finally set fire to the smoldering coals in her heart. Without thinking, she leaned into Marty, clasped the sides of his face with her hands, and pressed her lips to his, kissing him deeply. He didn't resist or pull away. This emboldened her, so she thrust her tongue into his mouth, met his tongue, and their kiss deepened, as they breathed each other in.

An intoxicating warmth she hadn't felt in a long time blossomed in her belly. It made her legs weak, made her lightheaded, almost giddy. She reached down, grabbed two fistfuls of his flannel shirt, and tried to pull him down on top of her on the futon.

Marty gently resisted, however. He reached out and braced himself against the futon, preventing her from pulling him down farther. They broke off their kiss with a gasp, and with such intensity, Julie had to blink several times to ward off a sudden rush of dizziness.

Sharp dismay pulsed through her, spiced with a touch of embarrassment. She'd let herself do what she'd wanted to do since first meeting Marty, but she also struggled with feelings of rejection, even though she knew Marty was being smart and showing some common sense. Even so, she couldn't help blurting out, "What is it? Did I . . . wasn't that what you wanted..?" Her face grew hot. "Omigod. I misread things, didn't I? You don't feel the same."

He smiled gently and cupped the side of her face, caressing her cheek softly with his thumb. "I do, Julie. It's just . . . I don't want to take advantage. You're tired, stressed out, emotional . . . and honestly? So am I. Plus . . . " he shrugged. "You know the credo. Especially when you're not much more than a year sober."

"I know," she whispered, her voice little more than a rasp. "I do. You're right. But I'm *not* imagining it, right? You feel the same. About me. About us."

His smile spread. "I do," he said softly. "I'm not sure how to proceed. Or if we even *should* proceed, given everything going on right now, and our backgrounds. But I *do* feel the same."

Julie felt herself smiling slowly. She wondered if she looked like a love-struck teenager, especially since she certainly felt like one. "Can we try? When this is over, can we at least try? If we're careful?"

Marty dropped his hand from her face, took her hands into his, and squeezed them gently. "Yes. We need to move slowly, is all."

She felt it rising inside her. A childish, girlish excitement at Marty returning her feelings, and all that could mean for their future. She felt short of breath, her heart had sped up, and she felt dizzy with what she assumed was supposed to be emotion.

But she must've been making a weird face, or staring or something because Marty's expression quickly shifted from happy to concerned. "Julie? Julie, are you okay? It's happening again. You're drifting."

Except she wasn't, this time. She saw him. His pinched, tense expression and she could hear his voice, tight with worry. She could feel him squeezing her hands tighter, she was still *there*, still in her body . . .

And yet she *wasn't*.

Julie opened her mouth to speak, but her throat constricted and she couldn't force any words out as she felt her mind shatter into a million pieces. She was in dozens of places at once. She saw through many eyes and felt a babble of voices and thoughts mixing into a cacophonous song in her mind. She wasn't just there with Marty in her trailer, she was all over Pleasant Brook. Waiting for the final feast in which they'd feed and feed until nothing remained, and then return to the dark to sleep until they were called forth again . . .

The burning on her forearm spread up her arm to her shoulder, down her wrist to the end of her fingertips, until her whole arm was numb and yet burning at the same time as the voices pounded in her head.

"Julie! Talk to me! What's wrong?"

The last thing she felt before the shakes came and plunged her into darkness was Marty's hands—cool, dry, comforting somehow, reassuring in their strength—gripping both sides of her head. But the sensation faded as a wave of other sensations—touches, thoughts, words, feelings, and an overwhelming buzz of sensory data from one big pulsing mind—washed over her.

Her head snapped back, hard. Her jaw clenched as she ground her teeth, and her throat closed completely. An electric jolt ran through her. The last thing she felt before the darkness was her body jerking as a mad puppeteer yanked her strings with insane abandon.

74.

GRACE WAS ONLY twenty minutes into her drive around town, looking for Scott when her phone rang. She pulled over to the side of the road, grabbed her phone off the dash, and saw SCOTT CARTER flashing on the screen. When she answered, she was greeted with the teenager's rushed, jumbling voice. He sounded breathless, panicked . . . and truly frightened for the first time. Almost terrified, even.

"Slow down, Scott," she said evenly, in an effort to put the frantic boy at ease, "start over. You were at Martinkovic Park, and something happened to Rory Jablonowski."

Scott paused. Took a deep breath, and began again. Grace listened, even though she already knew—deep in her heart—the kind of story Scott was about to tell. This was only confirmed as the kid stumbled his way through his story, coming to the end in a jumbling rush of breathless words.

"Okay," she said gently. "Where are you now?"

Scott swallowed. "*At the corner of Faber and Kinner Street.*"

He was on the other side of town, near the school. Only about a fifteen-minute drive. "Okay. I assume you're pulled over?"

"*Yeah.*"

"Great. Stay there. Lock the doors, keep the JEEP running, and don't get out until I'm there. Any of those things get close, put the pedal to the floor, get the hell out of there, and head back to my office. Otherwise, I'm on the way. Hang tight, kid."

"*O-okay.*"

Grace hung up. Put her JEEP into gear, and executed a sharp U-turn in the middle of an otherwise empty Jarvis Street. She tried to ignore the sensation of driving through a ghost town as she passed shuttered and silent homes and failed miserably.

75.

IT HAD BEEN a miracle Scott hadn't managed to wreck Rory's JEEP before finally deciding to pull over, park, and call Constable Matthews. The fear pounding through him had made it hard to think, hard not to slam the gas pedal all the way to the floor. It had been difficult focusing and paying attention to traffic lights and stop signs. Luckily, there weren't any cars out on the road. A fact which would've bothered him greatly if he'd given himself time to think about it.

Sitting in the idling JEEP of the now-dead and mutilated Rory Jablonowski, the fear which had pounded through him during his terrified flight from Martinkovic Park faded. He relaxed slightly, though a nervous energy still buzzed along his veins, humming with frantic questions without answers.

How did that thing read my mind?

Was it . . . looking for me? Like Jasper had?

How did it know I'd be there?

Even worse, Scott couldn't keep the horrible images of Rory's death out of his mind. Couldn't stop seeing the thing snapping Rory in half over its knee like the security guard was a dry twig. So preoccupied was he by these thoughts, he didn't notice the person approaching the JEEP until they knocked on the window. He jumped when he heard the rapping against the glass, and turned with wide eyes.

It was Constable Matthews. Scott stared at her. Mouth opening and closing, but making no sound. His throat felt tight and closed up, and he felt lightheaded. For a moment he couldn't breathe, and was sure he was going to faint, right then and there.

"It's okay," Constable Matthews reassured him. "Breathe."

Scott nodded. Took in several deep and hasty gulps of air. Swallowed, and when his throat finally loosened, pressed the window button and rolled it down. He managed, "I . . . I think it was after me. *Looking* for me, like Jasper was. I don't know how or why, but . . . "

He swallowed again and then finished in a steadier voice. "I think it was looking for *me*."

A shadow flickered across Constable Matthew's face, making her look even more troubled. "Why do you say that?"

In a halting voice, Scott told her what he hadn't over the phone. About how the thing had tried to look and act like his father, or at least what Scott had always imagined his father looked like. "I know it sounds stupid," he whispered, "but when I'm confused about stuff and trying to figure them out, I go to the old stage at the park and think about what Dad might look like. What kind of man he was or is. Why he left, why he never came back."

Constable Matthews nodded, eyes sympathetic. Scott continued. "It was like . . . it *knew* that. Pulled it from my mind and made me see what I thought Dad might look like. Like the thing did last night with Julie. If Rory hadn't . . . "

He swallowed, throat tight with emotion. He looked down, into his hands, which twisted fretfully in his lap.

"There wasn't anything you could've done, Scott," Constable Matthews whispered. "If Rory hadn't come along . . . you'd be gone. You'd be one of those things."

"And then I'd probably come after you," Scott added in a rasping voice.

"Very likely."

"I called Mom before I called you. On her phone, and The Whole's number. She didn't answer. She *always* answers, and I think . . . I think . . . "

"*Fuck.*"

Scott had tried to tell himself when Mom didn't answer either phone that she was too busy to pick up, (and even then, deep down, he knew that was a lie, especially with the way his mother had been complaining how dead the diner had been the last two weeks), but the almost wrathful despair in Constable Matthew's curse spoke a truth he couldn't deny. "She's dead. Isn't she?"

Constable Matthews sighed. "We don't know that."

"She is. I knew it. Didn't want to admit it."

"Goddammit. We should've told her. Should've tried, even if she didn't believe us . . . " Matthews shook her head. "Scott . . . I'm so sorry."

"What . . . " Scott sniffed, fighting to hold back tears which made him feel like a coward, as he looked up to meet Constable Matthew's gaze. "What are we gonna do?"

Constable Matthews shook her head, looking far more uncertain than Scott liked. "Sage is at the library. They were going to try and do some more research. Once there I'll call Marty and see how Julie's doing . . . "

Constable Matthews stopped as her smartphone rang. She held her finger up, pulled it out of her pocket, and glanced at the number. "Speaking of," she said, then answered, "What's up?"

Her eyes widened. "Okay. We'll be right over. Make her comfortable, get her some water, watch her breathing. Some seizures pass without any ill effects. Others don't so keep a close eye on her. Any idea what caused it?"

Constable Matthews fell silent as she listened (to Marty, Scott assumed). "All over her arm and the back of her neck? Scars. That are growing? And they feel like rubber?"

A shaft of white-hot fear slashed through Scott's heart. He blurted out, "Last night! When the one thing jumped on her back and its face started melting, it dripped on her neck. And she cut that other thing's fingers off. Its blood or whatever splashed all over Julie's arm. She screamed like she'd been burned, or something. Like it was acid. Sage got her into the shower and washed it off, but maybe . . . "

Matthew's lips pressed into a thin line as she nodded Scott out of the JEEP. "Okay, Marty. We're on our way."

76.

A **SOBERING FACT** of life: it's far easier than anyone realizes to develop a case of existential tunnel vision so myopic that one can only see—indeed, one only *chooses* to see—things directly in front of them. Anything and everything else is either blithely dismissed as inconsequential and irrelevant, or outright ignored. Thus, when the wolf is at the town gates, so long as it is careful and selectively picks off the weakest of the herd first, the ones no one will miss until it's too late, its threat is diminished and disregarded until it comes to the front door, because, of course: bad things only happen *elsewhere*, to *other* people. Not to us, in our hometown.

In this fashion, the people of Pleasant Brook—with the exception of Julie, Scott, Marty, Sage, and Constable Matthews—ignored the wolf crouched at their door. They went about their business and kept to their own as they always had because they were a quiet people who minded their business and kept out of their neighbor's affairs (even while gossiping about them over text, social media, email, or good old-fashioned telephone).

It was also safe to say that even though an official quarantine order had yet to be issued in Warren County, the remote schooling mandate and increased emphasis on social distancing had largely put the town into an even deeper state of retreat. Pleasant Brook's few shops remained open, as well as its two diners and two churches, but as the weeks passed—even before the horror came to Pleasant Brook—fewer and fewer people dotted the town's sidewalks as more and more of them sequestered themselves at home. Especially those who chose to work remotely.

Pleasant Brook's virtual schooling was a limping, halfhearted affair. Attendance had been spotty from the start. When it dropped off sharply in the week leading up to Halloween, the matter was discussed vaguely in likewise sparsely-attended virtual faculty meetings, though nothing conclusive or constructive was determined. Especially considering the growing number of teachers who were also not showing up for their own virtual classes.

Principal Williams of Pleasant Brook High knew the matter should be addressed, and he resolved to do so soon. Just because students were skipping virtual classes didn't mean teachers could do likewise. Oddly enough, however, none of the parents had complained about teachers not showing up for classes. He decided—all things considered in such trying times—that he'd let the matter lie and maybe address it *after* Halloween. Especially if the COVID infection rates had improved by then, and the county gave some indication of a return to in-person schooling.

The Whole in the Wall had remained in operation the entire time, but as Tiffany Carter could attest to, (if she were still human), the booths and tables had become more and more vacant as the days passed. Gone were the old-timers who'd eaten breakfast at the same table or booth for the past twenty years. Gone also were the teens skipping school to grab something better to eat than school lunches, or looking for a quick bite after late-night study sessions or sports practices (both of which had been canceled for the duration). No one was coming in Friday night for pizza after the football game, (because those had been canceled also), or coming in for Sunday brunch after church, as most of both the congregations had only attended church virtually since the remote schooling mandate.

This apathetic negligence spread throughout Pleasant Brook. Along the town's periphery, like a silent but aggressive tumor methodically eating away at cells. Trimming around the edges, biding its time.

More students and teachers stopped attending virtual classes. More calls went unanswered. More events—like Mary Ann Columbia's Book Love—were canceled with no reason, or attendants simply no longer showed up to a virtual format no one had liked, anyway.

Scott had been Jasper's only friend. It was safe to say, no one else had liked the Rileys. When they "skipped town," no one noticed, or cared, past those directly involved. Being from out of town, Rory Jablonowksi only had three or four local friends, and he hadn't talked to them much lately, not since the end of September. His landlord never interacted with him and would've only noticed him missing when the rent came due at the end of the month. By then, his landlord and all the other tenants would be beyond caring about such things.

Essential workers employed out of town stopped coming to work and wouldn't answer their phones. Their managers dully complained about people who didn't want to work and only wanted to collect government COVID assistance, and moved on to other concerns. And on, and on.

Until Halloween night, and the final feast.

Gerhart Trailer Park

77.

"**. . . THAT'S WHEN SHE** started shaking, jerking back and forth," Marty said quietly, casting a glance over his shoulder at Julie, sleeping on the futon, covered in an old knit afghan. "I was afraid she was going to choke on her tongue or something, the way she kept gagging and gnashing her teeth . . . "

Marty trailed off, staring at Julie. Grace gave him some silence and space, sensing how much the young woman had come to mean to him. After a few more minutes, Marty made a visible effort to compose himself and looked back to Grace. "After about ten minutes she stopped like someone flipped off a switch. I made sure she was breathing, checked her heartbeat and pulse as best I could. When I was sure she wasn't going to start convulsing again, I laid her back on the futon and got her settled."

Grace nodded, arms folded across her chest. She could see how worried he was despite his attempted stone face, so she spoke as gently as possible. "You said she kept repeating something over and over before she went to sleep."

Marty glanced back at Julie and nodded. "Two things. 'They're coming tonight' and 'the feast is near.'"

"Any idea what that means?"

"Tonight," they heard behind them, from the trailer's doorway. "They're coming for us tonight. All of us. Whoever's left in town."

Grace turned and looked at Scott, who'd apparently disregarded her request to stay in the JEEP. "Thought I asked you to stay in the car."

Scott shrugged, face blank, eyes hauntingly empty. "You did," he said simply, and nothing more.

Grace felt a pang of sympathy for the kid, washing away any irritation she might've felt. The blank expression on his face, the deadness in his eyes . . . it twisted her guts in a way few things did. Instead of saying anything more about the car, she asked, "What do you mean? They're coming for us all, tonight?"

Scott shrugged. "I think she's probably connected to them, now."

Grace opened her mouth—to say what, she didn't know—but she stopped when Marty turned and gave Scott an unreadable look and said, "Because of the blood or whatever that shit was, on her neck and arm."

Grace frowned and looked back and forth between them. "I think I understand but explain anyway."

Marty nodded at Scott, and said without a trace of sarcasm, "This is Scott's area of expertise, I believe."

When Scott didn't answer right away—actually looked scared, of all things—Grace laid a hand on his shoulder and squeezed firmly, yet gently. "He's right, Scott. You know more about this than the rest of us. Hell, *you* were the one who looked this stuff up on the internet, not us."

Scott still looked doubtful. Grace squeezed his shoulder again, and said, "Go on. We'll listen. We'll believe."

Scott nodded. Took a breath, and said, "I think she's connected with them now. Because its blood or whatever probably seeped through her skin before Sage could get her in the shower. Happens in lots of horror stories and movies, especially ones about vampires. A person gets bit or infected, but maybe doesn't turn all the way. At least, not immediately. They become connected to the head vampire or other vampires, or werewolves, or even zombies." Scott shrugged and said, "Like, uh, in John Carpenter's *Vampires*. Anyway, last night she said that stuff burned her."

Scott looked at Marty. "And you said she's got two scars that are spreading, and they look like burnt rubber. Maybe whatever we couldn't clean off her . . . "

" . . . got into her." Marty met Grace's gaze, eyes dark with worry. "And now she's connected to them. Or, even worse . . . "

" . . . she's slowly turning into one of them," Scott finished softly. "Can you show us the scars?"

Marty nodded, turned, and approached Julie, who was still sleeping on the futon. Grace followed, with Scott behind her. Not only did she feel sad the kid had to see this, but also sad *he* was the one who *asked* to see it.

Marty knelt quietly next to the futon, reached carefully across the fitfully sleeping Julie, and tenderly pulled her right arm free from the blankets covering her. He laid it across her hitching chest. She wore a loose, light hoody, and he gently rolled up the sleeve on her right arm to her elbow.

Grace didn't know what she'd expected to see, but whatever it was hadn't prepared her for the reality. Her breath whispered between her teeth as she hissed, "*Shit*," and her stomach rolled uneasily. Behind her, Scott muttered, "Holy fuck."

Julie's forearm had been bandaged. The wrappings looked fresh, indicating Marty had applied them recently. But the scarring the bandage might've once covered had spread all the way down to her hand, and up past her elbow, beneath the rolled-up sleeve, and possibly all the way to her shoulder, maybe even to connect with the scarring Marty said was on the back of her neck.

The skin had blackened and split. It bubbled up in places, looked melted in others. It also looked hard, like tire rubber. The cracks weren't weeping fluids, but Grace got the impression that if the rubbery skin was prodded too much it would, and the fluids would be a greenish-black ichor.

Marty glanced up at her. The look of helplessness in his eyes twisted Grace's heart. "It's gotten worse since I last checked," he said, voice rasping and distraught. "Especially the one on her neck. I'm not going to show you that one—don't want to disturb her—but it's spreading down her back."

"It doesn't look much like those things, though," Grace said, fighting to keep her tone neutral. "At least . . . not yet." She turned and looked at Scott. "You think she might be turning into one of them?"

Scott shrugged limply. Grace felt another pang for the boy, and also a wave of guilt. It felt shameful of them to be putting so much on a kid's shoulders. She and Marty were adults, for fuck's sake. He shouldn't have to carry this.

"I dunno," he said softly. "The info I found didn't say anything about how these things take people. And we've never seen any of them changing. Only after. Plus, maybe . . . "

"What?" Grace kept her tone gentle as she prodded him. "Maybe what?"

Scott took a deep breath, his features shifting, and Grace could almost *see* him fighting to get his fear under control. He breathed again, his face smoothed out, and he looked at Grace with an empty expression. "That thing at the park. It killed Rory. Broke his back, then . . . then pulled out his fucking *spine*. Maybe they usually kill you first before they change you. Maybe that's why it's not working on Julie, or working slower. She's still alive."

Grace looked back at Julie, who twitched in her sleep. Eyes moving rapidly under closed lids, face grimacing slightly in unconscious pain. "Working slower. Leaving her connected to them, but also . . . still herself."

"For now," Scott whispered.

Marty looked at her, expression curiously blank now, also. "You're thinking if we wake her up, she can connect with them. Tell us where they are, and what they're doing. Aren't you?"

It was slight—barely there, and then gone—but Grace heard it in Marty's voice, all the same. Accusation, and fear.

"I don't want to. Hell, no. But this is . . . things are . . . "

She swallowed and forged on. "Before I picked up Scott, I stopped at a bunch of places. Spent the whole morning knocking on doors. Not a single person answered. After three hours. I didn't check every house, but still."

"I called my mom," Scott whispered, looking at the floor. "She didn't answer. She always answers."

Though it was a woefully inadequate gesture, Grace reached out and squeezed Scott's shoulder again. He didn't look; he kept staring at the floor. She looked back to Marty, her chest full of emotion. "I don't want to wake her up. I don't. But I think . . . I think we may be . . . "

"The only ones left," Marty finished for her. "Or, at the least, the only ones left who can do anything to stop this."

"Why? Why don't we leave? Get the hell out of her, and go someplace safe?"

Grace looked back to Scott. He'd raised his head, eyes wide and glittering, jaw set, teeth clenched. She noticed his hands fisted at his sides, knuckles white, fingernails digging into his palm. "Why do we have to do anything? Let's get the fuck out of here."

Grace took in a deep breath. Approached Scott and took his shoulders into her hands. "We can't, Scott. Who knows what happens once they wipe out the town. Do they go away? Or do they spread? To Smyrna, and then further."

She knelt on one knee, bringing her to his eye level. Something she'd tried to avoid doing because she always felt it was condescending to treat kids that way. In this case, however, she felt it was necessary. "We can't save this town. You're right about that. Pleasant Brook is going to be another one of those weird stories about small towns disappearing overnight. But we gotta try and find where these things are. Stop them, at the source."

She squeezed his shoulders and forced a smile. "I haven't seen as many horror movies as you, but this is a big part of them, right? How the last people alive fight to make sure the evil doesn't spread."

Scott's left eye twitched as he stared at Grace. His gaze grew cold and remote as he said flatly, "Sure. Except those people don't usually make it out alive."

"Be that as it may. It's still a job that needs to be done. Besides," she nodded over her shoulder at Marty, "Marty's sure not leaving. And we're not leaving him."

Scott stared at her for a heartbeat, then nodded stiffly. Grace stood and looked at Marty. "Let's do it."

Marty nodded. Approached Julie, knelt next to her head, gently touched the side of her face, and called her name.

78.

JULIE SWAM IN a sea of buzzing voices and free-floating, abstract desires and hunger she'd no name for. She felt distinctly herself and part of something much larger all at once, but when she tried to think about it, tried to exert her thoughts and focus on what was happening to *her* as an individual being, her thoughts melted and softened, stretching out like taffy as her mind was swept away along a black river which had no end.

She felt herself, and she felt Them. She was alone; she was All. She felt scared, isolated but also alive and hungry, filled with a great need to consume as much as she possibly could.

Julie

Her sense of self was being split, fragmented into dozens of microscopic pieces, yet she was one, herself, Julie. She was Julie, and she was in her trailer, lying on the futon, yet she was More. She was bigger, larger, all-encompassing, and everywhere. She wasn't quite infinite—not like the hated Other—but she (they) wanted to be. They hated the Other and wanted to be everlasting like it. That's what they craved. To be infinite. To be everyone. To be everywhere, all people, all at once, one mind and many parts.

Julie

It's Marty

Can you hear me

Julie blinked and tried to open her eyes, but a dagger of blinding pain lanced her temples and drew a sharp gasp from her, which clenched her heart and made it skip, made her lungs spasm with fear. For the brief second she opened her eyes, it felt like she was looking through a fractal diamond, a kaleidoscope, her vision split into infinite strands of being. It felt like she was looking through hundreds of eyes all seeing different things, and the pain was overwhelming, made her feel sick. She thought if she opened her eyes again, she might puke.

She was sick.

That was it.

She was sick and needed to sleep. The buzzing voices crooned their agreement. Not in human words she could understand, but in feelings, sensations, impressions, and images. If she kept her eyes closed, gave up, and went back to sleep, she'd slowly slip away into the All and never be lonely or hurt ever again. All she had to do was let go and . . .

"Sleep," she muttered thickly, tongue feeling twice its size and fuzzy, too, her mouth dry and sticky. "Needsleep."

Julie

I know you want to sleep, and I want to let you. I do. But I've got to ask you a few questions. They're important. After, I'll let you sleep. Promise.

She distantly felt her hands, (but they didn't feel like hers; they felt numb, distant, unattached), reach up and rub her face. "Dontwanna," she whispered through someone else's mouth in someone else's voice, "wannasleep."

I know. After, you can. But we need you to do this. It's important. I need you . . . need you to find them. Can you do that for me? Find them, and tell us where they are.

Julie felt herself frown. She wanted to open her eyes and tell Marty, (she thought it was Marty talking; it sounded like him, though muted as if he was speaking from a great distance), how much she cared for him (loved him?) but she couldn't, for some reason. A great, oppressive weight held her down, pressing her mind under a heavy fog. Reminded her of the time (as a kid) when she'd caught mono and laid in bed sick for over two weeks, barely moving, always sleeping. She felt like that now, except . . .

voices

Fuzzy voices muttering incoherently in her head. So many of them, overlapping and mixing with each other. It sounded like she was surrounded by a great cloud of hissing, humming locusts, because they weren't *human* voices. The sounds she heard were jarring and insectile. They didn't express thoughts or human emotions, they were driven rather by hunger, need, and desire. The voices wanted to consume and procreate without end, nothing more.

She didn't want to think about them. When she did, images flitted through her sleeping mind of melting faces and bubbling flesh. One amorphous mass, not individuals, but a seething, roiling wave of not-flesh which wanted to roll over the world eating everything in its path until the Other finally took notice and forced it back into the darkness to sleep once more. She couldn't think of them. She didn't *want* to think of them. She didn't want to *know* where they were . . .

Julie, we have to know. We have to find them so we can somehow kill them. If we don't . . . we're done for.

Please.

She felt cool hands cup her face. Marty. Dear, sweet Marty. A black despair gripped her, almost forced her further under, because, with a dim sense of futility, she realized how foolish they'd been. They should've forgotten all that AA nonsense about no romantic relationships. They should've grabbed hold of each other and enjoyed what little time they'd had, because she felt—deep down inside—that their time was running out. If she *did* dive deep into those buzzing voices and that humming-locust song . . .

"Iwontcomeback. Wontmakeitback. Swallowedwhole."

She didn't hear anything for several minutes which felt like hours and years. Finally, she heard a soft, lovely whisper full of sadness at the edge of her thoughts, *I'm sorry, Julie. More than you can know. But we don't know what else to do, don't know how to make you better, and . . .*

There's no other way.

She nodded, (at least, she thought she did, it felt like it), and said in a rush, "Okayloveyoubye" and she dove into the humming current of voices which was flowing through her like a torrent of madness and chaos. She let it bear her along, and she thought *about* them, thought about where they might be, where they were nesting, (because Scott was right, that's what it was, nesting), as the buzzing voices rose to a fever pitch in her mind.

To anchor against the discordant inhuman voices filling her, she also thought about Marty and what they could've been, clung to the image of his face, in hopes she could hold onto herself amid the overwhelming cacophony of inhumanity long enough to help the only friends she'd ever had, with the exception of Conroy Ortega, of course.

Poor Conroy.

Poor Scott. Poor Sage, Marty, and

Constable—Grace—Matthews.

Poor Julie.

As the turgid river of tumbling and mingling thoughts bore her along, she clung tightly to those five names and their faces, even as the voices washed more and more of her away. As the voices flowed over her and through her, as her mind dissolved under their corrosive weight, (except the part of her mind holding on to the names of her friends), their history passed through her in flickering images and thought patterns. *Their* memories of everywhere they'd been and everyone they'd consumed. If Julie were awake and conscious and able to describe the feeling, she'd say it felt like a computer downloading software into her brain. A new operating system which would reformat the old and replace it with a brand-new program. She was inheriting its race memory, she somehow knew, helpless to stop it.

The images, memories, and sensations flowed through her, out of order and context. Ancient societies—ones in deserts, on mountain plains, in jungles and caves, even ice-locked lands—rose and fell in her mind, consumed by Them. Always it was the same. Someone called Them out of the darkness from their sleep. They consumed everything to make more of its kind, in a vain attempt to become infinite, like the Other it hated with every fiber of its being . . .

the Other

God

Yahweh. Elohim. Yeusha.

Is that . . . God?

. . . but soon enough the Other (God?) would find a way to hurtle them back into the darkness, wailing, screaming, gnashing their teeth. They would fall asleep in the darkness and wait until someone somewhere called them forth once more to consume, spread, but inevitably fall at the hands of the Other.

Towns.

Villages.

Islands. Kingdoms. Images of cultures and time periods which didn't run in sequential order. Small towns with horse and buggies, early cars, then primitive villages with no electricity, then men and women in caves, Native Americans in tepees, people living in log cabins, or in jungles . . .

A word, carved into a tree, flashed in the darkness, there and gone again, a word she actually remembered in some deep part of her: CROATOAN. The word swam away in the surging river of peoples, cultures, and places; most alien and strange to her, some of the *people* not even human, with bodies and limbs which looked too long, uneven, reptilian, even. It didn't matter, they all fell before Them, as They moved through time and space, and consumed everything They encountered, landscapes and plateaus beneath skies filled with black stars against an even blacker sky, and an entire CIVILIZATION carved from ice, until . . .

Pleasant Brook. Houses she recognized, the corn maze, Martinkovic Park, The Tipper Inn, The Whole in the Wall, The Cougar's Den, farther and farther back, until . . .

"Owen House. Started at Owen House. Empty now. They moved. Now . . . "

A run-down farm, the cemetery and its open graves and *eating corpses;* they were eating the dead and that's why eventually all towns and villages ended up empty because they ate the dead until there wasn't anything left . . .

CROATOAN.

Where are they now, Julie? We checked Owen House; it's empty. So is the cemetery and the Riley farm. Where did they move to? Are they all in one place?

"Yes," she felt herself whisper as she swam deeper and deeper into the river of twisting and melting faces and running flesh, "yes, resting, they have to rest . . . "

Where do they rest, Julie? Where is it? A pause, and then, *Is . . . is anyone left besides us?*

The answer came to her in a rush along the river of buzzing thoughts and alien mutterings, "A few. Not many. Most are part of the All, now."

Oh God. This she heard from farther away than the other voice. *Oh, shit. That can't be.*

And even further away, another voice, a smaller voice. *What about my mom?*

Hold on, the closer voice (Marty) said, *hold on*. Then, the closer voice said, chasing her as she sank even further into the twisting river of melting flesh, *Where are they, Julie? Where are they nesting? When do they rest?*

As she sank and more of her bubbled away and dissolved into a river which erased her thoughts like acid, she saw the side streets of Pleasant Brook, the library where . . . *Sage* . . . worked, saw more side streets, Main Street, until . . .

The river slowed to a stop.

She plunged down to its darkest depths, into the blackness at the bottom, where the currents of thoughts, alien desires, and voices met and nested, where they became one.

"The school," she whispered, "the school, down in the dark where no light reaches, and at the Time of the Other. That's when they rest . . . "

Julie slipped all the way into the darkness, finally losing hold of her friends' faces and names as her last spark flickered and dissolved as if it had never been.

79.

"THE SCHOOL," Julie whispered, face suddenly growing still, expressionless, almost as if it were made of plastic. "The school, down in the dark where no light reaches, and at the Time of the Other. That's when they rest . . . "

Her chest heaved once, with one last breath. Fell still, and Julie lay silent. Looking almost as if she was sinking into the futon. Her mouth hung open in a lopsided O, and her eyes stared blankly at the ceiling.

An oppressive silence filled the trailer. It fell on them, draped over their shoulders like a heavy shroud.

"Fuck," Grace whispered. "Is she . . . "

Marty nodded silently, lips pressed together tightly. He reached a remarkably steady hand to her face, to close her eyes . . .

He gurgled as Julie's right hand snapped out and struck with the speed of a cobra, latching onto his larynx and Adam's Apple. She squeezed, her fingers flexing and digging into his flesh like talons.

"Shit, shit! No!"

Grace's Glock was out of her holster instantly, the blocky firearm a blur in her hands as she drew down and aimed at Julie's . . . no, the *thing's* face . . .

The hand squeezed harder.

Marty's face turned a deep purple as his eyes bulged from their sockets. His hands flopped limply at his sides, twitching uselessly at the end of his arms. Something cracked deep in his neck.

Grace screamed and pulled the trigger.

Julie's face exploded into a geyser of blood, flesh, bits of bone, and spurting greenish-black fluid. A second before—maybe even a millisecond—her fingers clenched with inhuman strength and tore out Marty's Adam's Apple and trachea. Deep scarlet blood fountained from the gaping hole in Marty's throat. He slumped sideways to the floor, bleeding thick clots of blood onto the thin carpet.

Grace couldn't look. She *couldn't*, she kept screaming louder, hammering shot after shot into the thing's face. Each blast shredded its head to a pulp. Slammed it back into the futon, but after each shot, the flesh on its face kept surging, melting, reforming, and somehow the fucking thing was still moving!

It flattened itself against the futon. One of Grace's shots went too high and shattered the trailer's cheap wooden wall paneling. Before she could readjust her aim, the thing's body flexed, rippled, and leaped off the futon after her.

***

Scott burst forward without even realizing he was moving. His legs flexed and propelled him forward, operating independently of his mind, which was still frozen over with the image of Julie . . .

not Julie anymore

. . . tearing out Marty's throat. This vision burned itself into Scott's brain, like a video on loop, so he barely even understood what was happening when his shoulder slammed into Constable Grace's side and he wrapped his arms around her waist and yanked her out of the thing's path.

When they hit the trailer's floor—mercifully several feet from Marty's body, which was still pumping blood into the carpet—Scott blinked hazily, confused and groggy. Grace pushed him off her and to the side with an inarticulate shout. She once again brought her Glock to bear on the thing as it hit the ground where she'd been standing and soundlessly bounded at them.

Grace's gun thundered as she planted three consecutive shots center-mass in the thing's belly. The shots knocked its leap off course. It sprawled sideways, landing unceremoniously on Marty's corpse. It stood to launch another attack, but instead slipped and stumbled in the widening pool of Marty's blood.

Several crucial seconds passed.

Grace rose to her knee and fired again.

The shot hit the thing in the face, (a face which had already started reforming), turning it into a grotesquely blooming flower of splattered gore. The force of the shot slammed it back against the wall so hard it shook the trailer.

Grace proceeded to empty her Glock into it. Shot after shot, straight into its face. It twitched, jerked, and convulsed as the repeated impacts turned its face and head into nothing more than a stump of splattered meat and shattered bone oozing greenish-black slime.

After what felt like an eternity, the Glock clicked empty. Grace must've been waiting for it, however. Must've known it was coming. She simply dropped the Glock to the floor, where it landed with a sodden *thump* on blood-soaked carpet. She drew the stake from her belt—a stake Scott was just noticing now—and leaped at the thing twitching in seizure on the futon, stake raised high above her head as she howled.

She plunged the stake down at the thing's breast, slammed it *home*, with what looked like all her weight. It plunged deep, and after giving it one last hard shove, Grace backpedaled away, wiping her hands frantically on her pants . . .

One foot caught on Marty's ruined neck.

The other slipped in his blood. She toppled backward—ass over tea kettle, as Scott's long-gone grandmother would've said—and landed with a hard *thump*. This finally broke Scott's paralysis—the thought of Grace being next, of leaving him all alone—and he found himself scrambling forward, shouting "Get up! Get up!" as he frantically grabbed her shoulder and one bicep and tried to tug her upright. She didn't respond, staring at the thing thrashing on the futon, and when Scott looked up at what the constable was staring at, all he could do was stare, too.

The constable must've lodged the stake true because the thing was thrashing in eerie silence on the futon, melted lump of a head whipping back and forth, hands curled uselessly, fingers clenched into rigid claws. It kicked and flailed, its heels drumming the futon in staccato rhythms.

A rippling wave passed through it. The thing arched its back and went rigid as if flooded with a pulse of electricity. It bucked once and then fell still, arms falling limp at its side, heels giving up their rhythm, head coming to a rest, with what passed for its face staring at the ceiling.

As with Jasper—what *had* been Jasper—smoke wafted upward from it, as a sibilant hissing rose from the body. A terrible odor—the sickening-sweet smell of burning flesh mingled with the oddly chemical smell of burnt rubber—filled the air. And, like Jasper, the thing began to sag into itself as it melted away. Flesh or rubber or *something* sloughed off its head and hands, its ruin of a face slowly caving in. It took mere minutes for what had once been Julie, then one of those things, to melt into a sizzling, smoking, indefinable lump of matter inside blood and gore-soaked clothes.

The chest deflated more, sagging in on itself, loosening the stake. It slipped free and thumped onto the blood-soaked, thin carpet.

80.

TWENTY MINUTES LATER, Pleasant Brook Constable Grace Matthews and Scott Carter rode numbly in the constable's JEEP as they drove away from Gerhart Trailer Park and Julie Lomax's trailer, which was engulfed in flames from the fire Constable Matthews set. Flames lit by a lighter to the jugs of gasoline Grace had been planning to use on Owen House the night before.

It was windy, the flames roared high in seconds, and Scott had remarked numbly that it was likely the other trailers would catch fire, too. That didn't matter, however. They'd checked all the trailers first. They were empty, and of course, Sage was at the library. Grace lit the gasoline-soaked interior of Julie's trailer, tossed a match, left the trailer, and walked away without looking back.

Matthews drove silently, staring out the front window. Scott stared sightlessly through the passenger side window at nothing in particular.

As Julie's burning trailer receded in the JEEP's rearview, Scott finally asked quietly, "What now?"

Grace shook her head as she drove, hands tightening on the wheel. She opened her mouth, closed it, and shook her head, the only answer she could give at the moment, as she left Julie Lomax and Marty Crenshaw behind forever, and headed back into town.

Or what was left of it.

81.

THEY SPENT THE next hour driving Pleasant Brook's streets. Up and down Main Street. Down South Street and back. Around the block from Main to South to Henry Street. Back to Main. Grace stopped at random houses and knocked on their doors and rang their doorbells. Of the thirty or so homes they visited, no one answered. No signs of life detected. Not even a twitching window shade.

A surreal sense of dislocation and disorientation descended on Grace as she went from home to home. As she knocked on one unresponsive door after another, she was plagued by the fantastic notion these homes had been empty for *months*, rather than days.

She drove numbly away from the last house to check on stores, the churches, and The Whole in the Wall and The Tipper Inn, wanting to believe folks had withdrawn so deeply that they hadn't heard her knocking on their doors or ringing their doorbells. A good number of the doors had been unlocked, however, and many of them slightly ajar. Out of those doors, a chilly emptiness wafted.

Before checking the other stores, Grace pulled over and called the library first. Sage answered on the first ring. Grace was nearly overcome with the unexpected surge of relief she felt at the sound of Sage's voice. After confirming that not only had Sage locked all the doors and dimmed the library's lights, but also had the gun she'd given them the night before, Grace began a grim and futile check of Pleasant Brook's various small shops and businesses. Scott sat in the passenger seat, staring straight ahead, as he'd done since leaving Julie's trailer.

Rossman's Grocery and Deli on Main Street was empty and unlocked. No customers, no workers. Lights on, heat running, as if someone had opened the store for business in the morning, then simply walked out sometime between then and now.

Next to Rossman's, Pleasant Brook's small Radio Shack—one of the last of its kind—was dark, doors locked. Same with the laundromat next door. Pleasant Brook's modest travel agency—run by Patti Smith and her husband Ronald—was, like the deli, open with its lights on, but also empty.

Even worse, papers from both desks were scattered all over the floor. Several chairs in the agency's tiny waiting area were turned onto their sides. Grace's gut clenched at these too-obvious signs of struggle, and her Glock was in hand quickly.

She kept it drawn for the rest of her inspection, though she didn't need it. The pharmacy across the street was locked, empty, and dark. The Tipper Inn stood with its doors wide open. The lights were on, and beer bottles and shot glasses stood as lone sentries on the bar and on several tables. The Tipper was never open this early, and Jim Hutchins was as meticulous as they came. He'd never leave his place in such a state, even if he was on his deathbed . . . an analogy which made Grace faintly queasy, all things considered.

All the other businesses on Main Street were locked tight, their lights off. That in itself didn't mean anything definitive. So many of Pleasant Brook's shops and businesses which could operate remotely had been since the original quarantine. Other stores, however—like the hardware store, the Radio Shack, the pharmacy, and deli—were harder to rationalize.

As it had been when Grace had checked earlier, The Whole in the Wall was locked up tight, and dark, like almost every other place. No cars in the parking lot, none around back. As before, there were no signs of Tiffany Carter anywhere.

Grace's last two stops were both churches. First was Pleasant Brook Baptist, home of the inimitable Pastor Yorkins, on East Main Street. Down the road was First Methodist. Both were locked and dark, also. This bothered Grace terribly, though she didn't know why. She wasn't especially religious, and not just because most faith organizations weren't exactly welcoming to her orientation. She just wasn't wired that way, regardless of her sexual identity.

Still, the sight of both buildings of faith (even if Pastor Yorkins HAD been a colossal pain in her ass) standing as dark, silent monoliths proved extremely unsettling. Especially because both parsonages were locked and silent, too.

After rattling the parsonage door next to First Methodist, Grace got into the JEEP and sat still. She looked out the front window at the dark church, and whispered, "How is this possible? How could this happen so quickly?"

"'The dead travel fast.'"

Startled because Scott had remained silent this entire time, Grace looked over and said, "What do you mean?"

Scott didn't look at her. He kept staring out the front window, face expressionless, eyes dark. "The dead travel fast," he said again in a dull monotone. "It's from Dracula, by Bram Stoker. George Staub also says it in Stephen King's *Riding the Bullet.*"

Grace stared at Scott, unblinking, a cold emptiness swelling in her guts. "What does that *mean*?"

Scott shrugged. "I think we were right. When those things attacked my house? They probably moved on lots of other houses, too. Kind of like a coordinated, strategic attack. Probably the only reason why you and Marty weren't attacked is because you were driving around the whole time, on the move."

Grace's head spun. The surreal blanket of horror descending on her made everything feel distant and unreal. As if a thin layer of plastic separated her from the world, dulling her nerves, and anesthetizing her emotions.

Marty and Julie were dead.

The whole town was empty because everyone else was also most likely . . .

Her brain stuttered to a halt. "Sage," she whispered. "We need to get to Sage."

She started the JEEP up, pulled it out of First Methodist's parking lot. Scott remained silent, staring out the front window.

Pleasant Brook Library
Main Street
1:30 PM

82.

" . . . I CAN'T HELP but think this is my fault, somehow. That if I'd been suspicious of this strange feeling I had early on, acted faster, *done* something . . . "

Scott sat at one of the tables near the back of Pleasant Brook's small library, where Constable Matthews and Sage Hunter sat also, talking about the horrible events of the past few days. Of the past few *hours*. The two had some sort of past, Scott knew—he thought they once dated—and it was evident now in the way they conversed on autopilot, (as if communication between them was second nature), despite the awful circumstances they'd had to weather.

Scott yawned as he settled back in his chair and closed his eyes. He heard them talking in the back of his mind, but he wasn't listening. He felt empty, and numb.

Mom's dead.

She's gone.

She's not answering her phone, the diner's phone, or the home phone. Not answering texts. She's gone. She must be.

" . . . don't think there's anything *anyone* could've done," Sage responded in a voice which curiously sounded both reassuring and despairing. "With the way this town has been since the first quarantine? The place has been half-asleep since then. Almost in a coma. And then Warren County sent us back on remote schooling, the COVID numbers started rising again, so folks were staying inside more and more . . . "

Scott heard Sage sigh. "Easy for those things to sneak around without anyone noticing."

"My responsibility," Constable Matthews muttered, "and I failed them. Failed Julie and Marty. Failed the whole town."

The hopeless tone in Matthew's voice caught Scott's attention. He opened his eyes and looked toward the other table, where Sage and Matthews sat facing each other. Constable Matthews' face was painted with a multitude of expressions. She looked exhausted, with purple-black bruises under her eyes. Gaze clouded and heavy with guilt, but Scott thought she was angry, too. Angry at herself, probably angry at COVID, and angry at those *things*, too.

Sage, for their part, looked as tired and worried, but they looked more concerned about Constable Matthews than anything else. The librarian reached across the table, took the constable's hand, and squeezed. "Hell no. You didn't fail anyone. There wasn't anything we could've done differently. I think that once that fucking mask found its way here . . . we were *fucked*."

Sage let go of Matthews' hand and rubbed their temples. "Everyone's gone. All the people we knew and cared about. We're the only three people left. So what do we do?"

"The school," Grace said softly. "We go there and kill them. Question is . . . how?"

"Also," Sage added, "how do we make sure they'll all be there? Even if we can figure out how to kill this nest . . . how can we possibly account for all of them?"

"We can't," Matthews said, "there's no way. But there's also no way the three of us can track all of these things down one on one. Even if we *could*, there's be no guarantee we could get all of them that way, either."

"Julie said something about them resting all at the same time," Scott said softly, hating to be talking about this *shit* when folks as nice, caring, and as good as Julie and Marty were dead, but knowing they didn't have any other choice. "Maybe we can catch them all together, then. And maybe the First one will be there."

Constable Matthews met Scott's gaze with a look he couldn't decipher. "Go on."

Scott shrugged and shifted in his chair. "It's common in these stories. The first one turned is usually like . . . the leader, of sorts. Maybe we won't need them all there, as long as we get the first one. It's part of the vampire and werewolf myths, in some versions. Kill the original, kill them all. Although sometimes it's kill the original, and the rest revert back to human."

Sage looked at Scott with a guarded expression. "You think if we kill the first one, it'll save everyone else?"

Scott shook his head, a sudden and terrible sadness blooming inside. "No. These things kill people first. No coming back from spines being ripped out."

Sage pressed her lips together and nodded grimly. "Okay. So we need a time when they're all likely to be together, or at the least, when their 'First'—whichever one that might be—is most likely to be there."

"Like Scott pointed out, Julie said they rested," Matthews said. "At the time of the Other. That sounded important. Like—they all have to be inactive around that time. But what the hell is this 'other' business?"

Sage pursed their lips. "The 'Other' is a concept. The idea that there's some force which is so alien, so opposite, so different, so . . . *Other* that it's to be feared. It can't be comprehended or explained, it can't be dealt with or reasoned with, or stopped. It's 'Other.'"

Scott nodded, feeling the stirrings of interest in spite of the situation. "Used a lot in horror. Especially in Lovecraft's stories, or other stories of cosmic horror. There's always some alien monster from another dimension that's so inhuman—so 'Other'—that mere humans can't comprehend it, and are driven crazy thinking about it."

"As maybe you can guess," Sage added, "decades ago, the 'Other' had lots of negative and harmful racial and homophobic overtones. In literature—and in culture—being non-white and non-straight was often considered to be inhuman, alien . . . Other. Threatening the 'good and peaceful' status quo of the white straight world."

To his surprise, Scott found himself smiling slightly. "Like a Dionysian intrusion into an Apollonian existence."

Sage nodded slowly, a look of admiration spreading on their face. "*Danse Macabre*? By Stephen King?"

Scott shrugged. "Obviously."

Constable Matthews nodded slowly, expression thoughtful. "Okay then. So basically, something 'Other' is big, frightening, and incomprehensible. What the hell could these things be afraid of?"

The answer flashed in Scott's mind, as it sometimes happened in school on the rare occasions when his teachers were actually talking about something he found interesting. "God. It has to be."

He reached under his shirt, pulled out his cross necklace, (which he'd since threaded with a shoelace because the chain had broken in the corn maze), and laid it flat in his palm. "It burned Jasper. Sure, it didn't kill him . . . it . . . but it definitely hurt him. Same thing with the cross I made out of wood."

He looked up at Sage and Constable Matthews. "Julie's friend Conroy was covered with cross tattoos, and she said he was religious. They took him out without touching him." He paused, frowning slightly. "Not sure why they didn't go after the pastors in town before him, though."

Matthews snorted. "Easy. Conroy wasn't just religious. He was a *good* man. A real Christian who walked and talked his belief. Probably had more faith in his little pinky than Pastor Yorkins had in his whole body. Plus,

I'm not sure how 'Christian' Pastor Foley is . . . or was. He was mostly just inoffensive. If what you're saying is true, Conroy was a much bigger threat than those two."

She glanced at Sage. "Okay then. If God is the 'Other' then when is the 'time of the Other?' Like . . . God has a special time? Wouldn't that be Sunday or something?"

A light came to Sage's eyes as they said, "You guys have heard of the 'witching hour,' right?" After both Scott and Constable Matthews nodded, Sage continued. "We use the phrase all the time today without knowing where it comes from. In the 16th century, the European Catholic Church started prohibiting any activities between 3 and 4 AM because of their growing fears of witchcraft. For whatever reason, between 3 and 4 was the perfect time to get up to witchy shenanigans. Over here in the west, that time took on a sense of taboo because it was considered a mocking flip of the time when Jesus Christ died on the cross, which was supposedly at 3 PM. Between 3 and 4 became a time of supernatural peril. Also, there's always been the longstanding rumor that an unusually high number of mortalities in hospitals and nursing homes occur between the time of 3 and 4 AM, too. Never been verified, I don't think. Just one of those oral legends which gathers substance over time."

Scott nodded again, thinking. "Yeah. Lots of times in horror movies, 3 AM is always when the bad stuff happens. Like when the demons possess people, or ghosts haunt houses. Things like that."

Constable Matthews, however, looked slightly skeptical. "So the witching hour is at 3 AM. Because Jesus died on the cross at 3 PM. Which makes 3 PM the time of the Other? The Other, from these things' perspective, being God."

Sage shrugged. "It makes about as much sense as anything else."

Constable Matthews offered them a wry grin. "Ironic. That the three people in town who are God's least favorite folks are also the only ones left to try and take these things out. During 'God's hour,' no less." She snorted. "Hard to believe God would use bad old sinful folks like us."

Sage smiled in return. "Here's the thing. Stands to reason that if a God does exist, and does stand in opposition to these things, It . . . He, Her, Them, Whatever . . . would most likely bear little resemblance to the image believers have crafted and popularized over the generations. The ancient and original practices of following 'God' have most likely become as obscured as the rituals for invoking the Aspect of Samhain."

Grace nodded. "Okay then. So we bunk down tonight in my office—because it's almost 3 PM now, and we're not even close to being ready to take those things on—and then tomorrow, at 3 PM, we go into the school and kill those fuckers, and their fucking first."

"How?"

Scott's question was so abrupt, even he felt surprised at the way it popped out of his mouth. Constable Matthews didn't miss a beat, however, as she leaned over and clapped her hands flat on the table. "That's what we have to figure out next."

83.

THE RIDE TO Constable Matthews' office was quiet and tense. Scott rode in the back, while Matthews and Sage spoke in hushed whispers he couldn't hear, (or maybe, *chose* not to hear), while he stared out the window as the front porches and storefronts passed by. All of them dark, some with front doors creaking open, others with doors thrown wide to reveal rectangles filled with swirling darkness.

Front lawns looked neat and tidy as if nothing was amiss, and this was just another day. Scott wasn't sure what he'd been expecting. Signs of struggle, toys kicked askew and Halloween decorations torn down. He didn't see any of that, however. Only square, empty, picture-perfect postage-stamp front lawns bereft of life.

Orange and black crepe streamers and black and orange Halloween lights hung limp from trees and eaves. Plastic skeletons and Halloween animatronics stood silent vigil over the emptiness. Witches were frozen in the act of stirring cauldrons. Vampires lurked behind trees, ghosts dangled limply from their branches, and zombies reached up from front lawns. Jack o'lanterns on front porches and steps sat dark and unlit, as they had for days. Triangle eyes stared blackness as their jagged mouths grinned darkly.

The sidewalks of course were also empty. No one walking, (who was left?), no papers or leaves rustling along the sidewalk as if there wasn't a breath of wind to be found. Over everything a deathly silence hung. The town looked eerily preserved in October amber. As if everyone had walked away only minutes before.

It all passed in a Halloween-themed blur as they drove by. If Scott used his imagination, (which he didn't think he wanted to do ever again), he could see the Halloween props and still animatronics as frozen trick-or-treaters, caught also in October amber.

He stared dully out the window, thinking of a line from Ray Bradbury's *Something Wicked This Way Comes*. A kind of ridiculous line he'd always liked; about all things being 'printed on a boy's retina, forever burned there, forever detectable.' Or something like that. It had always sounded cool, but he'd never understood what Bradbury was going for in that line. Figured it was just Bradbury being Bradbury.

He understood, now. All the empty houses, windows dark, doors cracked open or swinging wide, the forlorn jack o'lanterns and Halloween decorations, never to be enjoyed or even seen by anyone in town, ever again. This sad abandoned Halloween tapestry, imprinted on his eyeballs, scorched onto his retinas, for all time.

The JEEP braked to a stop. Constable Matthews said, "We're here."

Constable's Office
2:30 PM

84.

GRACE PUSHED THROUGH her office's front door, walked past her desk, and approached the gun cabinet. Good thing she'd added to its contents over the years. Though the purchases she'd made every few years had felt moderately foolish at the time, they were about to pay for themselves in full.

At least they'd go down shooting.

***

Scott's eyes widened as the gun cabinet opened to reveal Constable Matthews' arsenal. Despite having shot the Jasper-thing a few days ago, he knew little about guns. Only what he saw on TV and movies, and from his experience messing around with his grandfather's shotgun out in the woods with Jasper. However, even with his limited knowledge, the constable's arsenal looked a little over the top for a town like Pleasant Brook. More like what you might find if Arnold Schwarzenegger was sheriff.

Matthews placed her hands on her hips and glanced over her shoulder at Sage. "When's the last time you went target shooting?"

Sage smirked. "Not since that day four years ago, when I was still dating you. And, if I remember correctly, the only 'targets' we aimed at that day were . . . "

Matthews cut her off with a gesture, scowling, but Scott could see a smile hiding in her eyes nonetheless. She reached into the cabinet, picked up a squat, black handgun, and handed it over her shoulder to Sage without looking. "Glock 19, then?"

Sage accepted the gun, squeezed the grip, and popped out the magazine. She looked it over, smiling, and said, "You always did give me the best gifts."

Constable Matthews ignored Sage and looked back to the cabinet. "Okay. We know guns won't kill them. But they cause damage and give us minutes, so we'll take what we can get."

She reached into the cabinet and pulled out two black, military-looking gun belts, both with two squat black handguns each. More Glocks, Scott assumed. She handed one to Sage and slung the other over her shoulder as she said, "Glock 19s. Most common kind of Glock. Standard magazine holds fifteen rounds. Figure we stuff mags into our pockets. We use all those up, we're probably fucked, anyway."

She reached into the cabinet and pulled out a rifle which looked even more like it belonged in an action movie and not in a small Adirondack town. She waited until Sage had secured the gun belt and had the two Glocks resting comfortably on their hips, then passed them the rifle, saying, "This is a Colt AR-15 Carbine police assault rifle. Semi-automatic. This one has a 30-round magazine. I have four of those. Can tape 'em together so we can flip them around in the middle of shit. Again, we go through all four mags . . . we're probably not making it."

"How . . . " Scott stuttered, swallowed, and started again. "How did you get all this stuff? And from *where*?"

Constable Matthews offered him a wry grin. "Friend of mine from the Bureau is ex-Army, and he's got contacts in the NYPD and the national gun show circuits. He's hooked me up with some good shit over the years."

"It's like . . . you were building an army or something."

Matthews smiled and shrugged. "Honestly, in the beginning I only meant to buy a few extra Glocks and maybe a riot gun, like the one I carry in the JEEP." She nodded at the gun cabinet. "That thing was barer than Mother Hubbard's cupboard at first. Even as small as this place is, that didn't sit right with me."

She glanced at the gun cabinet and shrugged again. "Guess I got carried away."

"What about me? Do I get a gun?"

Constable Matthews glanced at him, skeptical. He looked at Sage and saw their face had fallen neutral as if they didn't want to take a side. He looked back to Matthews, who was still looking at him, eyes narrowed. Finally, she said, "I don't want you going in there with us."

He folded his arms, snorted, and gave her a look he was sure would've gotten him sent to the principal's office. "What am I gonna do? Wait in the car? Lock myself in at home? We know that won't stop the First if it wants to get me."

Another odd look passed between Sage and Constable Matthews, but Scott ignored it and pushed on. "I'm safe with you two. And I'll be safer *with* a gun. You guys will be safer with me having a gun, too, because then you won't have to babysit me."

"No," Constable Matthews said dryly, "we'll have to worry about you shooting your foot or *us*, instead."

"Teach me. I'm a quick learner. We're not going until tomorrow, anyway. Plus . . . "

Scott took a deep breath because he was treading close to mouthing off to an adult, and then plunged ahead, anyway. "Do we have a plan? Where do we think they are in the school? How do we know? How are we going to make sure the First is there, and how are we going to kill them? I mean . . . "

Scott swallowed, faltering in the face of Constable Matthews' wide-eyed gaze. Somehow, he managed to blurt out, "Do we even know what we're going to do?"

Matthews stared. Blinked several times. Opened her mouth, closed it. Chuckled, and said with a wide smile, "Shit, kid. Way to show up the local law enforcement." She looked at Sage. "There should be floor plans and blueprints of the school in the town hall next door, in records. Maybe you can . . . "

"*We*," Scott said, emboldened. "We should go next door. Together. You never split up. That's, like . . . a *total* newb move."

Constable Matthews grinned outright. "Damn. We might get out of this, yet." She nodded next door. "Let's go."

85.

"ALWAYS HOLD THE Glock in a two-handed grip, elbows locked, solid stance. None of that one-handed action movie shit."

Grace aimed her Glock at the old two-by-four she'd erected in the high grass behind the constable's office, modeling her stance for Scott. The kid followed suit, doing an admirable imitation of Grace. "What if I can't get my feet exactly right," Scott asked as he aimed at the two-by-four. "I mean, if they're coming at me from every direction, am I going to make sure my feet are set every time I shoot?"

"If those things do come at you from every direction, you're probably fucked, so no. You're not going to worry about your feet then. More important will be at *least* trying to swing your shoulders and square up to what you're shooting at, and keeping those elbows locked." She paused and gave him a lopsided grin. "I mean, even if you do all that and they are coming at you from every direction you'll probably *still* be fucked, but the straighter and steadier your aim is, the better your shots will be, and the more you'll fuck them up."

"Gee, thanks. That makes me feel *much* better." Scott shook his head as he aimed, face tight with anxious concentration. Not for the first time, Grace felt a kind of grief over the destruction of Scott's childhood. Even if he survived this, (which was a monumental 'if'), an essential part of his innocence had been erased, and there'd be no getting it back. Grace knew this from experience, all too well.

There wasn't anything she could do about that, however. She couldn't even guarantee Scott would make it through what happened next. All she could do was give him the tools which might improve his odds. "If there aren't any active targets, keep your trigger finger along the barrel. Like this." She rotated her Glock so he could see her example. "When the action starts you're not gonna worry about this. But before it comes, all joking aside, you don't want to accidentally shoot Sage or me."

Scott nodded and did the same with his trigger finger. "What about the safety? People in horror movies are *always* forgetting to flip off the safety."

Despite the morbid circumstances, Grace couldn't stifle a smile. Kid had moxie, no doubt about it. "Well, that's where these movies screw up, depending on the guns they're using. No safeties to flip on a Glock. There's a little tab right *here* on the base of the trigger," she turned the Glock further to show him, "which is designed to hold your trigger finger up from an accidental fire, but if you pull it hard enough, you'll depress that tab all the way and the gun'll shoot. No safety to worry about on these babies."

Scott's eyes narrowed slightly as he took aim at the two-by-four. "Good," he whispered.

Grace dropped her Glock to her side and nodded at the two-by-four, "Go ahead. Pull the slide like I showed you, chamber the first round, and have at it."

Scott grabbed the slide and pulled it back, chambering the round a lot smoother than a kid his age should. Then, lips pressed together, he aimed and pulled the trigger.

86.

LIKE MANY OF the other buildings they'd explored, the town hall felt eerily abandoned. Of course, its "staff" consisted of Mrs. McHugh—a dour-faced sixty-five-year-old widow who believed keeping the town's records safe and secure was her God-given duty on this Earth—and Polly Summers, who'd graduated from Pleasant Brook High three years ago and shared a double-wide with her mother in Gerhart Trailer Park. It also could be accurately stated no one in town had ever much cared about records, archived census reports, or birth and death certificates, and no one had needed a new building permit in ten years or more.

So it wasn't like the "town hall" had ever exactly been bustling with activity on a normal day. The rare times Grace issued a ticket or citation (for parking in a handicapped spot, low-grade vandalism at Martinkovic Park, or those 'damn kids playing that godawful Five Fingered Death Punch'), it was usually by mail, or online. She herself only wandered next door to chat with Mrs. McHugh or Polly when she was bored out of her mind, which, before recent events, occurred at least twice a day. She'd never seen anyone else in the building all the times she visited. For the most part, the only people with any business at the town hall were Widow McHugh and Polly Summers, and even then, Grace was never exactly sure *what* it was they did all day, every day, five days a week.

Even so, the building felt like a mausoleum as Grace, Scott, and Sage crept through it. The air tasted stale and musty, as if no one had been there in several days, (Grace realizing, with a start, *she* hadn't paid one of her bored "social calls" since all of this had started), which only made things feel worse. All through the original quarantine, Polly and Widow McHugh had reported to work every single day, deemed "essential employees" by Warren County (essential for *what*, exactly, Grace had never been able to ascertain). Their absence now felt more ominous than if the building and its offices were in disarray.

The blueprints for the school turned out to be in Polly's small office, a small matchbox room with cheap oak paneling, a small desk in the middle of the room with a well-worn rolling leather chair behind it. They found the blueprints in one of the many drab, gray metal filing cabinets against the far wall.

On the filing cabinets stood several 5x4 pictures, of Polly with her mother Geraldine at Martinkovic Park, out to eat at The Whole in the Wall, and one with Polly and her infant daughter, whom Geraldine watched during the day. As Sage riffled through the cabinets, looking for the school's floor plans, Grace tried to avert her gaze from those pictures, and also tried not to speculate on these people's fates, especially little Bessie. She was only partially successful in doing so.

One hour later, after Scott's more-than-adequate target practice, the three of them sat around the small table in her office, where she usually ate lunch. The school's floor plan was spread out before them. Luckily, there wasn't much ground to cover. The school had never been large to begin with, boasting in its best years a maximum of two hundred students, K-12th grade.

"Okay," Sage began. "You said right before the end, Julie told you they were in the school. 'Down in the dark, where no light reaches.' That narrows things down nicely. All these hallways," she ran her index finger along the halls on the floorplans, "have banks of windows. The main office and principal's office all have windows also, and wouldn't be big enough, anyway. Classrooms all have windows, and even though they have window shades, I don't think that would be dark enough for them."

Grace tapped a large rectangle labeled GYM. "What about here? Maximum occupancy is about 150, but I doubt they're concerned about such things."

Scott shook his head. "There's windows all around the top of the gym, and no way to close them. It might get dark at night, but definitely not at 3 in the afternoon."

"Considering what Julie said about '*down* in the dark'—assuming that wasn't a product of her mind falling apart at the end—down implies . . . well, *down*. And since this is only a one-story school . . . "

She pulled back the floor plan to reveal another one underneath. She tapped the outline of the school, which had no demarcations for hallways, classrooms, or offices. "The basement."

Scott looked up and nodded, eyes bright. "Yeah. There's doors to the basement on either side of the school. I've never been down there, but there's always been rumors that a long time ago, a senior swiped a master key, made a copy, and then the key to the basement door was passed down every year to incoming seniors so they could sneak down there and skip class, get high, and basically party."

Grace chuckled, even laughed outright when Scott and Sage looked at her in surprise. "Oh, it's not a rumor. Went down there myself a bunch of times, senior year." When Scott's eyes widened, she grinned and said, "Only to get high, though. The guys weren't my type, of course. Neither were any of the girls because all *they* cared about were the guys."

Sage grunted, with a knowing smile. "*Anyway*. Do you remember much about what it was like down there?"

Grace shrugged, trying in vain to recall the handful of times she'd sneaked into the school's basement. "No. I got very high the few times I snuck down there, and remember, this was fifteen years ago."

She paused, probing her memory. "Dirt floor, a little uneven and rocky. Musty. Only lights down there were yellow light bulbs hanging from the ceiling which didn't light the place for shit. Lots of junk, like old desks, filing cabinets, and boxes of old textbooks. Occasional concrete support columns. Ran the length and width of the school, ceiling about eight feet high. Deep shadows in the corners. When you were high, you thought things were hiding back there, moving around, watching you. Kind of freaky and cool at the same time."

She glanced at Scott, offering him a wry grin. "Hope this doesn't ruin the image of your illustrious town constable."

Scott shrugged. "Mom gets . . . " He coughed, swallowed, and somehow managed to say, "Mom used to get high every Friday night after working all evening. No big."

Grace's smile and good humor faded, sorry to have—however unintentionally—conjured up bad feelings in Scott. She cleared her throat, looked at Sage, and said, "If that thing . . . the First . . . *is* down there with them, we won't be able to shoot our way through all the others to it, so we can stake it."

"Fire kills them," Scott said quietly. "We know that. Maybe we can roll some barrels of gasoline or diesel down there or something? Light them from the stairs?"

Grace looked at Scott, surprised anew at the kid's inventiveness, though she shouldn't be, at this point. "So you want to set the school on fire."

"Sure. The town's dead, right? We're all thinking that. Even if we survive, it's not like anyone's going to start this town back up, so they're not going to need a school."

Then he grinned. "Besides. It's every kid's dream to blow his school up. Isn't it?"

Grace snorted again, recalling a similar sentiment of her own days at Pleasant Brook High. But she shook her head and said, "Much as I gotta admit how I love that idea, I don't know how we'd get enough barrels down there to do the job, or how we'd even light them. It's not like they're going to stand there and watch while we take the time to roll barrels of gas down there, uncork them, pour them out, then light it."

Sage shrugged. “Might be enough flammable stuff down there to get it going, though.”

Grace wasn’t convinced. “Maybe. But I’m worried about how long it will take to light, and that it won’t spread fast enough to kill them all. Probably only smoke them out to another hiding place.”

“We could wait outside. Pick them off if they try to escape,” Scott offered.

Grace shook her head. “But we’d have to get outside fast enough. There’s not enough of us to cover all the potential exits, and we don’t know how to tell First apart from the others.”

Grace paused, the possible truth about the First—that it was Scott’s father, Bobby Lee Haskel—lingering on the tip of her tongue. Instead, she said, “Plus, it still puts us too close to them for my comfort.”

Sage folded the top floor plan back down and tapped the rectangular square next to CUSTODIAL which read BOILER. “Y’know, the school is *old*. Hasn’t been updated in decades. The boiler probably even longer.”

They looked up, brow wrinkled in thought. “Back when I was still dating only guys, I used to date one of the custodians. His boss then was a drunk, and Steve was always complaining that the boiler was so old, someday his boss was going to ‘fuck it up and blow this place to hell.’”

Scott’s eyes widened. “Shit yeah. *The Shining*. The book, not the movie, of course. Well, and the mini-series, too.” Sage nodded with a small smile. “Do you think we can . . . ”

Sage shrugged. “I don’t know. I’m probably going to have to Google it. I don’t know about this kind of stuff; I don’t even know what kind of boiler the school has, or what to even Google about it.”

Understanding dawned in Grace. “You want to rig the boiler to blow up.”

Sage smiled. “Why not? We’d be making a dream come true for every high school kid, ever.”

For a moment, they smiled.

87.

BECAUSE PLEASANT BROOK had never experienced much crime past drunk and disorderly, (Lester McDonough the usual and only offender), or traffic violations, it didn't have much in the way of incarceration. In the unlikely incident of someone committing a serious crime, they would've been remanded to the nearest state police barracks (there was one right outside Smyrna), or the Warren County Jail. What Pleasant Brook did have was a cell not much bigger than a small bedroom, with three bunks. Its only regular occupant—during Grace's tenure, anyway, and probably for ten years before—was Lester when he'd had too much to drink at The Tipper, or after indulging in too much home-brewed hooch.

Tonight, the cell served as a bedroom for the three of them. The three bunks were pushed against the walls and made up with what blankets and pillows were stored in the station. When they all bedded down around 9:30, Grace pulled the bars shut and locked it for probably the first time in over twenty years.

Scott only managed a thin sleep shot through with dreams of melting faces and grasping hands, so the slight *squeak* of the cell door sliding back woke him almost immediately. He shot up on the thin mattress, heart pounding and breath rasping, expecting to see one or more of those things creeping into the cell, hands reaching, grotesque faces leering as bulging eyes rolled madly . . .

Instead, he saw Constable Matthews about to close and re-lock the cell door. She saw he was awake and flickered a small smile. "No worries. Wanted to eyeball the street and alley from the windows. Back to sleep, kid."

Scott drew his knees to his chest. Even though he didn't think he could, he nodded and whispered, "Okay."

He was out fifteen minutes later.

***

Scott stood before the entrance of Pleasant Brook High School. All its windows were dark. It was hard to tell if it was day, early evening, or night.

The sky swirled with a myriad of colors. Orange, yellow, purple, red, gray, black. Something in him whispered it was morning, night, day, and twilight, all at once. That didn't make any sense, but it felt true.

He stood before the school, alone. Sage and Constable Matthews were nowhere to be seen. This registered absently, merely a footnote of his surroundings, nothing more. Their absence didn't seem important, or relevant in any way, because they weren't what he wanted. Were they? What he wanted was opening the school's front door and walking out to him, now.

His father.

Somehow—though he didn't know *how*—he thought this was what his father looked like . . .

had looked like

before

. . . not an image cherry-picked from one of his Father Comes Home Fantasies. No, this was the real deal. This is what his father looked like . . .

used to look like

. . . and not one of his made-up images. He wore jeans which were slightly faded in the knees and thighs. An untucked and unbuttoned red and black flannel over an untucked black t-shirt. The flannel's sleeves were rolled up, exposing tightly-corded, muscled forearms.

His father smiled. *Scott,* he said. *I'm so glad to finally meet you.*

Scott almost stepped forward, but hesitated, instead. Something felt wrong about this. He didn't know why. On one hand, this was everything he'd ever wanted. His father, and not only that but his father as a regular guy. Not a recovering drug addict, a war hero, or even career military. Just a guy who'd maybe made a mistake, maybe wasn't ready to be a dad, but was now ready, and wanted to try and make up for lost time.

Even so.

Why did you leave? Scott asked (in his mind, he realized, not through speech). *Why did you go away? Didn't . . . didn't you want to be my Dad*?

A look of genuine regret passed over his . . .

its

. . . face. *I wasn't ready, Scott. I was the BMOC around here, y'know? Big Man On Campus. Football star, town hero, all that shit. Then I screwed up and no one liked me anymore. Hell, they* hated *me. I had to go away, you know? Figure shit out.*

Scott shook his head slowly. He supposed he understood all that. Understood the need to get away from life to try and find oneself. Didn't he do that with horror movies and books, and hanging out at the amphitheater at Martinkovic Park, and hanging out with Jasper? But, still . . .

Why didn't you come back? Scott asked. *Why now, all these years later?*

The man . . .

his father

it

. . . looked apologetic. He spread his hands and said, *Here's the thing, kiddo. Your mom—Tiffany—she never told me about you. Never told me she was pregnant. But she's been feeling bad about it all these years, I guess. We . . . we been talkin, Scott. On the phone, and texting. She told me about you, said I had to come back because you needed me.*

He (it) shrugged. *So I'm here, Scott. I'm here,* he said, with a wide, white-toothed grin, *c'mon over here and let your old man size you up.*

An intoxicating warmth Scott had never felt before washed away that annoying inner voice which kept doubting. Scott smiled and stepped forward . . .

"Scott, no!"

***

Grace stood in the doorway of the Constable's office, watching the busy streets of Pleasant Brook bustling with activity as folks passed to and fro on the sidewalks. Some walked alone, others in pairs or groups, heading to shops, lunches, a friend's house, or wandering up and down Main Street's sidewalks. Cups of coffee or tea steamed in their hands. Cheeks and nostrils flushed red from October's nip, but eyes wide and glittering, and faces smiling in ways Grace hadn't seen since before the first quarantine. Everyone going about their business, enjoying another crisp fall morning in Pleasant Brook, population . . .

Grace frowned.

Something didn't feel right. Something felt out of place, off-kilter.

"Constable Matthews!"

Grace turned to see the balding and pear-shaped Bob Pacione approaching her, round face beaming, eyes wide and bright. "Constable! I wanted to thank you for doing such a wonderful job speaking at the town assembly last weekend regarding your partnership with the school's anti-bullying initiative. It was so brave, you coming out to everyone like that. You're an inspiration to us all. Don't know *what* we'd do without you."

Grace opened her mouth, confused, because for a moment, a memory flickered through her mind. Of being snubbed for the town assembly, and *not* being invited to be part of the school's anti-bullying initiative. Also, this had taken place about five years ago. She also briefly remembered something about Pacione being pissed at her for enforcing such strict COVID compliance . . .

covid
what the hell is that?

. . . but all those thoughts drifted away as she shook Pacione's pudgy, slightly clammy hand. "Thanks," she said hesitantly, not sure what to say, for some reason. "You know me. Here to serve."

Selectman Pacione nodded, grinning, and moved on. Relieved at his departure, Grace returned to her people-watching, as the folks of Pleasant Brook continued to happily pass by, chatting, mingling, commiserating over the things small-town people do. Probably also gossiping, though that didn't bother Grace much. It wasn't like they were gossiping about her, of course . . .

yes they do
all the time
at least, they did, *before . . .*

. . . so what was the harm?

Townspeople continued to walk by. Smiling, nodding to each other or Grace, greeting her warmly and enthusiastically. The town which normally ignored her and considered her, at best, an irrelevant nuisance. At worst, a dyke liberal pain in the ass who'd only been appointed because she was a hometown girl. Or because of gender and orientation politics. They looked for all the world as if they loved her. As if she was the most important and beloved of all Pleasant Brook citizens . . .

not true
they don't hate you
but they don't give two shits about you, either

Grace frowned as she glanced up and down the jovial, bustling crowd which moved along the sidewalks on both sides of Main Street. There was never this many people out walking through town, even on a warm day, or a town celebration. Even in the days before COVID . . .

what the hell is that?

. . . Pleasant Brook had always been a drowsy town, its citizens withdrawn and distant from one another, almost insular. Grace distantly remembered days standing in this precise spot and going *hours* without seeing more than one or two folks walking through town at a time . . .

This was a lie.

A fantasy image of what she'd thought it would be like to return to her hometown to work after failing as a big city cop in Utica, based on her rose-tinted childhood memories. A dream, nothing more.

The people flickered and faded away, leaving nothing but empty streets and barren sidewalks, along which dried leaves rustled and crackled in the wind. She began to feel dizzy. Her view of Main Street tilted on its axis, turning fuzzy, unfocused until it dissolved entirely.

She blinked and sat up on the bunk in the small cell in her office, struggling to shrug off sleep . . .

Grace looked up and saw Scott standing before the cell door, swaying back and forth dreamily. Something was on the other side of the bars, reaching through toward him.

Rage and fear pulsed through Grace, washing away the last vestiges of drowsiness. She leaped from her bunk, shouting “Scott, no!” as she stuck the riot gun through the cell’s bars and pulled the trigger.

***

Sage stood behind the front counter of the library, suffused with a warm glow of contentment . . . but still feeling slightly confused. Something felt off about the scene they were experiencing, but they couldn’t quite put a finger on *what*.

They *should* be ecstatic, of course. Their All Hallows Read Event was an enormous success. The library was filled with patrons taking free Halloween-themed and age-appropriate scary books. Children and adolescents with their parents and even teens who normally wouldn’t be caught dead in the library roamed the special area set up in the back, looking for their own scary book. Sage had every right to feel thrilled, except . . .

Something about all of this didn’t sit quite right. They didn’t know what. Something about the patrons themselves, who milled around the All Hallows Read display, picking up books, handling them, turning them over, then putting them back down again . . .

No one took any.

The patrons—children, adolescents, teens—weren’t picking up any of the books and taking them out of the library. In fact, when Sage looked closely enough, it became apparent the patrons weren’t doing *anything* at all, which made no sense. They were milling around the All Hallows display and throughout the library, but they weren’t doing anything purposeful or going anywhere. They walked in odd routes, barely missing each other, rubbing shoulders, aimlessly picking up books, handling them, and putting them back down.

Sage squinted, stepped around the front counter, and approached the nearest group of milling people, in the library’s main aisle. Sage couldn’t see any faces. It wasn’t possible, but even so. Every person walking back and forth turned their torsos slightly away, just enough so Sage couldn’t see their faces.

A deep sense of foreboding built inside. A warning, almost. That Sage should leave well enough alone. Enjoy the patrons teeming throughout the library . . .

teeming and writhing like maggots feasting on a corpse

That should be good enough. Sage should know their place and stay there.

That, of course, was the trigger.

Know your place.

After surviving an abusive childhood in a hyper-religious home and countless other abusive relationships before Sage finally understood who they were, and started living true to themselves, Sage had heard over and over: *know your place. Stay in your lane. Play your role. Don't step out of line. Be obedient. Submissiveness and compliance was next to Godliness.*

After years of living for others, Sage swore they'd never let *anyone* tell them those things ever again. They'd be damned if they told it to themselves.

Sage took another step forward. "Excuse me," they said in a slightly trembling voice, "I was wondering if . . . "

The patrons stopped as one. Turned in unison to stare. Sage's mouth hung open silently as an icy grip of fear made it impossible to speak. Their heart slammed, suddenly feeling heavy and twice its size. Their thighs quivered, knees and legs feeling watery, insubstantial.

Masks.

All the library patrons wore masks. The *same* mask. Made of rubbery, sagging, diseased flesh, with bulging eyeballs which glared and rolled in opposite directions of each other. Lank, thin and greasy black hair trailing from peeling scalps, and worst of all . . . gaping black mouths, out of which flopped twisting, muscled, and slimy serpentine tongues . . .

Sage raised shaking hands in a weak and pitiful defense. The things stepped forward, as one body, one mind. Sage's throat finally unlocked long enough to scream. A scream they heard from everywhere, crashing into her dream and shattering it to pieces . . .

"Scott, no!"

***

Sage jerked awake on the cell's thin mattress in time to see Grace shove the barrel of her riot gun through the cell door's bars and into the gut of a thing wearing a mask. The constable shouted and pulled the trigger.

The gun's roar boomed in the enclosed space and crashed against Sage's ears, sending a bolt of fiery pain through their temples. Holding the riot gun one-handed, the shot's recoil knocked Grace backward several steps, though she kept her feet, chambered another round, and stepped back up to the bars.

She had time. The first blast had not only thrown the thing back against the hall's opposite wall, it tore a hole the size of a basketball in its guts. Sage could see the shattered ribs, (which looked rotten with disease) poking out of tattered black-green flesh oozing clumps of matter (shredded intestines?) to the floor. She could also see what looked like the thing's spine, broken in two, which apparently didn't bother it at all as it pushed off the wall, its abdomen already filling up, knitting itself back together.

Scott stood at the cell door, still dazed, rocking back and forth on his feet, blinking, as if coming out of a deep sleep. Chunks of rubbery flesh oozed off the cell's bars, precariously close to Scott's hand. Fear *for* Scott pulsed through Sage—as they remembered what exposure had done to Julie—and they leaped forward, shouting, "Scott! Get back!" They grabbed his shoulders and yanked him back away from the gore-slicked bars, as the thing—its ravaged guts already reformed—lunged forward, its hands reaching through after Scott . . .

Grace was already moving. This time, she stuck the riot gun through the bars and at the thing's head and pulled the trigger. Like the one at Scott's house, its head exploded in a spray of blackish-green matter, spraying chunks of rotten flesh everywhere. Its hands reached up for its ragged stump of a neck and flailed as it staggered sideways and crashed to the ground.

Grace dropped the riot gun. Grabbed one of the sharpened broom handles they made and brought into the cell with them, and snatched the cell door keys off her belt as she moved to the cell door.

Sage finally found their voice. "What the *hell* are you doing?"

"I can keep shooting until I run out of bullets, and that thing will keep getting up," she said grimly as she unlocked the door, "I gotta end it, or it's gonna find a way in here!"

"No! What if there are more . . . "

Unheeding, most likely lost in adrenaline, Grace unlocked the cell door and flung it wide. She leaped out into the hallway, and with a cry, raised the broomstick spear above her head and brought its sharpened point slamming down.

88.

GRACE RAISED THE broomstick spear high above her head and slammed it down, driving its sharpened point into the thing's chest, plunging it through the stenciled name patch on its chambray work shirt. The patch read *Bob*, as in Bob Llewelyn, owner and operator of Pleasant Brook's only auto shop, *Bob's Auto*. In a weird way, this didn't bother Grace at all. Bob was—had been—a misogynistic asshole known for mansplaining repair quotes and overcharging his single female customers. Served the fucker right. She didn't feel an ounce of pity as she put all her weight behind the broomstick.

The wooden spear tore through the shirt and into the thing's flesh like it was made of rancid butter. The thing spasmed and jerked. Arms flailing, heels drumming the concrete, what was left of its reforming head whipping back and forth. Like Jasper and Julie, its skin hissed and bubbled, as a rank smoke which smelled like spoiled meat and burning rubber rose in a cloud of chemical stench. A savage kind of glee rose in Grace's heart as the thing's flesh melted and ran, as its body collapsed into itself.

"Grace! There's another . . . "

Grace looked up, reaching for one of her holstered Glocks, but too late. A heavy body hurtled from the back of the station and slammed into her right shoulder, sending her sprawling into the front office. She rolled and landed face-down. The thing was on top, its hands closed around her neck in a vise-like, unrelenting grip which cut off her air. Blackness crept around the edges of her vision, and as she fought the looming oblivion, she knew only minutes—maybe *seconds*—remained to her.

With a herculean effort, she threw herself up, bucking her body hard enough to cause the thing's grip to loosen slightly, and for the weight on her back to shift enough for her to jerk her Glock out of her holster. Blindly, she pointed it behind her head and squeezed off three rapid shots in succession, each report blasting and ringing in her ear.

The grip on her neck loosened. The thing fell away from her. She rolled onto her back, raised the Glock, and was about to pull the trigger again when she caught a splash of the thing's greenish-black fluids from its ruined head to the side of her face. Her skin instantly sizzled as if splashed by acid, and blinding electric pain arced across her face as she screamed.

89.

WHATEVER RATIONAL SENSIBILITIES Sage thought they possessed vanished instantly under a tide of manic fear as one of the things hurtled past the cell door and slammed into Grace, knocking her out of view into the front office. They didn't hear the ensuing struggle, the gunshots, or Grace's agonized howl, because they were solely focused on the things which had followed the other one, and were now scrambling into the cell with them and Scott.

Their mind white-hot with terror, Sage yanked Scott back behind them, against the wall, in a futile effort to flee. As the things advanced—oddly enough focused on her and not Scott—Sage pushed Scott away and to the ground in an even more futile gesture, their mind wanting to tell Scott to run, but failing, as they saw more things crowding the cell door. There was literally nowhere to go.

Sage reached for one of the holstered Glocks on their hip, but the thing in lead thrust out its hand and grabbed Sage by the neck. It lifted them effortlessly off the ground and pinned them against the cell's cold cinder-block wall. Part of them didn't want to fight; they didn't want to give the thing the satisfaction, wanted to stare defiantly, like maybe a strong, progressive, non-binary movie character would. A larger part, however, simply gave in to instinct and kicked and jerked, forgetting their guns as they dug their fingernails into the thing's hand, to no avail.

Its fingers—slimy, cold, not feeling like human skin at all, its touch driving Sage mad—clenched tighter around their neck. As Sage felt something crack and pop in their trachea, they felt a moment's peace, if only because they thought they were near the end.

This peace proved illusory. Its hand yanked them face to face with its hideous visage. Its jaws unhinged and opened impossibly wide, revealing an immense and wet darkness, out of which slithered a muscled, thick, and mucus-slimed tongue. Sage jerked and kicked anew as they realized death wasn't going to be so quick and merciful after all.

***

When Sage shoved Scott out of the way and to the floor, he tried to break his fall with his hands, but they slipped on the cool concrete and he fell face-forward, forehead cracking against the floor. The blow left him dazed. As he rolled onto his back, the frenzied signals from his brain to his limbs to *do something!* were scrambled by the pain throbbing in his head. All he could do was lay on his back and watch what happened next.

One of the things had Sage around the neck with its slimy hand, pinning them against the cell's back wall. Sage kicked, fought, dug their fingernails uselessly into its hands. The thing squeezed tighter. Like Sage, Scott thought the end would be quick and merciful. A simple snapped neck and then lights out.

Like Sage, Scott was wrong.

It yanked Sage's face close to its hideous, melted-rubber face. Opened its mouth *impossibly* wide. Its long, muscled, thick and rubbery serpentine tongue unfurled, dripping mucus and other strange fluids as it caressed Sage's cheek and wrapped—almost lovingly—around their head.

Smoke rose from Sage's flesh, which sizzled, filling the cell with the awful smell of burning meat. Sage's eyes widened, white with fear and pain, as they kicked and jerked even harder . . .

With one swift motion, the thing stuck Sage's head into its ever-widening mouth, all the way to their neck. Its jaws snapped shut and it bit down with a bone-splintering crunch, and also a soft *mushing* sound.

Sage's body spasmed once, trembling all over like an electric current had pulsed through it. Then they fell limp, as the thing continued to chew, sounding like it had a mouthful of crunchy granola cereal.

Too much.

It was too much.

Scott Carter, erstwhile horror fan who had seen it all, (even all three *Human Centipede* movies, and *A Serbian Film*), felt the lights go out, plunging him into a blessed oblivion as he slumped back to the floor, cracking his forehead hard, once again.

October 31st
Halloween
Constable's Station
10 AM

90.

GRACE CAME AWAKE violently, jolting upright off the cold concrete floor of the constable's station with the image of something looming over her, its face melting and sliding off, ready to coat *her* face and burn her eyes off with its flesh-eating rubber as it forced its way down her throat, filled her up, and made her one of them. She jerked upright with a shout, hand still miraculously clutching her Glock, and she pointed it wildly around her.

At nothing.

She was alone.

The constable's station was empty. She didn't move or try to stand, however. She sat, panning the room with a two-handed grip on the Glock. Eyes wide, heart pounding, her blood flushed with adrenaline.

Nothing.

She pointed the Glock down the short hallway leading to the cell and the back room. It also appeared empty, but shadows lingered there, and the back room was dark, so she couldn't be sure.

She swallowed. Tried to slow her breathing and her pounding heart. Something was wrong. *She* felt wrong. Out of sorts. Disjointed. She tried to attribute it to fear or a fight/flight response, but she knew that wasn't it. Something felt wrong *inside* her.

What?

She slowly got to one knee and then stood. Legs shaking, thighs quivering. The things had left her. She couldn't tell for sure because the back room was dark, and she couldn't see into the cell from here, but she thought—she *knew*—the constable's station was empty. The things were gone. Sage and Scott weren't here, either. She must've passed out because of the pain, and she'd been left here, untouched, but why . . . ?

Passed out because of the pain.

The side of her face and neck throbbed with an odd, cold, rippling ache. As she tried to turn her head, the skin on that side of her face and neck felt *strange*. Tight, restricted, unnatural. Also, it burned with a low-grade stinging which reminded her of a bad sunburn, or a burn from swimming in a pool with too much chlorine . . .

"Fuck," she whispered, as she remembered. The thing on her back, choking her. Pulling her Glock, pointing it behind her where the thing's head was, and firing blindly. Its blood—or whatever it was—splashed all over the side of her face and neck as she blew its head apart. She fell to the floor and howled in pain because it felt like her face had been splashed with acid. The pain was so intense she'd passed out. They'd left her here, untouched. Why?

Because.

She lowered the Glock. It dangled from her right hand at her side as she reached up a shaking left hand and tentatively touched the left side of her face and neck. The skin there felt like blistered, hardened, and cracking rubber. Along the left side of her face—somehow sparing her left eye—and down the left side of her neck, to her collarbone. She didn't need a mirror, (and didn't think she could stand to look into one), to know her skin had turned black and burnt-looking, like Julie's arm had been.

The strength left her legs as her muscles turned to water. She thumped to the ground and sat. Hands and Glock sitting uselessly in her lap. She bent her head, and even though she'd never been prone to crying—she couldn't even remember the last time she had—Grace Matthews, Constable of Pleasant Brook, and maybe the last person alive—wept openly, tears streaming down her face, shoulders shaking with great, wracking sobs.

91.

CONSCIOUSNESS CAME TO Scott slowly. Shifting from blackness through different shades of gray, slowly and painfully to a dim awareness, he floated up from oblivion to waking. When he opened his eyes, however, it was to another kind of darkness. A murky, subterranean darkness. Like that of an underground cave, or . . .

A basement.

Scott's mind worked sluggishly. He reached up and rubbed his face, trying to wake up and figure out where he was. He was sitting on the ground, that was for sure. A rocky, dirt floor. He was also leaning back against something hard, concrete, and rough. A pillar, of some kind.

He'd passed out. Him, the horror movie junkie, had passed out when that thing had bitten Sage's head off and chewed it like a mouthful of milk-soaked Raisin Bran. He'd passed out, had *stayed* out.

He blinked his eyes groggily as he rubbed his face some more. Something had put him under and *held* him under. He thought maybe those things had. If they could project images into people's heads, even make them *dream* shit . . . Scott supposed they could keep you asleep, too, for as long as they needed.

Which, of course, left the question. Why keep him asleep? Why was he still alive?

His hands fell away from his face as he opened his eyes, only for him to be greeted with a sight which looked born of the worst kind of fever dreams.

The school basement (because that's where he was, Scott knew) wasn't completely pitch dark. Dim light filtered through small, rectangular ground-level windows interspersed along the school's foundation. Those dusty, grime-encrusted windows let in enough light for Scott to see them—an uncountable number of them—all standing and staring at him. Heads cocked, like curious dogs. Bulging wet eyes rolling madly in their sockets, serpentine tongues flopping grotesquely in impossibly wide, gaping black mouths. Their hands hung loosely at their sides, shoulders slightly hunched.

They all stared at *him.*

Scott pressed himself back into the concrete pillar, its rough texture being the only thing which kept him from losing his mind to hysterical fear, as it dug into his back through his shirt, the pain keeping his mind focused, tethering him in spite of his mounting terror. He didn't know what was going on or why he was still alive or why they hadn't changed him yet, but he couldn't give in to the mounting terror building in his heart. Somehow, he needed to keep a clear head, if he had any chance in hell of . . .

A shift of movement rippled through the things. They parted, moving with one mind, (like a colony of ants, or a hive of bees), down the middle, allowing another one of them to pass. It was naked, and of course wore that awful, leering mask.

It approached him. Stopped about three feet away, then squatted until it was almost eye level, giving Scott the closest view he'd had yet of these things. This mask looked slightly different than the others. More . . . solid. As it wasn't made of melting rubber-flesh but made of something closer to wood. Its facial lines looked sharper, far more defined, and resembled more closely the picture he'd found on the website article about the Aspect of Samhain. More so than all the others, at least.

This thing was the First. It had to be. Also, it was the one who'd projected the vision of a man proclaiming to be his father.

Scott's eyes widened, as a weird kind of knowing pulsed through him. "D . . . Dad?"

The thing cocked its head like all the others, but instead of looking like a stupidly inquisitive animal, it seemed to sense his thoughts. Seemed to look right into his *brain* and know what he was thinking. Before Scott could even flinch, the thing leaned forward, reached out, and grasped both sides of his head. For a brief moment, unreasoning panic flushed through Scott, as he thought: *this is it, this is when he pukes that rubber stuff all over my face and I turn into one of them . . . !*

But it didn't do that. It simply held both sides of his head, squeezing firmly but oddly enough, not painfully, those mad bulging eyes staring at him, staring *into* him.

And then . . . came the *visions.*

Plunging through his head, his mind, like a cold, slashing knife, and the visions *hurt.* It felt like his brain was convulsing and spasming under the onslaught of images and sensations, and he opened his mouth wide in a silent scream.

92.

GRACE TIPPED BACK the bottle of Jameson she'd gotten from her bottom left desk drawer and chugged back a healthy swallow. The liquor burned its way down the back of her throat, but for some reason, it didn't taste quite right. It didn't taste like whiskey at all. It tasted rank and rotten, what she imagined rotten sewage might taste like. She gagged and sputtered, spewing some of it out and down her chin, and almost puked the rest of it up.

She forced it down. It burned toward her stomach, and when it settled into a nice, relaxing warm glow, she tipped the bottle back and forced herself to take another generous swig. It didn't taste so bad now, and she was able to get it down without gagging, even though it still didn't taste *quite* right. It tasted like dirty dishwater, with a rubbery taste underneath.

I'm already changing, she thought as she leaned back in the rolling chair at her desk, *already becoming one of them. That's why it doesn't taste right.*

Regardless, she helped herself to another nip from the bottle, albeit a smaller one this time. This sip finally tasted a bit more like whiskey, and weirdly, that made her feel better.

Her Glock lay in her lap. Her free hand flat on her desk, because she didn't want her hand on her gun, not yet. She was close to sticking its muzzle into her mouth and taking care of things for good, but she didn't want to do it quite yet. She wanted to try and think things over first, before going out on her terms, instead of becoming one of those things.

She had to assume Sage and Scott were gone. Most certainly Sage, based on the amount of blood Grace found in the cell. Scott, she had to believe, was most likely dead also, except . . . except . . .

You don't know that

You don't.

But the odds were against him being alive and, soon—depending on how quickly this stuff worked on her—she would become one of those things and be dead, also. It had taken less than 24 hours for Julie to turn, though Grace figured she was a bit more willful than Julie had been . . . though she didn't know if that made a damn bit of difference, at all.

She took her hand off the desk and laid it on the cool polymer of her Glock. The worst part was, she didn't even know if shooting herself would prevent her from becoming one of those things, now that she'd been infected. She'd seen their regenerative powers. Hell, she could blow her brains out, and that shit coursing through her veins would probably still bring her back. The best thing to do was stick to the original plan: waste them all. How the hell she was going to do that, she had no idea.

"Ahh, fuck it," she whispered, lifting the Jameson to her lips to finish it off, "fuck it all . . . "

She tossed the bottle back and took a deep swallow, but before she could empty it entirely, a white-hot pain speared through her head, feeling like an electric dagger had plunged directly into her brain. A blinding, pounding pressure filled her head, making it feel twice as large.

She only dimly heard the whiskey bottle shattering on the floor after it fell from her nerveless fingers. Her throat spasmed closed, clenching tight. She gagged, bent over, and spewed the whiskey all over the floor, even venting some of it from her nostrils, which lit her sinuses on fire.

None of that mattered, however, as an invisible psychic vice gripped her head and *squeezed.* She clapped her hands on both sides of her head, closed her eyes, mouth stretched out in a silent scream.

A torrent of images, sensations, and sounds bombarded her mind, flooding her thoughts with a deluge of words, sounds, pictures, and *memories* which didn't belong to her, didn't even make sense. Ancient cultures and peoples with rites and practices for which she had no context, geographies as different as day and night, (some human, some distinctly *alien*), empty European villages and American ghost towns out west, small communities living in the wilderness, what looked like early American colonies . . .

Their history, a tiny voice whispered inside, *this is their history, out of order and context, not told from a linear human perspective, but from an incomprehensible alien consciousness . . .*

Her thoughts drowned under a wave of more images and sensations, some eerily familiar, others completely foreign to her, until . . .

Pleasant Brook.

Main Street.

From the perspective of a car hurtling through a red light and plowing into the side of a red minivan filled with children, interspersed with point of view images of someone playing football; crushing helpless running backs and quarterbacks with vicious tackles, running back interceptions for touchdowns . . .

Kissing and making love with his girlfriend, Tiffany Carter.

Bobby Lee.

Bobby Lee Haskel.

Then the car crashing into the minivan again, boot camp in the Army, serving overseas, too many drunken brawls in the enlisted bars, getting discharged, going home, rambling across the country with another guy she recognized as Jesse Simpson, working odd jobs here and there, learning how to distill their own moonshine, until . . .

Returning to Pleasant Brook.

Squatting in old Owen House. Finding the *mask*. The original, the mask of Samhain, the mask of forgetting, putting it on, and then screaming, screaming . . .

All the images merged together into a spinning kaleidoscope of colors and sound, then they broke apart and dissolved into a deep, black nothingness that Grace wrenched herself from with a mental heave as she fell back into her chair so hard she almost tipped it over. As she pulled herself away from the darkness, Grace saw one last image—an image which sparked an impossible flare of hope in her heart, in spite of how doomed everything felt. An image from someone else's perspective, from some*thing* else—of Scott, scared and cowering against a concrete pillar in a dimly lit, subterranean space.

The school basement.

Scott was *alive*.

93.

THE THING LET go of Scott's head, stood, and stepped back. Scott gasped and jerked himself out of the river of images, sounds, and sensations which had almost drowned him. Feeling as if he'd been dunked into an ice bath, Scott drew his knees to his chest and hugged them, teeth chattering, mind reeling.

His father.

This *thing* standing before him *was* his father. In the torrent of memories which had flooded through his brain, he'd recognized the young cheerleader, the arrogant linebacker whose future was made . . . his mother, and his father, fifteen years ago. With the way the others had parted to let it pass, the way it had somehow passed its memories on to him—Scott knew it was the First. The one they had to kill.

Only Scott couldn't see how that was ever going to happen now.

The First, (Scott wasn't going to call it his father, he *wasn't*), stared at him. Head cocked to one side, eyes rolling, mucus-slimed tongue flicking and tasting the air. Scott didn't understand what was happening. Why he was still alive; why the thing had waited until he'd woken up to show him all those things, why it hadn't killed him yet and turned him. Was it possible that somehow—somewhere, deep inside—his father still existed? Had it sent the other things after him—Jasper, too—because it was his . . . father?

Shit.

His father.

But what was going to happen now?

Swallowing his disgust—and his pride—Scott looked at the First, (if that's what it was), and said in a surprisingly firm, steady voice, "Dad. You're my Dad. Aren't you?"

The First looked at him.

Head cocked slightly, hideous face expressionless. Undaunted, Scott pushed on.

"You and my mom. Tiffany. You dated in high school. You left. Why, Mom never told me. But . . . you didn't know, did you? Didn't know she'd gotten pregnant. Did you find out? Did she send you a letter or something? Or did you know she was pregnant, and you left anyway?"

The First cocked its head to the other side, tongue flicking the air, still expressionless, so far as Scott could tell. There was no way of knowing what it was thinking. *If* it was thinking anything. All he could do was desperately keep firing shots in the dark, and if his . . . his *father* still existed in some form, hope he hit a nerve.

"Maybe she didn't tell you. Maybe she knew all along, but for some reason, she didn't tell you. Did you guys have a fight? Maybe she was afraid to tell you? Maybe she did tell you, and *you* were afraid? Of having a kid, being a dad?"

Did those bulging eyes widen? Did its coiling tongue quiver the slightest bit? Scott plunged on.

"Why did you come back? Did she call you? Write you? Do you . . . do you know about Mom's drinking? Do you know why she drinks? Because of *you*. Because you *left us*. It's your fault Mom turned into a drunk. *Yours*."

Its right hand clenched and unclenched spasmodically. Something *was* happening. What, Scott didn't know. But he thought . . . he thought he was getting through, somehow.

"You were scared of seeing me. Scared of seeing Mom, scared of what she'd turned into, scared of explaining why you left, especially to me. You wanted to come see me, didn't you? But you couldn't. That's why you sent all the other things after me. Jasper, and then the others. Because even like this, you're ashamed. Ashamed you left us."

Both hands were opening and closing now, as its tongue whipped back and forth, and its eyes bulged even more. Of course, maybe he was imagining things. Maybe it was only wishful thinking. Regardless, he continued.

"I think you're afraid. Even like *this*, even in control of all these other things, all-powerful and shit, you're afraid of the kid you left behind. Afraid, and ashamed."

The thing that had once been his father stiffened; back ramrod straight, as if electricity was arcing up its spine. And then, three amazing things happened. Things which opened a sliver of hope in Scott's heart.

First, as Scott shifted, he felt something on his hip which he hadn't noticed before. The gun belt Grace had made him wear to bed. The left holster was empty, but the right one held a Glock. Somehow, these things had missed it when they brought him here.

Second: the other things in the basement—things which had once been townspeople, neighbors, shop owners, and fellow classmates—turned their bulging eyes to stare at the First. Almost as if they didn't recognize it, or as if they suddenly viewed it as a threat. Almost as if the First was no longer part of the hive, no longer one of them. In fact, Scott felt *sure* they were a step away from converging on the First, were in fact even stepping toward it.

Third: Something thundering into the building above with a deafening *boom* which shook the school to its foundations.

94.

GRACE HIT HER JEEP's brakes and brought it to a screeching halt in the middle of Main Street, gaping at what she saw parked askew, one massive tire up on the curb. The doors hung open, and it looked like it was empty. She took a breath and fought to clear her mind and tamp down her excitement, afraid that the link she now shared with the things—a link growing stronger by the minute—might run both ways, and betray her.

Even so, when she saw Miles Trevrow's bright yellow HUMVEE sitting crooked alongside Main Street, both doors open and abandoned, she couldn't help but whisper fiercely, "Fuck *yes*."

With no further thought, she shut the JEEP off, scrambled out the door, hustled to the HUMVEE, and hopped into the front seat. When it started up with a roar, Grace scrambled back out and hurriedly started transferring her supplies from the JEEP to the Humvee.

From the moment Grace realized she'd tapped into the things' hive mind—most specifically what was left of Bobby Lee Haskel's mind—she'd moved without thinking, obeying instinct, worried that trying to formulate a plan would not only tip off the hive mind of her actions but also might waste what little time and free will she had left. Though Grace had no way of knowing for sure, she thought that Julie linking up to the hive mind had sped up her transformation. If Grace knew what they knew and was seeing what they saw, her own transformation couldn't be far behind.

She'd gone immediately to the gun locker. Grabbed fresh magazines for her Glocks. Put on a shoulder rig and secured another loaded Glock in there. Didn't hesitate, grabbed a fourth Glock, and tucked it under her waistband. She didn't bother grabbing extra magazines, because if she couldn't get in and get out on what she had, it wasn't going to matter.

Next, she loaded the riot gun to capacity. Didn't bother stuffing more shells into her pockets. She'd empty the gun and toss it. After that—in a move which, on a normal day, would've made her feel like she was living in a bad horror movie—she snapped a quarter off the sharpened broomstick, then secured it onto the riot gun with heavy strips of duct tape, making an ad hoc bayonet.

Then, she simply walked out of the constable's station, got into her JEEP, and drove off. Last night, she and Sage had gone over the school's floor plan and had searched the internet for the boiler's specs, and how to set it off. Based on what they'd found online, if it was still the old one Sage's ex-boyfriend had complained about, blowing it would prove to be simple. Turn it on full blast, then smash the pressure relief mechanism.

The problem?

Not only keeping those things at bay long enough for her to rig the boiler, but also hoping she could get Scott out before it blew, and that all those things would still be inside when it blew.

However, as she drove toward the school—now rumbling along in Miles Trevrow's HUMVEE—she kept her thoughts off the plan as much as possible. She hadn't sensed any specific intrusion into her mind so far. No probing alien thoughts or weird voices, or any other indication they were aware of her in the same way she was becoming more aware of them. Only a low-level buzzing in the back of her head, like a dial-tone, or dead air on the radio. It remained that way, until about a mile before the school . . .

When she slammed on the HUMVEE's brakes, bringing it to a shuddering stop.

Scott's voice.

She'd heard Scott's voice in her mind. Speaking calmly, and forthrightly. She couldn't tell about *what*, exactly, but whatever he was saying was agitating them, and even better than that, Grace sensed they were distracted for the moment, all of them solely focused on Scott. She glanced quickly around where she'd stopped, knowing this moment wouldn't last long . . .

She glanced left. She'd stopped abreast of the Sip and Go, Pleasant Brook's only gas station. She smiled grimly, left the HUMVEE running, and hopped out to do some quick "shopping."

***

Ten minutes later, Grace put the HUMVEE in park at the high school's entrance. Next to her in the passenger seat and on the floor were four 5-gallon plastic gas containers, filled with diesel she'd "purchased" from the Sip and Go. She figured Jay—the gas station and convenience store owner—was probably dead, and would approve of her "purchases," considering her intentions.

Scott's voice still whispered in the back of her mind, though she still couldn't discern what he was saying. She sensed, however, that he was leading up to something, because the things' hive mind was getting more and more agitated, and it felt like *something* was stretching to a breaking point . . .

Scott fell silent in her mind.

Then, the most extraordinary thing happened. She felt the hive mind stretch, and then *fracture*. She could almost feel the tear in her mind, as one distinct part of the hive pulled and snapped free, and the rest turned on it.

"Now," she whispered.

Grace shifted the HUMVEE into gear and slammed her foot down on the gas. The huge vehicle lurched forward and roared into the school's parking lot. She gripped the steering wheel tight as the school's front entrance and short flight of concrete steps loomed. If the angle was wrong and there wasn't enough clearance and she'd made a mistake by not thinking this through ahead of time, she'd slam into the steps and probably bury the steering wheel into her guts, and this whole thing would be over.

Those thoughts fled, however, as the steps and entrance filled her vision . . .

The HUMVEE's huge front tires caught the bottom step and climbed. The HUMVEE barreled and bounced up the steps in a jarring, jouncing ascent. When the front tires cleared the top step, it felt like a gigantic hand grabbed the back of the HUMVEE and sent it hurtling forward. The HUMVEE's engine revved high, and it actually propelled itself into the air . . .

Straight through the school's double glass doors with a resounding crash she felt run from her jaw down to her spine. Miraculously, the HUMVEE landed on all four tires, pointed straight down the school's front hall. Operating completely on adrenaline and instinct, Grace floored it again. After the tires spun briefly on the smooth concrete floor, the HUMVEE shot off like a rocket down the hallway. Its engine roared and echoed mightily in the tightly enclosed space, barely fitting with mere inches to spare on either side. Lockers and empty classrooms whizzed by as the HUMVEE barreled down the hall, as the hallway's end rushed up quicker than she'd anticipated. She slammed on the brakes as hard as she could and yanked the wheel sharply left, throwing the HUMVEE into a slightly sideways skid.

She saw an image, then, of the HUMVEE not stopping, and instead smashing into the concrete wall at the hallway's end, with maybe the steering wheel *and* the transmission embedded in her chest. It would all be for nothing, and as the life leaked from her body, she'd feel the poison inside her work its darkness, spreading through her, until there wasn't anything of her left . . .

For a heartbeat or two, the HUMVEE's oversized tires shuddered on the slippery concrete as the wall rush closer. So certain was she of her fate, Grace closed her eyes and waited for the end.

The HUMVEE slid to a stop, however, in time for its front bumper to strike the wall hard enough to jerk her shoulders against the seat belt, nothing more. An almost dizzying relief pulsed through her, but she shoved it aside and forced herself into motion.

She grabbed the riot gun—on which she'd secured her makeshift broomstick bayonet, and which she'd secured to a shoulder harness—and slipped it over her shoulder. She grabbed two of the plastic cans full of diesel and kicked the driver-side door open. She slid out into the hallway to stand before an open door marked *Maintenance*.

An angry buzzing droned in the back of her head. The things had noticed her smashing the HUMVEE into the school, and they were coming. Whatever schism had briefly and inexplicably developed in the hive mind, they were now one again, and they were *coming*. She needed to move quickly if she stood even a fraction of a chance.

She stepped inside the small, dimly lit, and orderly (if somewhat dingy) maintenance office. She didn't stop, kept walking through it and to the open door in back, then ducked through that door into the boiler room. There it was, looming in the murk. An ancient-looking, rusting, metallic behemoth.

The boiler.

The buzz in the back of her head became more insistent. Grace scanned the shelves against the wall next to the boiler, and her eyes lit on the exact thing she needed. A hand sledge. She set the containers of diesel down, grabbed it, and hefted it. It would do the job nicely. She faced the boiler, looking for the pressure relief valve Sage had shown her on the specs they'd looked up last night.

There.

Grace hefted the hand sledge once more and swung. The impact of the sledge against the valve shuddered all the way up her arm to her shoulder, and she felt a fierce sense of satisfaction as the valve and its knob flew off with one blow. It clattered somewhere in the dark corners behind the boiler.

She stepped past the boiler to the breaker box on the wall. Flipped the lid open, and switched the boiler on. It thrummed alive with a heavy *whoosh*. She stepped back to the boiler and turned the controls all the way up. Another flash of satisfaction filled her as she saw the needle of the pressure gauge fly violently into the red almost immediately. She was about to bend for the containers of diesel at her feet when . . .

they're here

. . . she spun as the buzzing in the back of her mind rose to a crescendo. Jerking the riot gun up and around and firing without looking. Her blast caught one of those things square in the guts, blowing a messy hole in its abdomen and throwing it back several steps. The dripping wound was already healing, and the thing regaining its footing, so Grace leaped forward with a yell. She jammed the makeshift bayonet point-first deep into its heart, and drove it against the wall, pinning it there. It thrashed and flailed, smoke rising from its hissing, bubbling flesh. It sagged and melted into an indefinable pile of matter.

The buzzing in her head diminished, but there were more on the way.

She reached down and flipped the lids off the containers of gasoline. Didn't have time to pour them all over like she wanted, so she kicked them over. The acrid and pungent smell of fuel filled the room as the gas glugged out of the containers and into steadily widening pools on the floor. Mindful of stepping into them, Grace picked her way around the pools and headed for the door to the main hall, straight into another thing lunging for her, mad bulging eyes rolling wildly, black mouth gaping, ropy tongue slashing the air.

Grace pumped another round into the riot gun and blew its right shoulder away, driving it out into the hall. She leaped after it and drove her sharpened broomstick into its heart, slamming it back against the HUMVEE.

More buzzing in her head.

To her right.

Without removing the broomstick from the thing melting against the HUMVEE, Grace yanked the Glock holstered on her right hip and blasted one of the oncoming things in the face. It shuddered to a stumbling halt as its hideous face disappeared in a green-black spray of viscera and rotted flesh, its hands flailing where its face used to be.

Grace yanked the broom bayonet from the sagging mess melting into the floor next to the HUMVEE and charged the now faceless thing. She plunged the broomstick into its chest and, seeing another one coming up behind it, drove forward, legs pumping, pushing the broomstick bayonet through the thing's already melting body and straight into the one behind it.

Minutes later, she stood, heaving and panting, over smoldering piles of rubbery, green-black matter. The chemical smell of burnt rubber filled her nostrils and turned her stomach, but somehow, she kept her gorge down.

More were coming.

They'd left her alone at the constable's station because she was unconscious and infected and wasn't posing a threat. Now, she was attacking their nest, so they were defending it. She had to move faster before they came upstairs en masse. She holstered both her Glocks and slung the riot gun-broomstick bayonet over her shoulder and hustled all the way around to the passenger side of the HUMVEE. Threw open the door, reached inside and yanked out the other two cans of gasoline, turned, and stepped toward the basement door . . .

Grace!

She froze for a moment, clutching the gas cans, at first thinking she was starting to lose it and was imagining things. But when she heard her name a second time—in Scott's voice—she stopped, and listened to the buzz growing steadily in the back of her mind as Scott said, (presumably to the First, to get to her), *Grace, listen.*

95.

A PLOT ELEMENT in both horror movies and novels Scott had never been able to swallow was the uncanny calm displayed by kids like him in the face of horrific supernatural evil. Stephen King's adolescent characters in particular. Much as Scott loved King's stories, he didn't find that realistic at all. He certainly hadn't felt that way the last two days. Especially last night when one of those things bit Sage's head off and chewed it like a granola bar.

Which was why he felt surprised at the calm which descended upon him now. In the minutes after the gigantic crash which had shaken the whole building, and the engine, (definitely not Constable Matthews' JEEP), roaring down the Main Hall above and the screeching of tires at the end of the hall, all the pieces fell neatly into place, almost exactly like it did for all those cool, collected, calm kids in horror movies. Apparently, real life was a cliché-ridden shit-show built on stereotypes and motifs.

Regardless, as the things before him became *one* again, (he could *feel* the temporary rift he'd caused melting away), everything became clear.

Feeling a strange, almost otherworldly sense of purpose and even bravado, (damn, how cliché can you get?), Scott stepped forward, slipping the Glock out from its holster. He held it at his side, finger *on* the trigger because there weren't any friendlies down here. He called out in a strong, clear voice which surprised even him. "Grace!"

The things all stiffened as if he'd called out to them. They stopped moving toward the stairs to the main floor and turned to look at him, the First in particular. Flexing his grip on the Glock, he continued. "Grace! Listen to me! If that's you up there, it's because they left you last night. I was unconscious, but the only reason I can figure why they left you is because you're . . . you're infected, somehow. Like Julie. So maybe you're connected to them now. Maybe you can hear me, through them. I think you can hold out longer than Julie. You're stronger. More focused. You can do this."

Several of the closest things approached him, led by the First. His father. The rest, however, turned and headed for the stairs, and for Grace.

"Look, Grace . . . we're not gonna make it. There's no way. Maybe if I wasn't down here and we still had Sage, maybe . . . but it's not gonna happen. We still gotta finish it, though. It's gotta get *done*. You understand?"

He had no way of knowing if she heard him; if she was linked up to the things or not. One thing he *did* know, however, was she couldn't waste time trying to save him. They had to get this done. *She* had to get it done. Blow the boiler, blow this place to hell. Which meant he needed to distract these things heading for the stairs; he also needed to remove himself from the equation.

He couldn't kill himself. Didn't know if he had it in him. Besides, he didn't think that would distract these things. He could only think of one thing.

He raised the Glock and stepped toward the First, aiming the gun at it. He locked his elbow, like Grace taught him, with his grip tight on the gun . . . but not too tight. "You know," he said, "in all the alien movies when someone attacked the Queen, her brood came to her defense."

His finger tightened on the trigger. "I wonder if yours will do the same. *Dad*."

He pulled the trigger. Once, twice, three times.

Three holes exploded in the First's chest. It staggered backward, hands flailing. As its unnatural flesh was already filling in the wounds, the rest of the things turned and advanced on Scott, as he kept walking forward, pulling the trigger again and again.

96.

IT'S GOTTA GET DONE. *You understand?*

For a moment Grace stood there, frozen, wishing she *was* going insane instead of hearing Scott talk through one of the things in the basement. But the growing buzz in the back of her mind and the stiffening patch of what felt like hardened rubberized skin on her face and neck made denial pointless.

we're not gonna make it

but we still gotta finish it

"*Fuck.* All right, kid. All right." Grace set the diesel cans down. Reached out and threw open the basement door, half expecting a horde of those things shambling up the stairs toward her. She didn't see anything, so she reached down, grabbed both diesel cans, and with a grunting heave, tossed both of them down the stairs, hoping the cans' spouts were secured enough not to spill.

From her pocket, she pulled out a rag she'd already soaked with diesel, and one of the lighters she'd taken from the Sip and Go. Headed to the back of the HUMVEE again, flipped the fueling hatch open, unscrewed the gas cap, and stuffed the rag into the hatch as far as it would go. She flicked the lighter, bringing to life a dancing, flickering orange flame.

She paused for a moment—which stretched out into an eternity—knowing that once she lit that diesel-soaked rag, there wasn't any going back.

Gotta get it done

She lit the rag. It caught almost instantly. Before hustling away, she tossed the ignited lighter over the HUMVEE and into the maintenance, praying to a god she didn't believe in that the lighter would stay lit and land in the diesel she'd dumped in there.

As she grabbed the basement door's handle, she was rewarded with a low, sibilant *whoosh* behind her. She didn't look, however, a clock was ticking way too fast in her head as she drew both her Glocks . . .

Shots echoed down the stairs, in the basement. Three, four, five shots.

She leaped forward and descended the stairs as quickly as she could without tripping . . .

Which of course didn't make any difference when the HUMVEE's gas tank blew. A great cracking filled the air as everything shook and Grace pitched forward into darkness, surrounded by a roar which sounded like mountains collapsing and chasms opening deep in the earth.

97.

THOUGH HIS FIRST shots were perfect, dead center-mass hits on the First, Scott's next few shots—aimed wildly around the basement at the other things advancing on him—scored only glancing blows on shoulders, thighs, and legs, none of which had any effect. All of that fabled, preternatural calm had vanished, and Scott couldn't make himself slow down and take careful aim as he kept pivoting and firing. His hand and shoulders ached with each recoil, and he had no idea how many bullets were left. They were drawing in closer and closer, and in a few more seconds . . .

Thunder rippled through the basement in a concussive *boom*. The floor tilted sideways, and a great *cracking* split the air as massive chunks of concrete and masonry rained down. The capsizing ground threw Scott off his feet. He slammed shoulder-first into the rock and dirt floor.

He didn't move. Just laid there, curling into a fetal ball, covering his head with his arms, waiting for a large chunk of the ceiling to crush his head and put the lights out for good.

Minutes passed, however, and the end didn't come. Mortar dust trickled down and small pieces of concrete still fell, while the ceiling groaned and rippled with splitting and cracking sounds which echoed throughout the basement. The ceiling sounded like it was going to crash down at any moment.

It didn't.

Scott coughed and sat up, trying to rub the dust and grit from his eyes as he looked around. Surprisingly enough, it was easier to see, because the explosion or whatever it was had blown all the dirty glass out of the windows, which allowed more sunlight to creep in.

Scott's mind parked on that thought, the wheels of his mind spinning. If the sunlight was able to creep in, no matter how many of those things were hopefully crushed beyond regeneration in the ceiling's collapse, *some* of them might be able to scramble up the walls and out of the windows. That couldn't be allowed to happen.

However, as Scott scrambled to his feet and looked wildly around for his gun (which he'd lost) he didn't see *any* of the things. What he did see, however, were piles of greenish-black ichor and clumped matter inside ripped clothing. Apparently, there was a level of physical trauma besides a stake through the heart these things couldn't withstand.

"Yeah," Scott muttered weakly, "wooden stake through the heart, or drop a fucking building on them. No big deal at . . . "

A hand grabbed him by the hair and yanked his head back so hard Scott screamed, then threw him face-first to the ground, where his forehead cracked against the rocky floor. Dazed, foggy-headed, he didn't feel the hand grab his shoulder and roll him over. He only came back to himself when a crushing grip clamped onto his throat and raised him high into the air like a rag doll. Eyes bulging from their sockets, gasping but getting no air, clawing futilely at a hand whose rubbery flesh didn't feel human, Scott gazed down upon the hideous mask of the First, its eyes rolling wetly in what looked like rage.

Whatever brief connection Scott thought he'd forged with the First—his *father*—it was gone. It opened its cavernous mouth and pulled Scott's face close. Remembering too vividly Sage's fate, Scott kicked and thrashed anew.

98.

GRACE FOUGHT HER way back up through the darkness. A terrible pressure swelled in her head as she blinked and tried to move. Everything hurt, and for a moment, as she slowly lifted her head and felt it throb, she wondered if it was from a fractured skull, or something worse.

It didn't matter, of course. Fractured skull. Subdural Hematoma. It didn't even matter if the thing inside took over. The maintenance room had to be engulfed in flames by now, super-heating an over-pressurized boiler about to explode. The things would either be roasted then crushed, or crushed then roasted. It didn't matter . . .

Someone gagged and coughed, and she heard sounds of struggle. Grace grit her teeth against the pain, took a deep breath, and pushed herself off the ground, to a sitting position. Every muscle and joint in her body screamed in protest, but nothing felt broken, in her upper body, at least. She looked toward the gagging sounds . . .

One of them. The First, she somehow knew. Naked, it held Scott in the air by his neck and was bringing the boy's head to its gaping mouth. To kill him or turn him, she had no idea, but even that didn't matter, because soon it would all be over . . .

Something registered. She could see fairly clearly. Why was that? Shafts of light, coming from . . .

She looked and saw light streaming through the shattered ground-level windows. Empty windows that *thing* could crawl out of if it moved fast enough.

"Fuck *no*," she hissed between clenched teeth. She forced herself to one knee and tried to rise, but when she did, mind-numbing electric pain arced from her left ankle to her knee. She fell forward and barely caught herself on her right knee before slamming face-first into the ground.

She didn't bother glancing at her left ankle. Didn't want to, because she *knew* it was broken, and she didn't want to see it, for fear she'd pass out. Maybe it wasn't broken; maybe she'd torn ligaments or tendons, which would explain the burning all along her foot and ankle. It didn't matter, though. She had to get up. *Had to.*

Breathing in deep, marshaling whatever resources she had left inside, Grace forced herself up on one foot, left toes barely touching the ground. Her right thigh quivered and almost gave out, but somehow she managed to hold her position and not fall again.

She pulled her Glock—knowing in her heart it wouldn't kill it, and not caring—drew down on the thing, and emptied four rounds in the back of its head.

The thing twitched and spasmed with every shot, as holes blossomed in the back of its head and squirted that same blackish-green ichor all over its back. It didn't drop Scott, however, and the holes were already closing.

The broomstick bayonet. On the riot gun. Where the hell was it? She needed it. She could empty a whole magazine into that thing and it wouldn't make a difference. Where was the goddamn . . .

A sharp, dreadful crack echoed in the basement and filled Grace's heart with the coldest ice. She turned wide, frantic eyes on the thing holding Scott by the neck. Saw Scott's beat-red face, and empty, glazed over eyes. His head lolled on his crushed neck.

"No," Grace whipped her Glock back up, pointless as it was. "No, no, no, no!"

She emptied five more shots into the thing's back, then pegged another one in the back of its head again. It shook and jerked with every shot, but ignored them all. It tossed Scott's limp body aside like it was a bag of so much garbage, where it landed on a pile of rubble. Blood trickled from his eyes, nose, and mouth. The way he lay in a pile of jumbled limbs—like a discarded puppet with its strings cut—left no doubt in Grace's mind.

Despair of a kind she'd never known filled her. She stumbled, almost fell, and her scream ripped from out of her depths, coming from a heart torn in two.

"NO!"

All emotion left with her guttural cry. She wanted to give up. Sink to her knees and go to sleep. Let the thing in her mind take her, or let the other thing take her, whichever, it didn't matter. If she did, all the pain would go away, and she would descend into the darkness, beyond caring, once and for all.

finish it

gotta get it done

Footsteps crunched on grit and stone. Grace looked up and saw the thing walking away, toward the broken ground-floor windows, as of course it would. It knew the infection inside her would take over before long. She was no longer a threat because soon, she'd be one of them.

"Fuck that."

She drew down again and fired, but her shots went wide, or only glanced off the thing's shoulders, doing little damage as it advanced on the broken windows. The boiler should go any second, but it didn't matter, because the thing was going to fucking escape, and she could barely *move*, much less hop after that thing and stop it.

The basement ceiling cracked and groaned. It occurred to her, in that instant, how *old* Pleasant Brook High was. Even though the boiler hadn't blown up yet, the HUMVEE explosion might have been enough to cause significant structural damage, maybe enough to . . .

"Okay, God," Grace whispered, "You want me to believe? Show me fucking something, dammit. Show me."

The ceiling cracked and groaned more. Then, with the screeching sound of stone, metal, and wood grinding against each other, the south wall of the school—where the ground-level windows had blown out—gave way completely, collapsing in on itself. The ceiling above the south wall gave way, raining down debris, and where once had been broken windows leading outside, there was now nothing but an impenetrable pile of debris.

"Fuck yeah," Grace rasped. "Hail Mary, Father, Son, and Motherfucking Holy Ghost."

Her glee faded, however, as the dust settled and she saw the thing unharmed, facing the rubble where its exit had once been. It stood still, monolithic, staring.

"Fuck you!" Grace spat. "Won't be long now, fucker!"

The thing turned smoothly and stared at her from across the debris-ridden expanse, mad eyes rolling and bulging, awful tongue lashing the air in what looked like animal rage.

"That's right. *Fuck. You.*"

It broke into a loping run, straight for her.

She braced herself best as she could, raised her Glock, and opened fire. This time all her shots hit the thing in the gut, even its face. It didn't stop; however and kept coming.

Her Glock clicked empty.

Instead of drawing the other—it would do no good anyway—she scanned the ground, looking for . . .

Hope flared in her heart.

She bent, scooped her prize out of the rubble, and fell backward, hoping to create a least a little space between her and it. She landed on her back, crying out at the broken shards of concrete digging into her already tortured muscles, but she ignored the pain, drew *strength* from it.

The First leaped.

Mouth opening wide, tongue whipping. Grace screamed with rage and thrust the riot gun and its broomstick bayonet up and out. The First's momentum did the rest. It landed on the broomstick bayonet with all of its weight. The broomstick plunged into its chest and punched out its back.

Grace worked the broomstick back and forth, screaming all of her anger, rage, and sadness. The First, stuck like a bug on a pin, thrashed, arms and legs flailing in death throes. Its skin began to bubble, hiss, smoke, and melt.

To her dread amazement, the First's face stiffened, hardened, and didn't look real or like rubber anymore. It looked like the wooden mask in the pictures Scott found online, and when it slid off the oozing, melting face underneath, it clattered against the concrete floor and rolled away, an ancient artifact now, and nothing more.

Grace heaved the dissolving thing on the broomstick off her and to the side. It landed on the basement's debris-littered floor with a sickening, splattering *thud*. Her arms and legs shaking, Grace somehow got to one foot, her useless ankle still dangling, toes barely touching the floor.

As she watched the First slowly dissolve, a great weariness—a bone-deep fatigue she'd never felt before—filled her. All dead. The whole fucking town dead. Marty, Julie, Sage, and now Scott. Soon her, because despite their half-baked theories that killing the First would kill all of them, she still felt it, inside. The hive mind had gone quiet—she guessed all the rest were crushed when the ceiling collapsed the first time—but she could feel it inside her, all the same. If she changed before the boiler blew, if whatever she turned into somehow got out of here in time . . .

At that instant, a cold, gut-ripping pain tore through her middle. She bent double and gasped, the pain in her abdomen feeling like something was squirming inside her, trying to get out.

"No way. No fucking way."

Clutching her stomach, ignoring the alien cold spreading through her, she hobbled on one foot toward where she thought the stairs had been, as the buzz grew in her head. About ten feet away, she found them. Partially buried beneath chunks of concrete, but they were there. The two containers of diesel she'd tossed down the stairs before the HUMVEE blew.

The side of her face and neck—all rubbery and hard—burned with a cold, unnatural fire, and her guts squirmed with something which felt like greasy eels. Grace grabbed the two containers and tugged them free. Somehow, she managed to drag them both over to Scott's body, and the pile of matter which used to be the First. As quickly as she could—ignoring the growing cold spreading all through her—she uncapped one can and emptied it on both Scott, the remains of the First, and the wooden mask, choking back tears as the fuel's stink washed over her.

She tossed aside the empty container. Uncapped the other one, lifted it above her head as best she could, and dumped its contents on herself.

She closed her eyes, but the diesel got in there, and her eyes ached and burned. The fumes made her choke and gag and almost puke, but she didn't waver. She held the container above her until it emptied.

She dropped the can. Opened her eyes—which screamed in agony—and only registered dim shapes in her blurry vision, but that didn't matter. She wasn't going anywhere, anyway. She sank to the floor next to Scott. Took one of his hands, which already felt cold. She sat in the pool of diesel which surrounded her, Scott, and the remains of the First.

She dug her hand into her pocket and pulled out the other lighter she'd taken from the Sip and Go. Clicked the wheel, snapping alight a flame which burned a blessedly pure orange-red.

She looked at the mass of melted inhuman flesh that had been the First, and maybe even Scott's absentee father. The irony? She'd never liked Bobby Lee Haskel, anyway. An arrogant prick.

"*Fuck you*," she whispered. She dropped the lighter into the pool of diesel at her feet and sat there, holding Scott's cold hand, waiting for the warmth to wash away the alien infection growing inside. When the boiler finally blew and took the rest of the school with it, Grace knew she would be long past caring, and somehow, also knew . . . she'd see her friends again.

THE END?

Not if you want to dive into more of Crystal Lake Publishing's Tales from the Darkest Depths!

Check out our amazing website and online store
or download our latest catalog here.
https://geni.us/CLPCatalog

Looking for award-winning Dark Fiction?

Download our latest catalog.

Includes our anthologies, novels, novellas, collections, poetry, non-fiction, and specialty projects.

TALES FROM THE DARKEST DEPTHS

We always have great new projects and content on the website to dive into, as well as a newsletter, behind the scenes options, social media platforms, our own dark fiction shared-world series and our very own webstore. Our webstore even has categories specifically for KU books, non-fiction, anthologies, and of course more novels and novellas.

ABOUT THE AUTHOR

Kevin Lucia is the eBook and trade paperback editor at Cemetery Dance Publications. His short fiction has been published in many venues, most notably with Neil Gaiman, Clive Barker, David Morell, Peter Straub, Bentley Little, and Robert McCammon. This is his first novel. To learn more, visit: kevinlucia.blogspot.com.

Readers . . .

Thank you for reading *The Horror at Pleasant Brook*. We hope you enjoyed this novel.

If you have a moment, please review *The Horror at Pleasant Brook* at the store where you bought it.

Help other readers by telling them why you enjoyed this book. No need to write an in-depth discussion. Even a single sentence will be greatly appreciated. Reviews go a long way to helping a book sell, and is great for an author's career. It'll also help us to continue publishing quality books. You can also share a photo of yourself holding this book with the hashtag #IGotMyCLPBook!

Thank you again for taking the time to journey with Crystal Lake Publishing.

Visit our Linktree page for a list of our social media platforms.
https://linktr.ee/CrystalLakePublishing

Our Mission Statement:

Since its founding in August 2012, Crystal Lake Publishing has quickly become one of the world's leading publishers of Dark Fiction and Horror books in print, eBook, and audio formats.

While we strive to present only the highest quality fiction and entertainment, we also endeavour to support authors along their writing journey. We offer our time and experience in non-fiction projects, as well as author mentoring and services, at competitive prices.

With several Bram Stoker Award wins and many other wins and nominations (including the HWA's Specialty Press Award), Crystal Lake Publishing puts integrity, honor, and respect at the forefront of our publishing operations.

We strive for each book and outreach program we spearhead to not only entertain and touch or comment on issues that affect our readers, but also to strengthen and support the Dark Fiction field and its authors.

Not only do we find and publish authors we believe are destined for greatness, but we strive to work with men and woman who endeavour to be decent human beings who care more for others than themselves, while still being hard working, driven, and passionate artists and storytellers.

Crystal Lake Publishing is and will always be a beacon of what passion and dedication, combined with overwhelming teamwork and respect, can accomplish. We endeavour to know each and every one of our readers, while building personal relationships with our authors, reviewers, bloggers, podcasters, bookstores, and libraries.

We will be as trustworthy, forthright, and transparent as any business can be, while also keeping most of the headaches away from our authors, since it's our job to solve the problems so they can stay in a creative mind. Which of course also means paying our authors.

We do not just publish books, we present to you worlds within your world, doors within your mind, from talented authors who sacrifice so much for a moment of your time.

There are some amazing small presses out there, and through collaboration and open forums we will continue to support other presses in the goal of helping authors and showing the world what quality small presses are capable of accomplishing. No one wins when a small press goes down, so we will always be there to support hardworking, legitimate presses and their authors. We don't see Crystal Lake as the best press out there, but we will always strive to be the best, strive to be the most interactive and grateful, and even blessed press around. No matter what happens over time, we will also take our mission very seriously while appreciating where we are and enjoying the journey.

What do we offer our authors that they can't do for themselves through self-publishing?

We are big supporters of self-publishing (especially hybrid publishing), if done with care, patience, and planning. However, not every author has the time or inclination to do market research, advertise, and set up book launch strategies. Although a lot of authors are successful in doing it all, strong small presses will always be there for the authors who just want to do what they do best: write.

What we offer is experience, industry knowledge, contacts and trust built up over years. And due to our strong brand and trusting fanbase, every Crystal Lake Publishing book comes with weight of respect. In time our fans begin to trust our judgment and will try a new author purely based on our support of said author.

With each launch we strive to fine-tune our approach, learn from our mistakes, and increase our reach. We continue to assure our authors that we're here for them and that we'll carry the weight of the launch and dealing with third parties while they focus on their strengths—be it writing, interviews, blogs, signings, etc.

We also offer several mentoring packages to authors that include knowledge and skills they can use in both traditional and self-publishing endeavours.

We look forward to launching many new careers.

This is what we believe in. What we stand for. This will be our legacy.

Welcome to Crystal Lake Publishing—
Tales from the Darkest Depths.

Printed in Great Britain
by Amazon

28979848R00192